JENNY COLGAN

Talking to Addison

HarperCollins*Publishers*

HarperCollins*Publishers*
77–85 Fulham Palace Road,
Hammersmith, London W6 8JB

www.**fire**and**water**.com

A Paperback Original 2000
1 3 5 7 9 8 6 4 2

Copyright © Jenny Colgan 2000

Jenny Colgan asserts the moral right to
be identified as the author of this work

A catalogue record for this book
is available from the British Library

ISBN 0-00-766152-5

Typeset in Garamond 3 by Palimpsest Book Production Limited,
Polmont, Stirlingshire

Printed in Great Britain by
Bookmarque, Croydon, Surrey

Acknowledgements

Thanks to: Ali 'the golden' Gunn, Rachel Hore and Fiona McIntosh: all, for everything. Nick Marston, Carol Jackson, Lorna McDonald, Jonathan Lloyd and all at Curtis Brown, and Nick Sayers, Anne O'Brien, Jennifer Parr, Yvette Cowles, Claire Round, Phyllis Acolatse, Vera Brice, David North, Martin Palmer, Adrian Bourne and all the reps at HarperCollins. Plus: Katie Stone for her unfailing support, Ben Moor for the science as well as being Ben Moor; Salty Sandra McKay, originator of McKay BMS; Susan Hoyer; Jason Foxwell-Moss for the chess and one or two other things; James Crawford for his kitchen; Shappi Khorsandi; Karen Murphy MRCS, official medical adviser to TTA (although all inaccuracies and exaggerations are of course mine); Katrina McCormack, Lisa Jewell, and Robin and Dominic, my brilliant brothers. This book was written listening to *Equatorial* by Chris Hoban.

This book is dedicated with love
to my truly fantastic and long-suffering
parents – Mum, sorry I didn't take
my accountancy exams,
Dad, sorry about all the swearing.

Part I

One

A famous arctic explorer once said that polar expeditions were the most successful form of having a bad time humans had ever devised. Of course, he'd probably never answered an ad for a flatshare with a bunch of complete strangers. Although if it hadn't been for them I would never have met Addison. Hmm. Which, when I think of it, is kind of like saying, OK, I lost all my fingers and toes to frostbite, but I met some very sweet penguins along the way . . .

Thirty-six hours after I moved in to 12a Wendle Close, Harlesden, I realized I'd made a terrible mistake. Tiptoeing around someone *else's* home is weird enough, particularly if it's just after a late night and you can't remember their name or where they keep the Sugar Puffs or, say, you're a cat burglar. Tiptoeing around your own is discomfiting to say the least. But here I was, creeping into my own house and closing my bedroom door extremely quietly, heart pounding, after my very first quick jaunt to the shops, to make friends with my newsagent and see what flavours of Skips he had.

If I pressed my head against the thin wood veneer of the door I could just about hear my new best friends in the nearby ghastly open-plan Formica kitchenette.

'Well, I think we need a special *long-term* rota too. For cleaning the shower curtain and the drawers. And washing the skirting boards.'

'That's a great idea, Carol,' came another voice, deep with awe. 'Maybe we could do one big job every Saturday night and make an event of it. We could even get takeaway pizza!'

'And don't forget the nets!' screeched the unfortunately named Farah, who was about two foot tall and was always being mistaken for a monkey, or Martin Amis. 'I'll get my coloured pencils out and start drawing it up. This is going to be *such fun*!'

They all mewed.

'Didn't I just hear Holly coming in?' asked Laura, who was stolid and sat down a lot. 'That sounded like her bedroom door . . .'

Damn.

'No!' I attempted to telepathically send to them. 'It must have been the wind. That . . . mysterious indoor wind.'

'. . . Why don't we go and ask her what she'd like to do?'

I inhaled sharply.

'Yes, let's!' yelled Farah. And there was a pounding at my door.

'Holly? Holly, are you there?'

Carol, official leader of Scary Clean Freaks Incorporated, put her head round the door assertively. Was it only a week ago I had checked out her ankle chain and pondered whether we'd ever get on? She looked at me sneerily. I sensed that she secretly knew of the scientifically proven inverse relationship between me and housework (the more messy things were, the less inclined I was to do anything about them), even though I'd attempted to be pristine for my first few days.

'We were just wondering . . .' she hissed.

Laura sniffed, noisily, behind her. Laura sniffed *all the time*. I always wanted to tell her that it was OK; no one was about to make her do double PE any more. Carol shot an evil sideways glance like a viper.

'Ahem. We were just *wondering*, given that we're – ha – divvying up the rota, if there was anything you particularly liked doing?'

I eyed her steadily, not about to be intimidated by someone who ringed their lips with dark lipstick pencil on their skin.

'How about I take lightbulb-dusting and big spider removal?'

2

'Ooh, that sounds good,' screeched Farah from somewhere beside my knee. Carol dispensed another one of those Robert de Niro-to-doomed-gangster stares.

'We thought you might prefer loos, sinks and floors,' she said pointedly.

'Oh . . .' I said. 'You mean, *all* of it.'

'Ha,' she smiled. 'Don't get around to much cooking, do we?'

I realized I'd been outmanoeuvred.

I counterattacked. 'What are you going to do?'

'I'm going to co-ordinate,' she said. Laura nodded happily.

'Oh, *tough* one.'

'. . . that means I buy all the cleaning materials, arrange the rota, organize the external cleaning contractors, e.g. the carpet shampooers I've got coming in, arrange everyone's telephone hours and oversee everyone's painting choices. So we've all got *quite* enough to be getting on with, don't you think?'

I wanted to try one last stance – perhaps suggesting that Farah take the floors, after all, she was closer – but all I could say was, '*Telephone* hours?'

'I know, I thought of it,' Carol said proudly.

'It's a *great* idea,' said Farah, standing between Carol's legs.

'Basically, it means you can only use the phone or get phone calls at your set time each night. Then, when we get the bill in, you pay for all the calls in your time, and nobody lies about the expensive numbers.'

I stared at her.

'Well, that's going to cut down on my sex-line income.'

Laura's eyes widened with shock. Carol laughed politely, to show me that if I felt like fighting her, she was up to it.

'What's to stop me making phone calls on other people's time?'

'We're going to have a phone-lock that can only be opened by me. You come to me when you want to use the phone and I'll see if it's your hour or not. Really,' she said, shaking her head, 'your chores are *much* easier than mine, believe me.'

3

'Oh goodness me, I think I just heard my *mobile* go off,' I announced in a flurry.

'Excuse me,' I said, when they showed no sign of backing away from my door, 'I just have to, ehrm, excuse me . . .' Fortunately, the henchmen stuck next to Carol and backed away when she gave the signal, as my next move would have been to scream 'Fuck off! Fuck off! Fuck off!' whilst shoving them out of the door and pulling a hose on them.

I slammed the door behind them and sat on the bed. My mobile wasn't going off, naturally, but I took it out anyway and thanked this little machine. How could I ever have thought they were only of use to wankers on buses who thought that someone not on a bus might want to know when they were on a bus? Oh – and how the fuck was I going to get out of here?

Some people pick the wrong men all the time. I pick the wrong places to live. Well, OK, I pick the wrong men too, but anyway. So it was that after finally getting totally creeped out by my last landlord, in Hackney, who smelled of piss and used to turn up at random hours of the night to 'inspect' things (my knicker drawer included) – which followed the three girls in Dulwich who had all joined a beardy-weirdy religious cult and refused to allow men over the threshold, except for the cult leader, whom they all slept with whenever he wanted them to – I had ended up here, in a new house-share with three banana brains who all worked in the local hospital as phlebotomists. Apparently this meant they took blood samples from people. I assumed in Carol's case she simply bit them.

Anyway, they'd advertised in *Loot* for a fourth member to join a new household in tasty Harlesden, and, amazingly, I got it. Perhaps I was the only one who didn't blanch at the interview, when Laura came in and reported obediently to Carol that she had just bleached the teacups.

'And how often do *you* boil-wash the crockery?' Carol had asked me.

'Ehm . . . I find about every half-hour just about does it,' I'd gone for, and noticed her put a big tick on my application form, which had been broken down into sixteen handy sections. The relief of going from the dissipated seediness of Hackney – where they wanted extra rent if you got an inside loo – to a brand new 'executive' flat in the famous industrial waste area of North West London made it seem like a good deal at the time, but had blinded me to the obvious: i.e., all these people were mad, but because they outnumbered me in the house I was beginning to think that they were right.

I began to inspect my mobile for germs, and was getting really close up when it rang in my face.

I shrieked, did a comedy clown fumble, and dropped the phone under the bed.

'Are you all right?' said Carol's voice from just outside the door. She was obviously listening to everything. I shrieked again, swallowed some air, choked, coughed, and managed to wheeze, 'Fine, thank you.'

'It must be pretty dusty under your bed.'

'Yes, yes it is, thanks,' I said, sitting upright with the phone. Then I jumped – how the hell did she know where I was? I felt a cold hand of fear.

'Hello?' I finally choked into the phone.

'Do you know, I haven't made a woman scream like that for years,' drawled the well-modulated voice.

I relaxed slightly.

'Josh, you have never made a woman scream like that. In fact, have you ever made a woman?'

'Oh ho ho. Yes, of course.'

'In your country of origin?'

He paused.

'Not precisely.'

I'd been teasing Josh about this for as long as I'd known him, which was a l-o-o-ong time. Because he was attractive and also nice to girls, most people assumed he was gay. For someone with a posh background, a good job, and a nice haircut, he did horrendously badly with the opposite sex, which I couldn't

5

understand – not that I'd ever wanted to shag him myself; he was so *nice*.

Anyway, thank God he'd rung me back. Worriedly searching the ceiling for CCTV, I sat back on the bed.

'Josh, you know when you moved into Pimlico and I said I didn't want to move there because it was snooty London and you were moving in with Kate who hates me?'

'Um, yes.'

'Well, you know, how's it . . . how's the whole flatshare *thing* going?'

'It's going fine.'

'Right – GREAT! Right. How's that other guy you got in to fill the space doing?'

'Addison? He's just great . . . Well, quiet, and undemanding.'

That didn't sound much like me.

'Uh huh. So, no one's moving out or anything, then?'

Josh sighed. 'Don't tell me. Not another Turkish Lesbian Women's Collective?'

That had been Hoxteth, two years ago. I'd been kicked out for not liking chickpeas and buying that symbol of male forced dominance, sanitary protection.

'No. Worse.'

'The cat lady?'

'Christ. No, not worse than her. But still, pretty bad.'

I heard Carol's voice:

'Holly! Would you like some tea? Because it's your turn to make it!'

I ignored her.

'Josh, this is absolutely desperate. Listen, you know that little boxroom you were going to turn into a study?'

'The one you described as a coffin?'

'Yup, yup, that's the one. Ehm, have you . . . ?'

'Turned it into a study? Not since you were last here. I've leased it out as a bedroom, though.'

'NOOO!'

He laughed.

'You bastard! Josh, I know this is a huge favour – and please say no if you don't want to – but please, please, please can I come and live in your coffin? I mean, boxroom?'

'You've asked me this before, Holl,' he said with a sigh.

'I know.'

'Then you always dash off and the next thing I hear from you you're on the run from a postgraduate mathematics bad-minton team.'

'I *know*. I'm crazy.'

'You are crazy. Why didn't you just move in when I bought the place?'

'Because you're rich and Kate makes me miserable.'

'I am not rich, and Kate can't help being . . . Kate. Anyway, if that's how you feel . . .'

'No, no! I'm sorry! Please. Please. Please.'

There was a loud knocking at my door.

'Tea, please, Holly! It's in the lease!'

'It's the Gestapo!' I whispered. 'How soon can you come and get me?'

'I'll have to check with Kate and Addison.'

'Josh!' I screeched, near to tears. '*Please.*'

'OK,' he relented. 'I'll pick you up at about seven. Have you got much stuff?'

'Just a coffinful.'

'And no diving off again, do you hear me?'

'Yes, sir,' I mumbled meekly.

I could have snogged Josh, I was so pleased to see him. I wanted to grab hold of his legs round the ankles and sob with gratitude and pour unguents over his feet. Or is that glue?

Carol had not taken the news well, particularly when I retrieved my deposit cheque from the shiny silver box to which only she had a key (I distracted her by upending her Asda coupons all over the kitchen floor then making a dive for the key when she bent over). In fact, she had advanced on me until her face was only a few inches

7

from mine – well, her make-up was. Her face was probably about a foot away.

'Think you can just do what you like round here?' she asked menacingly.

'Yes, I do, actually. That's why I don't live with my parents any more.'

'So, who's going to take your room? You've got to sort that out.'

'Ah. Yes, well . . . I'm afraid you're going to have to sue me for my friends and acquaintances. Here, I've written down my forwarding address on this piece of paper –' I waved it reassuringly. It said: 1 Holly Lane, Hollywood, 020 8555 5555 – 'and don't forget to send those bills on to me!'

'We won't,' said Carol grimly. Laura opened and shut her mouth like a fish.

'Well, I think it's disgraceful the way you're leaving Carol in the lurch like this,' she announced, quivering. 'All the trouble she's been to.'

'And me!' piped up Farah from somewhere around my ankles. 'I did the rotas!'

'I'm sorry,' I said. 'My best friend's got cancer. I'm nursing him till he dies.'

Laura backed away, crestfallen.

'I'm *so sorry*,' she muttered.

'Oh really?' said Carol. 'What kind?'

I couldn't think. 'Ehm, nose cancer?'

'You're sick,' she said, turning to march out of the room.

'So are you!' I yelled after her.

She turned once more, her brutally permed hair a weapon.

'Well, at least I'm *clean* and sick.'

Fortunately, Josh's sporty little spitfire had turned up, and he was honking enthusiastically. Josh did *everything* enthusiastically.

I tore out of the house.

'Where the hell am I going to *put* anything?' I wailed, after

8

hugging him over-affectionately then examining his two-seater.

'I'm so sorry, darling. I meant to trade Bessie in for a Volvo but, you know, I just couldn't find the time.'

'Ha ha ha. Listen, would you mind sitting on my duvet?'

He gave me a look.

'Well, it's not like real sex, is it?'

It took us an hour and a half to crawl back into town. Even though it was only April, Josh insisted on having the roof off, so I had to hang on to everything I owned, like an earthquake refugee.

'Freedom!' I yelled into the air. 'I am never going to move into a crappy flat again.'

'Except for the one you're about to move into.'

'Josh, it could be a shed at the bottom of the garden, I don't care! I'm FREEE!'

'OK, steady on,' said Josh, obviously worried I was about to start leaning dangerously far over the bonnet and singing 'My Heart Will Go On'.

There are two schools of thought concerning the children of parents who divorce nastily just as you're approaching puberty. One school says, Well, life is like that – chin up, and maybe the seething atmosphere at home will spur you into staying late at the library and moving on to better and brilliant things in an attempt to pull yourself out of the flotsam. Lots of famous people have divorced parents. They over-achieve for attention. That wasn't exactly my school.

The *other* school says you should instantly become über-truculent and demanding, and put everything you do your entire life down to your bad upbringing. I tended to this school, it being rather easier and low maintenance, plus it tended to mean better Christmas presents, if dodgier exam results. It had worked reasonably well during my teens, but when your friends no longer *have* to see you every day in class and are too busy off doing horrid careers and stuff – well, so, now I was twenty-eight, and it was definitely becoming less fun by the day, especially when everyone I used to know had suddenly become fascinated by MORTGAGES, for fuck's sake. I just didn't get it. Boys and pop music – fascinating. Mortgages are what you get when you look up the dictionary definition of 'not fascinating'. Hence my precipitative flat-hopping.

To make matters even worse, I was starting to realize that my anti-establishment tendencies were beginning to marginalize me – not as a free spirit, as I'd always thought, but along with the old hippies and socialist workers and people who talked about smashing the state but couldn't actually get it together to wash their trousers – ever. It was extremely depressing. I mean, nobody likes washing their trousers, but I didn't want it to define my entire existence. To make matters worse, my father, who took up bringing home blonde women full time after he left my mum, had recently brought home one my age. Who also had a mortgage. And a sports car. Sigh.

Josh had a mortgage, but he was also a complete sweetie pie who could be endlessly relied upon in a crisis, as I knew and had shamefully abused in the past.

We finally pulled up in front of his dilapidated Victorian pile in Pimlico.

'I see you've still not got the builders in.'

'No, I couldn't afford them,' said Josh, hopping out of the car without opening the door and pulling up two bin-liners of my stuff. 'Until now,' he smiled sweetly in my direction.

'Ah yes, about that . . .' I followed him in, clutching my socks and pants bag, my cheese plant and Frank Sinatra the bear. One of the reasons that I'd wound up in Harlesden in the first place was that being a freelance florist and general under-achieving free spirit didn't exactly pay very much, and Pimlico was basically posh these days.

He told me, and I breathed a sigh of relief. The going rate for coffins wasn't so bad after all.

The flat was quiet inside. It was big and tatty and comfortable, and I'd always liked it. Josh had bought right at the top of the market and paid a stupid amount of money for it – apart from being infested with dry rot and woodworm and all sorts of other nasty moving things, it needed a new roof – but it was a good homey home. The kitchen was large, with nasty old units, a rickety table and four chairs in the middle, cracked floor tiles, and a huge window at the back which opened on to a rusty excuse for a fire escape. I pottered about in my tiny new room, mostly leaning against cupboards to get them to shut and stuffing things under the bed.

'Umm, sorry about the mess,' hummed Joshua when I went back into the kitchen for a cup of tea. 'It's not usually . . . Well, in fact, it is.'

'Great!' I said.

He smiled weakly at me. I leaned across the table.

'Josh, thank you. I'm sorry I forced you into this. I promise I'll be a good tenant. You'll see. I promise.'

He grinned back at me.

'Good. And I could do with the company, to be honest – Kate works all the time and Addison is, well . . .'

'Yikes!' I pounced immediately. 'Tell me the gossip about Kate.'

'Oh, she's a complete bitch, as ever,' said Kate, striding into the kitchen and dumping a Marks and Spencer's bag, an enormous briefcase, a Nicole Farhi raincoat and an expensive leather handbag on to one of the rickety chairs.

'Hello, Holly. Josh left me a message on my voicemail. Which I got about ten minutes ago. But never mind, eh? Welcome anyway.'

I went to give her a hug or something, but she was already en route to the bottle opener. Josh touched her lightly on the arm.

'How was your day, Skates?'

'Great. Great. As usual. Two sexist comments, four reports to do this week, one irregular forecasting, and I have to be in Dublin for 8 a.m. tomorrow morning, to give a presentation on a report I haven't even *read* yet. Then back in the office by noon to account for myself, two more meetings and a 4 p.m.

deadline for the Kinley account. Oh, and then a client dinner with a bunch of ghastly old bores who'll try and feel me up in the Met bar.'

Josh nodded sagely. Kate pulled the cork with a savage 'pop' and poured out three humongous glasses of wine.

'So, Holly, what are you up to these days?'

Kate had always intimidated me. We'd only really met because the three of us were on the same corridor of student halls. We'd both stayed friends with Josh – most people did – but never really got on with each other. She was rather more of a pull-yourself-up-by-the-bootstraps-type person – she didn't actually say 'lickspittle', but you could tell when she was thinking it.

She'd done business studies and got some hugely well-paid and prestigious job in the City, which hadn't helped relations between us particularly. I always felt she was just about to offer to buy a *Big Issue* off me.

Actually, that wasn't quite why we didn't get on. Specifically, well, you know in Freshers' Week, one is often, er, tacitly encouraged to get . . . Well, anyway. Originally, there were the three of us in a row on one of those grotty endless corridors that was distinctly not the Brideshead University model I'd always dreamt of. It was in Coventry for a start.

Students were still sharing showers, a good life lesson for future flatshares in how much YEUCH people are actually made of, and how, just when you think you've seen everything, there's always a new variety of repulsiveness.

Josh had opened his door on the very first day and sat there crudely beaming at everyone who walked past, a technique which probably wouldn't have worked so well if he hadn't been so blond and pretty. I wandered in there by accident, already worried by how keen my dad and Blondie had been to leave me, but faintly reassured by the seemingly enormous cheque now burning a hole in my pocket. It worked out to a lot of Caramac bars, although, as I found out four weeks later, not that many beers and taxis.

'Hello,' said Josh. 'This place is nice, isn't it?'

'It's a shit hole!' I said, looking around at the regulation stained walls, stained carpet and dodgy pinboard.

'Oh yes . . .' He took in the room. 'So it is. Oh well – only three years to go.'

'And a week,' I said.

'Of course. Hmm. What do you think the cooking facilities are like?'

'I don't know – what's a cooking facility?'

Through the paper-thin walls we could hear loud, fairly dramatic sobbing. We raised our eyebrows at each other.

'What is this, primary school?' I said, a tad callously.

'Maybe she misses her mother,' said Josh.

I sniffed derisorily, something I'd been practising throughout my teens to great effect.

'Come on,' he said, 'let's go cheer her up.'

'Ah, the beginning of my crazy university years,' I said, but I followed him dutifully outside.

Next door, perched on the narrow bed, with the door open, sat Kate, thin and a little pinched-looking, and dressed head to toe in immaculately ironed Benetton separates. Even though she appeared distraught with grief, she still had been composed enough to hang up lots of perfect shirts, I noticed.

'Hello there,' said Josh. 'I'm sure it won't be as bad as all that. When I went to boarding school I cried for my mother for four days. Mind you, I was six years old at the time.'

'My *mother*?' said Kate, spluttering. 'I don't miss my *mother*! I just can't believe I didn't do better in my A-levels than to end up in this shitty place!'

'Didn't you work hard?' I asked her. That was my excuse.

'Of *course* I worked hard!' she said, looking up. 'I had a fucking place at Magdalene.'

'Oh, I see. They only want really tall girls, don't they?' I said sympathetically.

'What the fuck's nervous anxiety, anyway?' Kate went on, ignoring me. 'I'll tell you what it is: it isn't enough to get your

13

exam marks upgraded. I wish I'd had a fucking full-on nervous breakdown. Then they'd have *had* to let me in.'

'Have one now,' I suggested. I knew she wasn't actually shouting at me, but she was certainly shouting in my direction.

'Don't worry,' said Josh kindly, touching her on the shoulder. 'Would you like to come out with me? I'm going ice skating at the Christian Union.'

'You're not Christian are you?' I said, disappointed. I'd liked him.

'No! But I sure can SKAAAAAATE!'

So the three of us ended up in one of those forced friendships that come together extremely quickly out of necessity in early college. Kate quickly decided that Josh was her own personal property, which annoyed me. OK, so both of them had flat stomachs and good posture, but I didn't like the assumption that as Kate was prettier than me I should butt out, especially as I didn't even fancy Josh and in fact assumed pretty much from the start that he was gay, rather than, as I later found out, completely and utterly confused.

Kate hadn't cottoned on to this, however, and insisted on treating me as an annoying kid sister hanging round with the grown-ups, her repertoire including: 'You again, Holly?' 'You don't mind, do you, but I've only got two cups?' and 'Sorry, Holl, but it's only a plus-one.' Soon their status as monied and classy students at a poor and common college became clear, and I started going out with a greasy sports science student who once tried to teach me kung fu and chipped my collarbone, so I pretty much left them to it – which doesn't mean to say that she didn't really fuck me off, Kate being the accepted sucking pig to Josh's sow and my runt. An analogy bordering on the disgusting, but that's how it was.

In time, of course, Kate realized that simply because her and Josh went to a lot of places JUST THE TWO OF THEM, it didn't actually mean they were a couple. But not before I got my revenge . . .

In a misguided attempt at collegiate unity, two socially inadequate but horrifically bouncy 'ents of-ficers' – to be involved in 'ents' of course meaning you are anything but – arranged a 'Corridor Convulsion' early on in our first term. There was a good and complicated reason for it at the time, but what it meant in effect was an excuse to haul in lots of weepingly cheap alcohol and stuff it down the faces of naïve but nubile eighteen-year-olds in the hope that they might accidentally strip their tops off and run down the corridor. Actually, maybe that was the official reason and it just sounded all right in those days.

Josh of course would do anything of a community nature enthusiastically and Kate was still in the 'gamely joining in' stage, before she realized that she could dress up as a giant antelope and it still wasn't going to make her sexually attractive to Josh, so we all trawled into the hallway to figure out what was happening.

What was happening was what happens anywhere with horribly diverse sects of shy and socially inept people away from home for the first time and unsure of their very identities: groups of twos and threes stood in small corners grunting nervously at each other and downing obscure former communist bloc spirits as fast as they possibly could. A group of rugby- or aspirant rugby-playing lads started getting rowdy in the corner, and the ents officers gibbered around, excited yet again at the possibility of not being one of the 29 per cent of students who *leave* Coventry certified virgins. What they didn't yet know was that 100 per cent of ents officers leave 100 per cent of all institutions certified virgins.

A petite, very pretty blonde girl who wore enormous fleeces and was clearly out to score with a rugby boy – Why? being the only unanswered question – became the first person, at around 10.30 p.m. and after a lot of goading, to take off her top and flee down the corridor, bouncing merrily, to massive applause. After that, about fifteen of the men immediately tried to do it with their cocks out – what *is* it about British men and being completely naked for no good reason? I've seen someone play the piano with his.

Anthropologists would have had a field day with all this, given, truly, how few of us that year had yet seen another buck-naked human being we weren't blood related to.

15

Finally, and it all starts to get a bit hazy around this point, pretty much everyone had done a quick streak and been accepted into the gang. Mine would have been sexier had I not stumbled over somebody's outstretched foot and made a noise which sounded like a fart (but *wasn't*) on my way down. Josh skipped along his, to yells of 'faggot', but generally good-natured ones.

And at last there was only one more person to go. Kate would clearly rather have died than take part in anything so vulgar. She had that faraway look in her eyes she got whenever she dwelt on what romantic and glistening evenings she could be having at Oxford *right now*. I started egging her on, and pointing out to people that she was the only one who hadn't done it, just in case she got away with it.

'Shut *up*, Holl,' Kate hissed.

'Kate hasn't gone! Kate hasn't gone!' I shouted loudly to the rugby players.

'KATE! KATE! KATE! KATE!' they started chanting.

Kate flushed redder than ever.

'Everyone else has,' I said petulantly.

'Go on, Skatie,' said Josh, who, due to his upbringing, was completely unable to understand why someone wouldn't want to take part in group-enforced humiliation in the name of fun. The rugby boys name-calling had failed to abate and formed an increasingly ferocious background.

'Oh, for fuck's sake!' said Kate, furious.

'KATE! KATE! KATE!'

Kate pulled up her top extremely quickly and made a sprint down the corridor. Immediately, silence fell. Quite simply, Kate had the flattest chest anyone had ever seen.

Of course, nowadays, that doesn't matter. Kate Moss resembles a boy who's been stung by two bees and nobody bats an eyelid. But when you're nineteen and desperate to find yourself attractive . . .

To cut a long story short, that was never a moment when anybody needed me to inadvertently expostulate:

'Christ, they look like two Pop-Tarts!' loudly enough for everyone to hear.

*   *   *

Kate handed me one of the glasses of wine.

'Sorry, I didn't hear that . . . what did you say you were up to again?'

'Ehm, I'm . . . I'm a florist.'

'Still! My goodness. Is it . . . fulfilling?'

'Huh?'

Fulfilling? I couldn't even conceive of what that might mean, and was standing with a confused expression on my face until I remembered that when Kate asked a question, she required a logical answer *quickly* – time being money, etc.

'Yes, it is,' I said. 'The pay is shit and the hours are crap and your hands are wet all day, but apart from that it's fantastic.'

She smiled thinly. 'Never mind, eh? You'd probably hate a career job anyway.'

'This *is* a . . .'

'Where do you work?'

'Actually, I'm freelance at the moment . . .'

Well, I couldn't commute to Hackney Flowerarama any more, but I did have a chum at New Covent Garden who was going to let me help out.

'Oh, so you're like a *temp* florist? How funny!'

I didn't know what to say to that, so I went and helped Josh, who was chopping onions for spaghetti bolognese. I could see Kate reflected in the kitchen window. She did look fantastic – tired, but fantastic. Her dark hair was glossy and tied back in a chignon, and she was wearing an expensive fawn suit. I wiped my hands on my pinafore and sighed.

'Tell me about your mystery flatmate. Is he away?' I asked Josh. Josh and Kate looked at each other and smiled.

'Away?' echoed Kate. 'Addison doesn't *do* away.'

'What – you mean, he's in the house?'

I felt nervous suddenly. I'd been stomping about merrily for two hours, singing and making loud noises in the toilet, and all along there had been an additional presence. Spooky.

17

'Oh yes,' said Josh. 'I'll probably leave some food out for him later on. He forgets to eat until he faints, so I put it by his door.'

Curioser and curioser.

'Can I meet him?'

They exchanged glances again.

'Ehm, best not.'

'Well, I'll have to meet him sometime,' I argued. 'What if he just pops up in the bathroom one day? I'll scream the place down.'

'You might do that anyway,' said Kate.

'Addison is very . . . well, sensitive. He's a computer buff, you see.'

Only Josh still used words like 'buff'.

'You mean, what – an anorak? A geek? Dork? Nerd?'

'Ahem.'

Josh gave a polite cough as a shadow flitted across the open kitchen door.

'Is that him?' I hissed. 'I'm going to see.'

Kate stepped in front of me and shut the door.

'What *is* going on?' I asked. 'Is he hideously deformed, like the Elephant Man?'

Josh patted me on the shoulder.

'Sorry, Holls. We're not doing this on purpose. Addison does a lot of highly technical, top-level computer work, and he hates being disturbed when he's working.'

'But he's in the flat.'

'He works from home.'

'And for about twenty-three hours a day,' muttered Kate. 'It's really easy to forget a hard day's work when you've got beeps and tapping going on all night next door to you.'

'Better than some things . . .' I started to say, then remembered that Josh's bedroom was next door to mine, and didn't.

'So, I mean, what's he *like*?' I started again. A man of mystery? Sounded good to me.

'Oh, you tell her, Josh. I'm absolutely exhausted,' said Kate. She took out her Psion and started stabbing at it, making me feel like a complete idiot. Then Josh and I shared our 'it's Kate' glance, and I felt a bit better.

'Well . . .' started Josh, stirring the sauce. I went and leaned on the cabinet next to him.

'He's quiet. Very quiet. In fact, I think he'd rather not speak at all. He was amazed when we didn't have e-mail in every room in the house so we could just communicate that way.'

I raised my eyebrows. At the table, Kate let out a long 'How can I be so busy and successful when there are people in my kitchen making spaghetti bolognese?' type sigh.

'Whenever he bumps into one of us in the hallway he acts like a startled rabbit, like he genuinely wasn't expecting anyone to be there. And he refuses to answer the phone or the doorbell. And he never eats.'

'Hence the food drops.'

'Hmm? Yes.' Josh artfully splashed a measure of red wine into the sauce, crying out 'Whoops!' flamboyantly when he got a bit on his professional apron. I really could understand why women had a hard time taking him seriously.

He caught me watching him.

'Am I being gay again?'

I smiled at him, colouring slightly. When we were at college, I used to tease him on a semi-continual basis when he'd bring his girl stories to me, but now I was his tenant, and it felt a bit uncomfortable.

'That was a very masculine dash of wine. But I am definitely fascinated by my new invisible flatmate.'

'Try taking the room next to his – it'll wear off soon enough,' growled Kate from the table, where she continued to do Very Hard Sums.

'Oh, can I?!' I yelped, before realizing the faux pas.

'Sorry, darling,' said Josh, 'but you're not – aha! – *coffin* up enough rent for that!'

Kate and I stared at him in disgust until he apologized.

* * *

Dinner was good. Josh liked to cook, and was good at it. He had a sinecure at his family's ancient law firm near Chancery Lane, which required him to turn up at about ten thirty looking well groomed, take long lunches and impress foreign clients with his Englishness and hand-made shoes, before retiring to the senior partners' offices at four thirty to partake of an early gin and tonic before heading home. Which was just as well, as he wasn't the most academic of characters: you wouldn't want him defending you in a murder trial whilst simultaneously admiring the court cornicing. The only thing preventing the absolute outbreak of class war was that he didn't get paid *that* much for it. It just stunned me that such things still existed outside of the kind of stuff Rupert Graves does in all his films.

Kate ate about three bites, wiped her lips ostentatiously with a napkin then declared she had mounds to do and retreated to her room with the remainder of the wine. Her good night to me was curt, to say the least.

I looked at Josh.

'*What* is with her?' I asked. I mean, she'd always been uptight, but this was real carrot-up-the-bum stuff.

Josh toyed with his spaghetti.

'Oh, it's that stupid job of hers,' he said. 'She works fourteen-hour days, then comes home like a bear.'

'What, pooing in the woods?'

'Grizzly.'

'Oh. Good spag bol.'

'Thank you.' Josh coloured prettily. 'So, anyway, I keep saying she should change it, do something less stressful, but she just bares her teeth at me and hisses something about me being privileged and how I would never understand what it means to fight for something.'

'Her dad's a GP, isn't he?'

'Uh huh.'

'Hmm. But she must make an absolute fortune. Why does she live here?'

Josh looked faintly amused.

'Charmingly direct as ever, darling.'

'Oh, you *know* what I mean.'

'I know. I'm not sure, really. She does make a stinking amount of money, though. Something like more in her bonus than I do in a year.'

Than I will in a decade, I thought to myself mournfully.

'We moved in together when I came down,' Josh went on, 'and she's been here ever since, so I suppose she likes it. It's only four stops on the tube, and pretty cheap.'

I remembered a rather better reason though. Well well well, after all this time. But then, even if she didn't still fancy him, I suppose if I was feeling stressed out, I wouldn't mind coming back to a nice warm flat and spaghetti bolognese and someone nice like Josh you could be rude to. Well, she certainly wouldn't get away with being rude to me.

'Would you *mind* getting out of that shower!' screeched Kate, banging her Clarins bottles on the door at five o'clock one morning (I was doing nights at the market). She carried them daily in and out of the bathroom, presumably in case I stole them.

'I don't know what can be keeping you in there *that* long. You can only smell of flowers, surely.'

She banged again.

'OK, *OK*, I'm *coming*,' I yelled back, frantically drying myself and wondering if I could stab her with a cotton bud.

'I have got a plane to catch, Holly,' she said. Because I have a career and you don't, she might as well have added.

'Oh no! The Euro will fall!' I opened the bathroom door dishevelled, wrapped in two threadbare towels which almost but didn't quite cover all my bits.

'Will it?' she said, instantly alert, then relaxed as her brain realized the context. She gave a tight smile, said, 'Excuse me,' and slipped past me, unbelting her Liberty robe.

Bitch, I thought to myself – one of my litany of dreaded 'thought retorts' – and headed for bed.

21

* * *

Over the next week or so I started to settle in. I was working part-time shifts at the New Covent Garden market, day and night, and as Kate went to work at 6.30 a.m. and returned at 9 p.m., I normally missed her, and steered well clear of the shower in the morning.

The house, though always untidy, was clean – for me, a perfect state of affairs. Kate paid someone to come in and 'do' once a week, which I disagreed with in principle but thoroughly enjoyed the benefits of. It began to feel like home, despite the coffin, which was nine foot by seven. Not the kind of place you'd let a cat visit, in case its brains got bashed to bits in a nasty swinging incident.

I was used to creeping in at odd times of night, and was always amazed to hear the faint tapping of fingers on a keyboard, random beeps and small buzzing noises from Addison's room.

I never saw him, but fantasized wildly about him. A monster? Kate and Josh's deformed lovechild, half man half robocop? Perhaps he was blind! That was why he crept around in the dark and didn't go outside. I had a brief romantic reverie of my being his life partner, caring for him, being his lover and his guide; 'Holly,' he would say, 'you, *you* are my eyes.' And, plus it would be a double bonus when I got to forty and wouldn't have to bother about how I looked.

Then, ping, I realized that the Internet is in fact an almost purely visual medium, and apologized in my head to all the blind people in the world.

Finally, after about a fortnight, I cracked.

It was about 3 a.m., and the house was completely still. I'd been unpacking tulips from 11 p.m., but the work had thinned out and Johnny, my gaffer, had sent me home. It took about ten minutes on Josh's bicycle – in the very dead of night I would glide down hills, hands free, and have to restrain myself from shouting out loud to fill up the rare London silence.

I had crept into the house, exhilarated and pink-cheeked from the spring wind. My hair was tangled, and I didn't feel sleepy.

22

My hours were so topsy-turvy, I didn't know when I slept. The television, however, was in the sitting room, which backed on to Kate's room – so, no Channel 5 soft porn for me. I was about to head through to the chilly kitchen to make some tea when I saw the omnipresent blue glow underneath the door, the familiar tap tap tap.

Well, sod it, I thought to myself. Two weeks living in the same house as someone and not seeing them is simply freaky and unnatural. There could be nothing wrong with just popping in and introducing myself, for fuck's sake. It was only . . . well, ten past three in the morning. I felt strangely excited, like playing ring-the-bell-and-run-away. If I got yelled at, I could always hide and say it was Kate.

I crept across the hall, instead of walking across it like I normally did when I came in late at night so everyone would know it was me and not a burglar; steeled myself and rapped gently on the door.

The typing noise stopped. Encouraged, I tapped again. 'Hello?'

There was no response.

Feeling like an idiot, I repeated, 'Hello?' leaning slightly on the door.

Clearly it wasn't locked.

Half horrified at what I was doing, I pushed open the door.

The large room was dark, but light streamed in from the moon and the streetlights. The place was also lit up with an unearthly green glow, which I realized, once my eyes adjusted, came from a huge VDU. The room was so filled with banks of electronic equipment it was like the flight deck of the Starship *Enterprise*. LEDs lit up and monitors bleeped quietly.

Sitting with his back to me was a very tall man, who resembled a normal man who'd been put on a rack and stretched out. His black spiky hair stuck up straight from his head, and I couldn't see his face.

He didn't turn round, although he must have heard me, because his back stiffened.

'Hello?' I whispered. 'Sorry to disturb you, but I saw you were still working and, well, I moved in here a couple of weeks ago and my name's Holly and I thought that, you know, since we lived together, we should perhaps lay eyes on one another.'

I swallowed. My voice seemed to echo in the empty room, and I felt like a complete dork. Then, when he didn't reply, I started to get annoyed. It wasn't like I was demanding anything unreasonable. This was only basic human contact, for fuck's sake! The way Kate and Josh tiptoed around him was ridiculous. He needed shaking up, if you asked me. He still hadn't even bothered turning round! That was bloody rude.

'Oh, I'm sorry,' I said. 'I didn't realize you were so rude. I won't bother you again. *Excuse* me.'

I turned to go. Slowly, I heard the revolving chair creep round behind me. I looked back.

A huge pair of dark brown eyes, blinking rapidly, regarded me with a mixture of curiosity and fear. I almost gasped aloud. He was . . . well, just spectacularly beautiful. Just, like, *Oh my GAWD*! Not in a pretty, boyband poofy kind of way, but that chiselled, sensitive look that cries out, 'I may have been staring at this computer screen for fifteen hours, but as my physiognomy suggests, I have the soul of a poet. And not one of those ones with hair in their noses that you see in the Sunday supplements.' Even from behind his glasses you could see that his eyelashes cast long shadows on his ludicrously high cheekbones and a frown seemed to pass over his exquisitely high forehead.

I managed to quell my first urge, which was to lie at his feet and present my stomach to him to be tickled, when I noticed he was wearing a *Star Trek* T-shirt. How original of someone who played with computers all day long to like *Star Trek*, I thought.

'Excuse me,' he said. His voice was quiet and soft, with no discernible accent – not like mine. I got very London, selling flowers every day.

He looked at his hands. His fingers were incredibly long – practically prehensile. I actually sighed.

'I was a bit caught up in what I was doing.'

He sounded apologetic, and I was in one of those brain-twisting moods whereby if you meet someone who is clearly your soul mate you feel an overwhelming urge to be rude to them.

'So you don't listen to people when they come to say "hello"? What were you doing?'

He stared at his hands again and didn't say anything. I thought for a bit.

'OK, shall we start again?' I announced. 'I'm Holly, and you're Mr Addison, I presume.'

'Not mister, just Addison,' he said quietly.

'Ooh, what a great name!' I said, reaching out to shake his hand. He didn't take mine, and regarded it with some alarm. 'Addison Madison?'

What? What magic potion had I just taken to turn me into the Moron of the Western World? I cringed.

He blinked. His eyelashes practically bounced off his sweetly pouted lips. 'Ehm, no . . . Addison Farthing.'

'*Farthing, Farthing – right*, of course, how *silly* of me,' I gushed, like I was interviewing him on a breakfast show. 'Of *course*.'

I was backing away and backing down big time.

'So, anyway, I thought, you know, time to say hello, pop in, have a chat . . .'

Addison continued to regard me impassively.

'So, here we are, having a chat . . . and it's been *lovely* chatting to you. Really. We must do it again some time.'

He continued staring at me as I backed out of the room.

'Great! Nice to meet you! Nice Starship *Enterprise*, by the way!' I said as I got to the door, but he was already turning back to his enormous screen and had clearly forgotten my very existence. Huge cables twisted round the table legs, heading off God knows where. The tapping started up again and I closed the door gently. Outside in the hall I leaned on the wall and let my jaw drop in wonder. Oh my God. No wonder Kate liked him locked away.

'*I* spoke to Addison last night,' I announced to Josh the next day. He was eating dinner and I was eating breakfast and trying to avoid his dinner – the smell of pork chops half an hour after I'd woken up made me feel a bit sick, I had discovered.

Josh looked up at me from an article he was reading in *Homes & Gardens*. I'd suggested *Loaded* as a slightly more useful manual for pulling, but it didn't quite suit him, somehow.

'And?'

'And?? *AND*?? Excuse me, but as landlord of this establishment, I do believe it is your duty to let me know when you're hoarding Johnny Depp in geek form on your property!'

'You never asked.'

'*Why* did I never think to ask?' I asked, slapping myself on the forehead. 'So many gorgeous computer geeks in the world, so little time. *Josh*! If it hadn't been for my extreme bravery last night I might never have met my future life partner! Ooh –' a thought occurred to me – 'and our kids get to be brainy, too!'

'He is very pretty, I suppose,' said Josh, a tad dreamily. I narrowed my eyes at him.

'Only in an objectively aesthetic way! Not in a romantic way! Not that there would be anything wrong with that! But I don't! Not that it's bad!'

'Stop, stop! You've got caught in the Richard Gere "I'm not gay/but it's OK" cycle of eternal justification. The only way to break free is to remove that plate of pork chops from my vicinity before I vomit on it.'

'Thank goodness for your magic spell-breaking powers,' said Josh, picking up his plate and moving over to the sink.

'You know, I must have him,' I went on. 'He will be mine.'

'But he doesn't *talk*.'

'That's OK. I can talk to you, or my mother. Addison is for *kissing* and *worshipping*.'

'So, like, there's no difference between me and your mother?' asked Josh gloomily, rinsing his plate off.

'Well, you haven't ordered me to help with the washing-up yet, so, perhaps there is.'

'Don't you have work to go to?' he asked, a tad crossly.

'Ah, *that's* more like it.'

26

'Fine. See you later. I'll just continue here on my lifelong mission of female identification.'

I popped my head back round the door.

'You know, if you meant that sarcastically, you should really take that pinny off.'

He gave me the V's.

'Bye, Addison!' I called out cheerily as I passed his door. There was a small break in tapping in response. I took it as a good sign.

Two

It was getting dark when I hopped on the bike and headed up to the market. Going out in the chilly nights was the worst; I knew I had several hours of rushing about with my hands wet to come, and all around me the nine-to-fivers were heading for home, fresh pasta and *The Bill*. And they all made twice as much as me. It didn't seem fair. Working in the market wasn't anything like working in a shop. Then, you got to choose things yourself and put them together, and if someone had been rude to you on the phone you could put a bug in their gladioli. Here, I had to check ten thousand tulips and try to work out which ones were the best.

I worked for Johnny, who was wizened and had been on the flower markets for four hundred and seventy years, as he never stopped reminding me.

'Aye, you never saw colours like that in my day,' he'd snort derisively at one of the more over-the-top hybrids.

'That's because everything was in black and white, then,' I'd point out to him. 'It was the olden days.'

'People used to eat flowers during the war, you know.' He was quite one for reminiscing. In fact, he was absolutely, bar none, the best person I'd ever met at making up things about the war.

'Hey, Johnny,' I waved to him as I whizzed round the corner. The lorries hadn't started to unload yet, so people were standing around, smoking roll-ups and gossiping about magnolias. The flower people despised the fruit people in the next set of bays, and they in turn thought the flower people were a bunch of big pansies who couldn't lift a box of melons if their lives depended on it.

'Hey there, lass.' He regarded me critically. 'You know, when I was your age, I was selling out the back of my own van.'

'Johnny, you have no idea how old I am. In fact, I'm nine years old. And I have my own van. I do this for fun.'

'I never met a lassie who knew when to shut up,' he observed mournfully, and threw me over a pair of heavy gloves.

I'd only been there a couple of weeks, and already I hated it. It was exactly like school. The girls all wore inappropriate clothing, smoked behind the sheds and picked on me. Either that or they were so stupid they had to be reminded every day how to pick up a box of flowers without drooling on it.

So I tended to slog away on my own, pausing only to hurl abuse at Johnny or to point out things to the drooling girls along the lines of 'Box – there! . . . You see box? Pick up box?'

The smoking girls teased me because I'd been to college, particularly Tash, their queen, this scrawny girl with thick black eyeliner who had a real mother-smoked-in-pregnancy look about her. Tonight she sidled up alongside me, observed my work closely for several minutes, and then said:

'Hmm, yes, I see now why that needed a degree – getting all those tulip heads in a line can't be easy.'

The rough boys all guffawed and I tried to laugh but couldn't. I hated her, and I hated being bullied, and however rude I could be to Johnny it wouldn't translate to this lot. They were rough as badgers' arses.

'Could you pass the sign-in sheet?' I hated it but sometimes I just had to talk to her.

'Sorry, love, I've only got a GCSE in general studies.'

All the boys laughed again, and one of them shouted, 'Oi, watch out, Tash, she'll trip on the chip falling off your shoulder.'

I grimaced and pretended to join in, boiling inside, but really I felt like when I was taken by some older girls to see *The Rocky Horror Picture Show* when I was eleven – it was all too trashy and I just didn't get it, but I was laughing along anyway. They were mean, mean kids. Because I didn't blow cigarette smoke out of my nose they called me TinBits.

'Please,' begged one of the lads, bending on one knee before me, 'your exquisite virginal majesty, might I just for one second peek up your skirt?'

'She's got her knickers welded to her bottom,' yelled Tash.

I very nearly flashed my tits at him just to piss him off, but instead made a hasty vow to myself to apply for every florist's job in a five thousand-mile radius.

For the rest of the night, Tash contrived to make fourteen derogatory remarks, upset my flowers four times and spend at least an hour talking about me (I suspected) on prolonged fag breaks with the lads. I was being bullied! I couldn't believe it! This wasn't fair.

My shift finished at 4 a.m. and I freewheeled home as usual, down the hill back to the big house. I crept in and saw the light on under Addison's door. The urge to see him again was overwhelmingly strong so I wandered into the kitchen and made two cups of tea. I didn't know how he liked it, so I put three sugars in for luck as I'd never seen him eat – he probably needed the nutrition. Then I ferreted around for a couple of biscuits to add to it, but the only thing going was a very lonely Penguin – Kate allowed herself one every fortnight. I took it anyway, planning to replace it, pronto.

I knocked on the door softly.

'Addison, it's me.'

The soft clicking noises stopped for a second. I could imagine him desperately trying to wrack his brains for a single person he could be expected to identify from a 'me'.

I pushed the door again and popped in.

'I made tea!' I announced, like a fifties housewife.

His short-sighted – oh, but beautiful – eyes swivelled round to focus on me. His glasses were sitting on top of the mother-ship console.

'Tea!' I indicated by holding the cups up and motioning like a lunatic.

He focused on the cup and followed its path as I went to place it beside him whilst I wondered if he was mentally subnormal.

'Not there!' he barked.

'OK, OK, put the gun down. How about I hand it to you?'

Slowly he extended his arm. I placed the cup in his hand, handle facing outwards – which meant burning a hole in my hand, but I didn't mind because when he took it, the tips of our fingers touched, and I swear I felt a bolt of electricity shoot through me.

I waggled the Penguin at him.

'Penguin?'

He stared at it for a bit then shook his head, so I ate it. After all, as he'd taken the tea, that implied a contract that allowed me to stay for a little bit.

I leaned over. His computer screen was covered in bizarre symbols, just like in James Bond films.

'What are you working on?'

He tried to cover up the screen, but as his arms were like matchsticks, it didn't have much effect. However, as the symbols meant as much to me as EC policy directives, it was a pointless exercise anyway.

'Ehm, nothing. Thanks for the tea . . .'

He sipped it, then tried to disguise his gagging reflex.

'That's all right. How was your day? Mine was shitty.'

And so I told him all about the nasty boys at the flower yard. Mainly for conversation really, because I knew the second I stopped talking there would be complete silence.

Much to my surprise he appeared to be listening – well, not doing anything else, which had to pass for it.

When I'd finished, I took another sip at my tea and said:

'So, what do you think I should do?'

He looked at me for a second, then cracked an absolutely heartbreaking smile.

'Not talk to anyone?'

A sentence! Almost. I grinned back at him, then decided to leave on a high note. I nodded with my mouth closed, mouthed 'good night' to him, and retreated, leaving him sniffing suspiciously at his tea.

'Success!' I crowed to Josh the following evening. 'He *talked* to me.'

'What did he say?'

'Well, he told me not to talk to anyone. But apart from that I consider it an outright success.'

'Oh, speaking of outright success, did you steal Kate's Penguin?'

Shit; I'd forgotten all about it.

'Mmmm . . . maybe.' I surreptitiously checked round the outside of my mouth in case there was any chocolate left there from last night.

'You're in trouble.'

'OK, OK, I'll just go out and get her one.'

'It's too late. Plus, she knows it's a blue one. I'd make myself scarce, if I were you.'

Unfortunately I wasn't working that night and, annoyingly, felt that cold thing you get in the pit of your stomach when you know you're going to get into trouble later.

'Argh! I am not in trouble! I am going to go out now and buy her fifteen Penguin biscuits and . . . and make her eat herself to death like in *Seven*. I am NOT going to let her intimidate me like this. She is so damn ANAL about everything.'

'Which is why she's one of the best corporate raiders under thirty in London –'

'*Just* under thirty.'

'I know what she's like. Be nice to her. She has it hard enough at work. Everyone is really mean to her.'

31

'Ooh, gossip? 'Fess up.'

Josh was an indefatigable gossip, although he wouldn't thank you for pointing out this particular trait.

'Well, she just has an overwhelming inability to spot married guys. I mean, they can have a bloody suntan ring round their fourth finger and Kate believes them when they say it's impetigo. And she's seeing this guy now who only phones her in two-minute bursts from call boxes at eleven thirty at night, and they do a lot of their dating in their lunch hours . . . Any day now she's going to find out he's another louse. Deep down, I think she realizes they are and it's all a big psychological mishmash.'

'Wow,' I said, nodding thoughtfully. 'That whole big psychological mishmash thing.'

And we each thought about our own for a second or two.

'So,' I resumed, 'she's grouchy all the time and it's not my fault.'

'I don't think she's that happy at having another woman around the flat.'

'I'm not exactly a threat,' I said, looking down at where the button should have been on my pyjamas. Fortunately, I'd known Josh a long time.

'It's not that. It's a territorial thing.'

I grunted. 'What, like cats have? I thought there was a funny smell in my room. Maybe she's pissed in it.'

'Ssh,' said Josh, as we heard the door open.

'Shit! I've forgotten to go out and get the Penguins!'

He winced at me as Kate did her normal arrival routine: an enormous sigh, an elaborate dumping of her expensive accoutrements, and a full-body lunge for the bottle opener.

Josh winked at me, and I smiled manfully.

'Hey, Kate, how's it going?'

'Shit! Holly, did you eat my Penguin?'

I cringed, which *wasn't* what was supposed to happen. I was supposed to say something along the lines of, 'Yeah – do ya wanna make somethin' of it?' and spit on the floor. Instead of which I said, 'Yes. Look, Kate, I'm really sorry, I'll buy you some more.'

32

'No, it's fine,' she sniffed, LYING. 'I've only been out working for twelve hours, slaving over a huge offshore investment, which is almost entirely my responsibility, something unheard of for someone under thirty . . .'

'Just . . .' I said, under my breath.

'. . . why on earth should I want or deserve a little bit of relaxation, which I've already bought and paid for, when I come home exhausted? I'm silly, really. I should just give it up and mess about with flowers and eat other people's Penguins all day long.'

She picked up the wine bottle and retreated from the room, continuing, 'Really, I must just be *so, so selfish*.'

Once she'd gone I beckoned to Josh.

'Hand me that bread knife.'

'Now, you remember what I said . . .'

'I heard what you said, and now I am going to kill her with a knife. GIVE it to me.'

'No.'

'I'm sorry. I don't think you understand the situation: I am going to have to kill Kate with a knife, and I'm asking you to pass it to me.'

'Sit down,' he said, handing me a plate of couscous. 'Ignore it. What else was Addison saying?'

'Nothing.'

'Don't sulk.'

'No, I mean it. Actually, nothing. Has he ever spoken to you?'

'Not really. He just turned up when we put the ad in, and he'd brought so much computer equipment we didn't have the heart to send him away again. Plus, Kate thought he was cute.'

'He's better than cute. Oh, did she try and pull him and fail?' I asked eagerly.

'No, she tried talking to him for ten minutes then ran out of attention span. Plus, also, he didn't show any of the normal signs of bastardy.'

'Ah, ooh, she is just SUCH a cow!' I exclaimed again.

'She's fine. Now, go out and buy the biscuits.'

'What! After all that – you must be joking.'

'Unless you want "all that" every night for the rest of your life, I would go and buy the biscuits.'

'Fine, fine, fine. I will go and buy the biscuits. Then, I will *pee* on the biscuits.'

I ended up heading to the gigantic supermarket which is open all night, all the time. I think they keep the staff caged there, like animals. They all have rickets from being out of natural light for so long.

I hate supermarkets. I can stand for hours in the shampoo section, stymied. Should I be putting fruit in my hair? What will happen if I don't? What *is* shampoo, anyway? Are there any more foods just out there waiting to be discovered? Etc, etc. As usual, it took me three hours to collect a more or less random selection of products, plus fourteen packets of Penguins. I'd wanted Josh to come with me or, ideally, volunteer to do it himself, but he'd started to get a bit shifty and got out work files to do stern lawyer stuff with – like, as if.

Finally I wandered home, feeling a bit mournful and stopping to put my bags down every five minutes.

When I walked in, the house was very quiet. Josh was locked away in his room – I hoped it was with his Playstation – and Addison had disappeared. I had never even seen him go to the toilet. I liked that. He was too unearthly for bodily functions. Men, or at least the ones I've always known, think that it's endearing to you if they fart a lot. Addison wouldn't be like that. And then, they'd smell of angel dew.

Feeling mildly nauseous, I backed my way into the kitchen with my sixteen bags, swung them round to dump them on the table and accidentally clobbered Kate on the side of the head. With the one with the tin cans in.

'Ow!' she growled at me.

'I'm sorry,' I cringed, though I wasn't really. But I didn't want her to think I'd done it on purpose.

'I didn't do it on purpose!'

'Oh, forget it,' she said.

I did a mental double take. That didn't sound like Kate. Surely she should be demanding my first-born child and threatening to take me to court.

'Really, I am sorry,' I said again, putting the rest of the bags down. I saw her properly for the first time. Her eyes were all red, and she was doing the giveaway, back-of-the-mouth sniff. As a world-class crier myself, I knew what had been going on.

'Are you OK?' I asked, as sincerely as I could, which of course meant it came out sounding like I was a confessional TV host.

'I'm fine, really.' She sniffed properly, and patted down her immaculately glossy hair. Now, there was someone who knew a bit about shampoo.

I started to unpack the shopping.

'What's the matter?' I asked, casually, as if I was a trained counsellor and did this kind of thing all the time.

'Nothing . . . nothing. Oh GOD.' Her face completely collapsed into tears. 'I HATE him. I really, really, really, really HATE him! And he doesn't even CARE!'

I put down the tin of Heinz spaghetti (where had that come from? Had I let a four-year-old do the shopping?) and sat down beside her.

'There you go,' I said, patting her lightly on the arm and saying the things you're supposed to. 'Don't worry. Don't worry. Absolutely, he's a bastard.'

'You don't even know him!' she snivelled.

'OK, is he a bastard?'

'YEESSS!'

I patted her harder. 'OK. Tell me, what happened?'

Her sobbing slowed down a little bit.

'I was seeing this guy, and I really liked him and I thought . . . well, stupid bloody me, eh, how dare I think that I could ever go out with someone who wasn't MARRIED?'

'Oh no!' I thought of what Josh had said. 'I'm really sorry. Didn't he tell you?'

'He said he thought I knew. I asked him to come out for my

35

birthday and he said he couldn't, he had to take Saffy to the dentist . . .'

'Who's Saffy?'

'That's what *I* said. Then he coughed and said, ehm, it was his dog.'

'A dog dentist.'

'Uh huh.'

'So you guessed from that?'

'Ehm, no. I believed him.'

'Ooh, nasty.'

She hiccuped. 'Then I went in to give him a surprise birthday present a day early . . .'

'But it's *your* birthday.'

She ignored me and sniffed even harder. 'And he'd left his wallet open on the desk . . . and I saw a picture of Saffy.'

'Not a dog?'

'A five-year-old girl!'

'Well, kind of a bit like a dog then . . .'

'No!'

'He could be divorced, couldn't he?'

'He isn't. I asked him. And now it's all over.' She started sobbing again.

'Why did no one else in the office *tell* you this?'

'I don't know! I don't really . . . talk to the girls in the office.'

I bet you don't, I thought. In fact, they probably set you up.

'Would you like some Heinz spaghetti?'

She thought about it for a moment.

'Yes, please.'

We sat and ate spaghetti in silence. I wanted to broach the topic of Josh, but I couldn't bring myself to. Also, whenever I'm in Kate's presence and trying to think of something to say, I always have a horrible compulsion that I'm about to accidentally mention Pop-Tarts, like Basil Fawlty and the Germans.

Kate appeared slightly coy and lifted up her fork.

'Ummm . . . would you like to come out for my birthday?'

'Sure!' I said. I was so relieved she wasn't giving me trouble,

I'd agreed before I realized what I'd just committed myself to.

Josh wasn't coming to Kate's birthday do. He was on parental duty. His parents were officially now genteel poor, living in a huge house they could no longer afford to run. They'd been cleaned out by that, Josh's education, and the education of his three sisters, who were all beautiful, and all completely stupid. Despite these extremely positive attributes, none of the girls had ever got married, which meant no new influx of old money into the fforbes' family coffers. The family, though, were holding up very well, marching on with some good stories and a lot of dogs and gin and tonics.

Which left, as far as I could make out, all of Kate's City friends and, ahem, me. Actually, I wanted to go. Young, rich, probably good-looking men . . . I liked the sound of it. Obviously, I was going to marry Addison, but that didn't mean I couldn't get taken to nice restaurants in the meantime.

Unfortunately, everything I had to wear was grubby – the market was going to make you dirty anyway, so it scarcely mattered – apart from my pyjamas, and I didn't think they would cut it. Finally, I dug up an old black summer dress which was so faded it could pass as grey, the colour *du jour*, apparently. It was too chilly, even in April, to wear it, and as I didn't have a tan it gave me an air of being clinically dead, but it really was all I had, which depressed me more than I wanted to think about.

I teamed it with my favourite daisy necklace and twirled in the mirror. I looked nine.

I was meeting Kate and her gang at some posh pub over an ice rink near Liverpool Street station. It was mobbed and full of braying, identical young men, who had rather better skin than the young men I'd grown up with but were just the same old wankers – with money.

'You've got to take it to the EXTREME!' one rather red-faced young man was hollering to his chum, two feet away.

'Quite!' the other, equally stolid, chap bawled back. 'That's why

I'm chartering a helicopter in the Canadian Rockies next season!'

'Uh . . . yars! Me too!'

The women were all eerily like Kate: their hair was shiny, and their lips were pursed. In fact, it was quite difficult to track Kate down in the thicket of size-eight Nicole Farhi, but I spotted her eventually. She didn't exactly appear overjoyed to see me, which pissed me off – I was feeling a bit off-the-beam as it was.

'Thanks for coming,' she said a little stiffly – reminding me that we were only forty-eight hours from wanting to murder each other. I nodded stiffly back, handed her a parcel and looked around. There were about eight guys in various stages of hee-hawing: my kinds of odds, I thought to myself. All around were champagne bottles and buckets.

'Great!' shouted one of the men. 'More champagne!'

I realized they were talking to me, and I panicked. Meanwhile, Kate had opened my present – a furry penguin. I'd thought it would be funny, but everyone stared at it in disdain.

'Oh, how *charmante*,' said one of the blokes, before the company stared at me one more time, cottoned on to the fact that I probably wasn't going to be buying them any champagne, then turned back to each other.

Kate gave me a half smile, and handed me a glass of champagne, then prodded the man to her right.

'*James*, this is Holly.'

James grunted at me. Kate leaned over to the person he was talking to, and nudged him as well.

'And this is James B.'

'James B.' I nodded.

'And over there are Jamie Egbert, Jim, and, ehm, Finn.'

Only Finn heard and tilted up his head. At first sight he looked a little odd, and I couldn't work out what it was. Then I realized that his tie was loosened, and he appeared to be wearing dirty spectacles. This reassured me, and I gave him a rather gushy grin, which clearly terrified him, as he instantly returned to staring at his glass.

'So!' said Kate brightly. 'This is all very nice.'

'Who are all these Jameses?' I asked her.

'Work colleagues, mostly,' she said.

'All of them?'

'Err, yes.'

'Birthdays can be horrid, can't they?' I said sympathetically.

'What do you mean?' she snapped.

'Nothing! Lovely champagne.'

I played with the glass for a second, then tried to lean into the two Jameses' conversation. They were talking ferociously about tax liability and the nastiness of the government for trying to extract money from their enormous pay-cheques to finance boring old services, and they managed to avoid looking me in the eye for ages whilst I tried to think of a ploy to enter the conversation.

'I hate tax too,' I announced when one of them paused for breath. 'Mind you, I don't pay more than ten pee in the pound.'

They raised their eyebrows at me. 'Really? What do you do with it? Is it offshore?' asked James 1.

'God, I wish I could figure it out,' said James 2. 'Did you form a limited company? What's your secret?'

'Ehmm . . . actually, most years I, just, ehm, fall below the threshold,' I mumbled.

Their faces registered shock, then instant embarrassment at registering shock – after all, they were terribly well brought up boys.

'Oh, lucky you,' said one of them, then clearly wished he hadn't. I felt an absolute pariah; you really shouldn't go drinking in the City unless you have at least one toe made of gold or something.

'What do you do?' asked James 2, regretting he'd ever bothered to focus on me.

'Ehm . . .' I thought frantically. This conversation, however demeaning, was the only thing I had going on, and it was about to finish two seconds after I said 'florist'. And they may all have been wankers, but they were handsome, rich wankers, so a girl has got to try. Now, let me see: Astronaut? Philosopher? Nurse? Ooh, they loved that.

'I'm a nurse,' I said. It was worth it just to see their little faces light up.

'Way-hey!' shouted one of them. 'What kind of nurse?'

I took another slurp of champagne. 'I work in the . . . waterworks department.'

James 2 turned white.

'Don't worry, I've washed my hands.'

'Oi! Jimmy! Egbert! Finn! Come and meet Kate's flatmate – she's a nurse!'

I hate boys.

Kate shot me a deadly look. I cringed at her. I'd only meant it as a laugh, but if she blew me out, I'd have to basically destroy myself with humbleness.

The other lads came over. They were a bit pissed, and up for ribbing someone they appeared to think was somewhat akin to a prostitute, but with an even kinder heart.

'Do you have to, like, you know, rub ointment in, like Joanne Whalley-Kilmer in *The Singing Detective*?' asked one of them, breathless.

'Sometimes.' I nodded sagely. 'Usually when I'm on night shift.'

There was a collective groan.

'Do, ahem, nurses still wear uniforms these days . . . ?' asked one of them, under the pretence of historical analysis.

'Oh yes. At St Mungo's our uniforms are white: it's like a hangover from the days when it used to be run by' – my *pièce de résistance* – 'nuns.'

'Ooh.'

'What do you find most interesting in your field? I mean, aren't you working a lot on prostate disease? Do you find this is becoming more of an environmental syndrome, or does it retain its genetic antecedence?'

Shite! This came from Finn, the one I'd noticed earlier, with the smeared glasses. Smart aleck bastard. A collective groan went up from the other boys. I wondered what a prostate was. I knew it was something to do with willies, but I didn't know what.

'Ehm . . . really, with the greenhouse effect it's all getting pretty environmental,' I stammered.

'*Really*? Is that true? How fascinating! Where else do you see this type of phenomenon . . . .?'

Annoyingly, the other boys were starting to turn their backs on me. They were obviously used to whoever this mega-nerd was, and sexy nurse was being replaced with scientist nurse. Boo. Kate was still throwing visual daggers in my direction.

'Oh, all over the place,' I said carelessly.

'Really . . . oh, I know you're off duty now, and I hate to bother you, but medicine is a real interest of mine and . . .' He flushed. 'Ahem . . . would you like to get together to discuss it sometime?'

'Sure,' I said. You really have to be a troll for me not to agree to go on a date with you. I've always figured it's a law of averages. Of course, that probably explains a lot about my life.

'OK! OK, brilliant,' he said, clearly surprised and a bit over-whelmed. 'Ehm . . . I know, what about the Natural History Museum?'

What? But you're a rich City person. I mean, surely I deserved the Oxo Tower at least?

'Next Saturday? Are you on duty?'

I reluctantly said no, I wasn't on duty, which at least was the truth.

'Great! I'll meet you there at two! OK! Fantastic! Brilliant!' Unable to stop thanking me, he retreated back to his group of Jameses, where I was disgusted to see him being slapped on the back by his friends. And I wasn't too proud of myself, either.

Kate came over. 'Well, you've certainly made an impression. Do they know you actually run a daisy hospital?'

'I'm sorry, Kate. No one would have spoken to me otherwise. AND, hey, it worked! I got a date!'

'Finn is not a date. He's a walking CD-ROM.'

'That doesn't sound too bad to me. What does he do?'

'He's developing string theory for stock markets.'

'Wow, I don't know what that is, but it sounds like he must be RICH.'

'No – wow, he must be DULL. Just a friendly warning . . . Oh, and he actually works for the University of London, doing a research project, so he's not even rich.'

'I'm going to the Natural History Museum with a *student*?'

'And he's going with a nurse.'

The 'party' didn't last too long after that. Bizarrely, the pub shut at nine – it was probably run by the banks, making sure their bonus-slaves didn't stay up too late enjoying their youth. So we found ourselves back round the kitchen table, slightly drunk, by ten o'clock, opening another bottle of wine. Kate was talking about how much shit she put up with at work, but I kept getting confused with all those Jameses, so I just nodded along generally.

Josh finally returned, a bit wobbly on his gin and tonics.

'I got a date!' I hollered, as soon as he walked in the room.

'No!' he said, clearly amazed.

'Yeah, a full-on *nerd* date,' said Kate, leaning into her glass of wine.

Josh sat down, his eyes shining.

'Tell me,' he said, 'how did he ask you?'

'Well, he just said, "Would you like to go to the Natural History Museum . . . ?"'

'Under false pretences,' said Kate.

'And you said yes,' said Josh, breathless with admiration.

'Yup!'

'He just said, "Would you like to go to the Natural History Museum"?'

'Apparently they let you in half-price if you don't know anything about science,' added Kate.

'And that's all it takes to ask a girl out.'

'That's all it takes to ask me out,' I said, before Kate pointed it out.

'Wow,' said Josh. 'It's that simple.'

'It's that simple.'

We all stared at our drinks.

'Kate,' said Josh, 'would you like to go to the Natural History Museum?'

Kate's head snapped up and she looked perturbed.

'Are you asking me out on a date, or are you just testing?' she said crisply.

'Don't be daft, this is practice. Do you think I can pull it off?'

'Oh,' said Kate. 'No, that would never work.'

'Right. OK. Fine,' said Josh.

'It's not a universal chat-up line,' I said consolingly.

'No, Holly is what's technically known as *easy*,' explained Kate.

'OK,' I said, rising somewhat unsteadily to my feet. 'If you're going to be horrible, I'm going to talk to my *other* friend around here, Addison.'

I lurched out of the kitchen, a tad unsteadily, and wandered across the landing, to the fast becoming familiar under-door blue glow.

I pushed the door ajar.

'Addison!' I said loudly, for the benefit of my ex-friends sitting in the kitchen. He did that gorgeous rigid back thing. God, I love that.

'What are you doing?'

I leaned forward, peering over his shoulder. To my amazement, instead of indecipherable computer babble, on his monitor was a picture of a hugely breasted fat lady.

He coloured and immediately dived for the escape button, but it was too late.

'Addison!' I said again, shocked. In my slightly drunk frame of mind, I felt deeply insulted. After all, here I was, and he still felt the need to . . . well.

'Addison,' I said a third time. He still wasn't meeting my eyes. 'Do you know lots of women?'

His beautiful dark gaze was focused solely on his computer keyboard.

'Because, you know, you might find . . . what you're looking for . . . closer than you think.'

I couldn't believe I was being such a tart. On the other hand, tart tactics were required when dealing with someone as shy as this. Plus of course I was pissed – that wonderful moral leveller.

I took his hand.

'You know,' I said, 'you're very attractive.' Really, I like to take all my chat-up lines from *Dynasty*, *circa* 1986.

His hand lay in mine like a piece of wet melon. Not noticing, I leaned over and kissed his forehead. He smelled of that wonderful Banda paper you used to get in schools: fresh and dry and inky.

He wasn't kissing back though. I realized this after say, thirty, maybe forty seconds. No reaction. Nada. Nothing. I kissed his head again. He didn't even move.

'So,' I said tartily, 'ehm, you know where I sleep . . .'

Sheesh. This was it. This was the pits. Robocop or the Natural History Museum. Even I hadn't plumbed my own depths before.

Amazingly, he simply took my hand off his forehead and squeezed it. Less amazingly (given he was a sober person who'd just been come on to by a mad harpy), he then handed it back to me and returned to his keyboard. I stood there for about ten seconds more – just to prolong the humiliation, I suppose – then retreated backwards slowly, whilst he busied himself with some computer stuff which, as far as I could see, had nothing more to do with big-breasted Betty.

'Oh God.'

'You'll get over it! You've got over worse stuff!'

'Like what, exactly?'

'What about that time you taught yourself to snowboard to impress big Eric and broke your ankle?'

Josh was failing to comfort me at the breakfast table. Not only this, but I had an interview today for a real live flower shop, which I had to do after the utter humiliation of basically prostrating myself in front of my flatmate. I wasn't sure that counted as extenuating circumstances.

'Anyway, I've done much worse things.'

'Like what?'

'I don't know . . . what about that time I got bitten by a dog?'

'Ehm, you know what, Josh? I don't think that really embarrassed the dog. So it does NOT compare.'

Kate of course had already gone to work, presumably clear-headed and 'motivated'.

'Yes, but I cried when I got my tetanus shot.'

'You must have been about eight years old.'

'Still embarrassing, though.'

'*And* they gave you a cream cake at the end of it, which really means that it does not compare. Now, ask me a question about flowers.'

'Ehm . . . what colour are tulips?'

'OK, ask me a question about a flower you've actually met.'

'I'll have you know I took the church prize in our village for flower arranging three times in a row!'

'You surprise me.'

'They were very . . . manly arrangements. OK, how do you grow a sunflower?'

'Stick it in any old shit and ignore it for months.'

We both paused for a minute.

'That's my life,' we both said simultaneously.

I couldn't believe a flower-shop interview could be so intense. There were three people in the tiny office at the back of the shop: an old bloke who might conceivably have been dead; a woman with very high hair, a monobosom and an imperious expression; and a sullen Indian girl with either a very large bogey or a bolt through her nose – it was hard to tell in the gloomy room.

'Now, here at That Special Someone, we take our customer care *extremely* seriously,' announced the big woman (I'd known she'd start the talking). 'Can you give us a particular example of good customer care you've been involved with in your previous jobs?'

I fucking hate job interviews. They are crap. They ask you all these bloody questions, whereas really they only want to know what you smell like, and how much you're prepared to say you agree with their bizarre views on racial hygiene.

'Well,' I began, modestly, 'once, these schoolkids came into the shop; one of their little chums had been knocked down by a car – on the school-run, ironically enough – and they'd clubbed all their pocket money together to buy him a princess bouquet, but they didn't have enough for the delivery charge. So, I took them to little Tommy myself.'

They were buying this. I couldn't believe it! The big woman was practically wetting herself.

'Yes?' she said. 'Go on.'

'Well, it turned out that Tommy's dad owned a major chain of conferencing suites, and we got the contract to do all of them after that.'

The bolt/bogey girl smirked worryingly, but the big lady was overwhelmed. Well, it wasn't exactly a lie – I mean, if charitable situations like that ever presented themselves, I'd like to think I'd rise to the challenge. None had, that was all.

'Well, that's just wonderful. Perhaps you can bring a little bit of that magic to That Special Someone, don't you think, Mr Haffillton?'

Mr Haffillton declined the chance to appear any less dead.

'I thought so. So, Holly, what about your horticultural qualifications?'

What about them? They didn't test you on telephone manner and Cellophane wrapping, the only two genuine skills required.

'Yes . . . obviously, I've been gaining experience out of London' – I took the bet they wouldn't know where Harlesden was, and I was right – 'but I'll be back down the Chelsea Physic Garden right away, you bet!'

'Not on our time, of course!'

'Ha ha ha! Of *course* not.'

46

God, I wish I didn't need this job, but Tash had given me a wedgie the other day and I'd had to hide and have a cry.

'Chalitha! Wouldn't you like to ask a question?'

Chalitha shrugged her black-clad shoulders petulantly.

'Come on now, Chalitha! We're all just one happy family here!' Big Lady grimaced at me as if Chalitha had just made some enormous joke.

'I dunno . . . What's your favourite band?'

I judged the situation carefully.

'The Sex Pistols.'

'Cool.' She nodded her head and turned to the old dead man. 'She'll be all right, uncle,' she announced. Aha. She turned back to me.

'The last girl liked Mariah Carey.'

Actually, the question clearly wasn't any more or less stupid than any other job interview question, and certainly got to the heart of the matter.

'I couldn't have worked with her,' I said confidently.

'No, can you imagine? She'd have worn little miniskirts and warbled emotionally all day.'

'I just spit,' I said reassuringly, then burst into a fake laugh when I realized Big Lady was staring at me with raised eyebrows.

'Ha! ha! Only kidding. Ehm, I think a happy work place is essential to provide the very premium in customer service, don't you?'

She nodded sternly. 'Yes. But this is a very efficient business. Naturally, we don't put up with any hanky-panky.'

'No, ma'am,' I said.

She loved the 'ma'am' thing, I noted instantly.

'Well, we'll be letting you know,' she said, rising imperiously to her feet.

'Thank you very much, ma'am.'

I practically walked out backwards.

I hung around that night, desperate for the phone to ring before I had to head up the hill – possibly for the last time.

47

'. . . Then I thought I'd say, "Tash, I'm sorry you didn't get better womb nutrition and have no prospects, but just LEAVE ME ALONE!"' I announced for Josh's benefit.

'And, for the boys, I thought I'd pity them too. Kind of like, "Isn't it a shame you're just so deeply ignorant?"'

Josh was chopping vegetables, but he stopped to look up at me. 'You don't think that's a little . . . well, you know, deeply deeply fascist?'

'I think it's only fair after what they've put me through. Really, I'm very humanitarian.'

'Ah yes, Mr Gandhi.'

'Exactly. I mean, it's not as if I'd ever have the balls to say any of it.'

'You could try, if you feel that strongly about it.'

Kate wandered in, and waved approximately, too exhausted to talk.

'Yes, and die in the attempt.'

I thought for a bit.

'Josh, you know, I lie all day long and think horrid things about people. Do you think I'm morally bad?'

Josh turned on the food processor for a minute to think about it.

'Don't turn on the food processor to give yourself time to think about it! You should know immediately!'

'I don't think you are.' This was from Kate. That was unexpected. 'I think you're normal. Lying all day long and secretly wanting to kill people is human nature.'

'Hmm, I don't know if I want to *kill* them, as such.'

'I don't . . .' Josh's forehead creased up in concentration. 'I don't think bad things about people. Or at least I don't think I do.'

Kate and I glanced at each other and Kate rolled her eyes. It was true actually. Josh was really quite 'good', in a primary school sense. The only reason we didn't hate him too was that he was a very easy tease and he cooked.

'Yes, but you're sickeningly nice,' said Kate. 'You're different and weird.'

48

There was a moment's pause.

'No, actually, I am thinking nasty thoughts about somebody now,' said Josh, turning the food processor back on. Kate and I shared a rare moment of bonding and grinned at each other when, thank God, the phone rang.

'JOSH! TURN THE FOOD PROCESSOR OFF!' I yelled, flapping my hands up and down.

'Oh yes, just boss around sweet old, pushed around "he's too nice" Josh,' he grumbled.

'SHUT IT!' I yelled, just as Kate picked up the phone.

'Holly Livingstone's office,' she said sweetly as I winced and lunged for the receiver. She held it at arm's length.

'Yes, she's here . . . May I ask who's calling?'

I jumped up and down on the lino in frustration and made clawing motions with my hands.

'I'll just see if she's free.'

Finally she handed the phone over.

'Hellayer!' I said in my best posh telephone voice. 'This is Holly Livingstone.'

'Hellayer!' said the voice back, so I instantly knew it was Big Lady.

'This is Mrs Bigelow' – oh, *that's* why I hadn't been able to remember her name – 'of That Special Someone. We've decided to offer you the post of Floral Executive. Nine to six, five days a week, alternate Saturdays off.'

Then she named the salary, which although more than I was getting for shift work down at NCG was still, I could practically guarantee, lower than that of every single person I went to college with, even that enormous girl with egg down her front and her glasses stuck together who treated English as if it wasn't her first language, even though it was, *and* the Art Historians.

'Great! That's great!' I stuttered, then remembered I was supposed to be the kind of person who would be fielding job offers constantly. 'I mean, I think that will be suitable. When would you wish me to start?'

'Saturday?'

Oh no. Saturday was my Natural History Museum date.

'Will Monday be all right? I wouldn't like to leave my former employers in the lurch.'

'Oh, yes,' she said, flustered. 'Of course, I absolutely agree. Employee loyalty is *extremely* important here at That Special Someone.'

So it was settled. Kate nearly slapped me for not renegotiating my salary offer when it would clearly be all such a high-ranking employee would deserve.

I debated with myself briefly whether to just blow off New Covent Garden completely, but couldn't quite bring myself to do so, and pedalled in an insouciant three-quarters of an hour late.

'You wouldn't have got away with those kinds of hours during the war, you know,' muttered Johnny as I swung into the forecourt.

'Actually, I'm sorry – I got bombed on the way here and had to stop and rescue some orphans from the rubble. Is that OK? Also, I quit.'

'Well, just get in there and get started.'

'Johnny, didn't you hear me? I just quit. I'll work tonight, then you can pay me and I'll be off.'

He stared at me, surprised.

'So, you're off then.'

'That would be my definition of "to quit", yes.'

He nodded his head slowly.

'What are you going to do?'

I decided to brighten up his evening.

'I'm going to join the army.'

'Are you really?'

'Absolutely. Going to continue with your valiant efforts to protect this country through the twin poles of duty and flowers.'

'Ah, get away with you, you liar.'

'I'll miss you,' I said.

He shrugged at me. 'No, you won't. In you go. Go clean up the daffodil line.'

I parked the bike and tiptoed into the vast shed.

'TinBits!' yelled one of the boys. 'Where have you been? Wanking behind the melons just hasn't been the same without you.'

It gave me a grim satisfaction to realize how little I was going to miss this place.

About halfway into the shift, the moment I'd been dreading arrived. Tash sidled up to me, her yellow teeth glinting.

'Bit late tonight, weren't we? Didn't learn to tell the time at college then?'

I didn't say anything.

'Forgotten how to talk as well?'

Oh God, I was too *old* for this.

'Piss off, Tash,' I said quietly. 'I'm leaving.'

'WHAT did you say?' she said. 'Hey, lads, did you hear this?'

I pretended to ignore her, and picked up my first box. Inside, I started trembling.

'Miss Degree here just told me to piss off. Didn't you?' she said, pointing at me.

'Tash, I really don't want any trouble. It's my last night, so you can go and find someone else to pick on, OK?'

'Oh, diddums. Don't want any trouble?' She pushed her hand up under my box, so the flowers scattered all over the floor.

'You think you're just a bit too good for us here, don't you?' she said.

'No,' I said, meaning: 'Yes, I hope so.'

'Catfight!' shouted one of the lads.

'You think you're just a little bit special; a bit above all this.'

'Fight! Fight! Fight!' the lads picked up.

'No, I don't,' I said, but caught my breath in surprise when she pushed me. The blood started to rush in my ears, but I certainly didn't know how to fight. I leaned down to pick up the box, and she kicked me in the shoulder.

After that, everything seemed to rush. Immediately the boys and the other drooling girls formed a circle round us, and I was trapped. I got to my feet, wondering what on earth to do. Tash was looking at me, laughing.

51

'Not quite so up on the smart remarks now, are we?'

'Oh, for God's sake, leave it, Tash.' I was trying to be reasonable, but my voice came out all shaky. Then, suddenly, like one of those flying vampires in the movies, she launched herself at me. I was falling backwards, and someone was clawing at my face and hair. A jumble of thoughts rushed through my head, not the least of which was: How embarrassing; my first fight at the age of twenty-eight.

My focus swam back in, and I realized she was sitting on top of me, getting ready to punch me. The boys were yelling, and I thought what a turn-on this must be for them. I tried to twist her off, but she slapped me hard on the side of the head. Oh God. My heart was beating a million miles an hour.

'JUST FUCK OFF!' I screamed. 'FUCK OFF!' She slapped me again, hard, then made her hand into a fist and drew it back to punch me.

She crunched into me with such force that my head rattled off the concrete. I was stunned by the violation and thought I was going to pass out; I wanted to. I couldn't see anything, but suddenly she seemed to float off me; the weight was lifted and I wondered if I'd died and was having an out-of-body experience.

The next thing I knew, Johnny was pulling me up, brushing me down and exclaiming, 'Girls fighting! I don't know.'

'I told you I was going to the wars,' I snivelled, then realized I was crying, and there was snot and blood and tears all down my face. Tash was being held back by two of the lads, who were killing themselves laughing.

'BITCH!' she shrieked at me. 'PATHETIC BITCH.'

I certainly wasn't going to respond in any way that was going to antagonize her. In fact, I wasn't going to stay another second.

'I'm going home,' I sniffed to Johnny.

'We'll have to get you cleaned up a bit, don't you think? Could be quite a nasty shiner.'

'NO!' I said. 'I'm going home NOW!'

'Do you want me to phone someone to come and pick you up?'

'No . . . I've got my bike and I just want to go HOME.'

'All right then . . .'

He walked me to the bike, clearly concerned. Then he asked me to hang on a minute, nipped into his office and came out again with an envelope, which he handed to me.

'Take care of yourself,' he said. 'You're not as tough as you think you are.'

'I think I'm as tough as a small mouse,' I said. 'And I'm *still* not as tough as I think I am.'

He clapped me avuncularly on the shoulder. 'Don't cycle too fast.'

I didn't cycle at all, but wheeled my bike down the hill, crying and feeling very sorry for myself indeed. The road was quiet at that time of night, with only the occasional car flashing past me. I was glad. I didn't want to be seen.

The house was cold and still, as usual. And after last week's débâcle, I certainly wouldn't be popping in to chat to Addison. Sniffing, I went off to the bathroom to clean myself up. I could feel my left eye very sore and swollen, and there were scratches over my eyebrow and down my cheek.

As I crept past Addison's room, I spotted an amazing thing. Usually his door was tightly shut, a warning against any interruption. Tonight, however, it was *open* – just a tiny, tiny crack, barely noticeable, but definitely open. Was he out? No, it was just that my ears had become so inured to the tapping I didn't hear it unless I was listening for it. Plus, of course, he never went out. And given that he did everything on purpose . . . he must have left it open for a reason. Could it be . . . could it be possible that he wanted to talk to me?

Desperate for some human sympathy, even of the completely mute kind, I pushed the door a little more. He was there, as ever, transfixed by the computer screen. As I walked in, though, he moved his swivel chair a little, turning away from the screen and towards me.

'Addison . . .' I said in a very small voice, and immediately burst into noisy sobs. 'Addison!'

His face registered shock as he saw me, and he stood up. For the first time I noticed how tall he was, how long his legs were. I gazed at him, my lower lip wobbling uncontrollably.

'Look at you,' he said softly.

'It wasn't my fault!' I snorted.

'Did you get mugged?'

'Ehm, no, I was in a fight . . . but it wasn't my *fault*.'

He nodded, as if it didn't surprise him for a second that I'd been in a fight.

'Come on,' he said, and I followed him into the bathroom. Completely helpless, I let him sit me down on the side of the bath and dab my wounds with TCP. Although my insides were still churning and I was very upset, nonetheless there was definitely something thrilling about Addison touching my face. This was practically a date. Then I caught sight of my face in the mirror.

'Oh my GOD,' I moaned. My eye was twice its normal size, and as pink and purple as a prize fighter's.

'Don't worry,' said Addison comfortingly. 'Sit still.'

'I can't . . . I mean, I've got a date and a job and – oh *GOD*. Ouch! Where did you go to medical school?'

'If it stings, that means it's doing you good.'

'Yeah, a bee said that to me once.'

'Ssh,' he said, uncoiling an Elastoplast on to my right cheek. 'It'll be a lot better in the morning.'

'Will it be gone in the morning?'

'Ehm . . . no, but it will be better.'

'Thanks,' I said, still gazing at him, my eyes still wet. For the first time ever, he smiled straight at me. I felt faint.

'Get some sleep.'

'OK.' I toyed with the idea of feigning a few internal injuries so that he'd have to undress me, but remembered the other night and wisely decided against it.

I slept for ten hours, all the adrenaline flushing its way through my system. When I woke up the next afternoon, I rediscovered the envelope Johnny had given me. Inside were practically two weeks' wages.

*   *   *

Josh couldn't believe I'd been in a fight. He was unbelievably jealous. We'd decided that beer was really the only response to my ordeal – or white wine spritzer, if you were Kate – and the three of us had repaired to a new pub round the corner which, ideally for my benefit, mistook having the place in practically complete darkness for atmosphere.

I had pondered long and hard about whether to try and smother my eye – now vicious shades of yellow and green – in foundation, but this had only made me appear even more like a startled panda bear than I normally did, so I'd nitched that and gone the other way entirely, making up my right eye with dramatic eyeliner and green shadow. From a distance, it wasn't too bad; I just looked like I'd escaped from a glam rock band, and sufficiently tarty and hard that you wouldn't want to get any nearer. Close up, I was terrifying.

Kate, once she'd established that I hadn't been raped or anything, could barely stop laughing. And Josh kept asking me stupid questions about whether or not the blood had rushed to my head. I pointed out that it had, and that it kept on rushing, straight out of my nose, and could he possibly be a bit more sensitive about it?

'Yes, these playground warriors can get a bit uptight about their traditional fighting techniques,' chided Kate. 'Watch out, or she'll give you a killer Chinese burn.'

'Ha ha ha,' I said, but stopped with my mouth hanging open as this unbelievably gorgeous guy loomed out of the darkness right in front of me.

Forgetting for a moment that I was tarted up like Marilyn Manson, I immediately tilted my profile up towards him, so that I could feel even more stupid when he swept right past me and went up and introduced himself to Kate.

Josh shot me a look of utter horror – how could this chap simply walk up to a group and introduce himself to a complete stranger? Then he sat back and waited for Kate to give the guy a good rude brush off. Josh really doesn't know much about women.

I mused for a moment that, if it weren't for my black eye, Mr

Deeply, Deeply Suave – who was wearing a grey cashmere top and a Burberry trench coat which matched Kate's exactly – would have been after me first, but I couldn't even kid myself: I got the nerdy scientist guys, Kate got the rich ones. He even seemed familiar, in an American way.

Sure enough, he was American, and soon Kate was giggling away – *not* one of nature's gigglers, but she was giving it her best shot – and chatting happily to him, and the very next moment a bottle of champagne had miraculously arrived out of nowhere and he was pouring her some. Not us, only her. I assumed she would remedy this deeply unfair state of events immediately, but when I looked at her I noticed she had subtly adjusted her body language so it seemed as if she hadn't even come in with us. And their heads were bent very close together. I was sure, still, that I'd seen him before.

Josh scuttled his chair round to me, muttering crossly.

'I'm sorry, but we appear to have been barred from the international Burberry convention,' I said to him, and he grunted. Then his face lit up.

'I know, why don't *we* have champagne? We can have fun, right?'

Kate and big beautiful thingy suddenly let out a pealing laugh.

'Josh, their definition of fun is probably comparing international money markets. But I would very much like another Becks, if you're buying. And some salt-and-vinegar crisps, which are essential medicine in the treatment of black eyes.'

Ridiculously, as the bar was trying to be trendy, it sold those cute teeny bottles of Moët & Chandon, and Josh returned laden with my beer, the crisps between his teeth, and a quarter bottle of champagne to himself, which he sipped morosely through a straw. I couldn't help laughing and had to restrain myself from rubbing him on the head with my knuckles.

'Don't worry!'

'How can I not worry? I'm twenty-eight years old and I haven't had a girlfriend for three years!'

'Or a boyfriend.'

'Would you *stop* with that already.' He pouted. 'Some of us just . . . take a bit longer to get round to things than other people.'

'What, like puberty?'

'Do you *want* to be homeless again?'

'No!' I said emphatically.

'And anyway, I've got a right to complain – you've got a date and Kate's obviously met her soul mate, and you'll all move out and have a squillion babies and I will die all alone.'

'I know!' I said brightly. 'When I marry Addison, we'll stay in the house and you can babysit our beautiful and brainy children.'

'Oh, right. And I'm the sad fantasist.'

'Not at all. He put this Elastoplast on my cheek. I'm going to keep it forever as a symbol of the first time we touched.'

Josh looked appalled.

'I think I'm going to be sick. Holly, *please* don't go all gooey over Addison . . .'

'Too late!' I exclaimed triumphantly.

'. . . I really think there's something a bit wrong with him. You know, like that weird form of trainspottery autism thing that boys are meant to get?'

He thought for a minute.

'I wonder if I could get it.'

'You could count things, I suppose. Then memorize them.'

'Ah yes. I can see the appeal.'

'Josh,' I said, 'don't worry about me and Addison.'

Kate, unsurprisingly – well, a little bit surprisingly, I'd have assumed she was a 'Rules' girl as it had the kind of anal, personality-smashing techniques she tended to like – chatted to the beautiful thing all night then swanned off with it to dinner somewhere. Le Caprice, I assumed. I had no idea what Le Caprice might be like, but it sounded the kind of place that people who wore designer underwear (I knew Kate did, because I stole a pair of her pants out of the drier once, but I couldn't get both legs in them) might go.

Josh and I hadn't stayed long. He'd decided he had to get back to gen up on some football scores.

I hung around the next morning, Saturday, to see if he'd come in or not and was disappointed to find that she had and therefore clearly hadn't gotten into something drunken and debauched, which would have been enjoyable for me. She swanned into the kitchen at around ten, carrying the *Financial Times* and looking composed and well rested. I busied around, pretending to be making coffee, and bursting to ask her what had gone on, however she calmly sat down and opened her newspaper. I tried to contain my frustration.

'Coffee?'

'Decaf, thanks, if you're making it. Black, no sugar.'

I looked over at her.

'That's a very pointless cup of coffee.'

She raised her eyebrows at me.

'Actually, it consumes more calories than it contains, like celery.'

'Aha.' I poured the water out. 'So *that's* what coffee is for.'

She smiled primly at me and went back to her paper. I tried again.

'It's *my* big date today. You know, at the Natural History Museum.'

'How nice for you.'

'Hey, maybe we could double date some time – Finn and I and you and . . .'

Kate put her paper down.

'Do you really think so?'

I tried to imagine the situation and couldn't.

'Oh, I'm sorry, aren't you seeing him again?'

She immediately bristled.

'Of course I am. I expect John and I will be seeing each other on a regular basis.'

'John? John what?'

She affected disdain.

'Oh, I don't recall.'

'Sounds made up to me.'

'What sounds made up?' mumbled Josh, wobbling in unsteadily like a new-born kitten.

'John Nobody – Kate's new love.'

'Oh God – another one,' said Josh, spooning sugar into his coffee.

'WHAT do you mean by that?' said Kate ferociously.

'I don't know – how many suave pretty-boy married men have chatted you up this year and not given you their last name in case you dig them up out of the phone book?'

'John is *not* married. I could tell.'

Josh and I glanced at each other.

Suddenly the phone rang, and we all jumped three feet. Kate hopped up, then, when she realized we were watching her, feigned a leisurely gait.

'Ehm . . . I'll get that . . . probably the office.'

'Probably Relate,' I said, 'calling you in as a witness.'

Josh and I peered round the kitchen door as she furiously motioned us away. Her expression quickly revealed her disappointment, however. She covered the mouthpiece with her hand.

'It's Addison's mother.'

'I'll get him,' I said quickly, and rapped on his door.

'Hrh?'

'Addison, it's your mum.'

'Can you tell her I'm out?'

'I don't think that's going to work.'

'He's in,' said Kate down the phone.

'Can you tell her . . . I'm . . . busy.'

'He's busy,' said Kate. 'Yes, he's eating. No, much the same. No, no sleep, no. OK, I'll tell him.'

She hung up.

'When's the last time you spoke to your mother, Addison?' I asked him.

There was silence from behind the door.

'Not since he's been here,' whispered Josh.

'I normally speak to her,' said Kate. 'She sounds all right most of the time.'

'Right.'

Kate bent down to pick up the post. As she did so, something slid out from the pocket of her exquisitely fresh Meg Ryanesque pyjamas.

'What's that?'

'Nothing,' she said, grabbing it, but it was clearly her little mobile phone.

'That pesky office, eh?' said Josh.

'Erm, right.'

I thought it would take me three minutes to get ready, but of course I had forgotten about my black eye, now puce and vermilion, and found myself in a desperate, excited rush whereby no matter how I tried I couldn't seem to get it together to leave the house. I'd forgone the Alice Cooper style for a prolonged attempt to whiten it out, which was now making me look like one of those eyebrowless sci-fi entities. I toyed with buying an eye-patch and pretending I was starting an early eighties revival, but it would take too much explaining, and, given that I'd only met this bloke for two minutes, I wanted to appear as non-mad as possible.

I still hadn't decided what to do about the nurse thing. After all, I had kind of got this date under false pretences, and it also meant he was a bit of a perv. I hummed and hawed and stomped around a bit, which was clearly annoying Kate. Normally on Saturdays she was up at eight, dashing to gyms and swimming pools and popping into the office and Joseph and the Fifth Floor at Harvey Nicks and going to exhibitions whilst Josh and I lay on the two squashy old sofas in the living room, watched black-and-white films, and ate Jaffa Cakes, but it was eleven thirty and she wasn't dressed yet. As well as the mobile, her pager was placed on the kitchen table and she seemed to have been reading the same page of the paper for some time.

'Holly, for God's sake, go. Otherwise he'll be hanging round the museum by himself all afternoon . . .'

'Nerds *love* that, though,' I argued.

'Just tell him. Tell him you were completely drunk . . .'

'Hmm, that's attractive.'

'. . . or temporarily insane. But please, stop hopping around the kitchen trying to make your mind up about it, because it's driving me crazy.'

'OK, fine. I'll go. Oh no, but what if he dumps me in the middle of the museum and I get lost amongst the brontosauri?'

'What if you don't go and you pass up the best thing you ever had?' said Kate in a surprisingly dreamy voice.

'What if he can only get off on the idea of people in uniforms? Yeugh.'

'Josh will lend you his old wetsuit. Now, just go.'

'In the wetsuit or not?'

'Out! Get out! Out! Good luck, it'll be fine. Now GET OUT!'

'Good luck to you too,' I yelled back.

'Oh God, I am ALL ALONE,' I could just hear Josh moan as I left the house.

Three

By the time I'd reached the museum in Kensington, I had decided, completely and utterly, that this was the worst idea I had ever followed through in my entire life, worse than the time I thought that that guy's motorbike would substitute for him not having a personality, and it took a wrist fracture to convince me otherwise. I tried to remember one single boyfriend I'd ever had who hadn't

61

accidentally made me break a bone, and gave up in disgust. Great. Even if he was nice I was still going to wind up in hospital somehow.

I wasn't even sure I'd recognize Finn. And he even had a stupid fish name. God, what was I doing? It was a nice, warm spring day, and I could be lying indoors on the sofa watching TV. But no, here I was, tarted up even though I looked like a road accident victim, going off to meet some spawny pervy speccy git who thought I was porno-nurse.

This is always the way with me. Plus, I have Teenage Daughter of Nastily Divorced Parents Syndrome, which means, as people like to tell me late at night when I make only the *teensiest* complaint about my love life, that everyone I ever date will be:

- The exact opposite of my father, as I hate him so much
- Exactly like my father, as I hate him so much
- Some sort of freaky revenge on *both* my parents
- Doomed to disaster right from the start as a way of trying to get my parents' attention
- Doomed to disaster right from the start as I have never learned how good relationships worked
- Doomed to disaster right from the start as some sort of genetic fate
- Doomed to disaster right from the start as I am a Bad Person.

That last one is my guess – plus, whose relationship has ever *not* ended in disaster? The best way out you can ever hope for is death . . . But this is why I'm not in therapy, although I wished I was on my way there – or anywhere – the second I saw Finn, standing awkwardly outside the entrance. He seemed as unhappy to be there as I was. God, why do we put ourselves through crap like this?

'Hi!' I said over-enthusiastically. 'Hi! Er . . . it's Holly . . .'

He looked at me confusedly for a second. For God's sake, he'd asked me.

'Hi! Oh, sorry, ha ha. My God, what happened to your eye?'

'Ehm . . . a mental patient hit me.' *Almost* true.

'Oh my God, you poor thing. What were you doing on the psychiatric wing?'

'Ehmm . . . just tidying up,' I said vaguely. Oh God, I couldn't put up with this for an hour and a half. When he went to pay for me, and I saw it was thirteen pounds for us to get in, I realized I had to act.

'FINN!' I screeched, as he handed over his Visa. 'Don't hand over that card.'

'No, really, I'll pay,' he said.

The swotty girl assistant held on to the card enquiringly.

'No, it's not that. Ehm, Finn, I think we're going to the Natural History Museum under false pretences,' I gabbled. 'Ehm, I'm not a nurse.'

He looked at me, confused.

'Sorry . . . are you a nursing student?'

'No, I mean, I'm nothing to do with nursing at all.'

'I think it's illegal to impersonate a nurse,' said the assistant helpfully. I shot her a hard stare.

'It was a . . . silly joke I was playing with . . . err, Kate,' I hastily improvised. 'She bet me I couldn't pretend to be a nurse all evening and . . . well, here we are!'

'Kate playing jokes,' said Finn meditatively. 'Never seen that happen.'

Neither had I.

'I'm so sorry that I dragged you all the way here . . . It was stupid. I'm really sorry. I'd better go.'

'Oh, great,' he said. 'You actually turn up to tell me you're going.'

'I'll go round with you,' said the swotty assistant eagerly. Finn must give off swotty scientist love vibes.

'Haven't you seen it?' I asked her rudely.

Then there was a silence.

'Well, bye then,' said Finn.

I looked at him again. He was wearing baggy old cords and a short-sleeved shirt with a pen sticking out of the top pocket, as well as a tweed coat, but – no leather patches. He seemed sweet, confused and not entirely unlike a grown-up Harry Potter. The assistant was already beckoning over her supervisor to tell her she was going on her break.

'I get in for nothing,' she whispered confidingly to Finn. Hang on, girlfriend! This was my date!

'Well, better make that one, please,' said Finn. 'Can you do a student concession?'

'For you, I'm sure,' said the girl, simpering greasily.

'Don't you want me to come then?' I said sulkily.

He turned round.

'I'm sorry, I thought you'd gone.'

'Well, you know, I'm here now.'

The assistant clucked her tongue against her teeth. Finn thought about it.

'Is your name actually Holly?' he asked.

'Yes. I promise.'

'What do you do, Holly?'

'Ehmm . . . astronaut?'

He smiled for the first time.

'Sounds good enough to me. Two please,' he said to the girl, who looked like she wanted to decapitate me with one of the velociraptor teeth they sold in the gift shop.

'So . . . who are you?' he asked, as we went up the rather sad lava-themed escalator.

'Really, nobody,' I said in shame.

'Nobody *at all*?'

'I'm Kate's flatmate.'

'Well, there you go,' he said. 'That makes you brave, for a start.'

'And I work as a florist.'

'Really?' His face lit up. 'I'm much more interested in botany than medicine, although of course one feeds so much into the other . . .'

'I don't know anything about botany either.'

'Really? Oh, you should. Did you know there's a kind of orchid that fills itself up with sticky stuff, like a pool. Then, when wasps come by, they go in and get so wet they can't fly out again. The only way out is through a tunnel at the bottom, where the wasp gets stuck and covered in pollen before he's let out. It's like a car wash.'

I was impressed despite myself, and more so when he led me to the case holding it, and pointed it out to me.

'See? There you go – do you see? *Orchidae Coryanthus*. It's kind of like a theme park for bugs.'

'So do you just know everything about science then? Is that what you do?'

'Good gracious, no,' he said, laughing at the very thought, as if knowing the properties of *Orchidae Coryanthus* off the top of his head could possibly be conceived as knowing quite a lot about science.

'No, really, I just dabble in some things. I am a kind of physicist.'

'A kind of physicist? I didn't know they had different kinds.'

'A few, yes. I'm into string theory.'

'You look at pieces of string to see what they do? Are snakes involved?' I asked, glancing anxiously at a particularly long and malevolent one stretched out in front of us, thankfully in a case.

'Well, on a very small level. You see, particle physics only works when we pretend gravity doesn't exist, but if you want to use quantum and not just classical theory, then string theory can help close the gap.'

'Oh, I see. No, hang on, that makes no sense to me at all.'

'OK, ehm . . . just think of the world as a kind of resonating guitar string.'

'Really?'

'It's a very beautiful theory,' he said. 'It means the world plays like music.'

'What, even the person who punched me?'

'Did they soar like a butterfly and sting like a bee?'

'No, she hit me like a cow.'

'Did you tell her you were a nurse too?'

'*Noo*! I'm sorry about that.' But he was laughing. 'I got bullied at my last job. So I decided to leave and someone was obviously going to miss me.'

'You poor thing. You should just tell people you walked into a bus shelter. That's what I usually do.'

'Why, do you get beaten up a lot?'

'No, but I do walk into bus shelters.'

We were standing in front of an enormous grizzly bear, and I took the opportunity of Finn studying it closely to study *him* closely. Well, it was all natural history, after all.

He was tall, and had extremely curly brown hair sticking out in every direction. He wasn't skinny and elegant like Addison, but well built and solid. Round dark eyes peered out of what were obviously bottle-thick glasses. I thought longingly for a moment of Addison's long lashes and dark pools, then snapped myself back to the present.

'Why are you called Finn?' I said, as he examined the grizzly's paw prints and I made little growly motions to myself. 'Are your parents famous shark people or something?'

'Ha! Good variation. Well, it beats the fish-finger theory. Actually, it's Feynman. My father was desperate to have a physicist in the family. Richard Feynman was a physicist,' he added, seeing my blank face.

'Why didn't he just call you Richard?'

'That would have been too obvious.'

'Wow. What's your middle name?'

'Lavoisier. Just in case the physics didn't work out.' He sighed, and I declined to question him any further.

We stood pondering the great blue whale for a long time, until I realized it wasn't actually real and got a bit pissed off with it. I was so full of relief, though, that the date wasn't turning into an unmitigated disaster that I managed to hide it.

'So why do you work at that wankerpit then?' I asked him.

'Where?'

'The City.'

'Oh, yes. I'm doing research there. It isn't very interesting.'

'It's interesting to me.'

'Really? Do you want to hear the advanced mathematics?'

'Ooh, is that the time?'

'See?' He regarded the whale glumly. 'Actually, I hate it. I'm trying to formulate whether the stock market works along roughly the same lines as other living systems, and all people seem to be interested in pointing out is that they have "considerably more money than you".'

'That must piss you off,' I said. 'If it helps, I'm probably poorer than anyone you know.'

'It's not really the money that bothers me,' he said grumpily. 'Want to go halfers on an ice cream?'

I'd started to feel that Finn and I were getting on surprisingly well. OK, his nose was a little pudgy, and he talked a lot about science, but here we were, doing a nice, adult, educational thing on a Saturday afternoon, and sitting out on the grass, eating ice cream and watching the duty tourists going crazy with boredom round South Kensington. He didn't seem like a perv, though. Which begged the question . . .

'Why', I asked, biting into my Magnum, 'did you ask me out?'

He looked at me, blinking in the mild sunshine, his eyes slightly enlarged behind the thick spectacles.

'Sorry?'

'Ehm . . . you know, why did you ask me on a date? If it isn't a nurse fixation, ha ha!'

'I'm sorry, I don't understand what you mean.'

However, he suddenly began to flush, and clearly did understand. I also began to understand something, and started to give him a run for his money in the flush department.

'Ermm, I didn't mean . . . I mean, sorry, but I just wanted

someone to go to the museum with; I normally go alone . . . I didn't mean for you to think . . .'

'What else would I have thought?'

'I don't know. I'm terribly, terribly sorry,' he stuttered. 'Really, it wasn't that at all.'

'Why not? What's wrong with me?'

'Nothing, no, nothing . . . but I would never just ask someone out like that. I mean . . . I'm so sorry.'

'Yes, you said that,' I said sulkily, standing up whilst trying to keep my ice cream upright – not the most elegant of procedures. Finn stared at me in disbelief.

'I mean . . . can't we be friends?'

'Finn, that's what you say when two people have actually *had* a relationship and it's been deeply passionate and then it all goes wrong. Which, despite the big fish, has *not* happened this afternoon.'

'Fine.' He shrugged. 'Well, once again I apologize for the misunderstanding, and it was nice to have met you. Oh, and the "fish" was a "mammal".' And he held out his hand.

I *hate* it when somebody does that. Some people just have no sense of the appropriate drama. I didn't take his hand but muttered 'bye' and stomped off, cheeks high with humiliation. And, naturally, I had to stand that way, waiting for the lights to change, two feet in front of him, whilst he watched me in amazement. Shite.

'I HATE bloody scientists and I HATE bloody dates which are the bloody Schroedinger's Cat of dates/non-dates!' I hollered, as I slammed through the door three bloody quarters of an hour later, after being thrust up against tourists' armpits as the Circle Line attempted to take the scenic route.

'Where are the bloody Jaffa Cakes?'

Josh was prostrate on one of the sofas watching Bette Davis with his usual devotion.

'It's Penguins, sweetheart – don't you remember? We still have a hundred and sixty-six to get through since you went to the supermarket. Date not go too well?'

'You *could* bloody well say that.'

I stomped into the kitchen. Amazingly, Kate was still there, and still in her dressing gown. This was unheard of. She had hooked up an extension line to the phone in the hall, and her mobile was now connected up to her laptop computer, and she appeared to be continually switching between the two. The pager lay to one side, discarded, as did two cold pieces of toast, and there was a fax buzzing away in the corner which I'd never noticed before.

'Hey there,' I said, but she made no sign to show she'd heard me. 'Can I eat this bloody toast?'

She shrugged her shoulders, so I ate it anyway.

'Any luck?'

She noticed me at last and looked up, her face drawn.

'Kate, it's only the first day. You know, no self-respecting bloke would phone you on the first day after you'd met. Especially one as cool and pretty as John . . . Thingy. You'd think he was pathetic and needy and you'd probably turn him down.'

Kate nodded like an idiot.

'But he said he would.'

'Yes, but he's also a bloke. Those two things cancel each other out.'

She regarded me with narrowed eyes.

'How did your date go?'

'Fine. Oh, and also, why didn't you tell me he was a prick?'

'Finn?' This startled her out of her reverie, although she still kept half an eye on the phones. 'What happened?'

'You were there at your birthday, weren't you?'

'Ehm, yes, I would have thought so.'

'You heard him ask me out, didn't you?'

'Well, I heard him ask if you wanted to go to the Natural History Museum.'

'That's a date, right?'

'Ehm . . . why? What else did he say? Dinner? A drink afterwards?'

'He didn't have to say anything! You don't ask someone somewhere just because you want to go there.'

Kate raised her eyebrows.

'Anyway, that's not the point. The point is that I reckon when he found out I wasn't a nurse, he changed his mind and made out that it was just a *friendly* thing all the time.'

'Really? Well, maybe it was. To be honest, though, Holly, it didn't seem very like Finn to just start chatting a girl up out of the blue. He got some ribbing for it the next day, and seemed a bit surprised when the Jameses started ripping the piss. Certainly, I'm not used to seeing him being that forward – quiet as a mouse, normally.'

'What? You *knew* about this?'

'Of course not. I'm just saying, maybe he didn't mean to ask you out, and you made an honest mistake.'

'Well, of course, you're being incredibly reasonable about it, because it's not you who had to listen to stupid theories of FLOWERS for two hours by that annoying, geeky IDIOT.'

'Oh well, it won't bother you that he doesn't want to go out with you, then.'

'It DOESN'T.'

We both sighed. Kate picked up the pager and checked to see if it was on.

'God, Kate,' I said, counting it out on my fingers, 'let's see: you gave him your home number, your office number, your mobile, your car phone, your pager, your e-mail and your fax number . . . ?'

She nodded miserably.

'I think we're just going to have to wait for the law of averages to kick in,' I observed, 'whereby he misdials another number, and gets you.'

Josh called a house meeting the next morning. Or rather, he ran up and down the corridor at 8 a.m. banging a ladle on a saucepan and yelling, 'Fire! Fire! Everyone out!' Then, when people put their

70

heads round their bedroom doors blearily, he grabbed them and pulled them round the kitchen table.

When I got in there I couldn't tell if Kate had even gone to bed or not; she was still sitting in the same spot, walled in by electronic communication devices. Amazingly, Addison was there too, blinking in the daylight. He seemed extremely uncomfortable.

I'd never seen him during the day before. Properly lit, he was even more beautiful: the strong curve of his upper lip, and the fathomless depths of his heavy-lidded black eyes making me want to rush back out of the room to put some lipstick on – until Josh caught me, and forced me back down.

'OK, everyone,' he announced, 'this has got to stop.'

I trembled for a moment as I remembered cutting my toe-nails in the bath, however he didn't point directly at me but continued:

'I want this to be a nice happy home for my friends, not some sort of love harpy madhouse,' he said, as sternly as he could, which wasn't very. We all stared at him uncomprehendingly.

'Just look at the situation,' he said. 'We're all obviously deeply bad at running our own love lives.'

'I'm doing OK,' I said, untruthfully and petulantly.

'Holly, you can't tell the difference between a love life and a school trip, OK? Addison, you just seem completely uninterested . . .'

Addison was tapping something into a computer about the size of a pea, and didn't even look up.

'. . . and Kate, I'm worried about your mental health.'

'Huh?' she said listlessly.

'What about you?' I said.

'Hum,' he said. 'And, yes, perhaps I could improve on my own love life.'

'Michael Jackson', I said, 'has a better love life than you.'

'So, we're just going to have to do something about it.'

'Like what?'

'I think we should have a house-warming. We've never had

71

one. And, I think we should all have to ask one member of the opposite sex.'

'. . . or the same sex, if you felt that way inclined,' I pointed out.

'Thank you, Holl, interjection accepted . . . We should all ask one member of the opposite sex who is definitely single and whom we think would be suitable for someone else who's coming – and then they ask someone too!' he finished triumphantly.

'What??'

Even Addison stopped tapping, looking up with a hunted animal expression on his face.

'It's called a singles party. I read it in *Vogue*. You invite a single person, and they bring along a single friend, who brings along a single friend, etcetera etcetera etcetera. It's a "fabulous and frivolous way to find a mate," says *Vogue*.'

He was clearly completely over-excited about his idea.

'Hang on a minute,' said Kate, still slumped into her chair. 'You realize that if we do that, within about five minutes you'll have invited every single single person in the entire world?'

'It's exponential,' mumbled Addison. 'But, if you got them all to stand close enough together, I think they could fit on the Isle of Wight.'

'What if some of them are burglars?' I asked.

'Guys! Have you no excitement?! No imagination?!'

'Addison,' I said gravely, 'can I ask you as my single friend?'

'Yes,' he replied. 'Ehm, can I ask you then, as my follow-up?'

'Yes! Ooh, that means I'll have to ask you again now.'

'No! No! Come on, guys! It'll be fun! Please! I'll hire the caterers!'

Josh believed *everything* he read in *Vogue*. As, of course, you should.

'You'll get caterers?' I asked, fatally. Well, I'd never been to a party before where catering didn't mean half a bowl of peanuts with a cigarette stubbed out in it.

'Oh yes – if it's going to be a proper party.'

'I doubt I'll be able to make it,' said Kate. 'John and I will probably be out that night.'

'Uh huh,' said Josh carefully. 'But say he's working abroad that night – you would come, wouldn't you?'

Kate shrugged her shoulders. 'I don't care. Sure.'

'But don't ask that Finny bastard,' I said. 'He'll make the punch explode or something.'

'Excellent!' said Josh. 'I'll get the invitations printed.' *Printed*? 'Shall we say . . . three weeks on Saturday?'

'Why are you doing this?' Kate asked him.

'This is our year,' said Josh. 'This is our summer. People always get it together in the summer. And we should all do it together this year, seeing as we're all here together, all single, all still young, all supportive of each other : . .'

I snorted under my breath.

'. . . I mean, by this time next year you'll be thirty.'

Kate didn't say anything but got up to leave the room, her face like thunder. As she reached the door, however, she accidentally on purpose dropped one of Josh's Wedgwood teacups – the family-heirloom ones he wouldn't let me use, only Kate because she was so careful – on the floor. It smashed everywhere.

'Jeepers!' said Josh.

'Oh, did I break something of yours?' said Kate. 'So sorry.'

I couldn't say that Josh's party idea didn't excite me. Here, finally, was a chance to get Addison on his own, without me being drunk, in a proper copping-off situation. I had started to dream about him, with the two of us managing to use his computer chair in a variety of surprisingly inventive ways. And he was my fantasy too; it normally went something like this: Kate and Josh decide to run away to sea to be sailors, leaving Addison and me to run the house by ourselves. After some delightfully romantic faffing around – he inadvertently sees me through a gauze curtain over the bath, we go to outdoor markets and laugh loudly, we somehow find ourselves having a glorious night at the opera, that kind of thing – we sit one night in front of the roaring fireplace (currently choked up with bird nests and also illegal, but never mind) and he rests his head on my shoulder and says, 'Holly, I have never experienced human companionship before, and now I cannot remember why, as I am clearly not weird or anything. But thank God I have found you. Please, never leave me.' And I say, 'OK,' and then we have Olympic-standard rumpy-pumpy. I ignored my worries in that area – e.g. the fact that Addison flinched if one so much as brushed past him – by telling myself that he would be a natural.

I could tell by a footfall where he was; by the gentlest tapping, how engrossed he was in his work; but somehow I couldn't go into his room during the day – it took the wee small hours and that quiet sense of magic you sometimes feel then. I wanted Addison and I to be special, and that meant not accidentally seeing his dirty underpants. I had it bad.

Kate did not get up from that damn table the whole day. Josh, who was humming about merrily planning party doilies, tried his best to be sympathetic.

'Skates, do you know what I think?'

'Hn?'

'I think there's a reason he didn't give you his full name.'

'Hn.'

'It was dark in that bar, wasn't it?'

'Thank God,' I added. I was trying to iron a shirt to wear for my first day at work, and making a crappy job of it.

'Was it dark in the restaurant you went to?'

'We went to Momo – it's pitch-dark in there. Proper Moroccan, you see. No electricity.'

'Not Le Caprice?' I said, disappointed. They both stared at me.

'*No one* goes there,' Kate said. She can't have been that depressed if she was still up to sneering.

'No, me neither,' I said, and tried to make the sleeves stay in the same place long enough for me to flatten them – unsuccessfully.

'*Well*,' went on Josh, 'I thought he looked a bit famous. Maybe

74

he was someone famous and was trying to hide it.'

Suddenly it struck me who John Thingy looked like – that guy from all those awful films where he had long hair and the whole world had been destroyed except him and he had to drink his own piss.

'Oh-my-God,' said Kate.

'You mean . . .' I said.

'Yes,' said Josh, shaking his head portentously.

'It's impossible,' I said. 'Although he did have an American accent.' I turned to Josh.

'You would have *noticed*,' I added. '*Somebody* would have noticed.'

'Oh my God,' said Kate again.

'Not necessarily,' said Josh. 'I mean, you don't usually expect to see major international film stars in South London. He must have been travelling incognito. Trying to see if you liked him for himself.'

'Oh my God,' said Kate again.

'I've heard they do this kind of thing all the time – haven't you seen *Notting Hill*?'

'He talked about Los Angeles quite a lot!'

'There you go then – proof.'

'Oh my God. I had a date with *Kevin Costner*!' Kate rushed off to the bathroom.

'*What* are you up to?' I asked Josh.

'Come on, what would you rather do: get dumped by some ferrety-faced married 'schmuckmeister or some ferrety-faced international superstar?'

'You're a good man.'

'Too good,' he said soberly, following Kate out into the hall, yelling, 'He probably got called away the next morning to give out an Oscar or something. Don't blame yourself! He'll probably make a film about you!'

'Yeah, and that one can be shit as well,' I thought, but I kept it to myself.

*   *   *

I was early the next morning, wearing my white shirt, which was almost spotless, and a pair of trousers. I only had one pair of trousers and couldn't believe that the person who invented the concept for women had done us any favours whatsoever, but they were black and smartish and looked quite a lot like what Chalitha had been wearing in the interview, so I was going along with that. I got a bit of a shock taking off on my bicycle, as the traffic was rather different at 8.30 a.m. than it was at 9 p.m., so I managed to get nearly killed three or four times and be hollering a gypsy curse on all white van drivers by the time I screeched to a halt beside That Special Someone. Mrs Bigelow was unlocking the door, and looked up with a faintly shocked expression on her face.

'Ah, Miss Livingstone.'

I dismounted in an ungainly fashion, which I think included flashing my pants at her.

'It's Holly. Hello again. Ehm, is there anywhere I can put the bike?'

She stared at me as if I was a Martian.

'No.'

We stood there, facing each other.

'OK then . . .' I checked around, and, for want of anything better, connected the bike to the nearest lamppost, in prime person-tripping and vandalism position. Mrs Bigelow watched me all the while, her several chins seeming to wobble reproachfully at me.

Finally, she opened the door and let me back into the shop I had seen only briefly the previous week.

It was small, with a floor covered in black rubber and the familiar heavy scent of flowers. Buckets of bouquets and posies sloshed around near the door, ready to be put outside for schoolchildren to pinch from. On the wall were several prominently displayed certificates from the Chelmsford School of Horticulture, made out to a Marilyn Gloria Bigelow.

She bustled through officiously.

'Now, here is the telephone,' she announced, pointing to the telephone. 'Incoming calls *only*, if you don't mind, unless you have to speak to suppliers, or me, or Mr Haffillton.'

'When might I need to speak to Mr Haffillton?'

She fixed me with a glare.

'Never! I am the only person who communicates with Mr Haffillton!'

I nodded my head as if this made sense.

The phone rang suddenly.

'Ah. Now, Holly, listen carefully: this is how we answer the telephone. Good *morning*, That Special Someone, how can I *help* you?'

Her helpful expression changed quickly, however, and she shot into the phone: 'You'd better make it quick, you procrastinating minx, or I'll be letting Mr Haffillton know, do you understand?'

Then she slammed the phone down and resumed her beatific smile.

'That was Chalitha. She's been a trifle . . . held up, but she oughtn't to be long. Now, through here, this is our staff room.'

There was a tiny chair behind a curtain, with a kettle on a shelf and a sink. There was no window, only a fluorescent bulb.

'We each bring our own tea, coffee, milk, cups and sugar; that makes life a lot easier, don't you find?'

I nodded in a way that indicated that in fact I found this the apotheosis of efficient tea-making.

'Ten minutes break in the morning and the afternoon, and forty-five minutes at lunchtime – quite generous, don't you think? Mr Haffillton always was most . . . generous.'

I tried to work out why she was talking in the past tense. Maybe he really was dead, and they just propped him up for formal occasions.

'The vans deliver at ten from the markets – *do* check the merchandise, they're never above trying to pass off those rancid African daisies, and it makes me *most* upset, do you understand? Then the orders for the day will be HERE –' she stabbed a long, deadly pink nail at the wall – 'and you start making them up immediately. Then you phone the collection boys . . .'

It seemed rude to enquire who the collection boys were –

'. . . They're positively indolent, *and* they get the tips, but we can't do it without them, unfortunately. Don't let them get away with anything, and keep an eye on them when they're in the shop. Now, have you got your NVQ in wedding floral artistry?'

I confessed that I hadn't. She let out a large sigh.

'Ohhh well. Perhaps we'll wait until we're on the job for that, shall we? Right, must be off, Chalitha will be in soon, one *supposes*. You *do* understand that I can't open the till until she gets here – you don't *seem* like a thief, dear, but they're everywhere, you know?'

'Where are you going?' I asked, worried that she was going to leave me.

'Oh, you don't think this is the only project Mr Haffillton has up his sleeve, do you? Oh no, I am the Executive Sales Director, and I'm extremely busy. But remember, be polite on the phone. And we do check all outgoing calls, you know, so don't think about trying anything – not that you would, I'm sure, but you never know, people have relatives all over the world these days. I'm sure that girl will be in shortly; normally we run an extremely tight ship, but she's officially been delayed, hopefully not in an accident or anything like that . . .' She appeared to fantasize about the possibility for an instant. 'No, I'm sure it wasn't. Now, you have got everything straight, haven't you? Orders off the phone, orders on to the nail, orders off the nail, orders through to the boys. I'm afraid you won't be able to take a break until Chalitha turns up, but then you don't appear to have any tea with you, so that won't be a problem anyway, will it? Bye!!!'

And she disappeared in a flash of polyester. I stared after her as she sped down the road, then slowly looked round the small shop. I remembered vaguely a TV show where people would be set up with new jobs, left on their own, and then gunge would be thrown at them, or someone pretending to be the President of the United States would phone up or something, and sighed. Also, suddenly, I was gasping for a cup of tea.

I wandered around the shop, picking at stray bits of ribbon, examining the stock – mostly dusty house plants – before the

78

day's delivery turned up, and praying that the phone wouldn't ring.

Worse happened, though. The bell at the door of the shop went off as an enormous greasy hulk stooped his head to come in. He was wearing a filthy old leather jacket and jeans holed and stained with oil, and his hair was long. In fact, he resembled a Status Quo fan from the eighties, and, as such, made me shudder. He popped his motorcycle helmet on the counter about a foot away from me and rubbed his stubble contemplatively with the heel of his hand.

''Oo are you?'

'I'm Holly Catherine Livingstone,' I replied, trying to sound insouciant. 'Who are you?'

He grunted by way of response. 'Where's Charlie, then?'

I had no idea whom he meant.

'Are you in the right flower shop?'

'What? Course I am. Are you?'

'Yes.'

We were at stalemate. He looked around cautiously, just in case he had, in fact, walked into the wrong flower shop.

'So 'as, Charlie, er, left, yeah?'

'He might have done . . . I'm new.'

He shook his head in disbelief. I noticed he was wearing one of those really visceral heavy-metal T-shirts – somebody's eyeball being punctured with a nail – and I tried not to concentrate on it.

'Yeah, all right then . . . sorry.'

'No problem!' I said, pleased with how well I'd dealt with my first customer.

'If you see 'er, right, tell 'er Gareth was looking for 'er.'

'Well, of course, I wouldn't know her if I did see her – but, as I said, no problem!' I replied jauntily.

He backed out of the shop, pausing at the doorway to look around it suspiciously one more time, as if I might have hidden her in one of the pot plants. Then he shook his head again, and the next thing I heard was a little hairdrier motorbike engine kicking into life. I patted my hands successfully, and started putting the

79

flower buckets outside, using a black marker pen to strike out all the unnecessary apostrophes.

Eventually, whilst bending down by the kerb, I realized someone was watching me, and straightened up very slowly. The longhaired, dark-eyed girl from the interview was studying me appraisingly. I wiped my hands on my trousers and spluttered a bit.

'Hi . . . Chalitha . . .'

'Chali,' she said dismissively, marching into the shop, 'that's what most people call me.'

'Ah,' I said, then thought about it. 'Ah,' I said again.

I followed her into the back, where she slung off a black PVC mac and started touching up her already heavy eyeliner in a mirror the size of a cigarette packet.

'Ehm, I think someone was in here looking for you.'

'Really?'

'A big bloke. I didn't realize it was you and told him you didn't work here. I'm sorry . . .'

'Did you? Was he big and greasy with stupid long hair, and did he smell?'

'Ehm . . . well, yes, to all of the above.'

'Excellent!' Someone smiled at me for the first time that day. 'Where did you say I'd gone?'

'Nowhere in particular.'

'Good. But specifics are better – he might follow me there. Next time, could you tell him I'm in Bhutan?'

'Not a problem.'

She grinned again.

'Did the old witch get you started?'

'She . . . ehm, Mrs Bigelow was very helpful.'

'Really? Maybe she's had a brain transplant. Cup of tea?'

'Yes, please.'

I followed her through to the little kitchen. Chali was about nineteen years old, and today was wearing tight black leather trousers and a ripped top. Her silky black hair came down to her bum – something I had always longed for as a child – and she had matching gold hoops in her ears, nose and lip. She was gorgeous.

'OK, always use *Biggie's* tea,' she instructed, picking up the box of Earl Grey. 'And if she asks you, deny it. You have to get your fun where you can around here.'

'How long have you been working here?'

Chali snorted and raised her eyes.

'One hundred and forty-seven years. Milk and sugar?'

'Yes, please.'

We took our teas back into the main shop and sat down.

'God, I had a killer night last night. Do you go clubbing?'

There is nothing I despise more than being made to dance in public in front of sulky teenagers in very little clothing whilst paying four pounds for a bottle of water.

'Yeah, you know . . . occasionally.'

'Right, where do you go?'

I searched my brains desperately, but all I could remember was the one down from my school where I grew up.

'Erm . . . Cinderella's Rockefellers?'

Seeing her disbelieving face, I hastily added, 'It's ironic.'

'Oh, cool. That sounds like a right laugh.'

'It is.'

'God, I got in at four this morning, E-ing off my head at Fabroche.'

I smiled politely.

'That's why this job isn't so bad in the long run – they don't care what you do, s'long as you turn up occasionally. Biggie gives you a bunch of shit, but you don't need to pay attention.'

She let out an elaborate yawn and went to open the door to the delivery men.

'Yo. Just dump them anywhere, as usual, boys.'

The two men brought in several boxes of flowers in different shapes and sizes and dumped them haphazardly on the floor. Chali ignored them, signed the chit without reading it and sighed theatrically at the pile. So far we hadn't had a single customer and the phone hadn't rung once.

I went over to start opening up the flowers. Sure enough, the African daisies *were* rancid.

'Who left the job before I came?' I asked, unwrapping the plastic carefully.

'Oh, no one,' she sighed. 'Really, you're here to keep an eye on me, because I was turning up later and later, and the shop wasn't opening at all.'

'Why don't they just sack you?' I said, before it had passed across my brain censor control. I cursed inwardly.

'They can't – Mr Haffillton's my uncle and thinks the sun shines out of my arse. *And* he only really runs it as a hobby – he's minted, and he likes flowers. You can't imagine how much that annoys Biggie.'

I started to feel a bit sorry for Biggie.

'So, do you feel up to babysitting duties?' She lit a cigarette.

I thought about it. Babysitting was definitely one up on where I'd just come from.

'Sure!'

'Excellent. Listen, do you know any singers?'

I thought about Josh singing in the bath and dismissed the image immediately.

'Not really.'

'Shame.' She tipped some cigarette ash into one of the flower buckets. 'That's what I *really* am, see? I'm just getting a band together.'

'What kind of band?'

'Kind of bhangra gangsta, do you know what I mean?'

I could see immediately why she thought I might know lots of people in those kinds of bands and nodded my head sagely. Finally the phone rang.

'Yeah? . . . Stodger. Yeah . . . No, I have left, yeah . . . No, I just came by to pick up some stuff, innit? I'm going to Bhutan . . . Yeah, it's in Peru, innit? . . . Maybe a year, maybe two . . . No, I don't think you can motorbike all the way there. There's an ocean or summink . . . No, I'll write to you. I will . . . Yeah. OK. Bye.'

She slammed the phone down, and reverted back to her normal voice.

'Where did you meet him?' I asked, genuinely curious.

'Oh, he said he was putting a band together,' she said dismissively. 'So I slept with him and everything, and next thing he's round here like effin' Hugh Grant every day of the week.'

I wasn't surprised. His gratitude must have been overwhelming.

The day passed in an easy round of selling the occasional bouquet, rearranging the occasional arrangement, cups of tea, and one and a half hour lunch breaks. I could tell I was going to like it here. Mrs Bigelow returned about four thirty.

'Hello, Biggie,' I said, quite innocently. She stared at me as if I'd just bitten her.

'It's Mrs Bigelow, as I thought you knew.'

'Erm, yes, sorry, Mrs Bigelow.'

'Did you have a busy day? You!' – indicating Chali – 'Cash up, please, madam, if it isn't too much trouble.'

''Ave you forgotten how to count again, Biggie? You ought to get out more.'

Biggie hissed at her and pretended to talk to me whilst watching Chali like a hawk. This didn't surprise me; Chali had already informed me that she used the float to supplement her meagre income, so I merely stared straight ahead in a neutral fashion until I was dismissed with a sniff from Biggie, suggesting that if I really, really behaved myself, one day I might get a set of keys.

It was bliss coming home when it was still light. I banged in the hall joyously shouting, 'Hi, honeys! I'm home!' and went straight through to the kitchen to start chopping onions for Josh.

I nearly threw up when I saw Kate was still there.

'*What???* Are you OK? Did you take the day off work?'

'No,' she said quietly, 'I left early.'

'What happened – did the junior doctors form an action corps and get you released?'

'No . . . I just felt like an early night.'

Josh popped his head round the door. 'Holly, is that you? Can you take over suicide watch for me?'

'OK.' I nodded.

'Oh, and if you're chopping those onions, could you do them a bit finer this time?'

'OK, MR PRISSY.'

I sat down carefully. 'Ehm, Kate, you know, sometimes, bad things happen to good people.'

'Bugger off.'

'Okey-dokey. Read my lips. He – is – not – going – to – phone – you. OK? You had a lovely night, he was clearly a dickhead and you will never hear from him again. But look on the bright side: at least you didn't take your knickers off, and that's what I'd have done, so reclaim your self-respect, girl. *Comprendez*? *Capisce*?'

Kate looked at me with pained eyes. 'Holly?' she said weakly.

'Yes?' Tough love. It always works.

'Would you mind watching the phone while I go to the toilet?'

'Argh. If he phones whilst you go to the toilet I am going to tell him you hate him and put the phone down on him, as it will save you the bother of doing it in two years time if you actually had a relationship with this man.'

'You don't know him!'

'Neither do you! You think he's Kevin Costner!'

She shrugged. I shrugged back at her and picked up the bag of onions, as she started manhandling her mobile and her pager into her dressing gown pockets and sidled backwards out of the room with the phone cord.

I hollered for Josh.

'*Do* something with her.'

'Sorry, darling – you know how much she listens to me. Why don't we all have a nice dinner and forget about it?'

'Huh.'

Kate marched back into the room.

'OK, that's enough,' she announced stridently, picking up the various bits of electric equipment.

84

'Oh no!' I whispered to Josh. 'She's reached breaking point! This is where she starts really beating up on herself for standing around waiting for a man to phone and then decides to get drunk, then phones up all her ex-boyfriends at four o'clock in the morning and berates them for treating her so badly, then falls asleep in a pool of her own vomit and wakes up overcome by self-disgust and remorse.'

'I give up,' said Kate. 'This is ridiculous. I am an adult, after all.'

Josh sniggered at me.

'Glass of wine, Holl?'

'And my old address book, please,' I replied glumly.

Four

Josh was explaining his party invitation strategies over dinner.

'OK, there's this girl in the office called Sophie, right? She's really gorgeous . . .'

'Is she blonde, posh and up herself?' said Kate, restored to near-normal service, and starving after her long vigil. How anyone could sit in a kitchen for forty-eight hours and forget there were one hundred and sixty-six Penguins in the cupboard was beyond me, but love does funny things. Kate was one of those people who complain that when they're depressed 'the weight just falls off me; I can't eat a thing; it's awful.'

'Ehm . . . well, she is blonde, and she did go to Cheltenham Ladies. Why?'

'No reason.'

'No, she is definitely not "up herself", as you so charmingly put it. In fact, she was in the top six of her year at the bar.'

'And she told you this, did she? You didn't find out from anyone else?'

'No, she told me.'

'Well, that proves it then,' said Kate, mopping up the remnants of her coq au vin. 'Definitely up herself.'

'She sounds nice,' I said comfortingly.

'Oh, she's brilliant. Normally she spends weekends in the country, but I've thought of a foolproof plan to get her to come to our party.'

'Oh no,' said Kate. She was obviously more used to Josh's seduction attempts than I was, but I did recall a few.

'It's not the one where you've got leukaemia, is it?'

'No!'

'Exchange student visiting?'

'No!'

'We're her possible half-sisters?'

'Oh, for goodness' sake!'

'Tell the truth, Josh.'

Josh hung his head.

'OK . . . um, well, I was going to tell her that you two were interested in reading for the bar, and could she come along and give you some tips.'

'What???!!!' we cried simultaneously.

'What's "the bar"?' I asked.

'And *that's* how you're planning on getting Sophie into bed?' asked Kate incredulously.

'Don't be disgusting.'

'Josh, you know, bed is not necessarily disgusting,' I said, refilling his wine glass. 'It's just been so long you can't remember.'

'I can't believe you think that that might get a girl to come to a party with you.' Kate was still amazed. 'Why don't you just ask her straight out if she'd like to come?'

'Ehm, well . . . because she might think I'm just trying to get her into bed.'

'But you *are*! You are, aren't you? Please say yes.'

86

'Yes, yes, of course. God, sometimes I think you lot would like to see me go and bugger Danny La Rue, but it's not going to happen.' He sighed. 'I hope. God, I don't know why it's all so damn complicated. I just want to, you know, meet someone nice to hold hands with, and talk about things.'

Kate and I stared at each other.

'Are you completely smooth in front, like an Action Man?' I asked him. He grimaced at me and went to fetch the rhubarb tart.

'Just ask her to the party,' said Kate. 'Look at you. You're cute. You're blond. You're posh. You're practically clones of each other . . .'

'Except you're not up yourself,' I added quickly, kicked myself under the table, then added: 'and I'm sure she isn't either.'

'. . . why wouldn't she come?'

Josh looked at us mournfully, holding the tart between his Heal's oven gloves.

Kate sighed. 'And yes, we will pretend that we are interested in the bar.'

Josh grinned and plonked the tart down with a flourish.

'Really, you won't regret it. You'll love her. Do you know, she stables her own ponies?'

'We love her already,' said Kate.

'And oh!' he said, as if he'd just remembered it. He got out of striking distance. 'She's a potential Conservative candidate.'

I snuck some coq au vin into Addison's room and didn't bother to tell him Josh had cooked it, in case he was into chicks that did that kind of thing. He waved a hand at me without turning round, which I'd learned meant he was in the middle of composing a particularly fluent line of code and was uninterruptible. I liked to think of him like Mozart, enraptured by his muse, except at the end of Mozart writing something he got lots of nice twiddly noises, and I had no idea what spilled out the end of Addison's frantic typing.

I sat down on the floor and started playing with a doll shaped like Jean-Luc Picard while he finished. I also picked at his chicken. Eventually, he turned round.

'How goes it?' I asked him, handing him a knife and fork. Addison stared at the food for a bit, then launched into it as if he hadn't eaten for a week, which would have surprised nobody.

'Hnfu bad,' he said, through a mouthful of pesto mash. 'It's boring really.'

'Not to me,' I said. I hoped he was designing something unbelievably hi-tech that would help disabled children and revolutionize the world.

'Well,' he sighed, 'I programme C++ and edit AVID.'

'Huh.'

'Would you mind not fiddling with that,' he said, indicating the doll. 'It's limited edition.'

'Sure,' I said, putting it down carefully. I forgive a lot in people whose eyelashes scratch their cheekbones.

'So . . . have you decided who to invite to the singles party yet?'

'Is that for real?' sighed Addison, putting down his forkful of carrot julienne. 'I hate parties.'

'Why?' I asked.

'Well,' he said, twisting himself nervously, 'I don't know if you've noticed, but . . . I'm actually quite shy.'

I choked, and tried to turn it into a cough.

'*Really*? No, actually, I hadn't noticed.'

'Yeah . . . I don't really like meeting people that much.'

I nodded sagely. 'Yes, I'm quite shy myself. In fact, you know, we could escape that night, go out somewhere else . . .'

'I don't really like going out much either,' he said apologetically. 'Do you think I'm weird?'

I shook my head. 'No. You know, really, it's not that great out there in the whole . . . big, world thing. You're not missing much.'

He smiled with relief.

'I'm really glad you moved in,' he said. A flame lit up in

88

my heart like a pilot light. I gave him my patented doe-eyed sincere look.

'I'm glad too.'

He smiled shyly. 'Ehm, actually, there was someone I wanted to invite.'

'Yes?' I said coyly.

'Come here,' he said, and beckoned me over to his computer screen. I got up, trying not to trip over the extension wires in my excitement. He clicked his mouse on a corner icon and suddenly a face filled half the screen. A big, flat, potato-like face. With a moustache. On the other half was what appeared to be a continuing dialogue in two different colours of text.

'This is Claudia,' he said.

I peered more closely at the pixels, just to confirm that it was, in fact, a woman and not the lumpy builder I'd originally taken it for.

'Who's Claudia?' I asked petulantly.

'Ehm . . . she's kind of . . . like, my girlfriend,' said Addison, blushing.

I sat down heavily, then got up promptly when I realized I was sitting on the remnants of coq au vin.

'Oh!' I said, trying to make my voice sound not too hysterical. 'I didn't know you had a girlfriend! Where do you keep her? Under the bed? Ha ha!'

'Well, we've never met.'

'Ah, that famous imaginary girlfriend?'

'No, she's real all right,' he said proudly. 'I met her on the Internet.'

Yes, well, I'd gathered that.

'How do you know that's her picture?' I said, squinting at the troll-like image. 'She could . . . you know, be really ugly or something.'

Addison smiled. 'I know,' he said. 'But, even if that isn't her . . . well, I wouldn't care.'

'As long as she's a girl,' I said. 'And not twelve.'

'No, there –' he pointed to the picture again – 'she's holding up her driving licence.'

She looked like the Rosemary West mug shot.

'She looks nice,' I said.

'She is. She knows more about *Star Trek* than anyone I've ever met.'

I started fiddling with the Jean-Luc Picard doll again.

'That's very romantic,' I said. 'So . . . are you going to invite her to the party?'

'Well . . . she lives in Baltimore . . .'

Hurrah!

'. . . and she doesn't much like leaving the house either . . . But, you know, I will ask her!'

'What does she do?' I stumbled on, torturing myself.

'She does C++ too,' he said proudly. 'She works on government defence programmes. She's got security clearance and everything.'

Wow. A fat agoraphobic bomb-maker four thousand miles away was doing better with Addison than I was.

'If neither of you leaves the house, and you live on different continents,' I mused, 'do you think there's a lot of future in the relationship?'

Addison shrugged. 'Well, you know, science can do a lot these days.'

I struggled to work out what he was referring to, thought it might be sperm, decided it couldn't be, realized it had to be, and nearly threw up.

'I bet you wish they'd hurry up and invent the teleport, eh?' I said.

'Actually, it's not worth the trouble to invent the technology to evaporate and replicate an individual,' he said gravely. 'You're on much safer ground when you work at speeding up transportation as quickly as possible.'

Snap! I suddenly realized that I'd pulled Jean-Luc Picard's arm off. I held it behind my back.

'So, this is serious, then?'

He blinked at me, but I got distracted and yelled before I'd had the chance to think about it: 'Oh my God, the face is coming to life!!'

At first Addison's eyes darted to where my trembling finger was pointing like some harbinger of doom in an Edgar Allan Poe story, but he quickly relaxed.

'Don't worry – that's just a little computer thing we do. When Claudia's typing to me, her picture moves like it's speaking.'

And sure enough, Claudia was making like a ventriloquist's doll while words were coming up on the screen. It was reminiscent of the *Bride of Chucky*.

'What's she saying?'

Addison went coy.

'Oh, just, "Hi, how're you doing?" That kind of stuff.'

I leaned over to the computer screen.

'"I salute you, Captain?" Is that you?'

'Maybe.'

'Can I say hello?'

'Ehm, best let me.'

'Otherwise it'll be coming out of your mouth on her end?'

'Uh huh.'

'Actually, you know, Addison, I think maybe you are a bit weird.'

My panic had somewhat abated. I was still pissed off, but hey, she was there and I was here, standing and talking to him – and he was about to tell her about me. She might even get jealous. Low tactics, certainly, but necessary ones.

Addison started to type and I peered over his shoulder.

'Hello there,' he started. Seemingly unsure of how to proceed, he pressed return.

'Rn't I yr Uhuru tonight?' shot back.

'Addison!' I exclaimed.

'What?' he said, embarrassed. 'It's like a pet name.'

'What, a pet whore?' I said, then wished I hadn't. 'I didn't mean that.'

'Of course you are,' he typed back, ignoring me. 'I'm here with a friend.'

'???????????????' came up.

'Holly, my flatmate.'

91

Ha, that'll get you, I thought meanly.

'IS THAT A GIRL'S NAME?'

'I don't know, is that a girl's moustache?' I said to myself.

'Y.'

'DOES SHE LIKE STAR TREK?'

Addison looked at me and I nodded my head vehemently, still hanging on to the mutilated Jean-Luc.

'Y.'

'FAVOURITE CHARACTER?'

Oh God, I didn't care.

'Scotty?' I said hopefully to Addison, who dutifully typed it in.

'FAVOURITE NEXT GENERATION CHARACTER?'

Oh, I was in deep doo here.

'Ehm . . . still Scotty, definitely.'

'What, you mean from "Relics" where they step back in time and meet mirror images of themselves from the original crew?'

'Yes, that one.'

'Wow.'

There was a long pause whilst we waited for Claudia's answer. Finally, the strange mouth thing crept back to life.

'IS SHE YR GIRLFRIEND?'

Even I was surprised. Addison looked distraught.

'Oh no. What should I do?'

'Tell her, "no"?' I suggested. 'Point out the word "flatmate". Oh, they don't have that in America, do they? They call it "roommate". Maybe she thinks "flatmate" means "lover"!?'

He practically stumbled over the keys to type: 'No, of course not! Don't be silly!'

Thanks a lot.

'How could I possibly prefer anyone to you? Even if she does recognize Scotty's performance in "Relics".'

I sighed and hid the *Star Trek* doll under a full-size Darth Vader head.

'So, I'll see you at the party, then,' I said to Addison breezily.

'Yes, OK then, I'll see you at the party,' was what he clearly *meant* to say. Unfortunately, the words didn't come out of his mouth but were typed at high velocity on to the keyboard. Before he could think, he'd pressed 'return'.

He stared at me open-mouthed in horror at what he had done.

'Addison, you're a true cyborg,' I said. 'Did you get your navel removed and replaced with a three-way socket? Where's your bar code tattoo?'

'It's not funny,' he said. 'I'm so much more used to typing than . . . She'll think I'm making fun of her.'

'Or she might come,' I said, for him. The mouth on the screen was no longer gasping like a fish. He was studying it intently. He actually seemed slightly hopeful.

'Well, if she doesn't come, I'll dance with you,' I said. 'Maybe they'll play some Kraftwerk.'

'I love them,' he said, still staring angstily at the screen.

'I knew that,' I said. 'Now, compose your letter of apology. In Klingon.' He smiled, and I beat a retreat.

I heard 'Holly, have you seen my Jean-Luc Picard doll?' being yelled after me, but I pretended not to.

Chali wanted to know exactly what kind of music would be playing and what kinds of drugs would be available at the party before she even attempted to decide whether to consider acknowledging the invitation.

'Snoopy Dogg Dogg? Vodka jelly?'

She sneered at me, whilst sloppily tying up a princess bouquet – not the easiest of double acts to pull off. Mrs Bigelow had 'just popped in' to see how we were doing and Chali had accused her of spying, whereupon there'd been a bit of a yelling match, so she was now putting together the deliveries very, very slowly. I was supposed to be watching her and learning, but all I was learning was how I would put bouquets together if I were underwater. It was the week after I'd found out about Claudia. I was dealing with it, but slowly.

'Is it going to be full of old folk?'

I hadn't considered asking my mother – she could get down and

93

frug with the best of them. Parents at parties stopped when you were of snoggable age – or at least, stayed upstairs praying – and started up again when you got engaged, there to continue for the rest of your life, I assumed. I explained this.

'No, I meant, lots of people, like, your age and that.'

I hit her with one of the thorny twigs.

'Mid twenties is NOT OLD.'

'Mid twenties, my bum. You're nearly thirty. And then, your life is over.'

'My life will *not* be over. Anyway, I won't be doing this when I'm thirty. Probably won't even be in the country.'

'Really? Why, what are you going to do?'

I had no idea.

'Oh, there's lots of possibilities. Lots of things.'

'Yeah, like climbing up on a shelf.'

'Shut up. Actually, you can't come to our party. It's only for mature, elegant individuals.'

'In smocks?'

Chali had on skinny little bootleg trousers and something chiffony. Her black hair curled in a long thick plait down to her waist. I was wearing a smock.

'Well, fine,' I said. 'If you want to miss out on all those City Porsche owners, that's up to you.' I hadn't forgotten the 'Gareth' incident. 'Or maybe you'd rather be going out with people who keep dogs on pieces of string.'

She didn't say anything for a bit. Then:

'You don't look like you've got lots of rich mates.'

'Well, you don't look like you jump up and down on the spot for ten hours a night and call it fun, but you do.'

'Hnn. Who's the DJ going to be then?'

There was a bit of controversy about this in the flat. Josh obviously wanted to do it, but if we let him, he'd play Scritti Politti all night.

'He's called Fatboy Josh,' I said. 'He's great. He's got a real, ehm, vibe thing, etcetera.'

Chali glanced at me suspiciously.

'Can I bring a friend?'

'You have to, that's the rule of the party. You have to bring a single friend.'

'All my mates are single.'

'OK. You know, Chali, I KNOW you're nineteen. It won't last. Get over it.'

'I wonder if I'll get droopy upper arms when I'm old, like you?'

'Maybe you'll die of a poisoned ecstasy tablet first,' I said moodily.

'What a way to go, though,' she replied.

'Are you coming or not?'

'I suppose we can drop in on our way out for the evening. You'll probably be finished about two, won't you?'

Two seemed to me an OK time to finish a party.

'Well, we can go out properly after it. Flint!'

I had no idea what flint meant, and I wasn't about to demean myself by asking.

'Flint!' I said, cheerfully.

Four hours before the party was officially supposed to begin, three of us sat tensely around the kitchen table. The house was immaculate, and Kate wouldn't let any of us move, so we were just sitting and staring into space. We were also forbidden from opening any of the wine or touching any of the little nibbly things the caterers had dropped off, which was in itself a form of torture. There were flowers everywhere, as filched by me. Filching was not a problem; Chali took so much she'd get the blame anyway. And, morally, they were paying me just above minimum wage, so these were my contribution to the party. Kate and Josh had paid for everything else, hence the embargo on the mini pizzas. It felt a bit unfair to ask Addison for a contribution, given that a party was being imposed on his living space, but he had bought his own bolt for his door. I assumed it was for the party and not, e.g., to keep me out.

It had been a really beautiful May day, which should have gotten everyone in a party mood, but as we'd been inside cleaning all day and filling the bath with ice for the beer before remembering that we were all hot and sweaty and needed a bath, we were a bit cranky.

'OK,' Josh was saying, 'so, the champagne has been delivered.'

'What exactly are we celebrating, again?' asked Kate. 'Our communal loneliness?'

'We could have a competition,' I added. 'See who's got the most frozen lasagne boxes in their bin.'

'Once again,' said Josh, quite heavily for him, 'we are celebrating our youth and success and the beginning of summer.'

'Through the medium of canapés.'

'I wish we had a croquet lawn,' Josh sighed.

'We've got a fire escape,' I pointed out. It was rusty to the point of extreme danger and if you fell off you would arrive in downstairs' midden of a garden and be eaten by triffids, but it was outside, and it belonged to us.

'Great. That ought to compensate. We can take bets on who's going to be the first person to fall through it. OK, Kate, where are we with the guest list again?'

Kate sounded bored. 'Elton John, Elizabeth Taylor, the Beckhams, the Olivers, and an assortment of weather girls.'

'*Really*? Oh no, I mean, ha ha ha,' said Josh.

'The Jameses, who are bringing their other mates from the office; Sophie and all your poncey lawyer friends; Holly's florist mate; some of the old college crowd, who will sit in a corner and ignore everyone else all night. And us. Including Addison. Maybe.'

'How many's that?'

'About fourteen.'

'Oh God; we're catering for two hundred.'

'Well, I like sausage rolls,' I said, staring at the massive platters of food. 'But maybe not for the rest of my natural life.'

'All that houmous,' moaned Josh.

'Well, they're all bringing people,' said Kate. 'The Jameses have got me to deal with if they don't. So, I wouldn't worry.'

'Please can I have a beer?' I said.

'No,' said Kate. 'You'll have passed out by the time every-one arrives.'

'On one beer?'

'On the beer after the beer after the beer after the beer after the beer.'

We stared into space again.

'*What* time do you think they'll be here?' whined Josh, for about the billionth time.

'Either you stop asking or I'll slap you on the back of the legs,' said Kate.

'Don't have kids,' I said, with a shudder.

'Why would I need kids when I have you and Josh?'

'What about Addison?'

'And my autistic son, Addison.'

'Maybe he can just be your son-in-law,' I said.

'You know, interestingly enough, the odds of you and Addison getting married are almost *exactly the same* as you being my biological daughter.'

I ballooned my cheeks and blew the air out of them slowly to stop myself from biting her.

'Well, can we go to the pub then? That's what *most* people do when they're having a party. Relax, throw a couple of things together, then just let people turn up.'

'Do they?' asked Josh in alarm.

'Yes,' said Kate. 'That's why *most* parties are rubbish.'

The phone rang. It was one of the Jameses, phoning up to cancel. Just as well he didn't turn up to tell us in person; Kate might have eaten him.

'Well, either you turn up tonight or you don't bother turning up on Monday morning,' I heard her say menacingly down the telephone. Josh and I looked at each other with panicked expressions on our faces.

'You can't sack someone for not turning up to your party!' we chorused, as soon as she'd slammed down the phone.

'Why not?'

'Ehm, because it's wrong?'

'Why? It was wrong of him to lie about his grandmother being ill.'

'*If* he was lying,' said Josh.

'He was lying. He's a very good liar. That's why I hired him. He'll be here.'

The phone rang again.

'I'll get it!' yelled Josh, anxious to spare some other poor bastard.

'Ehm, yes, she is. Hold on a moment. Who's calling please?'

Josh slowly put his hand over the receiver and turned to face us with a dramatic expression on his face. He was clearly making the most of the moment.

'Ahem . . . Skates?'

'Uh huh?'

'It's someone called "John" for you. Or Kevin Costner, if you will.'

Kate's head shot up as if she'd just been goosed.

'Oh my God! But I haven't had a bath!'

'It's the *telephone*, not the smell-o-phone.'

'Tell him you're not here,' I hissed. 'Be dark and mysterious. And Josh: stop making camp remarks.'

'A month ago I could have been dark and mysterious,' Kate hissed back at me, beckoning for the receiver. 'But now I am *absolutely desperate*.'

'Fair enough.'

'Hello,' she purred down the telephone. Here was one man who wouldn't be getting a sacking. A sucking, maybe.

'Really? Oh, what a shame,' she purred on. 'Never mind: how *was* America?'

'The elder one was fine but the little one's had a bit of a cough,' I said to Josh under my breath.

'I'm terribly sorry, but we're rather in the middle of a party . . .'

Josh and I made huge 'no' motions in front of the phone, shaking our heads and waving our arms.

'You could come if you like . . .'

Josh mimed extreme despair as she gave our address. I stuck my fingers down my throat and made elaborate vomiting motions.

'OK, see you later!' And she made that weird giggling noise again.

'Yes!' she yelled as she put the phone down, bouncing her fist off the table.

'Here we go again,' said Josh quietly.

'Kate, by way of celebration, don't you think we should open a bottle of that wine?'

'No!'

Four hours later we were still sitting at the kitchen table, although we were a bit smarter. Josh, bless him, had his dinner jacket on. Huge amounts of hearty teasing hadn't persuaded him to dress otherwise, so we were contenting ourselves by calling him by his surname and ordering him to bring us drinks. As soon as nine o'clock came, Kate had sanctioned the opening of the wine, and we fell on it like ravenous beasts.

'What if nobody turns up?' I asked, cramming a handful of prawn thingies into my mouth.

'I'll kill myself,' said Josh. 'My life will be of no meaning.'

'I won't care,' said Kate. 'John will be here.'

'Aha – two such brilliantly well-balanced attitudes. I'm going to get Addison. The party's officially started, and he promised to be here.'

I went and knocked on his door. There was the heavy sound of bolts being drawn back that made me think unpleasantly of right-wing militia groups.

'Hey there . . . are you OK?'

'Unh huh.'

'It's the party now. Don't you want to come and have a glass of wine?'

'Are there other people in the house?'

'Nope, not yet. Come *on*.'

'You know, once I was in a house that burned down.'

I stopped in my tracks and stared at him. A voluntary phrase about his own life was almost completely unheard of.

'Oh my God! What happened?'

He ignored me.

'So, I was thinking, maybe I shouldn't have the bolts, in case there's a fire . . .'

'Did anyone die in the fire?'

He blinked.

'Yes. My father. So, do you think I should take the bolts down?'

I was utterly dumbfounded and simply stared at him, my heart aching.

'I'm so . . . I'm really, really sorry.'

'It was a long time ago. Do you think Kate will let me have a beer?'

If she knew this, she'd let him have her car.

'Ehm, I expect so,' I felt completely disconnected, and simply followed him through into the kitchen. I had two alive and rudely healthy parents, even if they did live at opposite ends of the country and hate each other's guts, and a sister who drove me crazy, and this was all way beyond me.

I wanted to grab him and sit on his lap and never let him go. So, I did the next best thing and got him a beer. He didn't mention it again.

Five

At ten thirty, Josh announced he was heading into the bathroom to slit his wrists, and would anyone like a beer while he was in there, since we had one hundred and fifty, and there were still only four of us.

I wasn't adding to the party mood at all – and neither was the

100

music. We were letting Josh play 'Wood Beez' in an attempt to get it out of his system – post Addison's bombshell I was just staring into space. Oh my God, no wonder he was how he was. I was overflowing with love. I would make things OK for him. I would take care of him. I . . . well, I wouldn't light any open fires around him.

Kate was hyperventilating in case she'd given John Doe the wrong directions. Addison having collected his beer, dripping wet from the melted ice in the bath, had disappeared again. In honour of the occasion he was wearing shorts and a T-shirt with the cover of *The Wasp Factory* on it. Josh had loosened his bow tie in despair, and looked pleasingly *Brideshead*. I had debated with myself whether to tell them about Addison and decided no, there are better times to discuss enormous emotional trauma than right before a party. During a party, shouted out at high volume, whereby you'll completely forget about it the next day – that's fine.

Finally, at ten to eleven, the doorbell rang. Our collective sigh of relief was enormous, and Josh strode to the door manfully. There, attractive and composed, with a rather nice bottle of wine, was someone who couldn't have more been called Sophie if they'd had it tattooed on their forehead – not that a Sophie would ever entertain the possibility of getting a tattoo.

'Everyone, this is Sophie,' beamed Josh.

'No, really?' said Kate. I looked at her. She was usually beyond aggressive to women who crossed Josh's path. If the girls were nice, it was like watching *1984*. Fortunately they all tended to be blonde, posh and up themselves. Now I come to think of it, they were usually called Sophie as well.

'Nice to meet you. I'm Kate, and this is Holly.'

'Hellayerh!' she said, managing to use a quite extraordinary number of syllables. 'Naice to meet you! Nearw, which one of you is interested in joining the bar?'

Kate and I made Bugs Bunny-style simultaneous pointing motions at each other.

'Both of you? How farbulous!' She plonked down her pony-riding bottom. 'Gin and tonic, please, Joshua. I say, wasn't there supposed to be a party? Or was this just a ruse to get me to come along, hya hya hya.'

'No, actually, the ruse was . . .' I started, but Josh gave me an imploring look, so I shut up. Fortunately Sophie didn't appear to be the listening-to-people-when-they-talk type.

'The bar, yar? You know, I was in the top six of my year group there.'

'Were you *really*?' Kate said elaborately. 'Well, gosh, that makes you better than us.'

'Oh no, I'm sure it doesn't,' said Sophie, with a smile. 'First question though, is getting in. It's pretty tough. I mean, it's not quite "what does your father do . . . ?"'

'He works for social services,' I said promptly. Which was true.

'Oh. Well, you know, never mind. What about yours?'

'He's a GP,' said Kate, through gritted teeth.

'Oh, how very *mid*! That will do you no harm at all, ectually. Of course, my daddy's just a farmer, isn't he, Josh?'

'Eh?' said Josh, who was busy carving up lemons.

'I said, my daddy's just a farmer, *isn't* he?'

'Ehm, no, actually; Sophie's dad owns half of Cheshire! Ha!'

'Ha ha ha! Well, not *exactly* half.'

I glanced at Kate. Her face was a picture.

Josh brought over the drinks and sat next to Sophie, gazing at her adoringly.

'Next thing, you really have to grease up to any judges you know. Of course, I'm only doing it en route to a safe Tory seat – once we get rid of this bunch of charlatans, naturally.'

Thankfully, the doorbell rang. Kate and I both jumped up to get it, but I let her win. My heart sank when I heard an uncharacteristic yelp of delight. And, sure enough, she led in John, her face bright and glowing. He was definitely extremely suave, with a soft shirt on, which even though it *looked* just like an ordinary shirt in terms of buttons, collar, cuffs etc, was somehow also deeply, deeply tasteful and expensive. He was exceptionally handsome. He did resemble Kevin Costner, but in this light I realized it was Kevin Costner in his eighties baseball movies and not in his nineties post apocalyptic piss-drinking phase. He handed over a bottle of champagne and another of wine.

'You know Holly and Josh, of course . . .' We all nodded, although we didn't know him at all. 'And this is Sophie.'

I could hear from the faint tremor in her voice exactly what she was thinking: this is Sophie. She is blonde and she owns Cheshire. Do you prefer her to me? Well, do you?

John simply shook her hand, whilst Sophie giggled and blushed up at him.

'Oh, hello, John . . . Ooh, you're American. It's so lovely to meet an American.'

'Sophie was in the top six at her year in the bar,' I said helpfully. Kate and Josh both looked upset. 'But she's never met an American.'

'No, of course I have, Holly!' said Sophie earnestly. 'And I think they're really nice.'

'Well, thank you, ma'am.' John pretended to tip his cap at her. 'Any place a body can git a drink round here?'

'Listen to that lovely accent,' said Sophie.

Kate sidled up to me and grabbed the nearest thing that came to hand.

'Hit her with this and I'll throw her over the fire escape,' she hissed.

'It's a plastic colander.'

'So? Hit her a lot.'

The doorbell rang again, and I went to answer it. It was Chali and six complete strangers, most of whom were exceptionally scruffy, except Chali, of course, who was clearly their queen, and one other person who was unconscious and being carried. I was so pleased to see someone *I* knew that I went completely over the top, given that she was a work colleague and I'd known her for less than a month.

When I returned to the kitchen, the new age travellers in tow, Josh was still up fixing a drink for John, who was sitting between Kate and Sophie, who were both desperately trying to talk to him.

'So, here we are then!' I said stupidly. OK, so there were some people here, lots of booze, lots of food, music, candles and low lighting . . . yet, somehow, it didn't quite *feel* like an actual party. The temptation was to say, 'OK, everybody – start!'

'OK, everybody,' said Josh, popping open a bottle of champagne, 'start!' and he turned the volume up on 'Pray like Aretha Franklin'.

When the new age travellers saw all the canapés, their eyes lit up, they dropped the unconscious one in the doorway and leapt across the room, pockets ajar. Chali, however, stopped them with a raise of her hand. As we all turned to watch her, she felt in her minuscule handbag. I watched, fascinated to see what she would bring out – a home-made cheesecake? Crack cocaine? In fact, she brought out a CD with a pure white cover on it, cut off poor old Scritti, and inserted it.

Immediately the house started to bang as if it were about to fall apart, and the new age travellers all started to hop up and down. The doorbell rang again. The first person tripped over the guy in the doorway and spilt some of their booze. Prawn wingwangs were suddenly being crammed into faces and jammed into the carpet. Fags were lit.

'OK, everyone!' announced Chali. 'Start!'

Amazingly, after that, the place began to fill up. OK, I didn't actually know that many people who were there, but still, it was pleasingly noisy. I decided to get seriously drunk, to compensate for not knowing many people at my own party. I talked confusingly for a bit to some of the Jameses, who had all turned up from the pub in suits and ties, and seemed nervous. One had even brought Kate another present, in case it was a continuation of her birthday party. I told him it was mine and took the present, but disappointingly it was a gizmo-gadget for her hand-held computer that told you share prices on the moon or something. I tucked it away anyway, in case I ever had to give Kate something.

Then I bounced through to the kitchen, carefully avoiding old friends from college who would doubtless be very happy to ask me how my career was going whilst talking about their new cars and that endlessly fascinating topic, London house prices. And, in fact, if I wasn't very much mistaken, one of them was checking their watch, worrying about the babysitter. Argh.

Back in the kitchen, Josh was sitting at the table desperately trying to pretend that he was in a party of four when he clearly wasn't – Kate and Sophie were both facing directly away from him. I sat down next to him and poured us both another glass of champagne.

'How's it going?'

'Oh, fine, fine,' he said, in his usual enthusiastic tones.

'No, I mean with Sophie.'

Sophie was currently telling John why she was going to be the new Margaret Thatcher, but without the wishy-washy social policies. John appeared to be listening. Kate was wearing a very tight-lipped smile.

'Oh, yes, yes, coming along quite nicely.'

'Josh, she's completely ignoring you.'

'Well, that's perfectly normal, isn't it?'

I realized how hurt he was.

'No it's not! Either you should be in there fighting for her, or give her up as someone who's too up themselves. Look at that guy too! He's like a pig in shit.'

'I think they call them pigs in a blanket in America.'

'Really? Well, that's what he is.'

'So, you think I should win her back?' he asked, perking up.

'Well, I'm not sure you had her,' I said tactfully. His face fell. 'But, you know – yeah! Courtly love and all that.'

'Yes, right. That's exactly what I'm going to do. Sophie?'

'. . . that's why I love America: it's so classless,' Sophie was saying to a polite-looking John. 'Yes, Joshua? Oh, Joshua, *please* could you mix John and I another jug of Pimms?'

'Sure,' said Josh. I nudged him. 'And . . . I'll be wanting to talk to you when I get back!'

'Ooh, do you think I'm in trouble?' She nudged John flirtatiously.

105

Kate jumped out of her seat and came over to join me.

'Complete bitch!' she said loudly.

'What's that . . . you've got a terrible itch?' I said, conscious of our proximity to the other two at the table.

'No, didn't you hear me? I said, "What a COMPLETE BITCH!"'

'OK, OK, calm down. It shows he's not up to much either, doesn't it? And there are lots of other people here.'

'He didn't have much of a choice, with her sticking her BIG FAT BOVINE TORY TITS in his face.'

'OK, do you know what? I think we should perhaps go next door . . . Let's go dancing, shall we?'

I pushed a spluttering Kate out of the room. Josh's room was being used as a pot-smoking den, but the living room was full of people waving their arms in the air like they just didn't care, so we headed there. Chali was doing elegant Indian dancing to house music and looked fabulous. The crusties were all dancing round her like gnome servants. I collared one of them and shoved him and Kate together.

'OK! Dance,' I instructed them. The crusty immediately began to hop up and down in Kate's direction. Kate made a couple of sulky movements.

'Oh, you know, I can't be bothered. I think I might go to bed.'

'I think one of the Jameses and some young lovely have already thought of that,' I told her.

'Oh, for Christ's sake! What is this, a party for fourteen-year-olds? Did you see which one it was? I'll be having a word with him on Monday.'

'I'm afraid not,' I said, making a mental note to clear them out of there as soon as was humanly possible.

'This is turning into the worst . . .' started Kate glumly. Then her face lit up and I followed her line of gaze.

'There you are,' said the tall American. 'You just disappeared and left me with that pony-riding politician girl.'

He smoothly bypassed the crusty.

'In America we call that cruel and unusual punishment,' he said, and moved very close to Kate.

'Can I cut in?'

Kate could only nod mutely, and he put his arms round her, in that half-necking/half-dancing thing. And they were away.

Balls! He was nice! Noticing the crusty starting to bounce in my direction I hit a hasty retreat.

Back in the kitchen, hotbed of action, Sophie was still carrying on exactly as before. In his place, of course, Josh was listening to her with a dreamy expression on his face. Oh no. And, worse than that, the party was now swinging with a life of its own – the dancers were dancing, the snoggers were snogging – and, given the amount of that going on, I would say our singles theme was definitely a success – the potters were potting away . . . and I hadn't found my own group in time. Now I would have to be horrible puppy-like party hostess, bounding from group to group to try and gain acceptance. Arse! And I couldn't go home, as home now had three hundred coats in it! And Addison hadn't bloody joined the party after all. I didn't feel up to going and getting him, not after what I now knew. So, I pretended to be coolly surveying the atmosphere by the fridge, helping people get their beers, that kind of thing.

How annoying – after all, this was supposed to be a singles party, but I was the only one on my own. That wasn't how things should be progressing at all. I scanned the room, a tad crossly. In the corner was a tall person who was clearly a friend of Kate or Josh's, judging by the absence of acne scars and slouching. He was wearing a leather jacket and a dark top and, if a bit smooth for my taste, had a nice crinkliness around the eyes. Also, the bloke he was talking to had just disappeared.

OK, I decided. Kate had pulled. Josh was at least being shouted at by the object of his desire. Addison was nowhere to be seen. I had to at least *try*.

I ran my tongue over my teeth and walked up to him brightly.

'Hi there,' I said, as insouciantly as I could, which isn't very. 'Are you having a nice time?'

He looked around slowly and gave me a bit of a once-over. I can't bear that, but it was a singles party.

'It's OK, thanks.'

'Great, well, hi, I'm Holly and I live here.' I gave him a big beaming smile, then, as a nervous tic, ran my tongue over my teeth again. Then I realized I'd just done that, and shut my mouth abruptly. It made an audible noise, like a fish. He glanced at me for another couple of seconds, then seemed to make up his mind about something.

'Well, very nice to meet you, Holly. I'm Geoffrey – I work with Kate. I've been trying to find her, but I couldn't see her, so please tell her I did look in, and it all seemed very nice, and now I must go.'

He started to pull his jacket on. I could feel other people looking at us, and I started improvising desperately.

'Oh, right, Kate made you come, did she? Oh, you can't go – have you had some punch? Why don't you stay for a little bit? I'm sure she'll be right in.'

'I really can't,' he said. His eyes took on a wary, hunted expression. 'I – ehm – I'm double-parked.'

'Oh, did you drive here? What kind of car do you have?'

'Ehm, a Porsche, actually. Right, OK, James,' he yelled to someone I couldn't make out, 'see you Monday! Lovely to meet you!' and he disappeared stage left.

Fuck. I wandered my lonely way back across the room. My only thought was at least no one had seen me, but I looked up and Sophie was staring at me with a malicious look on her face. Fuck, fuck, fuck. I was so glad that, because he had been a bit of a wanker, I was managing to hate myself.

I poured another glass of wine and felt extremely sorry for myself. Then I went and checked in the mirror. Sure enough, I had a bit of prawn vol-au-vent stuck to my chin. Well, *I* knew it was prawn vol-au-vent. To the uninitiated, it could well have been herpes.

I limped back into the party a broken soul. Suddenly, however, out of the corner of my eye I caught a flash of movement by the fire escape . . . It couldn't be. Oh, thank God. There was Addison, sitting outside – outside! I wondered how his eyes were adjusting to the light. Then I noticed that not only was he outside, but he was most definitely talking to someone!

This was all I needed. I was pissed off. It was a well-known fact that Addison spoke only to me and, well, Claudia, I supposed, if you counted that as speaking, and I didn't. A horrid thought struck me – maybe it *was* Claudia. Maybe she'd taken Addison up on his invitation, after all. Oh God. That had to be it. All this time while I was pratting around and worrying about my bloody flatmates, he'd been pinched from under my nose! Cock! I might as well kill myself now.

I leaned over to try and get a better view from the fridge without being seen to actually stomp up and demand to know what she was doing here. Addison's thick black hair was in the way, though, so I leaned over a little bit further and, with a little help from the white wine and, I told myself later, deep despair, found myself falling straight on to the floor with an enormous crash.

The entire party stopped immediately – in fact, I could have sworn there was a record player somewhere, because it was like that noise you hear when someone skites a needle off a disc. A couple of the Jameses laughed, and I cursed them. Josh hopped up worriedly, whilst Sophie appeared faintly amused at Josh's poor old drunken flatmate. And the two heads on the balcony whipped round simultaneously, and annoyingly enough, the one who wasn't Addison was Finn.

'I'm fine! I'm fine! I could only conceivably have hurt my pride and I have none of that anyway!' I shouted immediately, to stop people cooing round me and making concerned noises.

'We once had a parlour maid who drank,' I heard Sophie say.

Addison loomed over me.

'You hurt yourself a lot,' he said carefully.

'It was the floor,' I muttered. 'It attacked me by surprise.'

He extended his hand to me. 'Are you all right?'

'Yes, yes, yes.' His large hand took hold of mine and I luxuriated in it as I stood up, accidentally on purpose falling against him. Casually – or, under the circumstances, as casually as I could make it whilst dusting myself down – I looked around the room and pretended to notice Finn for the first time.

'Oh, hello there . . . I'm so sorry, I can't remember your name.'

'Oh, really, are you very drunk?' he asked solemnly. I'd forgotten how annoying he was.

'No!' I spluttered. 'I just, you know, meet so many people it's hard to remember them all.'

'I see. Well, hello there, I'm Finn.'

'Well, yes, ehmm, I'm Holly,' I said, feeling increasingly stupid.

'Err, yes . . . I knew that.'

'So, how do you know Addy?' I said, in a way that might conceivably make it sound like Addison was my live-in boyfriend.

'Addy? Oh, Addison . . . ehm, I don't actually. I just met him – turns out we both went to see the eclipse. Fascinating man. Really, posited some very interesting theories . . . Why, is he your live-in boyfriend?'

'No,' I said crossly, but Addison was only three feet away. 'He's my flatmate.'

'Oh, right . . . nice bloke. Ehm, I know last time we met . . . I'm sorry about the misunderstanding.'

'What misunder – oh, that thing! Don't be silly, I didn't give it a second thought.'

I turned to Addison, in an attempt to convey how close we were. 'Thank you, darling . . . I'm quite fine now.'

'What?' said Addison. 'Oh, you were talking to me.'

'Shall we go back outside? Are you enjoying the outdoors, or do you find it a bit weird; you know, because sometimes the ceiling is blue and sometimes it's dark with little lights?'

'I'm not sure that fire escape of yours is too safe,' said Finn.

I turned round. 'Oh really? How do you know that: string theory?'

'Ehm, no, it's just completely over at an angle . . . Can I get you a drink?'

110

'No thank you . . . you might chemically alter it, or it might disappear into hyperspace.'

'God, you really stay pissed off at people for a long time, don't you? And also, hyperspace is only theoretical, so it couldn't really turn into the depository for your –'

'Of *course* I'm not pissed off with you,' I sniffed.

I was about to be sultry and elegant for once and wander off with Addison, leaving him there burbling, but suddenly a horrific sight caught the corner of my eye. It was Carol, hatchet-faced harridan of Harlesden, from whom I'd done a runner less than two months before. Fuck knows *what* she was doing here. Must have been a very distant single friend of a single friend. Dressed in a tight TIGHT pink dress which emphasized her orangey tan and carefully applied body make-up (blusher between the breasts, I noticed), she was running a long fingernail along the top of the units, checking for dust, and heading towards the fridge – where we were!

'Argh!' I said in a low voice to Finn. 'Quick, show me what's the matter with the fire escape.'

'What? Sorry, I didn't catch that –'

'Now!' I pushed him towards the kitchen door, practically hiding my face in his jacket. We collapsed down on the rickety brown metal.

'Ehm . . . OK, you see, here, when you sit down on it, it bounces?' said Finn.

'Huh? Oh, yes.' I stole a look back.

'So, I think the tension is probably unsafe . . .'

'I'm sorry, Finn . . . I just had to get away from someone over there.'

He craned his neck around to see.

'Who, her?'

'DON'T LOOK! Yes, her. I used to share a flat with her and she was mean to me. I'm trying to minimize the opportunities during which she can be mean to me again.'

'Oh, is she the one who punched you?'

'Ehm, no, that was somebody else.'

'Oh. Are a lot of people mean to you?'

'Yes. And none of it is ever my fault.'

'I see.'

I craned my neck round just a little to see if I could see her. She was about to open the fridge door when she spotted Addison, that well-known site of great natural beauty. I motioned to Finn to shush and leaned forward to try and hear what she was saying to him.

'Don't you think this kitchen is filthy?' she was saying. 'All this cookware, it simply gathers dust.'

Addison was facing us, and staring straight ahead, bright with embarrassment. She lifted up one ridiculously fingernailed hand. The claws grew bent over the top of her fingers and were painted bright pink, to match her dress. She was wearing three or four rings.

'Carol,' she said. 'Carol Patterson.'

Addison stared at us with a beseeching look in his eye.

'And this is my friend, Farah.'

He started staring at the floor.

'There are two of them?' asked Finn.

'Ehm, yes . . . Farah's on the short side.'

'I see. Oh my God, isn't that a monkey over there?'

'No, that's her.'

'Oh. Whoops.'

'Fine scientist you turn out to be.'

'So, one of the strong silent types, then?' Carol was saying, prodding Addison in the chest with her lethal fingernails. I winced.

'You could say that,' I whispered to Finn. He nodded.

'Ehm, as one of the hostesses, don't you think you ought to be circulating amongst your guests thereby saving Addison, rather than cowering behind the kitchen door spying on them? Just a suggestion,' added Finn hurriedly when he saw my cross face.

'She'll kill me! I never paid the phone bill.'

'You didn't pay the phone bill?' He looked shocked, then tried to retrieve himself. 'Oh well, I mean, right on, sister. Smash the state.'

'You are incredibly self-righteous, do you know that?'

112

'What? What did I say??'

But he was right in one respect. I would have to go and rescue Addison. Everyone else was ignoring them and he was a drowning man. And, as I knew, here was a man who'd been through enough in his life already.

I stood up shakily.

'OK, I'm going in. Do I look all right?'

'You look fine. Apart from that small piece of cheese attached to your head from when you fell over.'

I rubbed at my face. There was as well.

'Shit. OK, de-cheesed?'

'De-cheesed.'

'You stay here and guard the exits. This is going to be a lightning manoeuvre, so look sharp.'

Finn crouched in the doorway. I put my chin up, tried to pretend I knew what I was doing, and sashayed up to him. Well, I think it was a sashay. It might have looked like I had piles.

'Addy, there you are! I've been searching for you *everywhere*.' I put my hand territorially on his arm for the second time this evening. This time, however, he welcomed it.

'You *must* come and meet Finn.'

'But I've already –'

'Shut up,' I whispered *sotto voce*.

'Ohhh, I get it . . . YES PLEASE, I'D LOVE TO MEET FINN.'

Carol was staring at me. Her glitter eye-shadow had gone all crinkly as she tried to find a place for me in her mental card index.

'Look who it is!' yelped a voice from down below.

'Oh, hello, Farah,' I said, resisting the urge to punt her like a football.

'You!' hissed Carol dramatically. 'You owe us £57.20 for the council tax!'

'Ah, Carol, how lovely to see you again. I really missed you. You're looking fantastic. Really, I'd never thought of gold lipstick before, but it's certainly working for you – that "cheap" thing is so

113

in, isn't it? Now, please excuse me whilst I take my boyfriend over here, and then why don't you get the fuck out of my house and take your monkey with you?'

Is what I *so, so* wanted to say. In fact, I did say it, next morning in the shower, to Kate's Clarins bottles. And they trembled, let me tell you.

'Ehm, yes, sorry about that. I'm putting the cheque in, ahem . . . Excuse us; I'm really, *really* sorry,' I said.

'Why don't you just write me a cheque now?'

'Ehm, Holly, I don't . . . do you think we should leave Finn on his own?' said Addison bravely.

'No, Addison, you're absolutely right, we should . . .'

'Do you live here? Great, because I'll know where to come to get the rest of the money. I'm doing a course round here actually, so I can pop in most days, see if you're home.'

'No,' I said. 'Actually I'm only here visiting from Bhutan. That's Bhutan, Peru.'

This was turning into a complete nightmare. Addison was tugging on my sleeve like a three-year-old who needed the toilet.

'I mean, really! Talk about irresponsible. Do you know what she did?' Carol asked him. I wanted to scratch her, hard.

Addison shook his head, he seemed more and more agitated.

'Well . . .'

'Hello, everyone!' boomed a voice behind us. 'I'm Finn!'

Christ. The cavalry had arrived.

'And you must be Holly.'

It felt like we'd now been introduced four billion times.

'Yes, hi, hi. And this is Addison.'

Addison and Finn mutely shook hands.

'Wonderful. Now, as hostess, can you take me to the punch?'

And with one hand round my arm, and Addison tagging along on my sleeve, we speedily fumbled our way over the dead body in the doorway and quickly away from the punch, which was sitting on top of the refrigerator in plain view.

Outside the kitchen door, I rested against the wall.

'God, that was close.'

114

'Don't worry; I saved you.'

'I know. My hero. Oh my God – here she comes!'

'Quick!'

And we all tumbled into the front room, where the dancers were subsiding into dreamy swaying moves. Chali had her arms round the grubbiest of the crusties and they were half dancing, half smooching across the room. She jabbed me in the arm.

'He's in a band!' she yelled.

'Oh, brilliant! Are you going to shag him?'

''spect so!'

Over in the corner, looking, frankly, sickening, Kate and John were dancing as though they'd been welded together. She was staring into his eyes with an intensity half blissful, half rather frightening. I didn't catch her eye in case I broke her spell. And anyway, we did have a rather pressing problem on our hands.

'OK,' said Finn to himself, kneeling down beside the pile of CDs and running his finger along the spines rapidly. 'Think, Finn, *think*.' His face creased in concentration.

'Aha!' he whipped one out and jammed it in the CD player, shoving up the volume knob.

'What . . . ?' I started, but I could get no further, because the speakers suddenly boomed –

'ONE STEP BEYOND . . .' and WHOP, high-decibel Madness came crashing out of the speakers.

The drowsy dancers jumped as if they'd been slapped, and stared menacingly at the infidel who'd dared to contaminate the mood, but Finn was protecting the CD player with a fierce look on his face. Sure enough, within two seconds, the entire crowd of Jameses and, in fact, every single boy of *un certain âge* at the party (Josh excluded, natch) rushed into the sitting room and started bouncing up and down, doing leg kicks, putting on sunglasses, pretending to walk downstairs, playing imaginary saxophones and generally having a fabulous time.

'Dance!' shouted Finn at us. I'd been staring, open-mouthed, at the scene, but on his command, Addison and I began bobbing up and down gamely, and I started to laugh. The room was absolutely heaving with aftershave and testosterone, and the noise was frightful as lots of people in Paul Smith started yelling about how baggy their trousers were. Kate was looking daggers at me, until John leaned over and said something in her ear and she lowered her head and smiled, and hand in hand they threaded their way out of the sitting room. I doubted we'd be seeing her again tonight, and possibly never again if she played her cards right. Finn bared his teeth at anyone approaching the stereo until it became clear that anyone trying to change it now would either get pounded en masse, or die from aftershave inhalation before they got there. Then he came and hopped up and down with us. Addison was hopelessly uncoordinated and danced like a three-legged dog running. I tried to dance ironically, as it was music from the eighties, but dancing ironically can't really be done, and you just expend a lot of effort and get sweaty and, anyway, no one was watching, so I gave up and went back to hopping along with Finn. The three of us were right at the far corner and there was no way Carol was going to get through the line of crazy boys – stockbrokers by day, phantom flying saxophonists by night. And, sure enough, halfway through 'House of Fun', we saw her slamming the gate and storming off down the road, Farah galloping along beside her to keep up.

'Woo,' I said, when the three of us had finally made our escape and landed up, as tradition dictated, back in the kitchen. We were red-faced, and I kept giggling when I thought of the mayhem still taking place next door.

'Those City boys sure know how to party,' I said, opening beers for the three of us.

'You could have fooled me,' said Finn. 'They were talking about how they nearly got killed on their years off and whether or not they'd shag Sophie Rhys-Jones an hour ago.'

'Like I said; they *clearly* know how to have fun.'

Out of the corner of my eye, I suddenly caught sight of Kate's colleague again, enthusiastically chatting up one of those tiny

Natalie Imbruglia types – those girls you could keep in your handbag. The lying bastard! He looked up when he sensed my eyes on him and mock shrugged whilst I turned away and felt absolutely horrible.

Josh and Sophie were *still* on the other side of the table, and from what I could make out she was still talking.

'So, of course, Daddy didn't really want me to get a job – you know what these ancient families are like, just want to carry on the line, don't they? But I said, "No, Daddy, I feel a higher calling – I think the country needs me, and it's my duty. And I'll do it with or without your help." And of course he realized he was beaten then, and that's when he bought the little run-around and the mews, and got me into chambers.'

'You really showed him,' said Josh admiringly.

'I know. So, anyway, what was your family doing pre 1700?'

Josh told her.

'Mine were picking potatoes,' I said.

'Mine were being purged from somewhere,' said Finn.

'You always have to go one better, don't you?'

I turned to Addison.

'How are you doing? Did Claudia decide not to come after all?'

He shrugged. 'She was a bit pissed off at me.'

'Why? Not for talking to me?'

'A bit that . . . and a bit for asking her. She really can't get out of the house.'

'Is this your girlfriend?' Finn asked with concern.

'No!' I felt like saying. 'She's a big fat girl with a warty chin whom Addison has never met. Really, I'm his girlfriend. Practically.'

'Uh huh,' said Addison. 'She's . . . she's agoraphobic.'

'Oh, that's nasty. You know, I saw this study in the SA . . .'

And that was it. They were away again. Amazing. It was like they were talking some bizarre language of their own.

Suddenly, I became aware of an absolutely disgusting smell. I turned round and, sure enough, there was Chali snogging her record producer. I nudged her in the back.

'Chali . . . he really smells.'

'I know,' she winced at me. 'Feel this – I've been running my fingers through his hair.'

She held out her hand. It was distinctly sticky.

'Are you sure about this?'

'Are you joking? How do you think Celine Dion got her career?'

'I don't know – kissing dirty people?'

'Exactly!'

'Exactly *not*!'

'Anyway, what do you think ecstasy is *for*?'

The crusty grunted crossly and she gave him a huge snog. I felt my stomach turn and sat back with a sigh, picking up an entire bowl of toffee popcorn and proceeding to listlessly chew my way through it whilst watching Addison and Finn. They had their heads together. Finn looked like a ten-year-old being told the facts of life by the coolest guy in the school.

Madness definitely marked some kind of high point to the evening, and people had started to drift around in gradual bags-goodbye-mini-cab rounds (except for the pot smokers, of course, who weren't technically allowed to leave until 5 a.m.). One of them was even now blearily attempting to make one hundred and forty-seven pieces of toast. On seeing the first people leave, Sophie leapt to her feet, Josh springing equally quickly up to pull out her chair.

'Well, thank you, Joshua, for a charming evening. And thank you *so* much for agreeing to take on those extra cases. Really, you're quite the sweetie. You remind me of my girlfriends. Now, call me a cab, will you?'

Josh moved as a man under hypnosis to do her bidding. I made a mental note to remember her address for Kate so she could order her one hundred takeaway pizzas and put her telephone number on one of those prostitute cards you get in telephone boxes.

The Jameses came traipsing in one by one to make sure Kate realized how late they had stayed. Their faces fell when I told them she'd left already, but they perked up again when they tried to competitively book limos home on their gold cards.

The people we didn't know melted away too, leaving no trace of themselves behind, although taking lots of our traces with them, mostly in the shape of CDs and small ornaments. And finally it was pretty much just Josh, Addison, Finn and me, huddling round the kitchen table surrounded by piled ashtrays, empty cans, crushed food, broken plates, the denful of pot smokers in Josh's room (we hadn't told him about them), and the collapsed person, who was still blocking the doorway, but we'd periodically checked on his breathing, and he seemed OK.

'Well, I thought that went pretty well,' said Josh.

'I don't know,' I said, pouring us all a whisky. 'Nobody vomited all over anybody's bed. Nobody got pregnant. The police didn't even come once. It hardly counts as a party at all.'

'There's a bloke passed out.'

'Yeah, but somebody brought him. Doesn't count.'

'Oh, yeah. And I spent the whole night talking to Sophie! I thought that went rather well too.'

'What? Josh, she's at home right now measuring you up for a gingerbread house.'

'Didn't you like her?'

'Well, she's very . . . posh.'

'She's not that posh. She went to school with one of my sisters.'

'Oh, right. Josh, your sisters went to Cheltenham Ladies.'

'I know . . . but, you know, she *went to school*.'

'Are you going to see her again?'

'Well, I'll see her on Monday,' he said brightly. 'I've offered to take on some of her extra work.'

'So you're going to be her fag?'

'Oh, for goodness sake, Holly – I will *not* be letting her . . .'

'What?' I constantly begged Josh to tell me what public school boys got up to, but usually he would have none of it. Had he just let his guard down?

'*Please* tell us what fags normally do,' I pleaded.

'Nothing,' he said crossly.

Finn looked around.

'Oh, I'm sorry – I guess it's time to go . . . ?'

'Yup.'

'I'd better . . .'

'Where do you live?' I asked him.

'Ehm . . . Lewisham.' Lewisham was right over the other side of London.

'God . . . are you going to try and book a cheap flight?'

He smiled weakly.

'I'll call a cab.'

'You can stay over if you like.'

'Mmm,' agreed Josh. 'You can kip on the sofa.'

Then, I said it practically before I'd opened my mouth. It was purely a product of a disappointing evening, that bloke running away, everyone else pairing up, the white wine, Kate being madly in love and the whole damn thing, but I said it anyway:

'Or you could stay in my room.'

There was a stunned silence. I could have chopped off my tongue with a cheese slice.

Addison was wearing a confused expression. Josh was grinning hugely with excitement. Finn's eyes flicked to the side, as if to check that he'd heard what he'd just heard.

'Ehm, sorry?'

'And I'll sleep on the sofa!!!' I immediately added, hoping that would sort it.

'Ha!' said Josh. 'Is that what you *really* meant?' Finn still appeared distinctly nonplussed.

'Yes it is!' I said immediately. 'I'm just being a good hostess, Josh.'

'Oh, in that case, why don't you and Finn take my room? I've got a double bed, at least, and I don't mind sleeping on the sofa.'

'Oh, shut up,' I said. 'Why don't *you* sleep with him then?'

That was even worse. In fact, that was up there with the rudest things I had ever said in my life, including calling Marion Annis a big fat cow and getting detention. I couldn't believe myself.

'No need to get bitchy about it,' Josh said, bitchily. 'I was only . . .'

'Oh, *there* you are!' said a small, precise voice.

We all looked round.

'Madeleine!' said Finn, leaping up. 'You came!'

I could not fucking believe it. It was the swotty girl from the Natural History Museum.

'Yes. Sorry I'm so late. Crisis in the gerbil wing.'

'That's OK – it's good to see you. I think things are pretty much finished, but . . .'

'I'm just going off to shoot myself in the head,' I announced, getting up. 'Excuse me, everyone.'

After they'd gone, I slowly emerged back into the kitchen to apologize to Josh.

'Sorry about that, Holl,' said Josh. 'I didn't realize you were sweet on him.'

'I'm *not*,' I said in despair, giving Addison a wistful glance. 'It's just, he's the only other man I *know*. Who's not already going out with someone they met on the Internet.'

I gave Addison what I hoped was an appealing glance.

'Good night,' he said, horrified, and disappeared.

'Men find me DISGUSTING,' I hollered, with my head in my hands the next morning. 'I AM disgusting!'

'I too am DISGUSTING,' yelled Josh, who was sitting next to me. 'Everyone DESPISES me. Stop yelling!'

'How can I stop yelling? I HATE myself! AND my pathetic lifestyle. Is there anyone I DIDN'T try and get off with last night?'

'ME!' shouted Josh. 'Because I am SO DISGUSTING even YOU didn't want to get off with me!'

Suddenly, from the hallway, we heard the door open and somebody singing. We stared at each other, dumbfounded.

'Fuck off!' shouted Josh experimentally. He wasn't a swearer.

Kate put her head round the door, surprised. 'Hello, everyone! How are you? Anyone want some breakfast? I've got fresh croissants!'

'Oh, it's you,' Josh said wearily. 'Don't fuck off, then. Come in, in fact. We need cheering up immediately.'

Kate stepped over the comatose person who was still slumped in the doorway.

'Last night not go too well with Sophie then?' She didn't seem displeased. 'What's the matter? Aren't your parents related to each other?'

She hummed as she opened a carton of orange juice. I looked at her grumpily out of the corner of my eye and wondered what was wrong with the picture. Then it struck me.

'Ehm, Kate,' I said gingerly. She might seem in a good mood, but nothing was ever certain. 'Everything is clearly going fabulously well with, "John", yes?'

'Oooh, yes,' said Kate, switching on the coffee maker. 'Anyone want toast?'

'Me, please,' coughed the prostrate figure on the floor. We ignored him.

'Well, then . . . you know, shouldn't you still be there? Squeezing him orange juice and making him fresh coffee, given that we don't really give a toss what we drink, as long as it's got a side order of paracetamol?'

'Do you know, they should really make fizzy drinks with paracetamol already in them,' mused Josh. 'It would save a lot of time in the morning.'

'Yes, Josh, that's a great idea – they could call it Suicide Juice,' said Kate dismissively. 'Well, actually, I am back here because after a *glorious* night in a hotel . . .'

'Ooh, the Ritz!?' I said.

'The Sheraton. Practically the Ritz.'

'But, by the same token, practically a Novotel. Go on.'

'He had to fly to Brussels.'

'At nine o'clock on a Sunday morning?'

122

'Four o'clock actually. He's very busy.'

'He's very married!' yelled Josh. 'Oh God, forget it. Why listen to me? I'm disgusting. At least you get to have sex.'

'Married!!!' yelled the guy on the floor, suddenly jumping to his feet and staring around him wildly.

'I'm meant to be getting married!!'

'We all were,' I said. 'But then, society lied to us.'

'No, no, I mean . . . what day is it?'

'Sunday.'

'Oh my God, I'm meant to be getting married – today!'

'OK,' I said.

'No, no – to Carrie.'

'Oh.'

'Shit, I must have been so pissed – where am I?'

We regarded him with some amusement.

'Pimlico. The seedy end, but it's not far from the tube.'

'Where?'

'Pimlico.'

His face stubbornly refused to register.

'London?' Josh tried again.

The comatose guy turned ashen. 'London,' he said.

'Where did you think you were?'

His face twisted. 'Cardiff?' he said. 'Arrrggggghhhhh!' he said. Then he grabbed his shoes and vanished.

We rushed into the sitting room so we could see him scramble down the street.

'The tube's the other way!' yelled Josh.

'You've got a two in three chance it won't work anyway!' I shouted. 'You should cut your losses!'

'There's a cabbie who's going to get *extremely* rich today,' observed Kate.

'Oh, I'm sure he'll find his way back and have lots of wacky adventures on the way,' said Josh.

'No, Josh, you're thinking of all those TV programmes and films.'

'Ooh, so I am.'

We turned back to the kitchen to wearily start going round with the binbags.

'Oh God,' I groaned. 'I keep remembering other awful things I did.'

'Like what?' said Kate, perkily.

'Oh, some guy – actually, he said he works with you. Some oily chap. He was here . . .'

Kate went pale. 'Geoff? Geoff was here?'

'Yes, that was his name, the wanker. Anyway –'

'What did he say? Did he mention me?'

'He mentioned his Porsche. Wanker.'

'Oh God, it was him.'

Josh patted her gently on the shoulder as the penny finally dropped.

'The dog-dentist guy?'

'The married-with-children guy,' spat Kate.

'Well, you know, who cares?'

'Me! I wanted him to see me and John and how happy we were and then beg me to come back to him so I could say no!'

'Kate, has it ever crossed your mind that you might be the teensiest bit neurotic?'

'Are you joking? Why do you think I pay my therapist eighty pounds an hour?'

'To tell you you're neurotic?'

'Yes, and that it's *OK*.'

'Anyway. You didn't even let me finish the story of why I was so awful.'

'Huh! Thank God I'm only neurotic!'

'She asked Finn to go to bed with her,' said Josh.

'*Did* you?'

'God, Josh, that was *not* the way it happened, OK? It was a slip of the tongue and I didn't mean it.'

'No such thing as a slip of the tongue,' said Kate darkly.

'Oh, did your therapist tell you that as well? Was that before or after she explained why she wasn't a real doctor? Slip of the A-levels, maybe?'

'Do you think you might have an aggression problem?'

'My flatmates are accusing me of being a whore and *I'm* the one with the problem.'

'Holly, calm down,' said Josh. 'We didn't mean it.'

'And you started the conversation,' pointed out Kate.

I sighed. 'I'm sorry. I'm just so completely fucked off with myself.'

'Well, do you like him?'

'No! Well, you know no! He's nerdy and he has dirty spectacles and I want a real man.'

'Rrrright. So, why did you ask him to go to bed with you?'

'I *didn't*. I offered him my bed while I slept on the sofa.'

'Really? That's remarkably generous.'

'Well, I suppose . . . I didn't . . . I mean, it would have been quite nice to have someone to sleep next to, you know? Other than Frank Sinatra (the bear).'

Josh and Kate both nodded.

'I know what you mean,' said Kate. 'But would you shag him for a cuddle?'

'No!' I said shocked. Then, more shamefacedly, 'I might have . . . well, you know, let him have his tops or something.'

'I'd settle for just a snog with Sophie,' said Josh sadly, leading the way out with a bagful of rubbish. Kate smiled at me and followed on.

It was good to know they understood, I thought.

'Oh, but did she tell you she came on to Addison as well?' filtered along the corridor.

Bastards!

Six

Chali and I were in the shop, gassing away as usual, as I threw the roses together. I hated doing roses. One, they hurt, and two, they were only bought by teenagers and men who weren't very nice to their wives. Chali had decided to plait her hair with all the different-coloured ribbons in the shop and was intent on that, and chewing gum in the face of anyone who came in looking for service, so I was hovering near the front.

It was about a month since the party, although we were still finding bits of broken glass beside the washing machine. I had just about bitten down my embarrassment – i.e., whenever I thought about Finn, or Kate mentioned him, I didn't have to stuff my fingers in my mouth to stop myself from screeching out loud. Poor Kate, however, was on a huge anti-man mission, after John had failed to phone her *again*. She'd even shout at newsreaders on the TV, calling them 'lying bastards' apropos of nothing at all, and as for Americans, they were in serious trouble as a continent. Infuriatingly, Sophie had developed a habit of 'popping in' around dinner time, eating like Hector the Hungry Horse, dumping a pile of work on Josh, then disappearing. One night I thought I heard him cry. Kate accused him of being so emasculated his penis would disappear, 'which would be no bad thing, given the evilness of your entire gender.'

I had hardly seen Addison at all. After his momentary outburst of sociability, he seemed to have retreated again, and although I hovered late at night, the door was never open. I suspected I had frightened him – it was like *Badger Watch*. He might not reappear for months.

Chali had done better out of the party than anyone, though, as it turned out that the stinky guy really was connected to the music business, and had got her a gig doing backing vocals for a new band. So she was extremely excited and convinced her time had finally come.

126

'Loads of people start off being backing singers, you know.'

'Oh yes, I know,' I said. 'Alison Moyet did.'

'Who?'

'You know, "Alf" – Alison Moyet.'

'Nup. Was it pre-war?'

'Fuck off. Ehm, and that girl out of Fairground Attraction. She was a backing singer for the Eurythmics.'

Chali looked blank. I swore she did this on purpose.

'You have heard of the Eurythmics?'

'Holl, right, don't take this the wrong way, right, but maybe you shouldn't come to this gig.'

'Of course I'm coming. We all are. You might get plucked out from the backing singers like . . . who were you thinking of?'

'Lauryn Hill, of course.'

'Oh, yeh, I knew that.'

'Do you have to bring that girly blond mate of yours?'

'Who, Sophie? No, she's not a friend of mine.'

'No, not her, the bloke.'

'Josh?'

'Yeh. He'll stand out like a prat.'

'Wow. You're almost as horrible as a *real* star already!'

'Do you think you'll *ever* find a boyfriend?'

I was giving her the V's when the door opened with a ting, and I glanced up without enthusiasm. Chali didn't bother looking up at all. That's pretty hard to do – you have to ignore your own basic physiological reflexes – and she had picked it up from snotty club entry policies and practised really hard.

The punter stood blinking as his eyes adjusted to the darkness of the shop after the brightness of the June day.

'Hello,' I yelled from the other end of the shop. 'Can I help you?'

He looked up, and with a shock I realized it was Finn. He realized at exactly the same time, and took a step backwards in surprise. He was wearing long khaki shorts over his skinny English legs, and a flowery shirt with two pens in the top pocket.

'Oh, er, gosh, hello!' he said, with the expression of a man who's just been told he's standing next to an unexploded bomb and if he moves he'll detonate it. 'I didn't know you worked here!'

'Why would you?'

'Ehm, no reason.'

Chali snapped up from her hair-plaiting, sniffing the air for gossip.

'I'd like some, er, flowers, please.'

'Oh, well, you've come to the right place,' I pointed out. 'Gerbils all recovered then?'

'What? Oh, no. Ehm, these are for my sister; she's just passed her exams.'

'Cute,' whispered Chali, nudging me hard in the ribs.

'Shut up,' I hissed violently, then turned back to him.

'Right, right – driving test, is it?'

'She's just taken a double first at Cambridge, actually.'

'Is that good or bad?' I said, putting on a concerned expression, purely to annoy him.

He looked bemused. 'Ehm, well, it's *quite* good,' he said. 'So, you know, not funeral flowers or anything like that.'

'OK,' I said briskly. 'Bouquet, or all one style? Or, if she's a bit of a swot, she might prefer a house plant. It's got the Latin name on it.'

'I don't know . . . whatever you think. You know, I meant to ring and say thanks for the party.'

'Oh? Why didn't you? Maybe I could have embarrassed myself some more on the phone for you.'

'I don't know . . . I thought you might be . . .'

'Rude to you, like she's being now?' interjected Chali.

'What?' I said. 'I'm not being rude!'

Chali and Finn exchanged a glance.

'You are being a bit rude,' said Finn.

'Am I?'

'Darling, you're being a complete dog,' said Chali. 'Remember, you're not as young as you once were. You should take every opportunity that comes your way.'

I shot her a dirty look. 'OK, I'll stop being rude to him,

but for that last remark I'm now going to be rude to you. Piss off.'

She shrugged. 'Like I care. You'll be sorry when I'm famous. Won't she?'

'I expect so,' said Finn.

'See?' She nudged me. 'A nice bloke comes in to ask you out, you can at least be civil.'

'I didn't . . .' he began, then he stopped and smiled suddenly. 'This seems to keep happening, doesn't it?' he said to me.

'What?' I asked nervously.

'We're mistaken for . . . you know.'

'No . . . normally what happens is that I think we might be, then you gently point out that you don't like me.'

'I don't not like you!'

'You say *such* sweet things.'

His brow furrowed in concentration. Then he obviously made some internal decision and put his hand on the counter.

'Ehm, Holl, maybe, I don't know – would you like to . . . sometime . . . you know?'

'What?'

'I don't know, maybe . . . you know . . . ?'

'Look, Finn, unless you absolutely spell it out for me, I'll probably take it the wrong way and it will all end up horribly, OK?'

'Absolutely, yes, I see your problem.'

He took a deep breath and his eyes darted around the shop. Chali had grabbed my elbow in a fit of excitement.

'Holly, would you like to . . . consider . . . coming out on a date with me?'

'Yes, she would,' yelled Chali. 'In fact, she would like to bring you as a guest to my gig.' And she thrust a badly photocopied leaflet into his face advertising her band, the Bhangpigs.

Finn considered it closely, until I realized he was actually waiting for me to say something.

'What kind of music are you into normally, like?' asked Chali.

'Ehmm . . . Vaughan Williams?'

129

'Oh God, you're not a poof, are you? That would be so embarrassing, if I'd got Holl a date with a poof.'

'Why, would it make any difference if I was?' said Finn, stiffly.

'If you were going out on a date with me, it would,' I said.

'Oh, yes . . . sorry. I'm so used to City people being awful homophobes all the time.'

'That's OK. They can't help it; it's all that buggering at school. They liked it, and now they're ashamed.'

'Right. Yes. Anyway – well?'

'What about that woman who handles the insides of dead animals?'

'What about her?' said Finn.

'Are you inserting your penis into her vagina on a regular basis?' I wanted to ask him, but couldn't.

'She's not my girlfriend, if that's what you mean,' he said.

What was she then? Casual shag? Bridge partner? Wife? But I decided to give him the benefit of the doubt. Finn was not, I reckoned, a typical Lothario.

'A proper date?' I asked.

'Well . . . what does that entail?'

'Snogging,' said Chali promptly.

'Dinner,' I said simultaneously.

'Dancing,' yelled Chali.

'Flowers and chocolates.'

'Multiple choice, then,' he said.

'Yes, but it can be, you know, "all of the above".'

'I'll remember that.'

I smiled. 'See you at the gig?'

'Then dinner afterwards?'

'That sounds nice.'

He smiled shyly, then retreated out the door.

'Oh God, Holl, I'm *so* sorry, yeh? I really didn't mean to call him a poof, right, it was just, with that flowery shirt and everything . . . I mean, not that I mind poofs, right, loads of my mates are. But, you know, if I'd asked him out for you . . . He's nice, though, inny?'

130

Chali harangued me as I ignored her and took out a nice bunch of daisies and started wrapping them up, so that I could put them in Finn's hand with minimum embarrassment when he reappeared two seconds later to collect what he'd come in for. Which, of course, he did, blushing like a demon.

Later, I wasn't quite sure how I felt about all this. I had to admit, though, that there was something about a person who had seemed so immune to my charms, however average they might be, then changed their mind. I definitely felt like I'd achieved something – made some kind of stand for every girl who has ever made a fool of herself in front of a bloke whilst a bit pissed. They didn't usually come back after that, but this one had.

Kate and Josh took it with less than ecstatic excitement. Josh barely tilted his head from the sofa, where he was frantically working on a case. I'd never seen him do that before, but, clearly, it was Sophie. She was in Barbados. With whom, I didn't dare ask.

'Is this the guy you already haven't got off with twice?'

'Uh huh. So, you know, playing hard to get is not the only way!'

'Holl, are you sure he didn't just ask you the time or something, and you misinterpreted?'

'Ha ha ha. He actually came in to see *me*, remember?'

Kate put her head up. She too was up to the eyeballs, having thrown herself into her work to try and forget thingummy. It was annoying for us, because in her quest for the annihilation of all things American we weren't allowed to watch *ER* or drink Diet Coke.

'How did he know where you worked? He didn't ask me.'

'Well, OK, he happened to walk into the shop . . .'

'Oh, so you were lying?'

'. . . *But* he couldn't bear to walk out again without a date from me.'

'Wow, he's lucky he didn't decide just to pick up a bunch of daffs at the petrol station. You get some right boilers working in there.'

'Thank you, Josh. How's your lifetime of servitude coming along?'

'I think I'm earning Sophie's love, thank you.'

'Love is a very close emotion to contempt, isn't it?' mused Kate. 'As in, "How contemptuous am I of John?"'

'Truly madly deeply?'

She sighed. 'Yes, dammit. Did I hear the phone ring just then?'

'No,' we chorused.

'I'm so glad we spent all that money on the singles party,' I said.

'Well, it gave me one wonderful night,' sighed Kate.

'And me,' said Josh.

'And it got me a date, I suppose.'

'So, there you go. Well worth four hundred quid.'

'And the weeks of anguish.'

'And all the cleaning up.'

'And the loss of *Pet Sounds*.'

'And . . .'

'OK, everyone, shut up now,' ordered Josh.

'Please come,' I said to Addison for the four hundredth time. This was my secret pact with myself. If Addison wouldn't come to the gig, I was going to get off with Finn. But if he came, I would save myself for him. If he *said* he was going to come and then didn't turn up, I would still save myself for him. But if he point-blank turned me down – well, he might as well just thrust me into Finn's arms. I couldn't say I wasn't giving him a chance.

'*Pleeeeese* come. They use a drum machine.'

'But I don't want to.'

'How do you know? They might be fantastic.'

'Then I'll download their album on MP3.'

'What?'

'Never mind. Look, I just don't feel like going out, OK?'

'Addison, you know, everyone goes out sometimes.'

'Not me.'

'Did you . . .' I couldn't bring myself to ask him directly. 'Did you always stay in a lot?'

He looked at me.

'No. I just like it now.'

He clammed up. I didn't feel I could pursue the matter, but I was burning – unfortunate phrase – to know what had happened. Also, if I'd been in a house fire I'd probably live out in the middle of an enormous field and never go indoors at all. I just didn't get it.

'How's Claudia?'

'I think she's forgiven me for the party thing.'

'But you didn't do anything wrong.'

'I frightened her, and I didn't mean to.'

'She's a mentalist!' I thought, but I kept it to myself.

'She sounds like, you know, she has a few problems.'

'No, she can be quite funny, really. The other day, she told this . . . OK, how does Captain Jean-Luc Picard change a lightbulb?'

'What?'

'"Make it glow!"' He laughed heartily.

'That is hilarious,' I said gravely. 'Addy, *pleeese* come to this gig. Otherwise, you know, I can't answer for the consequences.'

'What consequences?'

'Well, you know, I won't necessarily be your next-door flatmate forever. I might, you know, go to the gig, meet someone nice, get married, move away. And who would you talk to then?'

'Claudia?'

As if in reply to some sub-ether summons, the grotesque face suddenly appeared on screen. Addison had obviously done something to it, because now the head rotated in 3-D. It was like that scene from *The Exorcist*, only Claudia didn't need the Oscar-winning make-up job.

'Ahh!' I yelped.

'Oh, there she is.'

Words started appearing on screen in upper case. I couldn't help reading them.

'IS SHE THERE?' it said.

'Whoops,' I said. 'Guess someone's a bit jealous.'

'No,' typed Addison.

'No? Why don't you tell her the truth? That makes me feel like I'm invisible.'

He shrugged at me.

'It's OK! You can talk, you know – she can't hear you!'

'OK. Ehm, I'm sorry – she does get a bit jealous.'

'Ha! Better not go and visit her – have you ever seen the film *Misery*? You'll come back with no legs.'

He didn't respond, and started typing away heartily.

'Well, GOODBYE THEN!' I said loudly. 'I'm off to the gig ON MY OWN. DON'T WAIT UP! BYE, CLAUDIA!'

He turned round briefly.

'Have a good time.'

'THANK YOU. I will try and have a good time ALL BY MYSELF.'

'I hope you meet someone nice. I liked that person that was at the party. Someone like him would be all right.'

'SHUT UP.'

I stomped out, leaving him rather puzzled.

I wasn't going by myself, of course. Josh and Kate were coming; (1) because they were interested in seeing Chali in a band and pretending they were hip young things, and (2) I needed the back-up in case it all went wrong with Finn.

I'd expected to be able to have a good laugh at Kate when she turned up for a gig in an Emporio Armani suit, but annoyingly she was wearing fashionably short jeans and a little top, and looked fantastic – there obviously was something in all this gym stuff after all. Josh wore a dark suit with a slightly louder tie than normal, but it wasn't as much fun to laugh at him.

It had suddenly turned cold, in typical English summer style, and the sky was grey and overcast. The gig was in a really nasty, scary pub in King's Cross, and didn't even start until ten. Lots of people who looked like they might have razors secreted about their person mooched about in front of us, and Scottish people yelled at us incoherently.

'Why are there so many drunk Scottish people here?' asked Josh loudly in his clipped accent.

'Shut up!' I pinched him hard, before we all got taken into a dark alley and duffed up. 'It's an exchange scheme. Edinburgh's full of pissed Cockneys asking people for ten pee for an eel pie.'

Chali had been nominally working today, but had spent the entire day in a fit of excitement, asking me whether I preferred the bolt or the hoop skewered through her eyebrow. She'd even tried to rope Mrs Bigelow into coming, who'd said she hadn't missed *Coronation Street* since Charles and Diana's wedding, and wasn't Chali a bit worried that people might mistake her for a professional, dressed like that?

At the door we were charged a revolting ten pounds to get in. Josh and Kate just handed it over as if it were nothing – which it was to them – so I tried not to grumble too much, but I did just have to try . . .

'Am I on the guest list?'

The bouncer, who was built like a brick factory for making shithouses, laughed in a way designed to show me how unfunny that was – like the Master does just after he's captured Dr Who and been offered a jelly baby.

'Are you from a record company, darlin'?'

'Yes!' I said immediately. Confidence is all. Josh stifled a giggle behind me.

'Which company is that then?'

'Ehm . . . Cross Scot's Records?'

He bent down and looked me straight in the eye. His one enormous eyebrow cast a shadow underneath his eyes. I tried to stare him out.

'Really?'

'Sure. Haven't you heard our latest number one –' I cast around for inspiration – "Piss in the Gutter"?'

He clasped an enormous paw on to my shoulder.

'No. Did you hear my last record, "Blood in the Gutter"?'

'No,' I gulped.

'No, sir,' I heard from Josh behind me.

'Well then, fuck off.'

I stared hard at the ground.

'Can I pay the ten pounds?'

'You can pay fifteen for cheek.'

'I'll get it,' said Josh rushing in. I squeezed his arm gratefully as he handed over twenty and waved away the change.

'Thank you for saving me, oh wimpy one,' I said, once we were safely inside.

'I only did it because I thought he was going to eat you.'

'So did I. This is going to be a great evening, I can tell.'

Inside it was boiling hot and absolutely heaving with people in weird trendy gear who looked much younger and immeasurably more self-confident than I did. I sighed. I was clearly missing the gene that made me want to hang about in places where the walls were wet with condensation. Right now I would kill to sit down.

Josh was fighting his way through the crowds to get to the bar, and the teenagers behind him were pointing and giggling at him as he went. After about six hours he returned with three slopping pints of watery lager in plastic glasses, and an extremely pained expression on his face.

'Well, it's not Harry's Bar,' was the only thing he said, sipping his pint with as much dignity as he could muster as we stood out like three banjos at a funeral.

'God, here's to not being students any more,' said Kate. 'They *have* to come here.'

'I wouldn't be too sure about that,' said Josh. 'That round cost me eight sixty.'

'Yes, but they put on added tie tax for you,' I said.

'This had better be the Beatles at the Cavern Club,' said Kate morosely.

'More like The Roaring Boys at Guildford Town Hall,' said Josh.

'Who?'

'Exactly. 1986. They were shit. And I tell you, it wasn't three pounds a pint, either.'

I looked around faintly anxiously for Finn. I wasn't going to get panicky quite yet, but I smoothed down my shirt and was vaguely conscious that my hands were sweaty.

'I'm going to give it five minutes, then I'm going home,' said Kate.

'You can't! You can't leave me! You paid ten pounds!'

'I'll come with you,' said Josh.

'But you paid thirty!'

In front of us, a bald bloke with enormous Doc Martens and braces slipped up on a pool of beer and what might have been sick, and fell on his arse. Instead of leaping up, he sat there, howling with laughter, as all his mates pointed at him and screamed, as if he'd just pulled off a spectacular comic coup.

'I'd pay a hundred to get out,' said Josh.

I glanced nervously towards the door again. The enormous bloke happened to be looking in at the same time. He caught my eye and sneered at me.

'You might have to,' I said.

Josh followed my gaze. 'I'm not scared of him.'

'Ehm . . . yes you are.'

'You didn't let me finish: I'm not scared of him more than I'm scared of everyone else in here.'

We huddled together for safety. The band were showing no sign of starting, and there were people wandering all over the stage and knocking into the drum kit. I hadn't seen Chali at all. I had a sudden premonition of a really terrible evening ahead and me being blamed for everything – whether we stayed or went.

Suddenly, stumbling slightly as he entered, Finn appeared. My overwhelming relief at seeing his handsome face was tempered with the fact that I wished he wasn't wearing a duffel coat and carrying a large satchel. It was like going on a date with Tucker Jenkins, without the raw sex appeal.

'Hello,' he said, forcing his way through the throng with the satchel. Then he was standing in front of me, pink-cheeked and messy-looking, his black curly hair all over the place.

'Hello,' I said, suddenly shy. It seemed for a second as though he was going to kiss me on the cheek, and he kind of leaned forward, and I jerked backwards at the wrong moment and hit my nose on his glasses.

Kate started to giggle.

'Hello, Finn.'

He turned to see her with her little tight trousers on.

'Oh, hello – you look, ehm, nice.'

'I don't sleep at the office you know.'

'Yes, well, OK,' I said quickly. I didn't want my date walking in and flirting with my flatmate, if that was all right with everyone.

'You look nice, too,' he said to me instantly. 'Here, I brought you these.'

He opened his satchel and brought out a box of chocolates. I stared at him in amazement.

'Well, if it's going to be a "proper" date,' he said, apologetically, and pushed them into my hands.

'Chocks! Top hole!' said Josh. 'I mean, ehm, wicked!'

I stood there in the crowded pub, holding the slightly battered box. 'Thank you. But, you know, where's my corsage?'

'Aha,' he said, and reached into his satchel again, fishing out a tiny sprig of heather wrapped in tinfoil.

'Some mad old Scottish woman outside wouldn't leave me alone.'

'Sounds like,' whispered Josh to me, 'the mad old Scottish woman knew a good thing when she saw it.'

I slapped him away like a fly, and let Finn stick the heather in my buttonhole. Then we stared at each other again, grinning like idiots. I was ridiculously chuffed.

'Would you like a drink?' I finally asked him.

'Let the lady buy a drink on our first date? Of course not!'

'You know this is a "proper" date, not a "sexist" date, don't you?'

'Oh yes, I forgot. Let the woman buy a drink on the first date?'

'Let the man get kneed in the bollocks on the first date?'
'Pint of bitter?'
'You'll be lucky. Warm watery lager?'
'Mmm, yes, please.'

As I got back from the bar, there was an enormous roar from the other end of the pub, and masses of people swarmed across the room. We followed in their wake, ending up in the crush down one end, where the stage was set up – the stage being about the size of a bath, into which had somehow been crammed a frontman, two big stacks of keyboards, a DJ with turntables and, at the back, Chali – a vision in see-through scarlet (part of me thought 'I wonder if she knows it's see-through?' before mentally hitting myself on the forehead for being an idiot) – and an extremely tall black woman, also in scarlet. They looked fantastic. The two boys on the keyboard and the frontman, however, looked ridiculous. It was impossible to see the DJ, because he had a hat pulled down over his face, but the frontman was wearing a silver suit c/o Martin Fry 1984 and had hugely magnified pores. I glanced at the others, warily, but before anyone had a chance to say anything, the guy in the silver suit leaned over the front of the stage, propped one skinny shank on the speaker and yelled:

'AAAAAGH! FLAY ME! SLAY ME! DON'T FORGET TO PAY ME! SHOVE ME! LOVE ME! WITH A PLASTIC GLOVE – EE!'

'Cripes,' I heard Josh say behind me.

The DJ made some retro scratching noises.

'BITE ME! FIGHT ME! TRY AND EXTRADITE ME!'

Finn and I nodded in appreciation at his syllable count.

'USE ME! ABUSE ME! PUT MY FINGERS IN THE SOCKET AND FUSE ME . . .'

'Ooh, nasty scan.'

The noise was unbelievable. I could hear my eardrums rattle up and down. I kept an eye on Chali to see when she got to do her bit, but she was languidly dancing as if she was

139

the most pissed-off person in the world – i.e., like a proper backing singer.

'PRICK ME! LICK ME! YOU CAN TRY AND DICK ME . . .'

'Here comes the catchy chorus,' I predicted to Finn.

''COS I HATE MYSELF AND I WANNA DIE/I CUT MYSELF AND I WANNA DIE/I HATE MYSELF AND I WANNA DIE/I'M ALL ALONE AND I WANNA DIE!'

The crashing keyboards rose to a great crescendo.

'WANNA DIE!' trilled Chali and the tall girl. 'WANNA DIE! WANNA DIE!'

Then everything cut off in a big wail of fake feedback. The singer took an elaborate bow.

'HELLO, KING'S CROSS!' he shouted 'IT'S GREAT TO BE HERE!'

The crowd went wild, except for us four, who just stared at him.

'I don't think that man wants to die at all,' said Kate eventually. 'Which is disappointing, as I, for one, would be very happy to see him dead.'

'It's kind of like Nirvana, isn't it?' said Finn. 'If they had never learned to play the guitar and, ehm, were, you know . . . shit.'

'Chali's good, though,' I said loyally.

'Yes, she is . . . I especially liked her "wanna dies".'

I nodded.

'Now!' The singer was still yelling. 'This is a song about how the state, right, it really tries to grind you down, right. So, just do your own thing, yeh?'

'I *thought* so,' said Josh.

'No, really, I'm sure those O-levels were quite handy,' I assured him.

'No, no, I mean, I *thought* I recognized him.'

'What?'

'He sounded different, of course, but, yes . . . it's Bladen-Start all right. I was in his house at school!'

'*Really?*'

140

'Yes, definitely. What was his first name again . . . ? Bladen-Start, Bladen-Start. Oh, yes – Tristram, that's it.'

'*Really?*' I said again. 'Fantastic!'

Onstage, Tristram was hollering over a drum and bass back beat:

'DON'T LISTEN TO WHAT THEY SAY/ IT'S ONLY BULLSHIT ANYWAY/SO GO GET PISSED AND HAVE SOME FUN/DON'T MAKE YOUR BED OR PHONE YOUR MUM . . .'

The crowd was going crazy.

'Thick as two short planks,' yelled Josh. 'His dad had to practically build a new college to get him into Oxford.'

'SCHOOL'S FOR WIMPS AND THE CONFORMERS/ FUCK ALL STUDENTS AND SIXTH FORMERS/LIVE YOUR OWN LIFE ON THE STREETS/ALL YOU NEED ARE DRUGS AND BEATS!'

'Yayy,' shouted the crowd.

'This sucks demon cock,' said Kate. I filled her in on what Josh had told me and her eyes gleamed.

'Go, Tristram!' she yelled, and burst out laughing.

'YOU DON'T HAVE TO! YOU DON'T HAVE TO! YOU DON'T HAVE TO! IF YOU DON'T FEEL LIKE IT!'

'Yeh!' yelled Chali, elegantly raising her arms.

'Shall we dance?' said Finn at my elbow.

'What??'

'You know . . . we're on a date . . . Isn't dancing the law?'

Tristram appeared to be trying to have sex with one of the speakers. The row at the front were hopping up and down trying to grab hold of his legs.

'OK?' I said tentatively.

Ceremoniously, Finn led me to the back of the crush. This end of the bar was comparatively quiet, away from all the spitting. Dumping the bags in a nasty pool of something, he bowed, then took me in a traditional dancing pose.

'What?' I said. 'What on earth are you doing?'

141

'Dancing,' he said, whirling me round.

'Finn!'

'You'll enjoy it more if you stop struggling.'

'Boys always say that though,' I yelled at him from the end of his arm, but he paid no notice and twirled me around again. Our pace was about a quarter of the beat that was lashing out from the stage, but fortunately everyone ignored us – they probably thought we were somebody's parents. I decided to give myself up to the moment and let myself be hurled about. Finn was an unexpectedly good dancer, and I enjoyed the experience of not being self-conscious and worrying about the music – (1) because what was playing wasn't music, and (2) we were so unhip that to this crowd we were invisible anyway.

'Where did you learn to dance?' I asked him breathlessly as he bent me back over his knee to the final chords of Tristram shouting:

'FUCK! FUCK! AND THEN SOME!'

Finn shrugged.

'Well, the boys on the football team stomped on my glasses, so my mum signed me up for dancing lessons instead.'

'And did that help your standing with the boys on the football team?'

He winced at the memory. 'I think I'm the reason why they took away free glasses on the NHS. I must have gone through five pairs that year alone.'

'Well, never mind – most of those boys are probably in prison now.'

'Actually, I keep bumping into them in the City, hollering for bottles of Cristal and slapping waitresses on the arse.'

'Oh, did you go to private school?'

'Scholarship.' He grimaced. 'Little Jewish scholarship boy. Really, you do get used to it. I wash my hair in the toilet even now.'

'Were you a boarder?'

'Yep. Banged up at eight for a ten stretch.'

I squeezed his arm sympathetically.

142

'It's all over now, you're free to go.'

He smiled. 'I know. And at least I know how to do THIS!' Without warning, as Tristram crashed into another song, he flung me over his arms and into a dramatic bent-back pose, and held me there. I looked up at him – he was smiling at me, and his dark hair fell over his eyes. For a very short split second, everything around seemed to go very quiet, and I thought he was going to kiss me. And for a very short split second, even stranger, I found that I wanted him to.

'Yo ho!' yelled Josh. 'You two seem to be having fun. Shall we join in, Skates?'

We straightened up immediately.

'OK,' said Kate. 'Although I'm due in Antwerp at 10 a.m.'

'Oh, hang on,' said Josh, wandering off. 'I want to say hi to Tristram again.'

'I didn't want to dance really,' said Kate. 'Can I go home now, please?'

The band stopped playing peremptorily.

'WE'RE TAKING A SHORT BREAK NOW,' hollered Tristram. 'BUT I'LL BE OVER BY THE BAR IF ANYONE WANTS TO GIVE ME A BLOW JOB.' The crowd pissed themselves.

'UNLESS, OF COURSE, YOU'RE AN A&R MAN, WHEREUPON WE'LL SUCK YOURS.'

'Maybe I won't go and say hello after all,' said Josh.

Chali came dashing up to us, with her usual tribe of filthy supplicants in tow.

'Hey there! I'm so glad you came!'

'You were fantastic,' I said. 'And you look brilliant.' Which, at least, was true.

'Thanks,' she said. 'This is Stitches, Cockroach, Wayne and the Weed Boy.'

'Hey.' We nodded.

'These are the guys that had the party,' she explained to them. One raised his hand in an exhausted fashion.

'Hey.'

143

'Are you enjoying yourself?' Chali asked Finn mischievously.

'Very much so.' He smiled, looking at me. 'Thanks for asking us along. You're singing brilliantly.'

'I know,' she said. 'Oh, here, have you met Sha?'

Chali's singing partner had segued up beside her, sipping a tall drink through a straw. Sha raised her eyebrows fractionally at us, which is all you have to do when you look like Naomi Campbell. Then her eyes lingered on Josh, who had just let his floppy blond fringe drop into his beer, and was wiping it out of his eyes with his fingers. She whispered something to Chali, who shrugged her shoulders and beckoned me over.

I was prepared for the question.

'No, he's not . . . probably,' I whispered to Chali.

'Wow – how did you . . .'

Josh was thoughtfully licking his beery finger and holding it up to the wind.

'. . . Never mind.' She shook her head at Sha, who walked straight up to him.

'Are you hanging around after the gig?' she purred.

'What?' said Josh. 'Er, no, I don't think – Ow!'

I glanced away innocently.

'Ehm, possibly . . .'

'Good. Wait for me,' she said, then turned round and stalked off.

Josh's eyes were on stalks. 'Gosh – do you think . . . ? Why do you think she wants me to wait?'

'She's probably a lawyer in her spare time and wants you to help with the legwork,' said Kate snidely.

'You've pulled, mate,' said Chali.

'Have I? I mean, do you think . . . ? Gosh!' said Josh, and lapsed into a happy stupefaction.

'Oh God, I really *am* going home,' said Kate, right in front of Chali. 'I just can't take it any more. Sorry, no offence.'

Chali regarded her coolly.

'Sorry, who are you?'

Finn and I winced at each other, but Kate merely turned the

chilly icemaidenometer up to eleven and announced, 'I'll just head out into a dangerous area and catch an unlicensed cab on my own then, shall I, Josh?'

Josh stared after her, blinking.

'What?'

But she was gone.

The second half passed in a blur. Tristram and his band crashed through 'THEY DESERVE TO DIE' (a long list, including fox hunters, religious fundamentalists and white people), 'IF DRUGS KILL, CAN WE FEED THEM TO THE PRIME MINISTER?' and 'I'M PROBABLY BISEXUAL, BUT I'LL KNOW FOR CERTAIN WHEN I GET ROUND TO GETTING OFF WITH A BLOKE'.

I barely noticed, however. I was standing close to Finn at the back, enjoying the closeness of us; the hairs on our arms were almost, but not quite, touching. Every so often, a lairy teenager would come crashing into us and send us hurtling into each other. I enjoyed this bit too; we would self-consciously apologize to each other, and hold each other's gaze a little longer than necessary. My insides were squirming, I could hear my own heart even above the condemned wailing of the band, and I was finding it quite difficult to understand why, after all, this geeky, annoyingly direct chap was having this effect on me. It couldn't just be because he was a good dancer, could it? I snuck a peek out of the corner of my eye. He was watching the band with an amused expression, but there was an aura of nervousness about him too. I assumed I was the cause of it, but I couldn't fathom which way – was he desperate to get rid of me, and had a prank instituted by Chali gone too far? Or did he feel the same way I did – nervous but, frankly, desperate for a kiss? And not just any old kiss – a proper, movie-star, blistering yet infinitely tender kiss, the type you reach your face up for so readily, and receive so rarely. I realized suddenly that I was fantasizing about him and had my tongue hanging out like a dog, and shook my head briskly to clear it.

The band rolled off eventually, Tristram headbanging in order to spread his circle of sweat as far as possible, and taking rather more encores than the audience had strictly demanded, including 'MY LOVE IS A FOETUS'. Finally, however, they were gone, and the audience started to drift away. Josh stayed rooted to the spot.

'Well?' I asked him.

'She said stay here,' he said rigidly.

'I'm not sure she meant the exact square centimetre.'

'You can't be too careful.' He thought for a second. 'I'm desperate for the loo, though.'

'Do you want Finn to stand there and pretend to be you for a minute while you get to have a wee?'

'No, thanks, I'll be fine.'

'Yes, until you go to kiss her and accidentally wet yourself.'

'That might happen anyway,' said Josh, suddenly spotting her sashaying across the floor towards us with a purposeful expression on her face.

'Shall we go?' said Finn to me, subtly.

'Oh! Yes, of course. Bye, darling. We'll want a full report.'

'Probably, nothing,' said Josh, but he held up his fingers, which were tightly crossed.

I crossed mine back at him, and waved at Chali across the room, who was berating her crusty army for something.

'See you tomorrow!'

She looked over, then laughed.

'I will be extremely surprised,' she yelled, 'if *either* of us makes it into work tomorrow!'

I twinged with embarrassment.

'Yes, well, whatever.'

Finn opened the door for me, and the huge doorman recognized me and laughed.

'You know, I might have guessed you two would end up together when you came in.'

'Matchmaker, are you?' I was still cross with him for taking the twenty pounds.

'Neh – you're the only two wearing shoes.'

I glanced at my feet. Finn was wearing desert boots, and I had a pair of Startrite sandals for grown-ups on. Everyone else was in neon trainers.

'You're very good at your job,' I said.

He tipped his head to me.

'Thank you, ma'am. Have a good night now.'

Outside, it had started to rain. Finn shrugged back into his duffel coat, and immediately appeared more prosaic. Then he caught my eye and smiled warmly. My stomach started doing the samba again.

'Now – dinner!' he announced. I stared at him.

'You know it's quarter past midnight?'

'No – is it really? I don't wear a watch,' he said disappointedly. 'Time is just so completely irrelevant.'

'Unless you're trying to eat in London after midnight.'

'God, if only Einstein had thought of that. It could have changed *everything*.'

'It could have changed us getting food poisoning,' I said, looking around. There were places open around the railway station, but they were frankly terrifying – unidentifiable kebab shops next to watery hamburger joints, with little tin ashtrays full of an evening's worth of anxious cigarette butts from prostitutes, drug dealers and runaways – the standard clientele of the King's Cross cuisine trade. I had been hungry, but one look at these places would put a scabby dog off its dinner. Also, I could have been starving to death, but if there was a possibility of kissing on the agenda later on, then I wasn't going near the oral hygiene minefield that was a kebab. These things need careful planning.

This may also have occurred to Finn, because we wandered about for a while, unwilling to end the evening, uncertain of what our options were. Finally, thankfully, we stumbled across a late-night coffee shop, and Finn acquired two great mugs of soapy coffee and thin slabs of chocolate biscuit cake and sat down next to me on the tiny moulded plastic chairs.

'My ears are still ringing,' I complained.

'Well, it was worth it just to see the start of a new phenomenon, wasn't it?'

'A phenomenal pile of poo.'

'Oh – I didn't know you were reviewing it for *Time Out*.'

I sipped my coffee, looking closely at his hands. They were long and wiry, with long pale fingers. One was holding on to the cup so tightly the handle was in some danger, and the other was drumming nervously on the table top.

'So, what do you want to do when you grow up, then?' I asked him.

He shrugged his shoulders.

'After I win the Nobel Prize, I thought I'd become the new Dr Who, and then go into space.'

'Don't you get to go into space anyway, if you're Dr Who?'

'Whoops, yes, I keep forgetting it's a documentary.'

'You'd be a good Dr Who,' I said. He would; he was the right mix of bright, confused and severely dishevelled.

'And you can still win the Nobel Prize, can't you?'

He sighed, and rattled his coffee cup. 'Not at thirty, I don't think, unless I come up with something quick. Physicists tend to peak when they're about twenty.'

'Wow, just like . . .'

'Yes, yes, yes, I have heard it. And I was too busy doing physics to pull . . . and, of course, I was doing physics, which rather limits your options in the first place.'

'Never mind,' I said.

'I'm sorry: do I sound like the most moany person in the world? I feel like I've just been moaning all night.'

'Well, it's closer to singing than Tristram was.'

'What about you? What are you going to be?'

'Hmm. Film star, I think.'

'Good choice.'

'Thank you. Although I'm not looking forward to all the porn I'll have to make before I get there.'

'Seriously. Are you a dedicated florist?'

I fiddled with a sugar packet.

'I don't know. It's OK. After my parents split up, neither of their flats had a garden, and I really missed it. This seems about the closest I can get at the moment. And I'd die if I had to work in an office. I couldn't handle . . . you know, the low-denier tights.'

He nodded. 'Why don't you go and work in gardens then? Or at least, you could go to an evening class.'

I stuck my hands in my ears. 'Not listening . . . la la la la la . . . I know that . . . la la la la . . . I am completely pathetic . . . la la la!'

He smiled, and folded his arms, waiting for me to take my hands down.

'I'm sorry, but . . .'

'La! La la la la!'

'Or you could . . .'

'La la la! La la la la!'

'OK, OK. Ehm . . . do you want to go into space?'

'You asking?'

He smiled again. 'Well, I'm a bit busy this month.'

'Oh, yeah, me too. Well, you know how it is.'

'I think I've got a window about 2017, though.'

'Really? That's amazing. I'm free that decade too.'

'Maybe we could go then, then.'

'Only if I get the window seat.'

'OK. But no opening the duty-free space dust until we get in to land.'

'You're no fun.'

Suddenly, I found myself yawning. It was after one, and the coffee-shop owner was looking at us grumpily over the top of a mop which, judging from the floor, he had no intention of using.

Finn seemed a bit crestfallen. 'You're right, I am no fun and am in fact boring you senseless. Can I take you home?'

I waved him away. 'Don't be silly, of course you're not boring me. It's just late, that's all. I'll get a night bus, don't worry.'

'A night bus? On our date? I think not.'

He jumped up and stuck his head outside the door and, amazingly, hailed a cab almost immediately.

'Cab,' he said, sticking his head back round. There was rain dripping off the front of his glasses.

The mood changed as soon as we stepped into the cab. A man, a woman, in a cab, after a date. There must have been millions of us doing exactly the same thing all over the world at that very moment, with the same nerves and worries going through all of us. All the way back we edged closer and closer together, but remained in almost complete silence. Occasionally, we'd smile nervously at one another. I wasn't really used to doing this without rather more alcohol in me than there was at the moment, so I was feeling terribly anxious. Finally, the cab pulled up, and Finn turned to me.

'Ehm . . . I'll just ask it to wait.'

Make your mind up time.

'You could . . . come in for coffee, if you like,' I said, staring hard at my hands.

'More coffee . . . ehm, great!' said Finn, paying the driver. I hopped out of the car, mentally checking what pants I had on. As we walked up the path, he reached out and gently took my hand, and I thought my heart was going to leap out of my mouth.

We went up the flight of stairs to the front door – underneath it there was a light on. We both saw it at the same time. And, just as I took out my key, Finn took me by the shoulders, and looked at me quizzically, as if checking everything would be all right. When I assured him with my eyes that it was, he leaned in very slowly and gently, and started to kiss me.

It was an international-standard kiss. Not desperately sexual, like one of those dog-humping-your-leg ones, and not coy either; strong, and sexy and very, very good indeed.

Eventually I pulled away.

'Your mother didn't put you in *that* class at school,' I said breathlessly.

'It was a very progressive school,' he said, adding, 'No, of *course* not!' when he saw my face.

I unlocked the door. 'Come in,' I said, taking him by both hands. 'Please.'

He followed me through the door. And we were gazing so intently at each other that I nearly fell over Addison, who was curled up in a ball by the telephone, silently crying his eyes out.

Seven

'What!?' I regained my balance, and let go of Finn's hands. 'Addison, what's the matter?'

He didn't look up. Finn crouched down beside him.

'Ehm, hello there . . . are you all right?' he asked, rather lamely.

I crouched down.

'Add? Addy?' I touched him lightly. With the desperation of a child, he grabbed me round the shoulders and clung to me as if his life depended on it. I glanced at Finn and grimaced.

'Would you mind making some tea?'

He nodded, and it was as if, on some level, we both knew that regardless of what was going on with Addison, making tea was not the same as having coffee.

I heard him clattering about unsteadily in the kitchen.

'What's the matter, Add? Speak to me.'

I took his chin in my hand. A sudden dash of fear ran through me like icy water.

'It's not Kate, is it? Kate came back, didn't she?'

He nodded miserably.

'She's asleep,' he sniffed.

'You mean she came in and didn't see you on the landing?'

'I pretended it was my contact lenses.'

151

Addison's glasses were as thick as beer bottles, and sitting on the telephone table.

'Wow. She must have been tired.'

'I'm tired,' said Addison quietly.

'Come on.' I hoisted him up. 'Come and sit in the kitchen and we can sort this out.'

I half hauled him into the kitchen and dumped his long frame into a chair.

Finn was still shuffling around the cupboards.

'Ehm . . . which tea should I use?'

I looked over my shoulder.

'The own-brand, obviously. The Earl Grey is Kate's, and she'd kill us.'

He nodded. 'And who is it lives off Penguin biscuits?'

'Ehmm . . . a penguin. Watch out if you want to use the bathtub.' I turned back to Addison.

'Oh, right.'

I picked up Addison's hand, waiting for the last few tear drops to squeeze their way down his cheeks and for him to become composed enough to talk to us without snortling. Finally Finn put down the mugs of tea, and a plate of biscuits that everyone ignored.

'Do you mind me being here?' he said.

Fatally, I looked to Addison for the answer to that question. What I should have done was say, 'No, I don't mind – Addison, do you?' But I didn't. I didn't make any sign that Finn and I were in any way connected.

Addison lifted his head a fraction.

'I don't mind.'

'OK,' I said, grasping his hand more firmly. 'What's the matter?'

'Well,' he sniffed, 'the phone kept ringing and ringing and ringing . . .'

'You never answer the phone.'

'I know. But it wouldn't stop ringing.'

'It's not Claudia, is it?' I said, wondering before I could stop myself whether she'd met someone else.

'Oh no – Claudia! I haven't spoken to her all night. She'll be wondering where I am.'

'Well, let her wonder for just a little bit longer, tiger. Who was the phone call from?'

'My mum.'

'Your mum? She usually phones on a Sunday, doesn't she?'

He nodded.

'Well . . .'

'She phoned to wish me a happy birthday.'

'Oh, when's your birthday?'

His face crumpled.

'Today. And I forgot!!!'

He burst into noisy sobs again. Finn and I looked at each other, concerned.

I put my arm round his shoulder.

'You know, Add, that might be a little bit flakey, but I wouldn't get too upset about it.'

'You don't understand. The date of my birthday and the date of the fire . . . I get them mixed up, and I always remember the wrong one.'

It was the seventh of June.

'What was the date of the fire?' I asked quietly.

'The seventh of July.'

'How old were you?'

'Eleven years and – sniff – one month.'

'Ohh, Addison.'

He felt chilled and damp through from crying.

'Drink some tea.'

'When I know it's coming, it's not so bad . . . but this year I forgot.'

I wondered how he could forget his own birthday. As soon as November dawned, I was jumping about like a bumblebee in anticipation. Well, it used to be anticipation. These days, it was more like dread.

'I forget mine all the time,' said Finn. 'I'll be up to my eyes in the lab and someone will shout out the date and I'll remember.'

Addison nodded.

'I usually schedule some really difficult coding . . . just to take my mind off things.'

'I'm sorry, mate,' said Finn.

'I miss him, Holly,' said Addison.

I thought for a moment he meant Finn, then cottoned on.

'Your dad?'

'He bought me my first ZX81.'

'Err . . . did he? That was nice.'

'And he taught me C+. Rudimentary, obviously.'

'Obviously,' said Finn.

'OK, scientist boys . . .' I thought for a moment. 'You know, Add, I think maybe this year we need to celebrate your birthday.'

He looked up. 'I don't . . .'

'I know. But I think maybe you should. In fact, I think you have to. I think, maybe, it's been too long since you had a birthday party.'

Finn nodded in agreement.

'But . . .'

'We'll make it on another date. We'll crown you a new birthday.'

He sat, silent and worried.

'Don't worry, it will just be us in the flat.'

'Will you be there?' Addison asked Finn.

Finn looked at me. 'Yes, of course he will,' I said.

Addison appeared unconvinced.

'Now, come on. We'll talk about it more in the morning. Let's put you to bed. You don't sleep enough; you must be exhausted.'

There was a sense of tired relief on his face, as if just being able to tell someone had helped; was all he wanted. Addison let me lead him off to bed as dopily as a child. Finn looked up with a hopeful expression on his face just as I left the room.

I turned back.

'I'm going to . . . sit with him while he goes to sleep . . . just to make sure, OK?'

He seemed briefly disappointed, but quickly covered it up.

154

'Right, well, I'd better be . . . you know, it's pretty late.'

'It is,' I said.

'OK. I'll just . . . see you soon? You know, date two?'

'Yes – ehm, I'll ring you about Addison's birthday,' I said. 'Thank you for a lovely evening.'

'Thank you. Ehm . . .' He was standing by the door, with his satchel in his hand, and he appeared to be about to say something, but then changed his mind, and didn't. '. . . Bye.'

'Bye,' I said, and watched him turn round and walk down the steps. He didn't look back at me.

I tucked Addison in and he lay staring up at me while I gently stroked his high forehead.

'Thank you,' he said. 'Sometimes, I think I'm going mad.'

'If you think you're going mad, that means you aren't,' I said. 'I think. Unless it's the other way round, in which case we're all in trouble.'

'You know, they just found an ammonia ocean on one of Saturn's moons,' he said. 'It's deep down, buried under a hundred light years of gas. You could never see it with your eye, or touch it, or even get close to it, and it doesn't make a noise. But they still found it.'

'And?'

'I don't think you can hide,' he said, indistinctly as he closed his eyes, clearly wearied out from crying. 'I think you still get found.'

'I think you do too,' I said softly, and watched him as his breathing slowed and became more regular. I watched his face for a long time: peaceful, but with a little white line of salt encrusted round his eye. And finally, when I got very weary too, I lay down beside him on the narrow bed, and I slept as well, my right arm flung across him, as if it would give some sort of protection.

I woke up the next morning with a start, and not the faintest idea where I was. Blinking heavily, the still sleeping Addison came into focus. Oh my God! Beside me, the fine lines of his face were outlined against the pillow, his eyelashes casting a shadow, and he had a line of stubble along his chin. He was absolutely beautiful.

'Hey,' I whispered, and he twisted towards me. Slowly, his huge eyes opened, registering at first shock, then a certain amount of good manners.

'Ehm . . . hey!' he said, smiling gingerly. I started to register a slight embarrassment.

'How are you feeling?'

'Ehm . . . better, thank you.'

I realized my arm was trapped under his, but didn't want to scare him by wiggling it away, so I gave it up to gangrene. We were in the extremely awkward position of waking up in bed together for the first time, and the fact that we hadn't done any naked stuff didn't seem to have any effect on how deeply embarrassing it was, which seemed unfair.

'Am I trapping your arm?'

'No! No, it's fine. Well, actually, yes.'

He moved and I was in that ridiculous position of lying on your side and having one arm too many getting in the way. I had an urge to slice it off, so we could lie facing each other in comfort.

'I . . . slept very well,' he said.

'Yes, me too.'

I hoped this was some sort of an invitation, but his body wasn't quite touching mine, and he seemed stiff. Well, his body language was stiff – I didn't know about the rest of him.

We regarded each other for a bit, until I absolutely had to say something.

'Add, you know . . . I'm absolutely desperate for the toilet.'

His face broke into a grin.

'Me too.'

'OK . . . I'll get up . . . Would you like some tea?'

'Yes please . . . Can I not have any sugar?'

'Not a problem.'

I crept to the door, preparing to sidle out of it like a jewel thief.

I listened for any movement, and when I didn't hear anything, gently opened the door.

Kate was standing opposite me with the phone in her hand and, as of precisely this moment, an extremely shocked expression on her face.

'What the fuck!??'

'Ssh.'

'Oh my God, I don't believe . . .'

'Shh! It's not what you think.'

'He obviously didn't find his contact lens,' she said, looking me up and down.

'I thought you were meant to be in Antwerp.'

'I was, you idiot. But instead I decided to have more fun by staying here and phoning the police. Where the fuck *were* you all?'

I shut the door behind me.

'What? I was . . .'

'In there, yes I'd gathered that. Josh isn't back – did you know? Or were you too busy shagging to check? How the hell was I to know you hadn't both been beaten up and left for dead? I mean, *Jesus . . .*'

'I'm sorry, you know, it's not the kind of situation you leave a note for.'

'Obviously not.'

'I *don't* mean that. Oh God, where is Josh?'

She raised her eyebrows. I remembered.

'Oh my God! Sha . . . Oh my God.' I grinned with delight. 'He must have gone home with her. Wow! You know, I can't get my head round that at all. Josh having sex – it completely changes my world view. Is water flowing upwards?'

'Well, you got off with Addison, so I wouldn't be relying on any magnets.'

I couldn't help grinning again. 'We didn't *get off*. We just slept together.'

Kate hit her hand on her forehead. 'I'm sorry, I keep forgetting you're *modern*.'

157

'Fuck off. No, I mean, really slept. In each other's arms.' I sighed with bliss.

'No monkeying?'

'No monkeying, I swear. Just good friends.'

'If you say so. God, I am *so* glad I have set back my entire career three years for this. Unlike some, I can't just take a day off when it suits me.'

She stomped into the kitchen. I followed her and put the kettle on.

'What do you mean, take a day off? It's only – shit!' It was after nine. Mrs Bigelow was going to have my arse for garters. I panicked, scrubbed my hands and face, pulled on a pair of jeans slightly too small for me and ran out of the house, only remembering halfway there that Addison would still be waiting for his tea. I closed my eyes again at the memory of him and nearly got run over by a white van. The driver had his windows shut, but I could lip-read the word he was using about me, and it wasn't a pretty one.

I swang round Edmonton Street, expecting to see the shop closed up, or Mrs Bigelow inside honking with disapproval, as Chali hadn't seemed as though she was on her way home for a cup of cocoa the night before, but everything seemed normal, and the gardenias out the front looked relatively healthy. I relaxed, and sauntered in.

'Woooooooh!' greeted me when I entered. 'Late night last night, had we?'

I shrugged. 'Might have done.'

Chali leapt off the counter where she'd been disdainfully painting her nails.

'Well? I want details. Width? Overcoat?'

'What on *earth* are you talking about?'

'Overcoat. You know, was he circumcised?'

The penny dropped.

'Chali, (1) you are a very dirty girl, and (2) nothing happened with Finn.'

She looked confused. 'But you had a late night.' Her eyes widened. 'Who with?'

'Well, you know my flatmate I've been telling you about . . .'

'You pulled him!?'

'Not exactly . . .'

I told her everything, but she wasn't quite as thrilled as I had hoped.

'So, let me get this straight: you blew off nice Finn for this completely fucked up wanker?'

'I didn't "blow off" Finn. Not everyone sleeps with their dates on the first night.'

'Yes, but you were about to.'

'No I wasn't.'

'You'd asked him in for coffee.'

'And that means "shag me", does it? Fine feminist you are.'

'How many times in your whole life have you asked a bloke in for a coffee, had a chat and not shagged him?'

'That's not the point! It's the principle!'

'How many times?'

'Well, you know . . . not many.'

'How many?'

'Nunce.'

'Exactly. But you threw him over for some complete weir-do.'

'Addison is not *weird*. He's damaged.'

'He's off his cake!'

'I know. But if you could see him . . .'

'I don't like handsome men. They make me feel insecure.'

'Is that why you hang out with all those disgusting crusties?'

'No, that's because I'm sleeping my way to the top of the music business.'

'Oh yes.'

'Speaking of which . . .'

She looked over my shoulder and I turned round.

A grotesquely fat, short man with slicked-back hair and sunglasses had just entered the shop.

'Hey . . . babyy! I was gonna bring you flowers, but I figured you already had some.'

159

His accent was mid-Atlantic via Birmingham. It made dogs whine and cover their ears with their paws.

'Bo!' Chali ran into his arms.

'Holly, this is Bo – he's a producer for the Shingles, and he's lined me up with an audition!'

'I'm very happy for you both.'

Bo put his arm round Chali and pinched her on the bum.

'C'mon, darling – I'm taking you out to brunch.'

'Is that all right, Holl?' asked Chali, snuggling up to him.

'Fine,' I said. 'I'll just sit here, planning how not to go out with, you know, *weirdos*.'

She stuck her tongue out at me and danced out of the shop.

I spent the day fantasizing madly. By lunchtime I'd moved us to Tuscany, with four children – no, actually, make that two children, otherwise I'd have a body like a beanbag. By two thirty, he'd developed some computer thingy and we'd become as rich as Bill Gates but without the acne. I'd even mentally rehearsed what I was going to say when I got home. I wasn't going to rush up to him and fling my arms round him. I wasn't going to move my stuff into his room. I wasn't even going to pull down his trousers, strong as the urge might be. I would simply wait for Josh to cook us dinner, then invite him in. Then we would all sit together, and it would be lovely. We could hold hands. I might even let him feel me up under the table. No, nitch that – that would be disgusting. All four of us would, for once, partake in intelligent, grown-up debate without any name-calling or slanging matches. Hmm.

I knew something was wrong when I walked in the door, but I couldn't put my finger on it. Kate was in the sitting room, staring out of the window.

'What's going on?'

'He's not back,' she said flatly. 'Josh isn't back. His work called and asked if we'd seen him.'

That was it. There was no smell of cooking.

160

'Wow. Well, you know, he'll come back when he's ready, I suppose. Aren't you happy for him?'

'What if he never comes back? What if she keeps him in sex prison?'

'Well, that's still better than Sophie, isn't it?'

'I don't know.'

I looked at her. 'You're really upset, aren't you?'

'I'm not upset. I'm just pissed off that he couldn't even phone to tell us whether he'd been killed or not.'

'You are – you should see yourself! You're upset. You're jealous.'

'Of course I'm not jealous! He's one of my oldest friends, and I just think he could have had a little consideration, that's all.'

'Kate is jealous! Kate is jealous!'

'Piss off, would you? Oh, and if you're going to start having sex in the flat, can you try and keep it down? Oh God, if you two are together now it's going to be rut city around here. And Josh is in sex prison. What on earth is the matter with my life?'

'I don't know. Maybe you scare men,' I said.

'Thank you, that helps, that really helps. My therapist says I come over as too independent to cover up my essential neediness. Do you think that's true?'

'I think your therapist talks through his bottom. Can you pay me eighty quid a week? Then we'll sit for an hour and I'll say, "Don't go out with married men . . . Don't go out with married men . . . Don't go out with married men," and then you can completely ignore me.'

She grimaced at me.

'Actually, I'll be pleased when you start shagging Addison. Maybe it'll keep you quiet for a bit.'

'I wouldn't be too sure about that,' I said, and left her to it.

So much for my dinner plan. Addison's door was tightly shut, which was a bit ominous. I stood in the hall, suddenly wracked with indecision and what last night might have meant, if anything. Maybe he'd want to forget the whole thing?

I tapped lightly on his door, and heard no reply.

161

My absolute first urge was to forget the whole thing. This, I suddenly realized, is what makes boys with whom you have had a positively wonderful time decide in that utterly logical boy way of theirs not to call you afterwards for no reason whatsoever.

You know what it's like: boys you have met, had a brilliant time with, possibly even slept with – but not in a seedy way; in a fun, adult, getting-to-know-each-other way. You know how many siblings he has, how he gets on with his dad, what stupid things he did at college; you've spent all night exchanging information in an intense and fascinating manner. You laugh, you eat in bed, you have a bath together, it seems almost churlish to ask him if he's going to ring you as you clearly are such soul mates – and then he doesn't ring you! And, worse than that, it makes *you* feel bad about yourself.

I should/shouldn't have gone down on him, you think (delete as appropriate). *Why* did I tell him I used to go out with a policeman who accidentally broke my leg? Just mentioning 'I like dogs' isn't instant boy code for 'I'm desperate for a baby', is it? Is it? Maybe it is!

For years this amazed me. I decided that, like in *The Matrix*, boys were living in a completely different parallel universe and were attempting to 'enslave' us whilst waiting for 'the one', probably a short-haired girl who would astonish you with her dullness and all-round podginess when you ran into them both at a dinner party a year later, displaying their engagement rings and talking about Ikea. The great scientific minds of the age should be working on it. But of course they're mostly blokes, aren't they? I suspect conspiracy.

It isn't all one-way, though – sometimes, due to alcohol, boredom or a sheer sense of pity, one has been known to take men home on a 'mercy mission' basis. This type you will gladly hide from forevermore, including plastic surgery and moving to minor South American countries.

Addison, naturally, wasn't one of those. In fact, he was someone

I'd been worrying about and thinking about for months. And here he was. Or, at least, here was the best opportunity I'd had so far. And I could suddenly understand why boys might think, 'Well, she's very nice, and I did have a brilliant time, but, you know, there's football on the telly and we've just ordered in a curry and – Oh, fuck it, I think I'll just wait around for someone a little dumpier. After all, I've got the whole of my thirties to get this sorted out.'

What I hadn't factored in was that if you live with someone it's slightly more difficult to avoid them for the rest of your life. Although, in Addison's case, not impossible. And I also hadn't factored in that the reason he hadn't opened his door might be that he didn't want to talk to me either.

Gulp.

I pushed open the door a little, my heart in my mouth. Addison wasn't there. His computer was switched off.

Oh no! He'd gone to South America!

Stunned and upset, I stomped into the kitchen to see where Kate had put the wine. Brilliantly, Addison was sitting at the kitchen table.

'Hey!' I said, more excitedly than I intended. 'You're not in your room!'

'No,' he said slowly.

'Why – did you think I was going to attack you?'

Aaargh! Why did I say that?

'Ehm . . . no. I just . . . thought I'd be here when you came home.'

Ooh! I loved him.

'Right – fine – ehm.'

I felt myself start to blush. He blushed in unison, until it felt like we were having a tomato competition.

'Josh isn't back then,' I observed, needlessly.

'No.'

'Looks like no dinner in that case.'

163

Addison shrugged. 'I don't usually care much about dinner.'

'Aren't you hungry?'

He thought about it.

'I suppose so.'

'Well then.'

I marched over to the cupboards and threw them open. I didn't seem to recognize anything inside them. What on earth was hoi sin sauce? Truffle oil?

'Ehm . . . what do you want to eat?'

He shrugged his shoulders.

'Whatever you're having?'

'What do you like?' I asked, as if he could name any of the world's major dishes and I'd whip it up for him then and there.

'I quite like cornflakes,' he said.

Perfect! (1) we had some, (2) I could make them, and (3) they are delicious. The man had taste.

'Coming right up,' I said. 'With sugar or *au naturel*?'

'What's the house style?'

'*À la maison* would be without sugar, using a luxurious amount of extremely creamy milk.'

'Can I have that, please?'

'Certainly, sir.'

I ceremoniously poured them out and we sat there, alternately scoffing and throwing shy glances at one another. It was bliss.

Kate stomped in in the middle of it.

'Oh my God. Is this dinner?'

We both nodded happily.

'Have you finished all the milk?'

We nodded again.

'Great great great great great.'

She seized the wine bottle and vanished. Addison and I grinned at each other.

'So . . . ehm.'

This was definitely a tad uncomfortable. Well, after all, I'd never actually officially 'lived with' anyone before, if you defined 'living with' as 'having the same door key as'. I'd always thought that one day I might, but those plans tended to include, you know, kissing them or something. We seemed to have gone straight from first meeting to end of year one. I mean, we might as well go out and get a Renault Espace. What if it was awful?

My old florist friend McKay has this theory. It's formally named after her, and it's called the McKay Button Mushroom Theory. And it goes like this: *always* sleep with someone as quickly as possible after you first meet them and decide they're a bit of all right. This can be within hours, although less than one isn't recommended.

Doing this saves you all the fuss and bother of finding out you have things in common, finding out you like them, realizing you're in love with them, and *then* deciding to seal the deal by bouncing the bishop and discovering that, after all this – the moonlight walks, the giggling dinners, the lingering glances – he has a penis the size and consistency of a button mushroom! But it's too late then! You're already in too deep! You've wasted all that time!

It's a good theory, and I had always tried to follow it as closely as possible. But it suddenly occurred to me that, actually, I had fallen hook, line and sinker for Addison before I'd so much as cocked a snook at his body, so to speak.

'Would you like to go for a walk?'

I was so wrapped up in my own thoughts I didn't hear him.

'Huh?'

'It's just that it's quite a nice night, so I thought when we'd finished dinner we could go for a walk.'

'Wow.' I pondered this. The ramifications of Addison actually suggesting to physically go outside were enormous.

'Are you sure?'

He swallowed. 'Why not? People go for walks all the time. Don't they?'

'Well, usually only when they need Rizlas, I think.'

'Oh, right well, we don't have to . . .'

'Don't be silly, I'd love to.'

He smiled shyly, and I felt something grabbing at my chest. I

165

found I couldn't eat another cornflake in his presence. I immediately came over all self-conscious and had an almost overwhelming compulsion to put some lipstick on.

'Hang on . . .' I said, getting up.

'Where are you going?'

'Ehm . . .' I didn't want to tell him I was going to slather myself in overpriced animal fats in an attempt to make myself more alluring. 'Ehm, I'm going to the toilet.'

Yikes! Shit! Oh no! I might as well have added, 'And I'm going to do the most unbelievably smelly poo whilst I'm in there, as that's what you'll be expecting if I'm out of the room for more than twenty-five seconds.'

I had broken my golden rule, which was never to let a man know I had standard bodily functions – ever.

Flushed, I fled the room, feeling Addy looking after me. In desperate haste I stole Kate's Clarins lippy and got a bit of cornflake on it. When I tried to wipe it off, it looked as though I'd just cut off one of my fingers and was bleeding everywhere – Kate tended towards the thin scarlet slash in lipstick – and there was substantially less in the tube than there had been before. I swore hugely to myself and went to brush my teeth, trying not to make too much noise. I suspect there's something a tad off-putting about hearing someone brush their teeth just before you take a romantic walk with them, don't you? It takes away the spontaneity, and it's a bit like saying, you know, normally I have really awful halitosis but, seeing as it's you, I'll make an effort just this once . . .

Catching sight of myself in the mirror I remembered my mother's old maxim: 'Always brush your teeth *before* you put your lipstick on.' I swore once more for luck, ran my hands quickly through my tangled dark hair and sidled back into the kitchen, pleading that he wasn't going to say, 'Nice poo then?' Of course, Addison is not as other boys. He stood up when I came in, and I just stood staring at him. I had never felt so paralysingly shy in my entire life. Well, I'd never felt particularly shy – but I did now.

'Shall we go?' he asked, gently. I nodded, and he swept us out of the door, gracefully depositing the two cornflakes bowls in the sink. It felt like that tiny split second where a rollercoaster stops on the top of the rails.

It was truly a beautiful evening; the sun was setting, the clouds were tinged pink, and after a momentary tussle at the gate, as neither of us knew which way to go, we headed down to the river bank near the Tate Gallery.

Two minutes later, whilst I was trying to rack my brains to remember the difference between a Pentium and a Mac – or was it a PC and a Mac? – so I'd have something to talk to Addison about, a familiar figure came lurching up the road, tie askew, hair distinctly ruffled and wearing a broad smile.

'Josh!' I hollered at him.

He grinned, and actually broke into a run towards us.

'I had sex!!!' he yelled, as he drew nearer. 'I had sex!!'

'And I'm sure the whole of SW1 is very happy for you!' I said as he reached me and pounced like an over-eager puppy. 'Well done. And, please, don't cuddle me until you've had a shower.'

'I had sex! With a girl!'

'What was it like?' I asked mischievously.

'Oh, you know – brilliant!!' He leaned over, out of breath. 'Guess how many times we did it?'

I hadn't wanted to know anything quite so icky, but I knew how much Josh wanted to tell me.

'A squillion?'

'Ha ha. No, guess again.'

'Oh, I don't know. Seven.'

'Fifteen,' he said proudly.

I looked at him through new eyes.

'Bloody hell, Josh.'

'It hurt a bit at the end,' he said. 'And I nearly threw up once. But, you know, I had some ground to make up.'

I nodded sagely.

'She must be a bit weary.'

167

'Not really — ehm, the first few were pretty speedy.'

'Josh,' I said, 'too much information.'

'Right, right, yes, of course.'

He took in Addison for the first time.

'Gosh — hello there, big fellow!'

Addison did his usual peculiar half-wince greeting and gradually Josh took in the scene around him.

'Oh . . . where are you two going?'

'It's such a beautiful night we're going for a walk,' I said firmly. No point in telling him the whole story — the neighbourhood had heard enough girly screaming for one night.

'It is wonderful, isn't it? Everything is wonderful. I think I'll come with you.'

'I think you won't,' I said, racking my brains to think up a quick rationale.

'I showered, I promise,' said Josh, wounded. 'Blood came out and everything.'

'Yeuch! Josh, for Christ's sake.'

'I think I might have ruptured something,' he went on, gloomily. 'Worth it, though.'

'No, that's not what I meant. I mean, you have to go home and see Kate. She nearly had the police out for you this morning. She was worried sick when you didn't come in.'

'Didn't you tell her where I was?'

'Ehm . . . you know, I forgot.'

'Oh,' he said, clearly puzzled. 'Well, yes, OK, I'd better be getting back then.'

'OK! See you later.'

He looked confusedly at Addison.

'You know, you seem a lot bigger standing up,' he said.

'Everyone does,' I said. 'Sex has addled your brain. OK, go home. But don't tell Kate too much — she'll go all neurotic and bitter.'

'I'd hate to see that happen,' said Josh. 'OK, goodbye.'

He leaned over and kissed me full on the mouth.

'Josh, *what* are you doing?'

'I've decided to be a bit more assertive in my relationships. Sha thinks I ought to be.'

'Hmm. Well, I'm sure Sha is right in many things, but just remember; there's a thin line between assertive and date rape.'

'Right,' he said. 'Good one. I'll try and remember that.'

And he scampered off towards the house, clicking his heels once in the air in the style of Morecambe and Wise.

I glanced at Addison and grinned and he grinned back.

'Well, things are going to be a little different round our house,' I said.

'It's the summer,' said Addison. 'It brings out the pheromones. It makes people do strange things.'

I took his hand. 'Is this a strange thing?'

He smiled. 'It is for me.'

'Bad strange or good strange?'

'I'd have to analyse it.'

'Maybe you could devise a computer programme to measure its effects.'

'Maybe.' He screwed up his eyes and stared into the middle distance.

'Well, on a probability of 97.2 per cent, I'd say I'd have to go with my intuition that it's good strange.'

We wandered hand in hand down to the river. The Thames, though positively filthy, was as smooth as glass and the lights of the bridges twinkled romantically in the distance. I hoisted myself inelegantly up on to the river wall and Addison plumped himself next to me with ease.

'Talk to me,' I said to him. 'We've spent months living in the same house and you know practically everything about me and all I know about you is that you have a computer girlfriend and you like Jean-Luc Picard.'

'Everyone likes Jean-Luc Picard,' he said.

'Exactly. So I can discount that piece of information as being on a par with "and you breathe in and out". So, come on, tell me.'

He shifted and looked uncomfortable.

'I don't really . . .'

'. . . like talking about yourself; no, I know that. But I'd really like to get to know you,' I said, as sincerely as I could manage. For some reason I suddenly reminded myself of the boys who tried to get into my knickers when I was eighteen. They were sweet talkers too. But this was different! I really cared! This wasn't just McKay BMS. I hoped. I wondered what boys called it. Fried-egg syndrome? Clyde Tunnel syndrome? Yuk. I shook myself, and a thought occurred to me.

'How about I ask you questions?'

He glanced up at me through his thick dark lashes.

'What do you mean?'

'We'll turn it into an interview. Like *Parkinson*. Then, if you don't want to talk about something, you can say, "You can read all about that in my forthcoming book," or attack me with an emu.'

'OK.' He nodded.

I gesticulated to some ducks on the river.

'Good evening, ladies and gentlemen and ducks. And tonight on *Parkinson*, as my very special star guest, with an entire programme devoted solely to him – Addison Farthing!!!!'

The ducks failed to go wild, but I clapped uproariously and Addison gracefully raised a modest hand in acknowledgement.

'Now, Mr Farthing, obviously we're feeling most privileged and excited to have you on the wall . . .'

'Call me Addison, please.'

'Well, yes, of course . . . *Addison*. So, *Addison*, the story in all the papers at the moment and what everyone wants to know is . . .'

He looked worried.

'What *exactly* do you do for a living? And, you know, I'm going to need that in phrases the ducks can understand.'

His face relaxed. 'Well, people want to know if you can join computer systems together to make the most out of them. So they get me to work out what's compatible and whether they can be combined for optimum effect.'

Half the ducks took off from the riverside.

'Well, there's a rude audience for you.'

'It is a bit boring.'

170

'No, no. Don't forget you're on the most popular show on the river.'

'Hmm.'

'OK.' I hit him with a slightly harder one. 'What were you like when you were small?'

His brow furrowed for a second, as if he couldn't remember.

'Don't you want to know – like, what's my favourite colour or something?'

'What's your favourite colour?'

'Light blue.'

'OK. What were you like when you were small?'

'Can I attack you with an emu now?'

'No. Tell me.'

And slowly, carefully, he did. In an odd way, I hardly listened to him at all. It was mesmerizing just to hear his gruff, low voice as a gentle wind blew across his dark hair and he stared out, straight past me. I kept thinking, 'I'm here! With Addison! We're here! Together!' After thinking about it for so long it was like going on a date with Brad Pitt – difficult to enjoy for itself, more for what it meant and how many people could see you while it was actually happening.

But I did hear him. His mother was Croatian, which accounted for those dark looks and high cheekbones, and his dad a lecturer. Only child, shy at school, good at science, chess club, played the piano, everything going fine . . . until, of course, they went on holiday to France just before he was due to start secondary school and everything went so terribly wrong. He started to stutter at this bit.

'What started the fire?' I asked gently, hoping against hope he wasn't going to say, 'Well, I set this firework off for a joke . . .'

'Wiring, they thought,' he said. 'It was all very confused, and the French authorities didn't really want to know . . . My mother's English has never been that great, and her French is worse,' he said, now staring hard at his toes. 'I don't even remember how it happened or how long it took. It was all a big mess, then finally we got home – someone dropped us off, I can't remember who –

171

and I went in the house and all I wanted to do was play the piano, for some reason. To play the piano like normal. Then I thought I had to stop because it was late and Dad didn't like me playing the piano late at night, it kept him awake.'

He stopped and bit his lip hard.

'Oh God, Addison.' I slipped my arm through his and held it tight. My head was spinning. I mean, I had wanted him to talk to me, but I hadn't thought he really would. I mean, what was it about me that was making him talk? I wasn't anything special. I couldn't quite see where I deserved these confidences. Unless, of course, he was in love with me . . . I was the first person he could speak to about these things – Oh my God. Oh my God!

Realizing I should perhaps be thinking less selfish thoughts when someone was pouring out something massive and deeply personal, I clutched his arm and rubbed my hand ineffectually up and down his leg.

'It's OK,' I said, in my best Mother Teresa soothing voice. 'It's OK. It's good to get it out.'

That sounded like he was vomiting. But he wasn't even crying, just staring very, very hard.

'Then I had to go to school, but they left me alone, pretty much. Then I got really into computers – the teacher let me sit in the lab during breaks . . .'

'What, you mean you missed out all that good smoking and swearing practice?'

'. . . then I got a degree in computer science and here I am. And I have been miserable for longer than I ever thought possible.'

He stopped short.

'I don't think I've ever said that out loud before.'

I looked up at him. 'It's probably a good thing that you did.'

He smiled weakly, and he was so adorable, I fell against him and gave him a huge hug, which he reciprocated. His hand touched my hair and I thought I was going to faint. We stayed like that for a while, whilst I considered kissing him and decided that revelations hour wasn't really the right time to start getting carnal. So eventually we drew apart.

172

'Do you think the ducks approved?' said Addison, as I pushed my hair back behind my ears.

'Who cares about the ducks?' I said. 'Bloody punters.'

He gazed out over the water.

'Thanks for telling me,' I said. 'I feel . . . honoured.'

I did.

'Oh,' Addison laughed, slightly embarrassed.

'That was down to Claudia. She's forever getting on at me to start living again; move on. Tell people, and get it out.' He looked at me. 'I'm very glad I did.'

What! *Claudia*!

If I'd had a mouthful of something I'd have spat it out.

I stared miserably at the ducks, thinking how much easier they had it than us. Then one began to peck another one really hard on the head and I remembered how much I'd miss *EastEnders* . . . but *still*. They had it easy. I was just confused. I mean, this was a date, wasn't it?

Addison turned towards me, excited.

'And you,' he said. Ah. This was getting better.

'But mostly her.'

Poo.

'She told me to get out, enjoy life, get to know people. Start over again. Then, you know, I met you, and it really seemed as if things were getting better, that I could get to know people.'

'Of course you can,' I said, more kindly than I felt. Actually, I felt like having a big fat tantrum, but it wasn't really that appropriate under the circumstances.

He shrugged. 'Then last night . . . I'd thought I was doing OK, I really did. And all the time I was just . . . sitting on it.'

'That's OK,' I said. 'Good to get it out.'

'You sound like Claudia.' He smiled.

Great. I sound like a pig.

'Last night was . . .' he looked shy '. . . really special for me.'

'Me too,' I said.

173

'And now . . .' He stood up unsteadily. 'Hey – I'm outside! It's a wonderful sunset! Wonderful ducks! Everything is going to be OK!'

He waved his hands in the air.

'OK, OK.' I smiled. 'You're feeling better. That's great.'

The sun was shooting deeply sexy pink things across the sky.

'No!' he said, towering above me. 'You haven't been locked in a room for fifteen years! It's wonderful!'

His happiness was infectious. Sod it, I thought. She's in America and I adore him. Sod it.

'It is wonderful,' I said, standing up next to him.

'It's brilliant!' he said.

'Yes, it is!' I said, flinging my arms out too.

I stared up at him, trying to manoeuvre myself into the most kissable position. The ducks started squawking and leaping up and down.

'Look at the ducks,' he yelled. 'They're celebrating.'

He started jumping up and down.

'We should celebrate too!'

'We should!' I tried a couple of experimental hops, then tilted my head up to his, and moved in for the kill.

'Huh?' he said, mid hop, peering down at me as I held up my face to be kissed.

'We should celebrate,' I said, reaching for him. 'Kiss me.'

Part II

Eight

You know those dreams you have, whereby you have to sit your O-level maths again, only you're naked and the whole test is in a language you've never seen before and they're making you take it in a swimming pool?

That's what the next moment was like; and will probably be like for my whole life.

Addison jumped back, nonplussed, when I unleashed my assault on him. Unfortunately, there wasn't a place to jump back to. It was that simple. One minute he was there, the next minute he dropped from sight. He didn't scream, there was just a scrambled yell, then a smash and a terrible, terrible thump as he crashed into the shallow, filthy water twenty feet below.

At first, I kept staring straight ahead, stupidly, my lips puckered, my brain trying to compute where the hell he was.

Then I screamed, then I realized that I wasn't the one with something to scream about, and leaned crazily far out over the wall. What I saw made my heart stop. Addison, his eyes closed, only his head above the water, was bobbing up and down on the waves. A bird had shat on his head. I'd killed him.

I was about to launch myself in when I heard shouts and footsteps behind me, and a strong hand grabbed the back of my dress, and a man hauled me off the wall. A group of people had gathered ridiculously quickly, and hailed a policeman, who, unusually, happened to be passing by, rather than taking part in the normal constabulary occupation of stopping disproportionate numbers of young black men.

The policeman ran over, then spoke brusquely into his radio, took off his hat and gingerly but quickly lowered himself over the wall.

I stumbled backwards.

'I've killed him! I've killed him!' I said over and over again, freezing hot and white cold at the same time. The man who had pulled me off the wall – and probably saved me – had disappeared back into the crowd. A woman came over from the spectators.

'Don't worry,' she said, putting a tentative, English arm around me. 'I'm sure you didn't mean to kill him.'

I started to hyperventilate.

Neither Addison nor the policeman reappeared over the wall. If I'd been thinking straight, I would have realized there was no way they could have shinned up the sheer drop, and the tide was low enough for them to wait there until the ambulance arrived. I thought that I'd killed the policeman too.

An ambulance and a police car drew up with a screech of brakes. In my blind panic I wondered whether or not they let you have books and magazines in prison. I tried to take a step forward, but my leg buckled from under me, and the woman kept hold.

'Do you need to phone anyone?' said a man with a dog, holding out his mobile.

I thought of a solicitor, but I don't have one. I phoned home, but all I could get out was 'Kaaaaa . . .' before launching into floods of tears when Kate picked up the phone.

'John?' she said hopefully.

'Kaaaaaa . . .'

'Holly? Is that you? What the hell's the matter?'

'Kaaa . . .'

The man with the dog grabbed the phone back off me.

'Hello . . .' He turned to me. 'Is this your friend?'

I nodded.

'What's her name?'

'K . . . K . . . Kate.'

'Kate, hello. Listen, I've got a friend of yours here . . . there's been a bit of an accident. Yes, she does have messy hair . . . No, somebody fell into the river.'

There was a very long pause. Then he mentioned the name of a hospital and hung up.

'Your friend will meet you there,' he said to me. I nodded mutely, shivering uncontrollably.

By the riverside, the ambulancemen were letting down a stretcher on a kind of mountain climbers' apparatus. The scene was now attracting more of a crowd and the atmosphere felt like that before a football match. In my hysterical state, I still noticed one man with his video camera out, and bitterly hoped he choked on the £250 he'd get from one of those morbid TV shows if they managed to tape Addison being dragged from the river with fish eating his eyes.

At that thought, I choked, stumbled forward, and thought I was going to faint. Everything went fuzzy round the edges, and a small child dressed up as an ambulanceman rushed towards me and put a white hospital blanket round my shoulders.

'Are you the other person involved?' he asked me, and I nodded.

'Come over here and we'll make sure you're all right.' He half led, half dragged me over to the back of the ambulance, and sat me down.

'Did you fall down? Did you hit yourself? Did he hurt you?'

I shook my head. A policeman who'd been hanging about trying to make himself look useful hurried over.

'Good evening, miss,' he said, taking out his notebook.

'Excuse me,' said the baby ambulanceman, 'but I'm the paramedic and I'm checking to see if she's all right.'

'I think you'll find I've got to establish what exactly the situation is here first,' said the policeman pompously.

'As soon as I've ascertained the clinical priority,' said the paramedic, just as snootily. I got the impression these two knew each other.

The policeman held up his hands. 'Fine. But keep it quick.'

'It'll get the clinical time it deserves.'

'OK.' The policeman sighed and had a look at his watch. The paramedic turned his attention back to me.

'All right. Ehm . . . how are you feeling?'

'I'm fine. I didn't fall, or hurt myself or anything. I just . . . Where's Addison?'

I started crying again.

'OK, OK.' He paused, then glanced at the policeman again. 'Right – how many fingers am I holding up?'

'Four . . . where's Addison?' I sobbed.

'That's right. Now, does it hurt when I do this?'

He pinched me on the leg.

'Ow! Yes! Where's Addison?'

'Now can I have a word with her, please?' said the policeman.

The paramedic stood back a bit sulkily. 'I diagnose that she's suffering from severe shock,' he said. 'She ought to have some oxygen.'

'In a sec,' said the policeman, then he crouched down beside me.

'What's your name then?' he said, in a deeply patronizing way.

'Holly,' I stuttered. 'Where is he?'

'Hang on,' said the policeman, and went and checked over the wall, where three men were hauling up ropes.

'Well,' he said, returning. 'He's not dead.'

I collapsed into noisy sobs again.

'I thought I'd killed him.'

It's a measure of how very upset I was that I said this in front of a policeman.

'Oh yes?'

'No, no, I didn't . . . I went to kiss him and he fell over.'

The policeman and the paramedic looked at each other.

'You must be some kisser,' said the paramedic.

'Can I see him?' I sniffed.

'Ehm . . . actually, you should sit down for a bit,' said the paramedic. 'But we'll take you both in at the same time.'

'Yes, and give me your full name and address,' said the police-man hurriedly, presumably in case I had deliberately thrown Addison in the river, forgotten to run off, and was just about to hijack the ambulance.

So I sat there for what can't have been more than five minutes but felt like hours and hours. Amazingly, a woman came out of one of the nearby houses with a flask of tea and gave me a cup. I snottered at her in gratitude, and she didn't even ask intrusive questions – in fact, she simply waited until I'd finished, took the cup and disappeared again. That just made me snotter even more as the last act of kindness anyone would ever extend to me after they found out how I'd ruined Addison's life forever.

Suddenly there was a huge clatter and lots of shouting. I glanced up to see the stretcher coming over the wall. On it, out cold, was a very pale, very unconscious Addison, with a white collar round his neck like he had fleas.

'Oh my God,' I said. The baby paramedic ran back to me, to open the doors wide and guide the stretcher in.

'Get in,' he said to me, and I staggered back, with my hands at my mouth.

They pushed the stretcher in feet first. One policeman and two paramedics were screaming at Addison. At first I thought they were angry with him and couldn't figure out why; then an iron fist grabbed at my stomach again as I realized they were desperately trying to wake him up.

'What's his name?' one of them barked at me.

'Addison,' I said quietly.

'MR ADDISON! MR ADDISON! CAN YOU HEAR US?'

'It's Addison, not Mr Addison,' I murmured, but they weren't listening to me.

One of the paramedics was shining a torch into his eyes, and the other banged twice on the partition of the ambulance – where I was sitting – then we took off. At the other end of the van, the three men continued shouting at him. One, my baby paramedic,

179

was looking at his watch worriedly. He spoke into a radio hanging down from the side of the van.

'ETA eight minutes,' he said. 'I think it's a GCS three.'

'Is that bad?' I whimpered. He didn't reply. Pretty bad then. I hoped a three was out of, say, five and not a hundred.

I ached to reach over and wipe the duck shit off Addy's forehead, but I didn't dare. As if reading my mind, the baby paramedic leaned over and wiped it off with a piece of blanket.

'Poor bastard,' he said, and I didn't like his tone of voice.

'WAKE UP,' the other paramedic was shouting very loudly, slapping Addison round the face.

'WAKE UP FOR US NOW, SIR.'

I put my head in my hands. 'Wake up,' I whispered to myself. 'Wake up, Addison, wake up.' Then I reached out and rubbed the bottom of his trainers. 'Wake up. Wake up.'

The ambulance screeched to a halt, and I realized we were there. I expected an *ER*-style assault on the back of the ambulance, but thought I detected a certain lack of urgency in the paramedics and the nurses when they opened the back of the van.

'They think it's over,' I thought to myself. 'They think he's braindead. And it's over.'

I felt numb now. It was too real with him beside me to cry.

They pulled him out, and a chunky, bossy-looking girl with greasy hair came out. She was wearing a white coat with various things – books, papers, pens and weirdy medical equipment – protruding from it and forming a trail behind her, underneath which was an unironed shirt and a very unprepossessing pair of trousers. She went up to Addison and did that torch-in-his-eyes thing again then hastened him inside. She motioned to me, and I followed them.

The hospital was new and shiny and noisy, with shops and cafés. It was like an airport. People in uniform were marching about with serious looks on their faces, to show they were serious people doing a serious job. Addison disappeared into a thicket of them, laden

180

with tubes and beepy machines. People were shouting and children were crying. I felt extremely disorientated. The chunky girl came up to me.

'Name?' she barked, rudely.

'Holly Livingstone,' I choked.

'Not your name, *his* name.'

'Addison. Addison Farthing,' I said, glad that this woman seemed to be doing her best to make me feel even worse than I did already.

'Has he been drinking? Drugs?'

'No,' I said.

'It's better if you tell us, you know. It could make all the difference.'

I seriously wanted to hit her, but daren't, in case she authorized some kind of new experimental medicine and killed Addison with octopus radiation.

'He hasn't taken anything, I promise.'

She gave me a look, just in case I didn't know she thought I was lying, then asked me if I was his next of kin. When I told her I wasn't, and didn't have his mother's telephone number, she gave a loud and exaggerated sigh.

'Well, let's just hope he doesn't require an operation,' she said. I reflected that it was a good thing we were in a hospital casualty department, for when I hit her with a brick.

'HOLLY!'

Kate and Josh came hurtling up the corridor.

'Is he here? What *happened*?' They threw their arms around me, whilst the podgy doctor stood by, tapping her foot.

'Are any of you next of kin?'

Kate looked round.

'I've contacted his mother, and she's on her way, but she lives in Lewes.'

My insides shrivelled even further when I thought of trying to explain to his mother what I had done to the only person (I imagined) she had in the world.

'Do you know what blood group he is?' countered the doctor.

'A negative,' said Josh surprisingly.

We all stared at him. 'It's on a sheet he gave me when he moved in,' he said, shrugging his shoulders. 'I don't know why, do I? He's the same as me, and it's rare, that's why I remembered, OK? Oh . . .' His voice went quiet. '. . . And he's an organ donor.'

Jesus. This just got worse and worse. I glanced at the podgy doctor to see if she would say, 'Oh, that's not going to be necessary', but she simply raised her eyebrows and said grudgingly, 'If you want to wait you can sit over there –' indicating a row of uncomfortable plastic chairs. Behind us, they were taking Addison elsewhere.

'But what are you going to do?' I asked helplessly.

She looked at me. 'Well, do you want me to stand here and explain it to you, or do you want me to go and see what I can actually do for him?'

What I actually wanted was to kick her in the nuts, but I retreated, and the three of us sat down in the corner, huddled together, terrified.

They both stared at me when I told them how it had happened. I had hoped that they would say, 'Oh, that could happen to anyone – once, I tried to kiss so-and-so and they fell out of a third-storey window – but they didn't. They just stared at me.

'Well, don't worry, Holl,' said Josh eventually, squeezing my arm. 'It'll make a great story to tell your grandkids.'

'Yes, when they ask why Grandpa's dribbling and has to wear his pyjamas all the time and can't walk and has to be fed with a spoon,' I said, swallowing hard.

'He's young and healthy,' said Kate. 'I might go and phone my dad, see what the prognosis is. Do you know where he bumped himself?'

I shook my head. 'No. By the time I saw him he was on a stretcher. I didn't see a mark on his face though. Well, apart from some duck poo.'

'Are you sure it was duck poo and not coagulated blood?'

'Or brains,' said Josh. 'Sorry,' he said, when we both glared at him.

'No, it was poo,' I said. 'But I didn't see the back of his head.'

Kate nodded. 'I couldn't ask Dad without knowing, and Dr Hitler in there doesn't seem inclined to help us out.'

'She's a witch,' I said. 'I specifically asked for Dr Greene.'

'Yes, she wouldn't be allowed in *ER* with those rat-tails tied up in an elastic band, that's for sure,' said Josh comfortingly. 'And you'd think, being a doctor, she'd know how to get rid of blackheads.'

'It's not that easy when you're inside under electric lighting for one hundred hours a week saving lives, you know,' said Kate.

'You know what I say . . . you can always make time for grooming.'

'You know, Josh, I thought having sex would make you less like a girl, not more. Maybe you're a lesbian.'

'Stop it you two,' I said, and I must have looked completely downtrodden, because they did. We sat there in silence for an hour and a half, pausing only to choke down some revolting substance which might have been from a coffee machine or a nasty medicine dispenser they'd installed for handiness. Josh leafed through some ancient *Women's Weekly*s, while I just stared into space. The policeman hadn't been back to talk to me – maybe they were waiting to see whether Add woke up, to decide whether they pressed for GBH or murder. Oh God. How did I get myself into these things? *How*? Kate took my hand, and squeezed it every so often, and I was glad of it.

People came and went across the hall – lots of people with cuts, and things held to their eyes, and a lot of yelping children. Only one other ambulance came in, and they brought out a woman so old you could see right through her, breathing through an oxygen mask almost big enough to cover her whole head. She looked very frightened when they all started yelling at her. I shivered, feeling awful and fluey and morbid. Suddenly, to my amazement, Tash limped in with a huge bruise on her head and scratches all over her face, accompanied by one of the boys from the flower yard. I hid behind Kate.

'What is it?'

'Big bully,' I whispered, 'at eight o'clock.'

'I'll fuckin' kill 'er the next time!' Tash was saying. 'No one fuckin' punches me.'

'She might be top bitch now though, right, Tash,' said her gormless companion.

'No fuckin' way,' said Tash and started to cry. 'And you can fuck off as well,' she said to the young doctor who'd approached her. 'Being fuckin' top bitch – it's all I fuckin' have! I'm going to have to have a fuckin' baby now!'

My eyebrows were in my hairline.

'She seems all right,' said Kate. 'Kind of person we could do with on the dealing floor. Never say die. I wonder if she needs a job?'

After an hour and a half, a young male nurse came and got Josh and asked him if he would donate some blood. He leapt up immediately. Kate asked them for information, but the nurse shrugged and said they would have to wait for the next of kin.

'That means they want to turn off the machines!' I yelled dramatically.

'Don't be ridiculous,' said Kate. 'They don't ask for blood then turn off the machines. It sounds like they might be operating.'

'Oh God.' I put my head in my hands. 'Oh my God. It's all my fault.'

Just then, a tall and fine-featured woman walked in through the sliding doors. She was so distracted she seemed to be sleepwalking, and her sallow features were pale.

'That's her. That's his mum,' I said immediately, grabbing Kate's sleeve. 'Oh God. Hide me again. Ehm . . . I'm going to have to go home.'

The woman at the reception desk was even now pointing us out and calling over a nurse. They both approached us. Kate stood up, and hauled me up with her.

'Mrs Farthing?' she said. 'We're so sorry. They aren't telling us anything.'

184

'Oh, that boy. Always trouble,' she said, with a heavy Eastern European accent. She attempted a weak smile. 'Under other circumstances, I would be happy to meet . . . Are you Kate?'

Kate nodded.

'Ah, see, we have spoken so often on the phone.'

Kate nodded again and smiled.

'Thank you for phoning me today. To think we worried so much about him getting out . . . and he goes out and – pfuh!'

I let out a strangled sob. She turned to me. 'And you are . . . Holly, yes?'

'I'm so sorry!' I let out. 'I didn't mean to!'

'What?'

'Holly was there when it happened, Mrs Farthing. She feels responsible.'

'Ach no – the clumsiest of boys. I'm glad he went out with you. Can I see him now, please?' she said to the nurse.

'Follow me. You two can come as well, if you like.'

We followed her in, me feeling acutely ashamed of my emotional incontinence in the face of Addison's mother's obvious dignity.

Addison was in bed, hooked up to all sorts of machines, in that way they always have people in soap operas. Except in soap operas they're usually up and about twenty minutes later and never even smudge their lip gloss. Addison had two black eyes and his neck was supported by some weird contraption. One of his legs was in plaster. Half his head was shaved, and across it were three great black stitches still wet with blood. I could see his heart beating – slowly – on a screen.

'Can I speak to a doctor please?' said Addison's mother. 'Or can you help me?'

The young male nurse seemed nice. 'I'll just get her.' I winced, thinking: surely that witchy girl couldn't be chief doctor, could she? Surely she'd just passed him on to the grown ups? But my worst fears were confirmed when she huffed in, looking as if to say how dare Mrs Farthing inconvenience her in this way when she had so much doctoring to do, goddammit.

'Do you want these two to stay?' she said, indicating us.

'Yes, of course,' said Addison's mother, and I felt like saying, 'Ah ha ha ha!' – if of course it hadn't been wildly inappropriate.

'Right then.' She marched over and stood by Addison's head.

'Mr Farthing fell backwards on to shallow rocky ground. He broke one leg in two places, but more worrying is that he appears to have sustained some level of head injury. A CT scan indicates that there may have been some bleeding in the brain . . .'

Addison's mum stiffened, but motioned her to go on.

'. . . and he hasn't yet regained consciousness. This means, really, we can't tell when he's going to wake up, or even if.'

Addison's mum drew a very long breath.

'It could be hours, it could be days . . . or longer.'

'I understand.'

Beside me, Kate stifled a very small sob.

'Until he wakes up, we'll be unable to assess the extent of his other injuries. And that's it, I'm afraid. Please ask the nurse if you need anything. We'll be moving him upstairs to a more suitable ward – naturally, we need all the space we can get down here.'

And with that she turned on her cheap wide-fitting pump and disappeared.

We all stared at each other in silence.

'What does she mean, "other injuries"?' said Addison's mother. Then she realized. 'Oh my God . . . she meant brain damage, didn't she?' Her hand went to her mouth. 'Oh my God.'

She sank down next to Addison on the bed, who of course didn't stir, and cupped his head in her hand.

'I can't . . . this can't . . .'

Kate was at her side.

'Don't worry, Mrs Farthing . . . people come out of these things all the time. Haven't you seen *While You Were Sleeping*? He'll come round and he'll be fine. I'm sure of it. Look at him.'

We did. He seemed incredibly peaceful and very beautiful on the crisp white bed. 'There's nothing wrong with his enormous brain, is there?'

Mrs Farthing shrugged. 'You are very kind. But, please, could you leave us alone for a time?'

'Of course,' Kate said, and pushed me out of the cubicle. I was still numb, and stumbled backwards into the male nurse, who saw my stricken face.

'Listen, don't worry too much,' he said. 'Loads of people come out of stuff like this absolutely fine, OK? Come in a lot – even though you think he's unconscious, sometimes they respond to voices and music – it helps. And don't worry about the demon doc.' He leaned in towards us. 'She never gets any, you know.'

We smiled wanly. 'OK, they'll probably move him to Baker Ward, which is a high-dependency unit – not quite ICU, but he'll be cared for there. You can come and visit him at any time, so try and come as often as you can. Oh, and bring your blond friend too – he'd brighten up anyone's day.'

And with a camp wave he disappeared behind a curtain.

Josh was sitting in reception looking very wobbly and pale. We rushed over to him.

'Are you OK?' I asked. 'Did they take a lot of blood?'

Josh stared at us blankly. 'Oh, that?' he said. 'No, that was fine. But do you know what? That nurse just asked me out . . . and I said yes. I think I'm going to faint.'

I hadn't thought I'd be able to sleep that night – indeed, I felt almost guilty even going to bed, just because I was in a position to decide when to go to bed and Addison wasn't – but I was so worn out I fell asleep instantly.

When I woke up, however, that awful stone was back – you've just been chucked, and you have to explain this fact to all your friends without admitting you've been chucked or downright lying; or you've got to sit your driving test for the fourth time; or you got off with your best mate's bloke, or . . . God, there were a lot of bad mornings in my past, but this was definitely the worst. I lay on my back gazing at the ceiling. He was going to be all right. He had to be. I would turn Florence Nightingale and nurse him ceaselessly round the clock, and when he came to he would be so grateful we would . . . ehm, get married or something, I didn't know. Anyway, it would be deeply moving, and he would be fine, and everything would be all right. Yes. Fine. I leapt out of bed to start my ceaseless vigil, planning on pausing only long enough to fuel up on Coco Pops. However as soon as my feet hit the floor, I heard Kate bang the saucepan up and down the hall.

'House meeting!' she yelled. 'Everyone up!' I groaned and rolled back on to the bed. If this was about that bloody toothpaste of hers again, there was going to be serious trouble, I told Frank Sinatra the bear. I was in the middle of an enormous traumatic dramatic crisis and thus deserved special treatment at all times.

'HOLLY? Get up for fuck's sake!' There came the sound of a saucepan being pounded against the door of my coffin. I swore mightily, and padded into the kitchen.

Kate was sitting there with an enormous cafetiere of coffee, which was cheering, and an expression on her face which was not. Josh emerged, eyes still full of sleep, with his hair sticking up in all directions.

'Gosh, I was having the oddest dream . . .' He saw our faces.

'Oh,' he said. 'Bloody hell!' he said, and sat down.

'Right,' announced Kate. 'We have a situation on our hands.'

'We know that,' I pointed out to her, pouring myself a cup of coffee.

'I'm not sure that you do,' said Kate, holding up a sheaf of papers.

'What's that?'

'This is the most up-to-date information on comas available on the Internet. And it's not good news.'

Josh leaned across the table. 'Let's have a look.'

And we did have a look, but it was just lots and lots of meaningless charts and long words like 'cerebral venicular expansion' and 'collateral sprouting'.

'Hmm, yes, I see,' said Josh.

'What?' I said.

He shrugged. 'She's going to tell us anyway,' he said to me in an aside. 'So, you might as well pretend you already know.'

'Ah. Yes, Kate, I see too.'

'Do you think this is funny?'

'No.'

'I've been up all night, you know. I haven't slept. This is the second night in a row I haven't slept because of trouble you two have got us in.'

'I say, that's hardly fair,' said Josh. 'Trouble *Holly* has got us in.'

I tutted, but only out of habit.

'So leave my coffee alone and make yourself some of your usual instant sludge and let me show you our plan of attack.'

'Kate, what are you talking about?' I asked.

'Right –' she said, and brought out an enormous magnetic whiteboard and stuck it to the fridge – 'this is our plan of attack'.

Day One

Kate had written 'Day One' in big letters on the whiteboard on the fridge door.

'Here's the deal,' she said. 'Basically, if Addison's going to get out of this thing, he's going to have to do it pretty quickly. Any more than a week, and he's probably going to have brain damage. Any more than a month, and he's probably not going to make it.'

'What?' we both gasped at the same time.

'He's going to be OK,' I said. 'He is.'

'Calm down, Holl, that just means you're officially in denial,' said Kate. 'We'll deal with that too. Now, the following things have been shown to have some probable effect on wakening people from comas: (1) An aggressive course of physical treatment (2) Committed attempts at rehabilitation from family and friends. OK? Now, this has certain ramifications for us, but the most important is that time is absolutely of the essence. We have several things to do, and we need to do them quickly.'

'What kinds of things?'

'These kinds of things,' said Kate, wielding an impressively stolen-looking whiteboard pen.

'Talking, number one.'

'I can do that,' I said.

'For several hours a day, in rotation.'

189

'Still not a problem.'

'Holly, it's OK, I've got a rota.'

'I hate rotas,' I said sullenly.

'Two, Music. Josh, we'll be relying on you.'

'Uh huh.'

'Relying on Josh? What, you're going to raise Addison with *The Pirates of Penzance*?'

'Lots of people rate *The Pirates of Penzance*,' said Josh.

'Yes, if they want to *put* people into comas.'

'Holly! I have a schedule, OK?'

'I hate schedules.'

'Three: touching and massage.'

'Ooh, I'm there.'

'He'll need constant stimulation and feeling; it can aid recovery.'

'Not a problem.'

Kate turned over the whiteboard, and the back was divided up into hundreds of small sections with our names written in them in different colours to itemize the particular task we'd be undertaking.

'OK then,' she announced. 'Here it is.'

Josh and I examined it closely.

'You're not asking Chali in to do music?' I said.

'Why not?'

'You're right – she'll piss all over *The Pirates of Penzance*.'

'Hey,' said Josh. 'I don't see you volunteering to do your famous pissed karaoke version of "Back For Good".'

'Yes you do,' said Kate. 'There, in the yellow.'

My first shift was, in fact, that morning. Actually, I seemed to have all the daytime hours, apart from lunch-time shifts. I mean, not that Kate thought my job was unimportant or anything. Still, it *was* my fault. And more, I realized: I really did want to see him. I wanted to see him open his eyes. And it might happen any minute!

I remembered myself long enough to phone in to work. And of course, things started going wrong almost immediately.

'I can't come in. I'm sick.'

'How sick are you? Are you phoning from hospital?' said Mrs Bigelow.

'No,' I said, wearily. 'But I really can't come in.'

'When was the last time you vomited?'

'New Year.'

'Fine. Then you're going to have to come in, because there's no sign of Chali and I can't have two chronically unreliable staff.'

'But . . .'

'But nothing. I'll see you here, or you needn't bother coming in at all. Ever again.'

I considered taking her to an industrial tribunal, but depressedly picked up my bicycle instead. I could steal the biggest bouquet in the shop and take it to the hospital after work. Kate was livid about me messing up her schedule before we'd even got started, but realizing she didn't have a choice in the matter, grumpily started rubbing it out with a duster and humming over it.

'My God, I can't wait to come into work now to hear the latest instalment of your life,' said Chali, who'd turned up by the time I got there. 'It's like *Brookside*.'

'No, it's like *The World at War*,' I said grimly.

'What are you going to do? Will they send you to prison?'

'I don't think so. Unless they can make kissing a crime.'

'Ooh, that sounds like a good title for a song.'

'Yes, in 1985. And thank you for your sensitivity.'

'Well, what are you going to do? Now you've thrown him off a wall, I mean.'

I fixed my sights on the middle distance in an attempt to appear noble.

'I'm going to nurse him back to health,' I said. 'I am never going to leave his side. When ascribed by Kate.'

'Does she know you're missing the first day? He might have woken up this morning.'

'I know that. I hope he hasn't . . . I mean, NO, I hope he has,

191

but, you know, once I get out of here I am never going to leave his side. I have to talk to him, comfort him, and massage him.'

'Massage him?'

'Uh huh. Physical contact is very important.'

'What, so you're going to, like, pull him off while he's unconscious?'

I narrowed my eyes at her.

'Of course not. Piss off.'

'I'm sorry. I thought maybe . . .'

'No you didn't. Chali, it was over the line.'

'The catheter line . . .'

I sighed.

'Look, is being completely sick your only way of dealing with this?'

'Ehm, yes, I think it is.'

'OK. But can you keep it for your gunge crew and not inflict it on me?'

'Yes, you're right. We're a flower shop, not a vegetable shop.'

I put my head in my hands.

'Oh, just fuck off and leave me alone.'

She tugged at my elbow.

'Why don't you go early?' she said. 'I'll cash up.'

'You're not allowed to cash up.'

'I promise I won't filch a thing. Just for you. And the weird guy in hospital.'

'Addison's *not* weird.'

'He's been asleep for twenty-four hours! That's pretty weird!'

'Chali!' I hit her with a daffodil, but it was her way of being kind, so I filled the basket of my bicycle up with gardenias and little blue forget-me-nots and paddled along the horrible busy road to the hospital at four o'clock.

Addison's mother was still there, looking white and strained. She clearly hadn't slept. Baker Ward had none of the frantic anxiety of accident and emergency; it was quiet and sombre. Machines beeped and hummed, and unconscious people lay around. These were mostly older people, whose big bellies bulged under the

192

sheets, but there were a few younger ones – all men. I wondered why. Maybe they just had the habit of falling off things.

I resolved to ask Josh's cute young nurse friend if I saw him.

'Hello,' I said quietly to Addison's mum. I was more composed today, determined to cling to my dignity, show that, whatever may have happened, I was completely committed to her son and would prove myself worthy of his love. When he woke up. Which he would.

'Hello,' she said. 'You're Holly, aren't you?'

'Yes, I am.'

'Call me Magda.'

'Magda. Yes, all right.'

I felt completely stupid and at a loose end, especially after my waterworks of the previous day. It wasn't easy to come on as noble and dignified so soon after that. We looked at each other.

'Ehm . . . Magda. Can I get you anything? Aren't you absolutely exhausted?'

'No . . . but would you mind sitting with him for a bit? I've been here since six this morning, and I need to stretch my legs and get something to eat. Do you mind? I'll only be down the hall.'

'Of course not. Stay as long as you like.'

She stood up, her hand still on Addison's pale one. The family resemblance was very strong.

'He hasn't moved all day,' she said. 'I think it's the longest conversation we've ever had.' She smiled wryly. 'I'm used to one-sided conversations with my son.'

'I'm sure he knows you're here,' I said lamely, and took her place.

The bruises round Addison's eyes had faded, and he looked less ghastly and more asleep. I wanted to tickle him to wake him up.

'The nurse is over there,' she said, indicating the desk. 'But I wouldn't recommend talking to the doctor. She's not very helpful.'

'I know,' I said. 'Right. Thanks.'

And she was gone, and the two of us were alone.

I cleared my throat nervously. I was due to be talking today.

193

'Well!' I said, feeling completely idiotic. 'Hello, Addison. It's Holly here!'

Unsurprisingly, he didn't stir.

'And I just want you to know how very sorry I am about what happened down at the riverside. But we're going to have to put all that behind us and concentrate on getting you well again, then the next time we kiss it can be . . . down a coal mine or something. If you want to kiss me again. Which you probably won't. And of course you'd be quite within your rights to feel that way.'

Oh no. This was all going a bit downbeat. I tried desperately to think of some good news.

'So, anyway, Chali sends her love. You've never met, but I'm sure you'd get on. Well, OK, so not get on, as such, at all, but you know, she's a person I know and you're a person I know and, well, she sent her love. Though not, as such.'

This was proving harder than it looked. I remembered back to old documentaries about people in comas. Wasn't I supposed to put stereo headphones on him and play lots of Cliff Richard records? But hadn't I hurt the poor guy enough?

'Ehm . . . oooh, and the big news of the day is that Josh has been invited out by a bloke. And he said yes! Which, as you know, comes only two days after him sleeping with a woman. So that's pretty exciting for us – we might be able to categorize Josh once and for all. But he's a bit scared and stockpiling lots of Vaseline products –'

'Is that true?' said a bleached blond head sticking through the curtains. It was the male nurse.

'You can't be supposed to listen to people talking to coma victims!' I said, annoyed. 'Anyway, I thought you worked downstairs.'

'I do,' he said. 'I came to check on your friend here.'

'Uh huh?' I said suspiciously.

'And see if he had any visitors.'

'He does,' I said. 'Me.'

'So I see. Hi . . . I'm Stephen.'

'Hello, Stephen. I'm Holly.'

194

'Yes, I know all about you,' he said.

'Oh,' I said, feeling that horribly disconcerted way you do when you drank too much tequila at a party and spoke to someone for ages and they come up and say hello the next day and you can't remember who they are. 'Well . . .' I said.

'But never mind about that. Tell me more about that yummy flatmate of yours.'

He was the first person I'd met in the last twenty-four hours who didn't think I was evil, so I was perhaps more willing to confide in him than I might otherwise have been.

'Josh is very sweet and a bit undecided.'

'Really?' he pouted. 'I prefer it if they're straight.'

'Well, you know, he probably is. He slept with a girl just this week.'

'Huh.'

'But he did agree to go out with you, didn't he?'

Stephen smiled shyly.

'Don't take him anywhere scary,' I warned. 'He's very innocent. Don't take him anywhere he has to put on a harness, or dance around in his underpants.'

'I thought I'd take him to dinner,' said Stephen. 'Is that OK, or do you have to write him a note?'

I smiled. 'OK. How's Addison doing?'

'Is he your boyfriend?'

'Kind of.'

'He's cute.'

'Isn't he?' We looked at him for a bit.

'He's going to be OK, isn't he?'

'I'm sure of it,' said Stephen, getting up to go.

'IS HE HERE?' The curtain was pulled back with indecent haste, and the greasy doctor stormed in, rushing over to the bed and bending over Addison's head. 'STEPHEN, GET ME A SPATULA, STAT!'

'What? What is it?' I jumped up, horrified. The doc shot me a dirty look. 'Could you step outside for a second, please.'

'Why, what's the matter?'

Stephen returned, out of breath, with a small piece of plastic.

'I'm not leaving until you tell me what's the matter,' I shrieked.

'You can stay,' Stephen said, coming round behind the doctor, who shot him a dirty look too.

'OK,' she said, slapping on a pair of unsavoury plastic gloves. Slowly, she prised open one of Addison's eyes and shone a light into it.

'What's she doing?' I hissed to Stephen. He shrugged his shoulders. That did not instil a sense of confidence.

The doc turned to me. 'What's his refraction index?'

'Duh huh huh?' I dribbled. What was she talking about? What was going to happen if I didn't know?

'I can't see anything,' she said to Stephen, 'can you?' He leaned over.

'What are you looking for?'

'It says on his chart that he's extremely short-sighted. Dr Costello thinks he may still have his contact lenses in.'

She leaned back off the bed, slightly shame-facedly.

'I didn't . . . see them yesterday.'

I picked up Addison's glasses, which were lying by his bed.

'He wears these.'

'Right, right, of *course*, I knew that. Just checking. OK. Ehmm. All clear.'

She tore off the gloves dramatically, then disappeared.

'*What* was that?'

Stephen shrugged. 'If you forget to take out someone's contact lenses and they're unconscious for a long time, the eyes get oxygen starvation and they can, you know, rot.'

'*WHAT*?'

'But it's OK.'

'Dr Hitler tried to blind my boyfriend and you are telling me it's OK?'

'Hey, you know, she caught it.'

'He could have worms coming out of his eyes!'

'Ehm, don't forget he may be able to hear you.'

'Oh, for fuck's sake!'

196

I sat back down beside him.

'I have to go.'

'I know. I'll say hi to Josh for you.'

'Cheers.'

'Oh, Add,' I said, when he'd gone. I put my head on his shoulder. He smelled of starch, and hospital beds. 'It's not easy self-sacrificing myself for you, you know. What if they've forgotten something else? I'm not going to know what it is, am I?'

My fingers idly tapped out a rhythm on his.

'You know,' I said, 'this is worse than the time I went to meet that guy who I thought looked like Andrew Ridgeley and I tripped up at the railway station and nearly fell on the track and that guy caught me and I broke my big toe. Still, at least it was me that got hurt. And, you know, it's not fair if you have only just woken up to life and everything and you get it whisked from under you. And if that's the case and there is a God then he's a SKANKY OLD MAN.'

I said this last bit a little louder than I intended, because all of a sudden this rasping voice came: 'No I'm not!'

I jumped five feet, yelled, 'Fucking hell!' and looked all around, in case it was God.

'Is that God?'

'Yes,' rasped the voice. It appeared to be coming from somewhere to my left. I peered out from behind the curtain. In the next bed along was an old, old man who looked very sick indeed. He was hooked up to a ventilator. I went over to him.

'You're not God.'

'Close enough,' he wheezed. 'He's on his way.'

'Huh.' I pondered for a bit. 'You are a skanky old man though.'

'That's true. But on the inside, I'm divine.'

'Cool. A man said that to me once.'

He laughed, and it wasn't a pleasant sound.

'So, can you help my friend Addison?' I said eagerly. Any port in a storm.

'Unfortunately, I move in mysterious ways.'

'Is that a maybe?'

'Harrumph. Yes. It's a maybe. Now, could you put some whisky down my feeding tube?'

'I don't think that sounds very safe.'

'I'm God, you idiot. I'll be fine.'

'Mr McClockerty! Are you talking again?' Dr Hitler arrived out of nowhere. She eyed me with her standard look of suspicion tinted with hatred. 'Please don't speak to the other patients. It's not good for them.'

'She wasn't talking, nurse, she was praying.'

'I'm not a nurse, I'm a doctor. And it's time for your medicine. And you can have a big vein or a small vein – it's your choice.'

The old man sighed and lapsed into silence.

'I'll just get back to Addison,' I said, more crawlingly than I'd intended.

'You do that,' she said, in the same crawly tone of voice.

Inside the cubicle I sighed, and experimented to see whether I could actually sit on the bed, but there wasn't space and I was terrified of disrupting a tube, like in that *Airplane* film, so I settled for dragging over the low and uncomfortable hospital stool and leaning over it, resting my chin on the bed. And for want of anything better to talk about, I told Addison about the time I'd shared a flat with a so-called terrorist who'd decided to go on dirty protest.

Around seven thirty, Josh turned up, looking even more dapper than usual – I couldn't work out what it was until I realized he was wearing a cravat.

'Did I miss the waking up?' he said eagerly.

'No.'

'Great! I mean, oh.'

He came and stood by the bed and made as if to touch Addison, but didn't, of course, being English and male.

'No change then.'

'Not in him,' I said. 'You, however, appear to be wearing a cravat.'

'Ah. Yes. Well, you saw the schedule, didn't you?'

'Uh huh. I hate schedules.'

'Well, it's time for me to . . .'

It dawned on me . . .

'No.'

''Fraid so.'

'It might make him worse.'

He turned to me stiffly.

'Arthur Sullivan and the great W. S. Gilbert have never in the history of the world been known to make someone feel worse.'

'Now, Josh, you know that's not true. What about that production you were in of *HMS Pinafore* when that guy in the audience pretended to faint and got carried out on a stretcher and fell off the stretcher and twisted his knee?'

'He didn't pretend to faint.'

'He limped into Casualty screaming, "It was worth it to get me out of there!"'

'Well. Anyway. It was on the rota.'

I sighed. Josh cleared his throat.

'Sing it quietly at least,' I said. 'Dr Hitler will probably get your neck amputated if she hears you.'

'Well, music can soothe the savage brow.'

'Yes, *music* can,' I said, sitting down disgruntledly in the corner chair. 'Not whatever it is you do.'

In fact, Josh had an exceptionally pleasant baritone voice, but it didn't stop me sitting there making 'rumpety pumpety rumpety pumpety' noises in the background as he sang:

'I am the very model of a modern Major-General, / I've information vegetable, animal, and mineral, / I know the kings of England, and I quote the fights historical, / From Marathon to Waterloo, in order categorical; / I'm very well acquainted, too, with matters mathematical, / I understand equations, both the simple and quadratical, / About binomial theorem I'm teeming with a lot o' news, / With many cheerful facts about the square of the hypotenuse.'

'WITH MANY CHEERFUL FACTS ABOUT THE SQUARE OF THE HYPOTENUSE,' I groaned.

'Thank you,' said Josh. 'Do you think it's working?'

'I had hoped', I said, 'that he would have gotten up now, just to point out how many more facts he knows than you about the square of the hypotenuse.'

'This verse might help,' said Josh.

'I'm very good at integral and differential calculus; / I know the scientific names of beings animalculous: / In short, in matters vegetable, animal, and mineral, / I am the very model of a modern Major-General.'

'IN SHORT, IN MATTERS VEGETABLE, ANIMAL, AND MINERAL, HE IS THE VERY MODEL OF A MODERN MAJOR-GENERAL,' I hollered.

We both took a peek at Addison. It didn't seem to be working.

'That's God's music!' shouted a voice from the next bed. I stuck my head out of the curtains.

'That's not God's music! Hymns are God's music!'

'God's music is whatever I say it is,' hacked God. 'Which today means it's Gilbert & Sullivan. And Climie/Fisher.'

'You are truly a wrathful God,' I said.

'I know. Now, tell him to sing again before I turn you into a bush.'

Josh raised his eyebrows, but one of his uncles thinks he's the Duke of Wellington, so he's pretty used to it.

'Ehm . . .'

'I know our mythic history, King Arthur's and Sir Caradoc's; / I answer hard acrostics, I've a pretty taste for paradox, / I quote in elegiacs all the crimes of Heliogabalus, / In conics I can floor peculiarities parabolous; / I can tell undoubted Raphaels from Gerard Dows and Zoffanies, / I know the croaking chorus from the Frogs of Aristophanes! / Then I can hum a fugue of which I've heard the music's din afore, / And whistle all the airs from that infernal nonsense *Pinafore*.'

'This is *all* nonsense,' I grumbled. 'And how come you can remember this rubbish and not your pin number?'

'Look, Holl, I thought this would be the best thing for someone as brainy as Addison so I spent all day learning it, OK?' said Josh hotly.

'OK, OK, I'm sorry.' The nurses had come and joined us from the nurses' station and seemed to be enjoying it.

'I forgive you,' came the rasp from next door, joining me in,

'AND WHISTLE ALL THE AIRS FROM THAT INFERNAL NONSENSE *PINAFORE*.'

'Which is also good,' said God. 'I'm glad I made it.'

'Shh,' said one of the nurses. 'Let him finish.'

'Then I can write a washing bill in Babylonic cuneiform, / And tell you ev'ry detail of Caractacus's uniform: / In short, in matters vegetable, animal, and mineral, / I am the very model of a modern Major-General.'

'IN SHORT, IN MATTERS VEGETABLE, ANIMAL, AND MINERAL, HE IS THE VERY MODEL OF A MODERN MAJOR-GENERAL.'

Josh looked strained. 'I can't remember the final verse though.'

'OK, we'll do that last bit again.'

And Josh and I stood, and God raised an ageing hand, and the nurses joined in and we all chorused:

'IN SHORT, IN MATTERS VEGETABLE, ANIMAL AND MINERAL, HE IS THE VERY MODEL OF A MODERN MAJOR-GENERAL!!!!'

Josh gave a smart military bow.

'WHAT is going on in here?' screeched Dr Hitler, pounding up the ward. The nurses scattered like pigeons in the road, leaving us staring guiltily at the floor.

'Uhm . . . apparently music is good for helping . . . uhm . . . you know . . .' Josh was trying on his best Hugh Grant, but he didn't appear to be getting anywhere.

'Yes, through *headphones*. This is just plain disruptive. Was Mr McClockerty involved?'

'Ooh no . . . God – I mean, Mr McClockerty warned us against it.'

'She speaks the truth,' came the voice.

'But we did it anyway,' I concluded, shooting an evil glance next door, then concentrating on the floor.

'Oh, but, Doctor,' said Josh, gazing at her imploringly. He came up opposite her and took both her hands.

'Take a pair of sparkling eyes,' he started, very softly.

'Hidden, ever and anon, / In a merciful eclipse / Do not heed their mild surprise / Having passed this Rubicon, / Take a pair of rosy lips; / Take a figure trimly planned / Such as admiration whets / (Be particular in this); / Take a tender little hand, / Fringed with dainty fingerettes, / Press it – in parenthesis – /Ah! Take all these, you lucky man / Take and keep them, if you can!'

Amazingly, Dr Hitler started to giggle and blush. Maybe Josh was right about Gilbert and Sullivan after all. The nurses started to creep back out of their holes to watch the bizarre spectacle. Josh took a deep breath and went on:

'Take a pretty little cot / Quite a miniature affair / Hung about with trellised vine, / Furnish it upon the spot / With the treasures rich and rare / I've endeavoured to define. / Live to love and love to live / You will ripen at your ease, / Growing on the sunny side / Fate has nothing more to give. / You're a dainty man to please / If you are not satisfied. / Ah! Take my counsel, happy man; / Act upon it, if you can! / Act upon it, if you can!'

There was a round of applause. Dr Hitler coloured and looked away.

'That's as may be,' she said finally. 'But –'

'Doctor!' shouted one of the nurses at one of the far beds. 'Come over here! It's Grant! I think he's moving!'

Josh and I stared at each other as the entire ward staff threw itself to the other side of the room.

'Fucking hell!' we said in unison and raced over to have a look. A nineteen-year-old was lying on the bed, blinking in the daylight with an extremely confused expression.

'First motorbike,' said one of the nurses to us in a hushed voice. 'When they sell them to young guys they just put a long bit of elastic on the back so that when the boys fall off them five minutes later, they come right back to the garage.'

'Gosh, really?' said Josh, not concentrating. The curtain was swiftly drawn round, however, and we were forced back.

'I've done it again,' said God.

'Have you really?' I said. 'We reckon it was Josh's singing, and we just need to find the right song for Addison.'

'And anyway,' said Josh, 'why did you put him in here in the first place?'

'Mysterious –'

'– ways. Yes, we know.'

God stared at us wistfully.

'Do you know how you could best please God whilst the nurses aren't looking?'

'Sponge bath?' I said.

'The whisky's in the cabinet,' he said. 'Just pour it down this tube here. Not this one, or I'll choke to death on the stuff. What a way to go though.' He hacked strenuously at the idea.

'Nuh huh,' I said. 'I am in enough trouble already just on bed number four.'

He nodded.

'I know.'

'Yes, well, you're omniscient, aren't you?'

Addison's mother came back into the ward.

'I am sorry,' she said. 'I fell asleep in the doctors' canteen. It was so full of doctors sleeping.'

'Don't worry about it at all. Really, you know, he was no trouble.'

She looked at her son.

'I always wish he were more trouble.'

'I know what you mean.'

She sat down and cupped his head. 'You can go now,' she said quietly.

'We'll be back tomorrow,' I said.

She nodded, and we crept away.

Kate met us at the door as we trooped in.

'Well done, chaps,' she said. 'Did you sing?'

Josh nodded.

203

'We're pretty much on schedule then. And I made dinner.'

Josh and I glanced at each other suspiciously. There wasn't any smell of food. I wasn't allowed near a stove, but Kate was pretty much an unknown quantity. I suspected sliced raw green things. Bugger it.

'Here we go.'

In the kitchen was an enormous pile of boxes from Marks & Spencer. There was chicken in port wine, squash, confit, bananas and gravy, and pork in mustard, cumin, champagne and figs, as well as a box with julienne carrots in it, and a box full of mashed potatoes which had cost a couple of quid. Josh was practically speechless.

'Choose away.'

'Kate, this isn't food.'

'It better be; it cost me more than dinner at Bank.'

Josh picked up the various boxes as if they were active jellyfish.

'I don't think I can eat this.'

'But I went to so much trouble!'

'You went to Marks & Spencer!'

'That's trouble! Have you ever seen it at six thirty in the evening? I could have been killed!'

'OK, calm down,' I said. 'At least we're not eating through tubes.'

'I'd rather have this through a tube,' said Josh sullenly. 'At least it could bypass my taste buds.'

'Kate, I don't mind. I'll eat anything. Thanks for getting it.'

'Don't bother yourself,' she said huffily, and stormed out.

'See?' I said to Josh. 'As if today hasn't been hard enough. Don't upset Kate. That's my job.'

'I didn't mean to upset her,' he said, putting his apron on. 'I was only teasing.'

'You *know* Kate doesn't take teasing very well from you,' I scolded. He looked immediately penitent.

'Skates!' he hollered through the door. 'I need you to help me chop things. Come here immediately.'

Amazingly, she came back in, slightly red in the face.

Between them, they took all the pre-packaged rubbish, chopped it all up, liquidized it and turned it into a slightly odd but warming soup and pasta sauce, and we all sat down at the table at last.

'Sweetcorn in pasta sauce,' I said. 'Not been done enough.'

'Shh,' said Josh. 'Please don't remind Kate that this pasta sauce cost £30. But, hey, the boxes will come in handy.'

'What for?'

'I don't know . . . sledges for hamsters?'

'All right, you two,' said Kate. 'How was he? I assume no better or you'd have said, but we now have only six days, as far as I can see.'

We told her about the accidental waking of another patient, and her eyes lit up. 'So, it's obviously Josh's singing. We just need to find the right song.'

'Oh yes, well, that shouldn't be a problem. Six days to sing him every song in the world.'

'I know,' I said. 'Why don't we go in his room and dig up his record collection and sing that?'

'Nice one,' said Kate.

'Thank you.'

After dinner had been cleared away – and Kate overwhelmingly thanked to a nauseous degree – we crept into Addison's room. It was eerier than ever without him there. The computer seemed to be working away on its own, blinking and whirring. The screen was off.

'I don't know where he keeps his albums,' I said, looking around in dismay. If Kate hadn't been there I would have gone up to his bed and smelled it.

'Over there?' said Josh, pointing to a pile of CDs underneath his desk. He went over to pick them up, and stumbled slightly on a *Star Wars* figure. This made him grab on to Add's desk, where he accidentally touched the computer keyboard, causing the screensaver to go off.

Instantly, Josh and Kate screeched.

'Guys, guys . . . relax,' I said, as they backed away. 'Perhaps this would be a good time to introduce you to Addison's *other* girlfriend.'

Clutching each other, the two peered closer at the screen. As if in agitation, Claudia's huge head was spinning even faster today. Down the side she had typed 'WHERE ARE YOU?' in increasingly large and panicked fonts.

'CHRIST!' said Kate. 'I know he likes sci-fi, but that's ridiculous.'

Josh cottoned on slightly quicker.

'You were losing out to that?' he said, putting his arm round me.

'No!' I said. 'I was playing the long game.'

We stared at Claudia for a bit.

'Somebody's going to have to tell her,' observed Kate.

'Why?' I asked.

'I don't know . . . given that Addison is probably the only person she knows in the world and he's just deserted her . . . I mean, Holly, how much blood do you want on your hands?'

'For fuck's sake,' I said.

'Go on, Holl,' said Josh. 'You have to.'

Josh and Kate retreated – the yellow-bellied bastards – and tentatively, I sat down in front of the computer screen. The chair was far too high for me – my legs dangled off the floor. I felt Add's presence very strongly, and missed him even more.

'Hey,' I typed.

Instantly there was a flurry of text on the screen, mainly along the lines of where had I been, bastard? Oh, fantastic. So, not only was she horrible in my head, she might actually be horrible in person too.

'This isn't Addison,' I typed. The flurry stopped. Then, after a pause:

'Is this Holly?'

'Yes.'

'WHAT HAVE YOU DONE WITH ADDISON?'

Ah.

'Nothing,' I typed. 'He had an accident.'

206

'WHAT DID YOU DO TO HIM?'

'Nothing. He fell off a wall.'

'All by himself?'

'Not exactly.'

'You set about trying to steal my boyfriend then you throw him off a wall?'

I really wished people would stop saying that.

'Have you any idea what it is like to be me?' she typed.

Thankfully not. Being me was bad enough at the moment.

'I've been housebound for six years. I only eat what I can get delivered, which is why I'm the weight I am. I never look in a mirror, because I know what it's going to say. Both my parents are dead. I hate my job. Addison and *Star Trek* are the only friends I have. Did you know that?'

'No,' I typed, feeling hideously ashamed.

'No, you wouldn't even think about it, would you? I expect you thought Add would be pretty easy to steal away from me, didn't you? You didn't even think about his problems, about whether he was ready to go. You just thought: Horrible old Claudia, she'll be easy to . . .'

'Hey, one secnod,' I typed, too cross to spell. '(1) If you've never met someone they are NOT officially your boyfriend. OK? And (2) do you want to go on and on about yourself or do you want to know how he is?'

There was a long pause. I really wanted to find the button to stop the head spinning, but I couldn't.

Finally:

'How is he?'

'He's not good. He's in a coma, in fact.'

There was a long pause.

'I hate you.'

Strange as it may seem, no one had ever said that to my face before, not even my parents.

'You know, I didn't have to let you know, you know,' I typed anxiously. 'I could have completely ignored you.'

'I wish you had.'

'Well, at least you know that it's not because he didn't . . .' I
didn't want to say it, but I supposed I owed her that much '. . .
love you.'

The head stopped spinning, and she didn't type any more.

'How did it go?' asked Josh later.

'Oh, no problem at all. She was fine about it,' I replied.

Nine

I was making up a funeral wreath. This, at least, felt apt. I let out
a sigh as a tear dribbled down my nostril.

'I hope you're not making up family wreaths in company time,'
observed Mrs Bigelow in passing.

'What an unfeeling bitch,' said Chali loudly.

I was grateful to her for voicing my thoughts from the impunity
of being the boss's niece.

'. . . that Lassie really was,' she finished abruptly, as Mrs
Bigelow's eagle eye found her. 'Nice wreath for Mr Collins, by
the way.'

'Thanks,' I said. 'I hope his family like it, although of course I
have never met any of them.'

Mrs Bigelow gave her traditional sniff and went off on one of her
mysterious expeditions. Chali and I kicked back immediately.

'Still not much change then?' said Chali, pouring tea. I told her
about Josh's near miss with the Savoy song book. Her eyes lit up.

'Hey, you know, we could do that!'

'What?'

'I'll get the band in. We could come and play. Maybe get the
local papers down – *London Tonight* something like that.'

'*London Tonight* aren't going to want to cover your band!'

208

'Are you joking? They'd cover the St Winifred's School Choir if it filled up some between space. Oh, this is a fantastic idea.'

'Chali, you know, I really appreciate the offer, but I just don't think the hospital is going to want long sessions of anti-establishment art wank – I mean, rock. I mean, what if you tried to plug the amp in and pulled out someone's life-support system?'

'Pleeeasse. And anyway, I'm not with that band any more. My new band is going to be much more acoustic.'

'Oh yes? Like what?'

'Like . . . the most acoustic thrash-metal band you've ever seen.'

'Chali, this is a terrible idea.'

'Gutters!'

From the tiny back room, a filthy little blond-dreadlocked chap appeared. I hadn't noticed him when I'd come in; only, it became obvious, because he was covered in so much soil.

'I need you to go and get Mr Spangle.'

'*Who's* Mr Spangle?'

'Oh, he's Mr Big for this new band.'

'Mr Big Spangle? What's the name of the band?'

'Mr Big and the Spangles.'

'Chali, thank you so much for your kind offer, but I don't think the hospital's going to . . .'

'Only trying to help.' She shrugged, and turned her back on me.

'Hugnerh hugnerheh?' said Gutters.

'No, she doesn't want to help her boyfriend.'

'Huignerf heg a *hay*?'

'No, I don't understand it either.'

Gutters shot me a look of disdain – which was rich, coming from someone who had a filthy half-smoked roach dangling in their hair at nine thirty in the morning. I sighed.

'OK. Fine. You speak to Mr Big and I'll get Josh to speak to Stephen.' Josh's date was coming up. He was looking paler every day, but seemed to have braced himself, so to speak.

'Hey!' yelled Chali. 'World domination at last.'

'Yes – so many bands get started in the high-dependency unit of St Hugh's.'

'Well, there was . . .'

We thought for a while.

'Dr Hook?' I asked.

'The Cardiacs,' said Chali decisively.

'You're right.'

'Well, book us then.'

There was a crowd of people around Addison's bed. I broke into a run immediately. Stephen grabbed my elbow before I got there.

'Don't worry,' he said.

'What are they doing, giving him the last rites?'

'No, nothing like that. Candice Piper is here.'

'Who?'

'You know – haven't you seen *Emergency Pets in Danger*?'

'No!'

'You must have – it's that game show where they take a pet who's been ill and put them in a situation that requires the attention of the emergency services. For every minute the pet stays out of trouble, the owners double their money. It's brilliant – *everyone* watches it.'

'Not me.'

'Huh. Anyway, she's the presenter.'

'What's she doing here? Addison hasn't got any pets. Well, he's got an American pot-bellied pig.'

'She's come to talk to coma patients. It's for their Christmas special.'

'But it's June!'

'Yes, it gives them time to film someone waking up after Candice has spoken to them.'

'Bleagh! Bleagh bleagh bleagh!'

'It's good publicity for the hospital.'

'Hospitals don't need publicity! If no one came, that would be a good thing!'

'Well, anyway, that's what's going on. I'm just up to report back to the girls downstairs. They want to know what Candice is wearing.'

'Is that her? The one in fuchsia?'

'I know – divine, isn't it? See ya, darling – oh, see if you can't get into the shot. And, if you can, ask her which moisturizer she uses.'

Candice was wearing skin-tight fuchsia just in case anyone within a forty-mile radius hadn't immediately recognized her. She had an enormous blonde head and a minuscule, stick-like body – in fact, it was lucky she wasn't wearing black and white, or you could have taken her for a Belisha beacon. She had so much make-up on she looked like she'd been airbrushed, and a low husky voice that sounded too big for her frame.

I wandered slowly up to the group. Magda, Addison's mother, was standing off to one side with a pale and worried expression. Kate was next to her – I'd forgotten it was Kate's night on the rota.

'What are you doing here?' she hissed at me when I sidled up.

'What do you mean, what am I doing here? I'm always here.'

'Well, tonight's your night for cooking and learning "Please Release Me" on the recorder.'

'But of course I'm going to see Addison! What do you think I'm doing here – showing off?'

Kate stared pointedly at the TV cameras and shrugged.

'Oh, for fuck's sake!'

I was furious. Kate really did think I was showing off. Candice didn't seem too thrilled either. She was trying to have a conversation with Dr Hitler.

'Can't we just close his mouth? It would make him seem more asleep, more attractive.'

'As his breathing tube is currently keeping him alive, I'm going to have to say no. We're trying to make him better, not encourage anyone to adopt him,' said Dr Hitler.

'Just for a second or two, while we get the shots . . . ? You know, like in America, where they just have those two little tubes going up the nostrils? That doesn't look bad at all.'

'No!'

'Go, Doctor Hitler!' I muttered under my breath.

'Well, I'm going to have to phone the producer,' said Candice, bringing out her mobile phone.

'I'll have that, thank you,' said the doctor, and whipped it off her. 'It interferes with machines.'

Candice's face was a picture.

'God, you'd think you lot were doing us a favour, letting cameras in here. Roger, get me a tall skinny latte, *pronto*.'

She walked round to the side of the bed we were on.

'Who are you?' she demanded brusquely.

'We're his flatmates,' said Kate before I could say anything.

'And I'm his girlfriend,' I added quickly.

She looked me up and down. 'Really?'

I brushed a leaf off my dress. 'Yes,' I said defiantly. Kate was glaring at me.

'Hmm. Lacking a bit in the personality stakes, is he? You know – Superbore?'

Now it was Magda's turn to look furious.

'No!' I said. 'And what are you doing here anyway?'

'Well . . . the show's called *Coma Alone*, and it's going out at Christmas. The idea is that I go and visit coma patients, and we really impart to the viewer what a very . . .'

'Lonely?'

'Lonely, that's right. What a lonely position it is to be in. Especially at Christmas.'

'But Addison's not alone!'

'Of course he isn't.'

'And I don't think he'd notice if it were Christmas,' murmured Kate.

'Right. OK, I *see*. Now, would you mind just getting out of the way while we film?'

Without waiting for an answer, Candice started clipping on a microphone, and a woman ran forward and began patting at her immaculate, robot-like hairdo.

'Roger? Yes, OK, start it rolling, thank you.'

That, as we found out, meant: Roger, forcibly push everyone out of the way and tell them to be quiet in a very loud voice designed to show that working in TV is a VERY IMPORTANT THING.

We moved back and stood in the corner.

'I had no idea this was happening, you know,' I said to Kate. 'I just wanted to see him.'

'Here at St Hugh's,' Candice started, 'lie the near corpse-like bodies of the unloved, the nearly dead and the unwanted at Christmas time.'

'Well, why are you so pally with Stephen all of a sudden?'

'With who?'

'That nurse. Josh's boyfriend.'

Candice moved round, the camera still on her, and sat on the bed, picking up Addison's hand.

'Like beautiful statues they lie here, almost asleep, were it not for the many tubes coming out of their mouths.'

'I wasn't asked to be a beautiful statue,' grumbled a voice behind me. I peered backwards. It was God.

'Hey – you got Michelangelo and Leonardo da Vinci and he got Candice Piper – you're winning, OK?'

'OK.'

'He isn't Josh's boyfriend,' I said to Kate.

'Well, he's about to be.'

'So what?'

'So what? So why is Josh Mr Popular all of a sudden?'

'Don't you think he deserves it? He's had a long enough dry spell. You've been edgy ever since he met that backing singer.'

'Edgy, who's edgy?'

'Who cares for these, these modern-day zombies? Well, today here with us we have Doctor Flowers, who has dedicated her life to the relief of those who can't even say thank you.'

Dr *Flowers*?

Candice smiled tenderly at the camera. I growled under my breath. 'Cut!' said Roger. 'That was great, darling.'

She dropped Addison's hand like a snake and jumped down off the bed.

'You've just got to keep a professional attitude, that's what I say. Now, where's that bloody doctor? And for God's sake, Make-up, can't you at least get her to comb her hair?'

'I'm here,' said Dr Hitler – or Dr Flowers, as I supposed I should call her. She was flushed red. For the first time ever I felt sorry for her.

'And I happen to think that what I do for a living is a *little* bit more important than make-up, don't you?'

Maybe I didn't.

'Suit yourself, dear,' said Candice. 'For some of us it's professional pride, for others it's . . .'

'. . . being too busy saving lives?'

They stood round the side of Addison's bed glowering at each other. The big light went on again and Candice broke into an enormous glowing white grin.

'So, Dr Flowers, thank you *so* much for having us here.'

'Always a pleasure, Candice. Thanks for coming in. Anything you can do to help these kiddies will be great for St Hugh's.'

'Well, we'll certainly try, Doc! So, anyway, what can you tell me about . . .' She indicated Addison.

'This young man. Well. Yes. I'm afraid he's an object lesson to people planning on standing on high walls over hard things like stones – don't do it!'

'Right. And, you know, if there are kids watching at home, what would be your advice to them if they're thinking about climbing on high walls?'

'Ehm . . . don't do it!'

'Right. Or you *could* end up like him.'

'Hey!' I said.

'Cut! Who the fuck was that?'

'Just . . . you know, don't treat my boyfriend like a piece of meat, OK?'

'That's how I treat all my boyfriends. Ha ha ha!' laughed Candice.

Roger came over and nudged her, and they had a quiet discussion for a second. Then Roger beckoned me over. I dragged my feet – if they were going to chuck me out, it wasn't happening without a sulk – but he sat me down with his best 'I may have an important job in TV but that doesn't mean I don't care' face on.

'You know, we're all terribly upset about your boyfriend.'

I glanced over. Candice was signing autographs for several of the nursing staff, and giggling.

'Yeh? What's his name?'

'Look, obviously you're upset. What Candice thought was that perhaps we could take you aside when we film the next bit and interview you about . . . how emotional it is for you, your long lonely vigil at the bedside of your beloved, that kind of thing.'

'We've only been here three days.'

'Yeh, well, whatever. We think it could really add something to the piece.'

A thought occurred to me.

'Well, there was something we were thinking of doing that could really help . . .'

And I told him about Chali's band.

'Hmm,' he said. 'Hmm, ya. Maybe we could have it as the finale . . . can they do something really sad? Do you think they know "O Little Town of Bethlehem"?'

'Probably not.'

He called Candice over and explained the idea. Candice looked me up and down again, as if unable to believe that a thought or fully formed sentence could have come out of my mouth.

'What are the band called?'

'Mr Big and the Spangles.'

'Oh yes, I've heard of them.'

I was surprised at this, but I found out later that Candice had to pretend to have heard of everyone, in case they were incredibly cool and she looked like she was missing out.

'So, they'll be all right then?'

'Yeh, sure, that'll be fine. Jazz up this piece of crap anyway. Oh, sorry.'

'Don't mention it.'

Really, it was going to be worth it just to see Dr Hitler's face.

'What was all that all about?' hissed Kate.

'Oh, yeh, we were talking about you and Josh.'

'*Really?*'

'No!'

Candice went through her piece to camera twice more, then the entourage moved off to paediatrics.

'Have you got any undersized children?' she was saying as they left. 'Maybe we can poke them a little, get them to move about a bit.'

Dr Hitler stalked past us and slammed the ward door behind them.

'I hope I'm not going to have to ban *all* visitors,' she said, brusquely changing Addison's drip.

We stared at her in horror.

'You couldn't do that!'

'Really, am I the only one thinking of the *patients* around here?'

We left Magda crooning a Croatian lullaby to Addison. We figured he'd probably have had enough excitement for one night.

Josh was at home steaming vegetables.

'Are you trying to lose weight?' asked Kate accusingly.

He blinked at her.

'Maybe just a bit. Why?'

'No reason,' said Kate miserably, and went off on her own.

'She must really be missing that John guy,' mused Josh.

'Everyone's missing somebody,' I said pointedly, and toyed with a wet string bean. And ached for my own wet string bean.

'Who do I have to sleep with?' asked Chali excitedly.

'No one!'

'You asked for a gig and got it, just like that?'

'Yup. And they need me – I'm like, grieving widow.'

'You did tell them what kind of a band we are?'

'What kind of a band are you? They want you to do "O Little Town of Bethlehem".'

'We can do "Little Girls Dead in the Park".'

'Oh God. Maybe this wasn't a good idea after all.'

Chali grabbed me. 'And there's going to be TV people there and everything?'

'Lights, cameras, make-up people – it could be your big break!'

'And I don't even . . . I mean, surely somebody wants a blow job?'

'Somebody always wants a blow job,' I said, to the consternation of the man picking the largest, tackiest bunch of red roses we had out of their bucket. 'I mean, just look at him.'

'I think that's a "brown wings" bunch of roses,' said Chali. 'It's the biggest one in the shop.'

'I wouldn't like to be his girlfriend tonight.'

'Oh no. Sore.'

The man hastily paid for his purchase and scampered off.

'You're not really a filthy heavy metal band are you?'

'Oh yes we are. I don't suppose they'll want to hear "I Wish I Could Die Every Day"?'

'Ehmm . . . what about "I Wish It Could Be Christmas Every Day"?'

'This could be tricky.' Chali nodded her head. 'I'm going to have to give this some serious thought.'

'OK, well, they're shooting next Monday, so be ready.'

'Huh! Even the roadies know me as "ever ready".'

'Especially the roadies, surely?'

I was amazed by how quickly my life had fallen into a routine. I got up, I went to work, I slacked off, then I went and sat with Addison for as long as I could. That was it. Plus occasional refereeing between Kate and Josh. It terrified me to think that this could go on for years. At what point, say the worst came to the worst, would I feel obliged to pack it in? Would I end up like Miss Havisham, doing the same thing every day, waiting for a kiss that was never going to come? Watching his beautiful face grow sunken from lack of use? Or worse, even – I pictured myself looking stoic but noble, as, with trembling hand and swelling choir, the machines were slowly switched off . . .

Two days after the attractive television incident, after daily hours of reading, talking and humming occasionally, I went in one rainy afternoon, shaking my head like a dog as I stomped up the stairs, through the familiar antiseptic-and-poor-people hospital fug. Patients cluttered around the doors, still smoking cigarettes with their drips in. Everyone looked as grey and worn as an old bra strap, including, I supposed, me. My grooming standards, never tip-top at the best of times, were gradually deteriorating. Putting on make-up felt like a betrayal.

As I paused at the door, Stephen crept up behind me and tapped me on the shoulder. In my reverie – I was standing at the graveside looking elegant, I think – I wasn't paying attention and jumped six feet in the air.

'WHAT?'

Stephen looked hurt.

'Nothing. I just wanted to ask you what you thought of my new streaks.'

The top of his hair had gone a tacky, eighties-style blond, which didn't fit in well with his black spiky style.

'Club Tropicana?' I asked. He nodded. 'Are you going in for the super-gay awards?'

He smiled modestly. 'Are they really that good?'

'You're hyped up about this date, aren't you?'

'No.'

'Go on, admit it.'

He shrugged. 'Well, it makes a change from preaching to the converted.'

'OK . . . good luck.'

'Do you think I'm going to need it?'

'Stephen, I have known Josh for ten years . . . and I have no idea.'

'Oh well, it'll be a shoo-in, then. It's the really hetty bastards you have to watch out for.'

'Oh,' he added almost as an afterthought, 'and there's a new visitor today.'

'No, that's me – I just forgot to wash my hair,' I said.

'Behind the curtain. Definitely a fully signed-up member of the dweeb-o-rama brigade.'

Oh my God. It dawned on me instantly who the visitor had to be – let's face it, Addison's wide circle of friends had already been more or less exhausted. I winced when I thought of the alacrity with which I'd chucked Finn out on his ear when confronted with Add in the hallway – it seemed so long ago.

I peeked tentatively round the curtain of Addison's bed.

Finn was sitting on the bed, his corduroy trousers hitched up, his satchel on the floor, facing Addison, who looked as dead as he usually did. Finn was concentrating hard on something balanced on the sheet between them.

'OK, right, knight to knight's rook four,' he was saying. I realized he'd set up a chessboard between them. He stared at it for a long time.

'Oh, good move, Add.'

I moved closer, and inadvertently tripped on a trolley containing various dodgy stainless steel things that extracted Addison's poo or something. At least they were clean.

'Shite!'

Finn jumped up, upending the chessboard and scattering pieces everywhere.

'Jesus!'

We stood staring at each other, surrounded by detritus. The curtain was whipped back by Dr Hitler.

'What the hell is going on in here?'

Finn and I looked shamefacedly at each other.

'Oh. You,' she said to me. 'Do you actually *want* him to get better?'

'I thought the loud noise might . . . wake him up?' I said pathetically.

'Been reading up on the clinical trials, have we?'

'No . . .'

'I'm sorry, Doctor . . . it won't happen again,' said Finn.

'Oh? Who the hell are you?'

'I'm Dr Feynman Levy,' he said, proffering a hand.

'Oh . . . right,' she said, clearly disconcerted. She pushed back her thick hair and grinned at him almost coyly. 'I'm sorry . . . I didn't realize there was work going on.'

What *was* this magic effect Finn had on weird scientist girlies?

'Is she bothering you?'

What? I shot her a dirty look. Finn laughed.

'Yes, actually, she bugs the hell out of me. But I'm sure it would be OK if she stayed.'

'Well, thank you very much, Mr Cat Doctor,' I said when she'd gone, casting Finn a backwards glance that implied she'd quite like to square the root on *his* hypotenuse.

'I'm not a cat doctor.'

'Cats . . . wool . . . whatever it is.'

'String.'

'Huh.'

'Well, I got rid of her, didn't I?'

'I suppose so.'

'Next time I'm sending locusts,' came the voice from the next bed. I popped my head out.

'Hello, God.'

Finn popped his head out too.

'Are you God?'

God did his best to appear modest.

'Well, you know . . .'

'Huh. I don't believe in you,' Finn said.

'Really? Most people, a place like this – they at least make an odds-on bet.'

Finn nodded. 'I see your point. Well, very nice to meet you. Ehm . . . would you mind telling me how the universe works?'

'Worth a shot,' he said to me quietly.

'Anything's better than that spaghetti thing you believe in,' I said.

'*String*.'

'Hmm,' said God. 'Really, you wouldn't like it if you knew.'

'Trust me – I'm a physicist.'

God contemplated it for a bit.

'Well, you know, to demonstrate it properly I'll need a bottle of whisky.'

Finn glanced at me, and I shook my head fiercely.

'I don't think . . .'

'Ach, you physicists – all the same. You think you want to know, but you don't really – it'd put you out of a job.'

And He immediately fell asleep, snoring loudly.

Finn smiled at me.

'Well . . . hello again.'

'Hello,' I said shyly. 'Ehm, I'm sorry I didn't . . .'

He shushed me. 'Not at all. I didn't realize . . . until Kate told me.'

We looked at Addison.

'It's very sad,' said Finn.

'Kate thinks she's got it worked out,' I said. 'Lots of singing and stuff.'

'I hope so.'

I moved round to the other side of the bed and picked up one of Addison's hands, trying to warm it. Finn started crawling around, picking up chess pieces and metal implements.

'Can you give us a song?' I asked.

'Absolutely not. Really, I've got a note from my mother.'

'What were you doing when I came in?'

He held up the board. 'Well, there's this game, you see, which was invented in the Middle East . . .'

'No, I know that much, you pillock. I mean, why?'

He shrugged. 'Well, I can't sing, so . . .'

'Do you think it's helping?'

'I can't tell . . . Still, he was winning.'

221

I picked up one of the pieces. 'How do you play this anyway?'

'You don't know how to play *chess*?'

'No, and I didn't buy my teacher a Christmas present either. Or hang around the computer lab at break-time.'

He looked embarrassed. 'Yeah, like I really missed out on learning how to smoke cigarettes.'

'Oh my God – I know what you are! You're a Teacher Pleaser! Teacher Pleaser!'

He hit me with a castley thing. 'Thank you for adding another five years on to my therapy bill. Now, do you want to learn or not?'

'OK,' I said, sitting down. 'Did it upset you that you were too well behaved to get detention, when it would have meant more school, which you would have loved?'

He ignored me. 'OK. This is a prawn. This is a bish. And these are horsies. Horsies can jump.'

I eyed him suspiciously.

'What do the bishes do then? Swing both ways?'

'Yes, in a manner of speaking.'

So I sat next to him on the bed, and he taught me to play chess. Despite desperately doing his best to lose, it was physically impossible. I blamed all my moves on Addison and said he was psychically guiding me, but unfortunately not quite enough to save my queen from suicide missions.

After the third game, when I had taken to making all my lost pieces have little biting fights with each other, he said, 'So . . .' in that way that means, 'OK, enough fun and games young lady.'

'So . . .' I said. He looked at me, imploring me in a boyish way to, you know, talk about things and that, being the girl and everything.

'So . . .' I said. He glanced at Addison lying in the bed.

'I suppose I should be glad that it was him and not me.'

'What?!!'

Finn cringed. 'I'm sorry. I was trying to . . . you know . . . introduce the . . . Forget it.'

'That was well out of order.'

He hung his head even lower.

'I can't believe I even . . .'

'I think at least a hundred, possibly two.'

He glanced up. 'What?'

'Lines.'

Finn looked relieved.

'You know, I really really do hope he gets better, and that it works out fine for you.'

'He will,' I said fiercely, grasping Addison's hand. 'He has to. Otherwise . . . I'm going to set fire to the Houses of Parliament or something.'

'I know,' said Finn, and smiled his shy scruffy smile at me.

'God! I mean, we would never have got together, would we?'

'I don't know what you mean,' I said, crossly.

'Well, we're just so . . . chalk and cheese.'

I shrugged. 'Why, because you're such a big swot?'

'Maybe.'

I smiled at him.

'Are you seeing Madeleine?'

He shrugged. 'Now and again. She's finishing her PhD in cellular mitosis.'

'Wow. I can see how attractive that might be.'

I held out my clenched fists.

'Pick a prawn.'

'You can't wear pink! Are you crazy? That'd be like, if it was me going on a first date, wearing stockings and suspenders that you could see and a big T-shirt saying "Take me now".'

Kate and Josh both stared at me.

'. . . And that only happened the once. Josh, put the shirt away and go and put your grey top on.'

Kate sighed. 'Look, do you think you two girlies could get ready next door? Some of us have got *work* to do.'

'Ooh, bitchy,' said Josh. Then, to me: 'Oh my God, it's started!'

I smacked Josh on the head and dragged him into the living room to put some eyeliner on him.

'What did you do that for?'

'I don't know . . . practice?'

'I mean, why be nasty to Kate?'

'What? She's been super-nasty to me all week!'

'And it never occurred to you why that might be the case?'

'What do you mean?'

'Well, don't you think she started being particularly nasty to you when a certain someone started going out on dates . . . ?'

I waited for the penny to drop. One, two, three . . . ooh, there it was.

Josh's face was stricken.

'Oh my God.'

'Uh huh,' I said smugly.

'No wonder she's . . .'

'Yup.'

'But Stephen is *never* going to want to go out with her.'

I squeezed his shoulder. 'Please,' I said, 'just go.'

'What? What did I say?'

'Nothing. Now. Off you go. Have a wonderful time. Worry not.'

He paused.

'I am a bit worried, you know.'

'That's a healthy response.'

'Tell Skates I didn't mean it.'

'I will.'

'And tell my parents I love them.'

'Josh, you are *not* going on a date with Dennis Nilsen.'

'I know. But if I come back different then I just wanted to be . . .'

'You will never be different, J.'

'Fine. Good. Right. OK, bye then.'

'I mean, you walk funny now.'

'Piss off!'

He wiggled out the door.

* * *

Kate was sitting at the kitchen table, disconsolately pushing her computer mouse around.

'Don't tell me . . . you're playing patience as a displacement activity?'

She smiled wanly.

'So my therapist tells me.'

I sat down next to her.

'What else does your therapist tell you?'

'Well . . .'

'Go on, tell me. I've always been fascinated.'

'Yeah, you know, nosiness isn't always a good thing.'

'You're pointing that out to me? Or is that a piece of therapist wisdom? Either way, it's far too late.'

Kate sighed. 'What does my therapist tell me . . . ? Well, basically, I pay her eighty pounds an hour and she tells me that everyone is a bastard except me. Or rather, she agrees with me that everyone is a bastard except me.'

'You're joking!'

'Not at all. That's pretty much it. I go in and tell her who's being horrid and she agrees and says it's not my fault I'm so sensitive. Everyone. In the world. A cunt. Except me.'

'Wow,' I said. 'Actually, I can see why that might be appealing.'

'It's not designed to be appealing. It's the world of big business.'

'Are you sure you haven't just been watching too many films from the eighties?'

'Did you come in for a reason?'

'Yes. Message from Josh.'

Kate glanced up, momentarily startled.

'He didn't mean what he said.'

'That's it? That's the message?'

'Yup.'

'Bastard.'

225

'He's not one, though, is he?'

She looked at me sharply.

'What do you mean?'

'That's where your therapist runs into trouble. Josh doesn't have a bastard bone in his body.'

'So?'

'So, well, you know . . .'

Kate grabbed hold of a wine bottle which seemed to have just materialized.

'So, he's gay. OK, so it doesn't matter. All right?'

'He's not gay,' I said. I checked my watch. 'Well, not yet.'

Kate poured herself a large glass of wine but neglected to ask me if I wanted one.

'All this time. All this time, you know? "Everyone's a bastard, Kate. They're all bastards except us. The bigger the bastard you can find, the better you're doing."'

She contemplated her wine glass and sniffed loudly.

'Then I meet . . . then I *realize* that there is one guy in my life who is not a bastard, and what happens?'

'He goes out to find out what it's like to have other men touch him on the bottom?'

'Well, *exactly*!!'

I annexed some of the wine.

'Whatever happened to John then?'

'Nothing happened. I just realized that he was yet another in a long line of penis heads and that, you know, the person I really liked was . . . on my own doorstep.'

I squinted at her.

'And?'

'OK, so, and, I ran into John – or should I say *Arnold* –'

'I knew it!'

'– and his poxy wife at a bankers' conference. But that's got nothing to do with it.'

'OK,' I said, holding my fingers up in the air. 'Hold on a second. Exhibit one: you have never moved out of this house, despite having more money than Stella McCartney makes in a year during which people want to eat food, listen to music and wear clothes all at the same time. Exhibit two: Josh has started having sex. Exhibit three: you have stopped having sex altogether. Exhibit four: when *do* you turn thirty, exactly?'

She looked at me crossly. 'In eleven months and eight days, although I don't see why that's got anything to do with it.'

'Ha! I'm a genius,' I said. 'QED. You'll probably be married in a year.'

Kate sat back in her chair, staring into space. 'But . . . even if, I mean . . . I mean, how do you know he even likes me?'

'Kate,' I said, trying not to sound patronizing and failing – I even patted her on the hand – 'what's not to like about you?'

Ten

'It's not that I *want* children necessarily . . .' Kate and I were sprawled across cushions on the sitting-room floor. It was later the same evening, and there was still no sign of Joshua. We were commiserating with each other. There were rather more empty wine bottles around than I remembered seeing earlier.

'I mean, I'm independent, have a good living, got everything . . .'

'You're desperate, aren't you?' I asked her.

'Well, I wouldn't want to say desperate exactly . . .'

'Pining? Fretful? Terrified of an empty life with cats and no meaning?'

'Well, something like that. Why, don't you want one?'

'I think I'm too clumsy for children. I'd drop it down the stairs, like I did with that bottle of port Josh was given for his christening.'

Kate nodded. 'Yeh. Or like that time you left your shoes in the fridge.'

'I think I'd manage not to leave a baby in the fridge.'

'Yes, but probably best not to risk it, eh?'

'Prob'ly.'

Kate looked at her watch.

'You know all those girls called Sophie?'

'Those were different girls?'

'You know what I mean.'

'Uh huh.'

'Well, why don't I ever get a bit of that adoration from Josh?'

'Because you're a real person?'

'I mean, if he liked me, why didn't he walk around with a piece of toast stuck to his jacket, like he did with them?'

'Because he might have a chance with you?'

'Oh, thanks very much.'

'Hear me out, hear me out. The boy's terrified. It's taking him just that little bit longer to get over puberty than everyone else, OK?'

'But *why*??'

I settled back on the carpet. 'How the hell should I know? You're the one with the MBA. Maybe *no one* gets through puberty.'

'Shit,' said Kate. 'Still, at least I got to get off with a film star.'

'Exactly. Now all we have to do is get Josh through his rites of passage –'

'So to speak.'

'Yes, well. And make sure Addison gets to actually *hit* puberty. Then we'll all be there. Maturity Central.'

'It's a horrible word, puberty.' Kate was staring at the ceiling. She'd twisted the tin foil from the cork into the shape of a big heart.

'It is. As a word it practically smells. Too close to pus and pubic. I'll tell you what's a nice word, though.'

'What . . . Josh Junior?'

'Euch! Really, no, I was thinking of Penguin. As in Penguin

228

biscuits. As in – there are some in the kitchen, do you feel like going and getting them and calling them dinner?'

'Just because we're lying on the floor having a discussion doesn't mean I've forgotten that little incident, you know.'

'I bet a mature person wouldn't mind a bit.'

She eyed me crossly. 'Mature people don't eat Penguins.'

'OK.' I pushed myself up off the floor. 'You go buy biscuit shares. I'm going to eat them.'

'Can I have a red one?' she called after me.

'I bet Josh is saying that right at this very second,' I said as I came back in, but I wished I hadn't when I saw her face.

We tried to stay up till Josh came back but it was impossible. Well, we could probably have managed it, had not Kate degenerate into passive-aggressive mode, alternately ignoring me, then suggesting I get a career in the City. Then we watched some American import Friday-night TV, designed to make anyone who was already miserably at home on a Friday night feel worse about themselves by watching what glamorous young Americans were getting up to.

As I was the only one who had to go to work the next morning, as soon as I started to feel sick from eating too many biscuits I sloped off to bed, and I heard Kate follow shortly afterwards. I tried to listen for the door opening, but I didn't hear Josh come home.

The next morning I was woken horribly early by the phone. I left it for a bit – Kate was usually conscientious enough about these things to sort it out – but no one was moving, so I opened the door with my hand – easy enough given the size of my room – wrapped myself up in a sheet and pulled myself into the hall like a caterpillar.

'Reghh?'

'Helllaaayyyrr!'

I shook my head to clear it. What was Princess Anne doing phoning at seven o'clock on a Saturday morning?

'It's *Sophie*.'

Oh God! This could be interesting!

'Oh, *hello*, Sophie. This is Holly.'

'Yars, well. Joshua, please.'

'Ah, that might be a bit of a problem . . .'

'Where is he?'

I so longed to tell her the truth, just to set her little Alice band on end, but I didn't dare.

'He's . . . in the country this weekend.'

'Oh yars, ahem, so am I, *naturally* . . .'

That was odd, as I was sure I'd just heard an ambulance siren going past her flat.

'Can I take a message?'

'Maybe *you* could help.'

I curtsied and put the V's up at the phone.

'Maybe . . .'

'Well, I hear Joshua's tenant is ill.'

'Yes . . . ?'

'The thing is, my father thinks that it would help *considerably* with my nomination if I were to be seen to give money to a hospital . . .'

'What nomination?' I asked stupidly. 'Are you going in for the Eurovision Song Contest?'

'Oh, Holly, you can't waste qualifications like mine, you know! Everyone says so! No, for when I enter the *hais*.'

'Sophie, it's very early. What on earth are you talking about?'

She sighed.

'Look, are you *sure* Joshua isn't around?'

'Yes! Do you want me to tell him you called or not?'

She sighed again.

'I'm going to be an MP. Eventually. Once this disgusting government has been overthrown. So we need lots of nice pictures of me handing over cheques to those grateful, ghastly NHS types, yah? And we thought we'd do it where that dorky tenant of Josh's is – keep it all friendly. Yah?'

'But that's evil!'

'Yars, well, there's a natural class of government, Holly. So, don't worry yourself about it. Now, which hospital is your little friend in?'

'I'm not telling you!'

Sophie's sighs were becoming increasingly less world-weary and more irritated.

'Well, you can either ensure your friend gets the best treatment modern medicine can buy, or you can just ignore him . . . let him linger. Up to you, really.'

'It's St Hugh's,' I said, involuntarily.

'Well done. I'll bring the photographer. And tell Joshua I'll need him to help out – maybe I can let him pose as my boyfriend. Always politic to have an attractive partner. And that should please him, don't you think?' She laughed conspiratorially.

'You're pure evil!' I gasped again.

'Yars, welcome to the real world, darling. OK?' And she put the phone down.

It was not turning into a good day. At work, a bug bit me, then when I went in to see Addison he was upside down. Literally. Only the underside of the bed was visible. At first I thought they'd cleared him away altogether and not bothered to tell me. I simply stood and stared, my heart in my throat. Then I noticed the straps on the bed and the fact that the beeping machine was still beeping in a vaguely reassuring manner.

Stephen wasn't anywhere to be seen either – I didn't even want to think about that – but one of the younger nurses told me they had turned Add upside down to stop him getting bed sores. I hadn't thought it was for fun, like a fairground ride, but it did make me worry about how long they thought he was going to be here for – like, did they really think he was going to be here long enough to make his skin fall off?

I approached the bed. I'd bought a *Scientific American* to read out to him, and there weren't many other visitors around. After saying hello to God, who told me that it was the sixth day and God was having a rest – I said wasn't that Sunday and he said no, he had

231

just declared it was Saturday and the Jews had always been right about practically everything anyway – I couldn't quite find a good position where I could be sure Add could hear me, so eventually I simply scooted down under the bed where I could lie on the ground facing up at him.

OK. This was weird. This was definitely weird. Addison's pale skin flopped loosely around the straps – it struck me that Japanese comics and a certain class of Englishmen tended to find that kind of thing quite sexy. Our respective positions were definitely on the unusual side too, although there was about a foot between us. It reminded me of the old James Bond film where they have sex in space at the end, except the towel covering them goes down instead of up.

The first thing I noticed was that Addison no longer had a tube in his mouth. This could only mean one thing – he was breathing! This was wonderful news. Well, it would have been more wonderful had he been awake – and there was a definite pool of spit and crustiness around his mouth – but still. This had to be a good sign.

'Hey!' I said softly, reaching my arm up to tickle him. I don't think tickling is well known as a coma cure and, unsurprisingly, it didn't work.

'You look like Superman. I bet if you were awake, you'd love this. I should take a photograph, so you can see yourself flying.'

Always so thin, he seemed to have got even thinner in the last few days – his ribcage was a series of angles.

'OK,' I said. 'Here we go. *Scientific American*. The latest scientific news from the country that doesn't believe in evolution. What do you fancy – "How Broadband Internet Access May Influence Social Metamorphoses"? You know what . . . that's probably a bit late for you. Ooh, how about "The Theory Formerly Known as String" by Dr Michael Duff?'

Addison showed no objection, so I launched in:

'"At a time when certain pundits are predicting the End of Science on the grounds that all the important discoveries have already been made, it is worth emphasizing that the two main pillars of twentieth-century physics, quantum mechanics and Einstein's general theory of relativity, are mutually incompatible. General relativity fails to comply with the quantum rules that govern the behaviour of elementary particles, whereas on the opposite scale, black holes are challenging the very foundations of quantum mechanics. Something big has to give. This predicament augurs less the bleak future of diminishing returns predicted by the millennial Jeremiahs and more another scientific revolution . . ." Blah blah blah.'

I yawned. 'You love this, don't you? You big weirdo.

'"Until recently, the best hope for a theory that would unite gravity with quantum mechanics and describe all physical phenomena was based on strings: one-dimensional objects whose modes of vibration represent the elementary particles. In the past two years, however, strings have been subsumed by M-theory. In the words of the guru of string theory, Edward Witten of the Institute for Advanced Study in Princeton, N.J., 'M stands for Magic, Mystery or Membrane, according to taste'. New evidence in favour of this theory is appearing daily, representing the most exciting development since strings first swept on to the scene."

'Oh my God!' I sat upright, and accidentally hit Addison on the nose, but it didn't make him bleed or anything. 'I wonder if Finn knows about this? This could really cack his work up!'

I was genuinely worried for him. I mean, he'd spent years on this.

'What do you think? Should I phone Finn and tell him it's all a bunch of crap! Oh no! And, he'll think I'm just doing it to annoy him.'

There was a chuckle and suddenly a pair of brogues appeared beside the bed. A familiar person crouched down beside me, clutching a chessboard.

'You would really ruin an entire theory of the universe just to annoy me?'

'Oh no!' I said. 'Have you read this? You're in serious shit!'

He smiled again. 'Well, sometimes the paradigm changes, and you have to go along with it and add new ideas to your thinking. Let's just say that my "spaghetti" is now looking more like "ravioli".'

'Phew,' I said. 'So, you really do make it up as you go along?'

'Pretty much.'

'All those years of hard sums were for nothing then?'

'Well, I can work out twenty-four hour clock times.'

He leaned in to take a look at Addison. 'How's he doing?'

'Do you want to come in and see? His breathing tube's out! Isn't that fantastic?'

Finn looked concerned. 'Not really. Can I come under and see?'

'Sure!' I budged up. OK, this was now treble weird. I was in a bizarre sex sandwich between Finn and Addison, who was strapped up and completely unconscious.

'Weird huh?' I said, trying to break the ice.

'Well, not weird exactly,' said Finn, obviously completely unaware of our physical proximity. I cursed myself for being a sex maniac. 'It's just, they were probably hoping that if they took the breathing apparatus away it would stimulate him to breathe for himself . . .'

'Which it did . . .'

'. . . which in turn would stimulate him to wake up. Which it doesn't appear to have done.'

'You mean, this is *bad*?'

'It certainly implies that he could conceivably be under for longer than they thought. If his physical problems sort themselves out but he's still not conscious . . . that's not good, Holl.'

'Jesus,' I said, blinking back tears. 'I didn't realize.'

'It's OK,' said Finn, taking my hand. 'It's not over.' Then we stiffened as an unmistakable pair of scuffed pumps bossily made their way across the ward to Addison's bed.

'This way,' said Dr Hitler bossily. A shuffling bunch of shoes followed her. Without even being able to see them, they sounded like students. The curtains were drawn back abruptly. Finn and I looked at each other and winced. It was too late to move – we were already surrounded. Finn tightened his grip on my hand and

234

we tried to stay stock still. I could hear my heart beating like a hammer.

'Right. If you'd like to examine the charts, what we're seeing here is a state of unarousable neurobehavioural unresponsiveness, currently in progress for ninety-six hours.'

How many days did that make it again I wondered? Finn shot me an incredulous look.

'*Four*,' he whispered.

'We're going to have to start looking at an intensive physiotherapy programme to forestall the onset of heterotopic ossification, although of course that's not exactly a primary concern.'

'When they catch us, they're going to put us in the cooler!' I whispered to Finn.

'Just remember,' he whispered, 'whenever they ask you a question, answer in German.'

'Thank you.'

'No! That's what did for Richard Attenborough!'

'How are we going to escape?'

Above us, the medical students were pontificating on poor old Add, or having a competition to see who could shout the longest words the loudest – I couldn't tell.

'Maybe they won't notice us.'

'Don't say that, you'll immediately have to sneeze or something.'

Our eyes went wide as we both realized how dusty it was underneath the bed and how, indeed, we did both have to sneeze. We'd cursed ourselves completely. We held on to our noses as our eyes watered and blinked. Finn squished his nose up like a rabbit, which meant that if I wasn't about to sneeze, I was certainly about to laugh.

It came like something out of a cartoon, when the Acme Company delivers an enormous box of pepper to someone. We simultaneously 'ATCHOOED' all over the place.

'He's sneezing! That's a conscious sign!' said one of the students.

'It sounded like a double sneeze though,' said another.

235

I sighed as, slowly, the owners of the six pairs of legs came into view. I closed my eyes and squeezed Finn's hand tightly (not the hands we'd sneezed into). He squeezed back.

'WWWEELLLLLL!' said Dr Hitler, as if she'd just found out I was born in a handbag.

'And so . . .' said Finn quickly, 'this is what we mean by the word *down*, and where we were before was what we mean by the word *up*.'

'I've been confusing those for *years*,' I said, scrambling out from under the bed and dusting myself down.

'Thank you, Dr Levy! So, this is *up*, yes?'

'That's correct. No more falling down for you!'

'Wow! Shall we go *down*stairs?'

'Indeed. And perhaps we can practise *near* and *far* by first attempting *far*.'

We started walking quickly away from the bed.

'Remind me again of the distinctions between *fast* and *slow*?' I asked.

The medical students watched in disbelief as we made our exit.

'It is at times like these when you may find your belief in the Hippocratic oath severely tested,' said Dr Hitler loudly, so I could hear.

'It's at times like this when you may wish Anthony Edwards was actually QUALIFIED,' I said loudly, as Finn shooed me away.

Finn had to go off to some boring thing at the Royal Geographical Society. Well, it may or may not have been boring, but I certainly wasn't invited, and – guess what – Madeleine was. How charming for them both. I stomped off home by myself, picturing Finn surrounded by hordes of smarty pants bespectacled lovelies, then got cross with myself for picturing it, then felt horribly disloyal and nasty, like those men you see in the drink-driving ads who leave their girlfriends after they've been in disfiguring accidents. So finding an atmosphere at 44 Bisthmus Road that you could make into ice sculpture was hardly ideal.

'Hey!' I said tiredly, walking in the door, hoping against hope that just *once* my flatmates would leap up, remove my coat and coo with endless sympathy at my burden before presenting me with gin and tonics and home-baked cakes. There was no reply. I wished we had a dog – or, better still, one of those Japanese robot dogs that could make you a gin and tonic *and* be pleased to see you.

I leafed through the post – you never know, despite acres and years of evidence to the contrary, someone might decide to send a nice surprise out of the blue – then, empty-handed, slouched through to the kitchen, trying not to think about the fact that it was Saturday night and I had fuck all to do. I didn't even have a meeting of the bloody Royal Geographical Society to go to, for fuck's sake. Josh was sitting slumped at the kitchen table with his back to me.

I eyed him closely. It wasn't a 'having trouble coming to terms with my new sexuality' slouch. On the other hand, he wasn't wearing a Jean-Paul Gaultier sailor's outfit either.

'Yo?' I said, experimentally. Josh waved an exhausted hand.

'Hey.'

I stepped round the table and sat opposite him. '*Well?*'

He raised his arms Gallicly. 'Well???'

'Well, go on . . . you are going to tell me, aren't you?'

Josh heaved a sigh.

'I suppose so.'

'Hooray! Do you want to wait for Kate? Please say no. Tell me first.'

'I don't have to wait for Kate. She's already here. She's sulking in her room.'

'*Oh.*'

There was a pause whilst I debated with myself how much I wanted to talk about Kate. Not at all!

'Well, *tell* me then.'

Josh gave a sigh.

'OK. Well, we went to Snows . . .'

'*And?*'

'Do you want to hear this or not?'

'I want to hear whether you did it, not whether you both had starters.'

Josh sat up suddenly.

'Holl, do you think I'm homophobic?'

'Well, given that you openly date men, probably not.'

'No, I mean, really.'

'I don't know — try this multiple choice. Do you call homosexuals a) botty burglars, b) uphill gardeners or c) darling . . . I don't know, do I? I don't think so.'

'OK. Well, then, ehm . . . I don't think I'm gay.'

'Because why?'

'No reason.'

'Josh! You did it, didn't you?'

He squirmed. 'Well, maybe.'

'You did! You're a cheap date! Oh my God! What was it like?!'

'What do you mean, what was it like? It was like going to bed with a man.'

'Oh, yeah, right. But you know, I *like* doing that.'

'Well, I didn't like it. It was all . . . hard, and hairy.'

'Hard and hairy are usually seen as positive attributes — Robin Williams excepted.'

'Huh. Well, I definitely didn't like it. I think I like . . . soft, and kind of mushy.'

I nodded understandingly. 'Yup. That'll be girls.'

He nodded. 'So.'

'Well then, aren't you pleased?' I said. 'Now you've sorted all that out? You can get on with having lots of meaningless relationships that end up in degradation and heartache, just like the rest of us!'

'I know,' he said. 'And that does feel good. It's just . . . well, Stephen is so nice, you know. I hate to let him down like this.'

'Ooh no,' I said. 'Stephen's my friend, and I won't have you pretending to be gay out of politeness. It's not fair to drag someone on like that. What about Sophie and you? God, the way she treated you, I could have told her where to go when she rang this morning . . .'

'Sophie rang?'

'No!'

'Oh my God! Why didn't you *tell* me?'

'I don't know . . . Because you were out being Big Gay Al?'

'I'm just going to ring her . . .' he said, diving out of the room.

'Oh, well done,' I said, and gave myself a sarcastic round of applause.

As soon as I could hear him buzzing excitedly on the line, his vowels elongating by the second, the door creaked, and Kate popped her head in, red-eyed.

'*Well?*'

'Well what?' I said to annoy her.

'Well, is he or isn't he? I haven't been able to sleep, you know.'

'You sounded asleep this morning when I had to get up to answer the phone,' I grumbled.

'How can you say that? I've . . . never felt like this before. Please don't scoff at me.'

'What about the dog dentist bloke?'

'HOLLY!' she said, exasperated.

'OK, OK. Do you want the good news or the bad news?'

Kate sidled in and sat down.

'Good news, please. Is he in love with me?'

'Ehm . . . well, he's not gay.'

'Good! OK, what's the bad news?'

'Guess who he's on the phone to . . .'

She looked at me for a second.

'It can't be.'

'It is.'

I explained Sophie's evil scheme. Kate was clearly furious. Then she gave me a pleading look.

'No!' I said immediately.

'Well, you know . . .'

'You want me to overthrow a chance of Addison getting some

extra money to make him better so that you can try and get off with Josh without any competition.'

'And stop the world being overrun by over-privileged fascists in parliament!' said Kate, scandalized. 'Do you think I'm completely heartless?'

'I don't know. But I am taking Sophie's money, I'm afraid.'

'Class traitor.'

'Haaa!' I turned on Kate, just as Josh bounced back into the room like the Andrex puppy.

'Guess what, everyone! That was Sophie!'

'Oh, I thought someone was dragging their fingernails down a blackboard,' said Kate.

Josh ignored her.

'And she's presenting a cheque to the hospital wing where Addison is! AND I told her about the television cameras coming to film Holly, so she's going to do it on Monday afternoon!'

'No. No no no. Please, not on TV,' I said.

'But think,' said Josh sincerely, 'this money could change the lives of hundreds, if not thousands –'

'– of prospective Conservative candidates,' said Kate. 'Josh! Holly! Please don't let this happen!'

'But . . .'

'And *I* think . . .'

'No way!'

We were well on our way to a full-blown barney when the doorbell rang.

We stopped scrapping, and looked at each other.

'Well, it's not Sophie, because she's in the country,' said Josh. I sniffed.

'And it's not John because he's NOT JOHN,' said Kate sourly.

They both looked at me. Even though I knew it couldn't possibly be Addison, I felt a sudden thrill of anticipation as I tiptoed to the door and down the stairs.

'Hello?' I asked tentatively.

'Jhnghf?' came the noise from the other side of our admittedly heavy door. I opened it nervously, preparing my face.

'Hello,' said Addison's mother, smiling nervously at me.

I obviously didn't prepare my face enough because it must have looked a bit disappointed.

'I am sorry . . . this is a bad time?'

'No! No, this is absolutely the *best* time!' I said, ushering her in.

'I made a goulash . . .' I noticed she was carrying a heavy bowl.

'Why, that's brilliant. Kate, Josh . . .'

I brought Magda into the kitchen. Both appeared surprised then managed to make themselves look pleased. I kicked myself for not sorting my face out better downstairs.

'I hope I am not intruding . . .'

'No, of course not,' we all said, in a totally over-the-top way, so that even though it was true it sounded false.

'Sit down,' said Josh, springing into gentlemanly action. 'Why don't I open a bottle of wine?'

We all made appreciative noises as Magda handed over her goulash. It became clear that she was simply in search of a bit of companionship, and there was nothing mysterious at all about her visit. Except for the obvious, which Kate asked her as soon as we were all sat round the table eating.

'Ehm, Magda . . . how did you know we'd all be in on a Saturday night?'

Magda shrugged tactfully. 'I just . . . no, really, I did not know.'

'I think the thing that worries me most,' said Magda when we had moved on to the sitting room to finish the wine, 'I think . . . is when he wakes . . . he will be different.'

'What do you mean?' asked Josh.

'No, I know,' said Kate. The imposition of an external – and maternal – force on us had made us be civil, and that had gradually relaxed into actually being pleasant – maintaining huff status, as everybody knows, being simply too exhausting and bothersome. 'I read about it. Sometimes people wake from

241

periods of unconsciousness with different personality habits. One guy woke up speaking French.'

'Oh, whereabouts in France?' I asked, then wished I hadn't.

'Yes, that is the kind of thing I mean,' said Magda. 'Or that he has amnesia.'

'Oh, that would be *great*,' I said. Then, after a pause, I decided to get up and make the coffee.

'Wow. Addison with a different personality,' mused Josh, voicing our thoughts.

'You'd never shut him up.'

'Yes, he'd be off climbing mountains all over the world then boasting about it,' said Kate.

'Or he'd become a hippy and go and live in a field and kiss rabbits.'

'Or write poetry with a quill pen.'

'Or become a Radio One DJ,' I chipped in from the kitchen.

'Or a consumer affairs television presenter!'

We mused on the amount of opposite personalities Addison could have.

'I think I'd like my son back the way he was,' said Magda.

'Me too,' said Kate.

'Me three,' I said in a small voice.

Eleven

Six forty-five on Sunday morning. I lay fuming, listening to the phone blare at me. Wasn't it enough that my bedroom was small enough to cause carbon dioxide poisoning if you didn't keep a window open without having to suffer assault by phone?

Nope. Definitely no one else was moving. It suddenly occurred to me that it might be the hospital and I swore and performed my patented duvet jam roly-poly manoeuvre into the hall.

'Rrgh?'

'Is that Holly Livingstone?'

'Ehmm . . . yes?' I jerked awake. I always snap to attention when somebody uses my full name, in case I'm not listening and get arrested for something I didn't do.

'Oh, yes, hi, this is Roger Montserrat? I'm the producer for Candice Piper's show?'

'Hello,' I said grumpily. 'Don't tell me – you're at a coke-fuelled TV party and haven't been to bed yet?'

He pretended to laugh loudly.

'Actually, we thought we'd find you at the hospital.'

'It's six forty-five in the MORNING.'

'I know . . . it's just, one of the male nurses said you were very dedicated.'

'I am FUCKING dedicated. Didn't you hear me? It's six forty-five in the . . .'

'Quite, yes, all right. Anyway, just wanted a little chinwag about tomorrow?' He had one of those annoying nasal voices that turns everything into a question.

'OK,' I said, leaning against the telephone table and preparing to give a faintly sanitized history of my relationship with Addison. 'Well, we met . . .'

'What colours were you planning on wearing?'

'What?'

'Candice is most particular that no one clashes. She was planning on pistachio, so we'd be most grateful . . .'

'Hang on,' I said, shaking my head to clear it. 'What colour is pistachio? Pale brown?'

'It's green.'

'Green? Like, rotting nuts?'

'Ha ha ha. So, if you just steer away from the primary palettes, I'm sure everything will go perfectly smoothly. We haven't heard from your band's agent yet, but we'll be expecting you all around two, OK?'

'Hang on!' I said, panic-stricken. 'What am I actually going to *do*?'

He seemed stupefied by the question.

'Just . . . you know, dear, you'll be on *TV*!'

'Doing *what*?'

He sighed. 'Just turn up in non-clashing pastels and prepare to try and make yourself cry, darling. OK? We'll handle the rest. Remember: it's all for the best and you'll be on TV! Brilliant, eh?'

I went back to sleep and had one of those horrible early-morning nightmares – I was being pursued by Addison tied upside down on a board whilst trying to find a non-green smock in my wardrobe, which was inexplicably turning into a bowl of spaghetti. I finally got up when I heard Josh banging about in the kitchen washing up. Not having to do the washing-up – well, I was taking my small bonuses where I could find them.

I had to phone Chali about the next day. It occurred to me that if I was going to be there and she was going to be there, there was a small shop opening problemo, and I needed her advice.

Of course, a big troll thing picked the phone up.

'Chali?'

'Ugh??'

'CH-ALEE, PLEASE,' I said, enunciating very slowly.

'Ugh, uhu.'

After half an hour, Chali came on the line.

'Yes? Buster, stop that.'

'What's he doing?'

'You don't want to know. There's snuffling involved.'

'You're right. I don't want to know. Do you want me to phone back?'

'No, don't be silly, we're only having sex. Is this about the band?'

'Are you still ready to go ahead?'

'Is it still on? Oh, that's brilliant! We've written a special song.'

'What's it called?'

244

'"The New Coma Suture".'

'Oh God.'

'No, it'll be cool. It's still thrash, but I add an air of eastern exoticism.'

'What are we going to do about the shop?'

She thought for a moment.

'God. I'd ask my uncle, but apparently he's down to absolutely no faculties or marbles whatsoever. Hmm . . . Buster, lower.'

I hung on the phone. After about a minute she said, 'I've got it!'

'What?'

'We go on strike! We've got rights, haven't we?'

'I don't know about the right to take a day off to be on TV.'

'No, no, we should. Form a protest.'

'What for – communal tea bags?'

'Come on, Holl – Christ, we barely make minimum wage.'

'Yes, but you steal.'

'Not the point. I'll phone old butterbum now. Terrorize her into accepting our demands.'

'Hadn't you better wait a bit, in case she does accept them and we still have to turn up?'

'Good point. Fear not. I'll see you tomorrow.'

'Two o'clock,' I said. 'And don't wear anything pistachio.'

She snorted. 'God, could you *be* any more middle-aged? Buster, *stop* that.'

'Urhgh.'

'Oh no, don't stop *that*.'

I put the phone down.

'I rather *like* pistachio,' said Josh, holding up two ties whilst doing his Sunday night ironing.

'Josh, you don't know what you like, so shut up,' said Kate.

'Also, nobody must come,' I said. 'If I have to humiliate myself in this way, I'd rather do it alone.'

'Sophie asked me to come, so there,' said Josh, selecting the mulberry tie and poking his tongue out at me.

245

Kate heaved a sigh and pushed her salad around her plate with a fork.

'Not coming, Skates? Don't you want to be part of the television extravaganza? It'll be a laugh.'

'It's not *meant* to be a laugh,' I said.

'And of course in a very good cause . . .'

'I've got work,' said Kate finally. 'Do you think the Stock Exchange stops because someone's in a coma?'

Josh and I looked at each other.

'Depends who it is,' he said. 'I mean, if it was the Governor of the Bank of England . . .'

'Or the Pope, maybe,' I chipped in.

'. . . or your flatmate and friend,' said Josh.

'Look, just can it, OK?' said Kate. 'You and *Sophie* go off and have a brilliant time. Why don't you get famous, like that woman who couldn't drive a car? Make a record? Go to parties with Keith Chegwin? I really couldn't give a fuck. But just leave me alone, OK, Josh?'

She got up and stormed out of the room.

'Wow, has Kate got problems with her love life or something?' said Josh, peering after her.

I couldn't sleep. Every time I closed my eyes my mind began whirring through an exhausting litany of things that might happen, including:

- I get fired (because I deserved to be)
- I wear the wrong colour and they make me wear an old man's pyjamas
- The band get us banned from TV
- Candice makes nasty personal remarks about me
- Josh and Sophie get engaged and I have to cook for myself
- It doesn't work for Addison. Because, as I don't need

Kate's flow chart to remind me, he is running out of time.

When I say I couldn't sleep I . . . well, I managed to sleep pretty late into the morning, then scrambled up in a panic. The house was quiet. Outside, it was threatening to turn into the most beautiful day. I wandered over and confronted my wardrobe. I had no idea I had so many green things. Black wasn't going to work either, not sitting next to someone with pitch-black hair who was as pale as death. I'd look like the Crow of Doom, perched on his shoulder. Is there a Crow of Doom? It didn't matter, I discarded all black and grey items forthwith. And navy – I could never tell the difference. OK. There wasn't a lot left now, and rather a lot of that seemed to be pink. I sighed. If only Kate ate less salad and more sausage rolls, I could have borrowed something of hers. I picked up an old T-shirt that said 'Free Nelson Mandela'. Well, it would have been a good message to get out on TV, but perhaps a little unnecessary now. Finally I settled on a stripy top and a plain long skirt, in a vain attempt at 'willowy'.

Before I left the house, I crept into Addison's room.

'Don't worry, guys,' I said to his stacked computers, 'I'll bring him home.'

Someone had turned the monitor off, so there was no Claudia. I walked around slowly, patting things. Magda had taken lots of his *Star Trek* stuff and put it round his hospital bed, so Add's room wasn't as cramped as usual. I picked up a small Han Solo figure.

'You're coming with me,' I said. 'You're known for getting people out of sticky situations. We need you now, Han.' And I put him in my pocket.

'Look at you,' I addressed the computers again. 'Enough power to run the space shuttle and you can't do a damn thing for the person that loves you the most.'

The computers winked at me.

'And don't be cheeky.'

I shut the door behind me quietly.

From the moment I stepped inside the hospital, I could tell there was something going on. Staff who normally slouched about the corridors were bustling officiously up and down. Everyone was moving a bit quicker than normal and had suspiciously clean hair. Yup, the TV cameras must be in.

I was so used to weird goings on in the high-dependency unit that I almost didn't notice when I walked through the familiar swing doors. This, however, was something else altogether. For starters, there was an enormous Christmas tree in the middle of the ward. Big, cheap and nasty plastic wreaths had been randomly placed on the walls, with what were obviously large empty cardboard boxes hastily covered in cheap wrapping paper, so you could still see the flavour of crisps the boxes had held. I nearly retched when I saw Addison's bed. Somebody had dressed him in garish red pyjamas, but that wasn't the worst thing – they had also seen fit to hang some mistletoe above his bed.

'What?' I said out loud. There were about four times as many people as there normally were on the ward, and about twice as many nursing staff. Stephen spotted me and came to my rescue.

'Excited?' he said.

'To the point of vomiting,' I replied. 'What are you doing here?'

'It's my day off,' he said. 'I came in anyway. Plus, there's this particular sound recordist . . .'

'You tart!' I said. 'I expected to find you crying your eyes out over your lost love.'

'Who, your friend?' He grinned wickedly. 'I don't think so. It was a lot of fun to watch, though.'

'You're an *evil* tart!'

'Sweet!'

'Still, at least you helped,' I said, hitting him with a bit of tinsel.

'Good. Now, do you want to come over and join the party?'

I looked around – Chali and her menagerie clearly hadn't arrived yet, but the television crew was bustling around. Several other families were also with their patients, hovering nervously. Not one person was wearing green. Candice – a vision in snot – and Dr Hitler were in front of the nurses' station, talking very intently to each other in the way that people do when they're trying to pretend to the outside world that they aren't having a row.

'All I'm saying,' Candice was whining as Stephen and I walked over, 'is that I don't see why we can't just change that little room into make-up. God, it's only for a day.'

'And all I'm saying is could you please stop talking nonsense about things you don't understand, like how much we use the disinfecting room and the importance of clean things to sick people,' Dr Hitler hissed back at her.

'Hi,' I said. They both straightened up.

'Yes?' said Candice snottily.

'Ehm . . . I'm meant to be in your show.'

'Oh, well done. Why don't you go and speak to Roger, and I'll sort out any autographs later on, OK? . . . Look, Doctor, surely you have an operating theatre or something we could use?'

I glanced at Stephen and he made the thumbs-up sign at me.

'She's *such* a bitch,' he said. 'I *love* her.'

Roger was nowhere to be found so I went over to Addison's bed to try and remove the mistletoe.

'What's going on?'

I leaned across to the next bed.

'God, if *you* don't know, what hope is there for the world?'

'None. You're all doomed and you're all going to hell, especially the Protestants. And the Liberal Democrats. And David Essex.'

'You're a very grumpy God today.'

'Well, I'm not feeling well and they keep shining lights in my eyes. It's like being back in Japan in '44.'

'Why don't you ask them to close the curtains?'

'Not Christmassy enough, apparently.'

'Oh. Well, they're making a TV show and they're having a band play to try and wake up some of the coma patients. Then hopefully they'll piss off and leave us alone.'

'Huh,' said God. 'Well, at least I get to wear my best pyjamas.'

'It's still a beautiful world,' I said.

'HOLL!'

A vision in silver came clopping up the ward in enormously high-heeled shoes.

'Aha – one of my angels!' said God.

'Not exactly,' I said. 'Chali? What's the matter?'

'Nothing. Well, my shoes are killing me. But apart from that, everything's fine. Mrs Bigelow is FURIOUS.'

'That's not fine.'

'Oh, yes it is. She's opening the shop by herself! I almost wish we weren't here, so we could see how she's getting on, doing a day's work for a change.'

'I'm sure she's finding it tough,' I said. 'Probably won't even have time to paint all ten fingernails.'

Chali stopped suddenly in front of Addison's bed, and looked at me.

'Is this him?'

I nodded.

'Oh, God, Holl, you didn't tell me he was so gorgeous.'

'Ehm, I think you'll find that's pretty much *all* I told you.'

She gently stroked his face. 'God. Wow. Hey, is this mistletoe?'

'No!' I grabbed it off her. She pouted.

'Well, his pyjamas are horrible, anyway. Where can we set up?'

'How many of you are there?' I said with some concern as a line of grubby blokes filed through the ward door, each carrying a piece of sound equipment or an extension lead.

'Ah,' said Chali. 'Well, when I told Mr Big . . . lots of people wanted to get on TV. So, the band's a bit . . . larger than it was.'

'How much larger?'

'Well . . . there was five of us . . . ?'

'Uh huh.'

'Now there's about fourteen.'

'Fourteen?'

'I'm still the only vocalist. Mr Big is on lead guitar. Two bass players. A rhythm guitarist, four drummers and five backing singers.'

'Jesus, Chali, we're trying to wake these people, not punish them.'

'It's my big break, remember? And don't worry, I'll make sure they're OK,' said Chali pleadingly.

'Urhg! Chocolates!' At the other side of the ward, one of the Spangles was half-inching gifts from a critically ill person.

I let out a long sigh. 'Well, it's not me you have to convince. There's a guy called Roger who . . .' As I spoke, Roger himself appeared.

'Quick, come and meet Roger.'

Roger was walking around half in a daze carrying a tray of designer coffees.

'Hi.'

He looked at us both with a complete lack of recognition.

'It's Holly Livingstone,' I said. 'I'm not surprised you don't recognize me during daylight hours.'

'Oh, yes, hello.' He took me in for the first time.

'Oh my God. Stripes?'

'What?'

'You're wearing stripes. I'm sorry, that won't do at all, yeh?'

'Yeah, well, forget about that. This is Chali Sanghara, lead singer with Mr Big and the Spangles.'

'The carol singers, right?'

'Ehm, well . . .'

'Great . . . just set up anywhere, yeh?'

And he ran away from us towards Candice, brandishing the coffee.

Chali and I looked at each other, and she shrugged and went over to help the band set up in the far corner. One of the gnome army, his mouth covered in chocolate, leaned down to plug in his amplifier, eliciting a screech from Dr Hitler, who was getting increasingly puce and agitated at her ward being turned into a three-ring circus.

Last to arrive were Josh and Sophie, who entered the scene

251

like some weird couple from a genetically perfect future. Their matching blond hair gleamed in the sunlight through the windows. Sophie was ostentatiously carrying a cheque the size of a playing field, bearing her name in huge letters, and a quite enormous number of noughts.

They'll never fit that under the banking counter, I thought mutinously. 'Hi, Josh. Hi, Sophie.'

'Hey,' said Josh. 'How's it going?'

Out of the corner of my eye, I'm sure I saw Dr Hitler smack one of the gnome army.

'Hmm. Not bad.'

'I must go and talk to Candice,' said Sophie. 'I'm hoping to bring her on board as one of my celebrity supporters.'

'I wouldn't bother,' I said. 'She's a bit of a bitch.'

Sophie, however, had already swanned her way over there. Josh and I waited a couple of minutes for the expected rebuff, but within seconds Candice and Sophie were blathering away like old friends.

'Sophie really does get on with *everyone*,' said Josh proudly.

'OK, everybody!' A loud voice rattled around the ward. I looked up. Roger was standing on someone's bed, hollering through a megaphone.

'Get *off* that!' shouted Dr Hitler.

'It's OK – they're asleep!' shouted Roger. 'Now, everyone, just a few ground rules. First, please stick to your own corners. We're only filming a short ten-minute segment, so this shouldn't take more than eight or nine hours. During that time please do not change clothes or your hair and make-up, for continuity reasons. Unless of course you cry and we want you to do it again, in which case you'll be taken off to make-up. We're going to film Candice, then the band, then the cheque, OK? Refreshments will be provided; once we've finished filming you, you will find a sandwich waiting for you at the door. Please don't take more than one. Oh, and please, on no account address Candice unless she speaks to you. In fact, we'd rather you didn't make eye contact with her. So, keep quiet, keep out of the way, and, who knows

– you might be on TV and have a nice souvenir for your loved one, if and when he or she is returned to you. OK, do we have any questions?'

Someone asked what if they needed to go to the toilet, and Roger requested that they didn't for the duration of filming, prompting a mad dash for the bathroom. Then Sophie very loudly asked if she was expected to say a few words when handing over her fifty thousand pound cheque. Roger glanced at Candice, who nodded and, behind Sophie's back, managed to mime something that looked as if it meant they could chop it out later.

'Of course,' said Roger. 'You're a very important part of the show.'

Sophie preened herself.

'Anyone else?'

One of the drummers played a 'ba boom – cha!' Roger wasn't amused.

'OK then, everyone. Places, please.'

I started looking around for what might be my place, but a tiny girl with an enormous walkie-talkie came up and manhandled me on to Addison's bed.

'Candice will come and talk to you, probably!' she said, as if Candice was Santa Claus.

'So, good luck! I'm sure you'll get on.'

'I'd rather get off,' I mumbled, but she had whisked away to shove some other people about.

The whole ward went silent and the Christmas tree lights were turned on. Candice strolled over and sat two beds down from Addy's, alongside a young lad called Carl who'd nicked a car, smashed it up, and had been in here for a year. He was fifteen. It wasn't pleasant.

She turned towards the camera and lit up with an enormous beaming smile.

'So, I'm here with Carl Foster and his mother, who are spending another "coma alone" Christmas this year. Mrs Foster . . . how *did* you feel when you first heard Carl had been in an accident?'

'Well, I felt terrible, yes, really bad,' said Carl's mother, who was shrunken and nervy.

'Right. Right, that must have been awful. And how did you feel when they told you he was in a coma and might never regain consciousness?'

'Yes, well, that was really terrible. It was really bad, yes.'

'Do you feel sad that he might never have a chance to grow up, get married, have a family, have a career – that he's missing out on so much?'

'Yes. Yes, really, it's terrible . . . really, you know . . . really bad.'

Candice turned her attention to Dr Hitler.

'So, Doctor, in a case like Carl's – what's the likely outcome?'

'It's very difficult to say,' said Dr Hitler, who looked like she'd smeared her glasses especially for the occasion.

'What – don't you know?' said Candice.

'Well, there are a number of possible outcomes. He could wake at any time, or he could be in a vegetative state for many years.'

'And you don't have anything better to offer Mrs Foster?'

Dr Hitler coloured. 'As I say, comas are very unpredictable things.'

'Right. Well . . . *thank you*, Doctor.'

Candice turned to face the camera.

'So, remember, kids, if you're thinking about joyriding tonight, you'll probably end up like Carl. Don't do it!'

'Yes!' said Sophie, who was standing nearby. 'When I become PM, I'll make going into a coma the punishment for joyriding!'

Candice moved on.

'Many of our stories here are tragic. Some are uplifting. And some, like our next stopping point, are even . . . romantic!'

To my surprise she sat down next to me.

'So, Holly, you've got a funny story to tell of how Addison came to be in this state, haven't you?'

'No.'

'You know – leaning in for a kiss and then – whoops!' She chuckled. I sat there stony-faced, unable to believe she would bring this up on TV. I caught sight of Stephen out of the corner of my eye wearing a contrite expression and shot him a dirty look, the grasser.

'No,' I said again.

'Cut!' yelled Candice. Roger hurried over so they could both have a go at me. Candice started:

'Now listen, ehm . . .'

'Holly,' I said.

'Yes, Holly. We've all got a job to do here, you know. And we can either make it hard or make it difficult – it's up to you.'

'We've got all day,' said Roger. 'And tomorrow and, you know, the day after that . . . But all these dedicated nurses and doctors here, they really want to get back to work to help sick people – like your boyfriend, yeah?'

'I mean, Christmas is a time for unselfishness,' said Candice.

'It's June!' I said. She ignored me.

'. . . and I'm sure everyone in this room would like to see us make the best programme we can as a tribute to the amazing work of . . .'

'And I need to go to the toilet,' shouted one of the Spangles.

'OK, OK,' I said. 'I'll do it. It'll be like one of those hostage videos they send back from the Middle East.'

'*There* you go,' said Candice. 'That wasn't too difficult, was it?'

Roger pressed Candice's shoulder. 'You're so diplomatic,' he said to her. 'Ready to go in three . . .'

Ping! Candice lit up her amazing smile again.

'So, Holly – you've got a funny story to tell of how Addison, here, came to be in this state, haven't you?'

'Yes I have, Candice,' I said dutifully.

'Would you like to share it with the viewers?'

'Well, we were . . . I was trying to kiss him on the top of a wall, and he fell over and hit his head,' I muttered.

'Oh! That is just so heart-warming,' said Candice. 'Even in the midst of human wreckage, there is romance.'

She turned back to me. 'Well, here on Babbleon TV, we thought

255

that, since this started with a kiss, perhaps another kiss could wake the Sleeping Beauty . . .'

This made no sense to me whatsoever.

'So, why don't we all wish for a little bit of that Christmas magic for Holly right now . . . Go on, Holly, give him a kiss – you never know!'

'What?' I said.

'I'm not sure that's a particularly helpful course of treatment,' said Dr Hitler, watching critically from the sidelines.

'For all our viewers . . . just to try and get a little bit of Christmas magic into all our hearts.'

'*Whaat?*'

The room was completely silent as everyone stared at me. Feeling like one of those poor deer who have the option of tearing off their own legs or dying in a trap, I slowly turned towards Addison.

Even in this, my darkest hour, I was still conscious of how my bottom might appear directly facing camera, and inched my way sideways towards his face. His stupidly immobile, beautiful face.

'What if . . .' I was thinking to myself. 'What if it did . . . ? Not that it could, but, what if . . . ?'

I whispered to the next bed: 'God, if you felt like doing any miracling, this would be a very good time.'

God snored back at me. For some weird reason I heard Enya music in my head. I hate Enya.

The ward was holding its breath. Slowly I leaned over and kissed him gently on the lips for the very first time. It was almost as if there was nothing there at all. Actually, it was like kissing a fish.

The silence held. I drew back. Addison didn't move. Not a nerve, not a flicker. Goddammit. God*dammit*. Candice came up to the bed and sat beside me.

'Are you OK?' she asked. 'Are you crying?'

Witch. Of course, if you ever want to make somebody cry, those are the only two sentences you need to use. She laid a supposedly comforting arm on me and, with the other, indicated for the cameraman to rush over and stick his camera in my face, which he did.

'And we'll be back with more tragic and heart-warming stories from the ward that time forgot after this break,' she managed to say whilst still patting me on the arm. 'Cut!'

Josh and Stephen comforted me as Candice whisked round the beds of those patients who weren't too old or ugly to be on TV, and the band set up.

'But why did you think that would work?' said Sophie.

'Oh, shut up, Sophie,' I said, more vehemently than I intended.

'Ooh, temper! Better watch out, or no fifty thousand pounds for you.'

Even Josh looked a bit surprised at that one.

Chali was removing her silver top to reveal a minuscule silver bra underneath.

'Ah, appropriate,' I said, sniffing, when she rushed up to me.

'I think we're just about ready,' she said. 'Would you like to meet Mr Big?'

'Oh my God, I thought that was a Muppet,' I said, as a tiny skinny creature entirely covered in hair came bouncing up.

'Hey – touching scene, man,' squeaked Mr Big.

'Thank you,' I said. 'I do everything for my public.'

'I've given the list of songs to Roger,' Chali said. 'But I don't think he's read it.'

Roger was in fact lighting a cigarette for Candice. Really, we should have clubbed together to buy Dr Hitler a skateboard so she could speed from crisis to crisis even quicker. And a foghorn, so she wouldn't have to wear her voice out. Roger got up on the bed with his megaphone again.

'Right, everyone, well done. Little treat for you now; we've got some friends in who are going to do some lovely carol singing.'

The Spangles had lined themselves up against the back wall. Mr Big's guitar was larger than he was. The drummers seemed to have one very long eyebrow between the four of them. Chali was already contorting herself into deeply erotic poses. Anything less

257

like a bunch of carol singers but still in human form was difficult to imagine.

'So, if you would like to clap as much as you can and perhaps sing along . . . who knows what miracles might happen here? Music is good for coma patients, so the louder you sing, the better their chances are!'

Everyone arranged themselves into optimum carol-singing position. Except Josh and I: we put our hands over our ears.

There was an expectant hush. Chali raised her lovely arms above her head and, as she brought them down, there was a huge crash of drums.

'O LITTLE TOWN OF BETHLEHEM!' she screeched. 'HOW ILL WE SEE YOU LIE! AMONG YOUR DEAD AND BLOOD-SOAKED STREETS, THE CORPSES PILING HIGH!'

People looked a bit stunned, then started to shuffle uneasily.

'Oh God,' said Josh. 'This is going to be even worse than I thought.'

'Good,' I said.

'YET IN THE DARK STREETS SHINING AN EVER-LASTING LIGHT / THE POWER OF ROCK RULES ALL THE WORLD / AND ROCKS WITH YOU TONIGHT!!'

BOOM! Mr Big launched into a massive squealing guitar solo that threatened to break the windows. He thrust his pelvis forward and placed his foot on one of the amps. Some of his sweat broke free and dowsed the nurses. I saw Stephen lick a bit.

'OH MORNING STARS TOGETHER PROCLAIM THE LORDS OF SOUND! / THE KIDS ON THE STREET GIVE HAIL TO THE BEAT AND LET THIS ROCK GO WILD! / KNEEL AT THE ALTAR OF HEAVY NOISE AND GIVE THE LORD HIS PRAYERS! / THAT YOU WILL DIE WITH A GUITAR IN YOUR HAND AND THE BLOOD OF A VIRGIN SLAYER!'

Roger and Candice were looking stunned and whispering feverishly to each other. All the relatives were becoming distinctly upset and querulous. Interestingly, Dr Hitler was tapping her feet and nodding her head almost imperceptibly. Chali took a quick breath and launched back in:

'HOW NOISILY, HOW NOISILY . . .'

'OK, OK!' Roger started shouting through his megaphone. 'That is quite enough.'

Of course, nobody could hear him. The drummers went into a prolonged drumming competition. More and more hospital staff were poking their heads round the doors.

'THE LORDS OF ROCK KICK ARSE!'

'Stop this!' screamed Roger.

'WE HATE THE PIGS WHO STOP OUR GIGS / JUST FOR SAYING THE WORD "MOTHERFUCKER"!'

'Yay!' said some of the nurses.

'MOTHERFUCKER! MOTHERFUCKER! MOTHERFUCKER! MOTHERFUCKER! MOTHERFUCKER! MOTHERFU–'

The music suddenly came to an abrupt screeching halt. Roger stood there with the cables in his hand.

'I think that's quite enough of that, don't you?' he shouted, visibly trembling.

'No!' shouted the nurses and Dr Hitler.

'Cut! I said Cut!'

'More!' shouted Stephen, and the drummers started to play a low, insistent beat that was soon joined by slow handclaps and whistles from members of staff. The drummers played faster and louder and the stamping grew more pronounced.

'STOP IT!' Roger was shouting through his megaphone. 'STOP IT IMMEDIATELY! AND CUT THOSE BLOODY CAMERAS.'

'Get me out of the building,' hissed Candice from behind us. 'I *asked* those tight bastards for security. "I'm a target," I said. But did they believe me?'

'MR BIG! MR BIG! MR BIG!' the room was now chanting.

Chali was wrestling with Roger to try and plug the amplifiers back in. The noise level was unbelievable. Then suddenly, cutting right across the top of it, there was an ungodly scream.

Twelve

Instantly, there was silence. My first thought was that a combination of Chali, her silver-foil bikini and her wrestling with Roger over the plug socket had caused some ghastly accident. But it soon became clear this wasn't the case; she was staring around as confusedly as we were. It wasn't Candice, because she was still screaming into her mobile phone about helicopters and riot gear. Dr Hitler had reached out when the scream came and managed to grab one of the gnome army. She hadn't let go. I looked slowly around the room. By the first bed, Carl's mother was gesticulating and shaking.

We moved towards her.

'He opened his eyes!' she said. 'He opened his eyes!'

A very perplexed-looking teenager was taking in the world around him.

'Is it Christmas?' he was saying groggily. 'Have I been out until Christmas?'

'No, no, it's only June,' a nurse reassured him.

'Oh, thank God,' he said.

'Of course, you missed last Christmas . . .' the nurse added.

Candice raced towards the scene at the speed of light.

'Did you *get* that?' she screeched at the cameramen. They nodded. 'Right. Fine. We can dub some real carol music over it later.'

She sat down beside Carl and switched on her beaming smile like headlights.

'So, viewers, we have indeed witnessed a miracle here. Through the healing power of music – and who knows what little sprinkle of Babbleon TV magic – Carl here has been returned to us! So, Carl, how do you feel?'

'Ehm . . . Terrible . . . like, you know, really bad, yes,' said Carl.

'Shit,' I said, slumping next to Addison. 'Shit shit shit shit shit.'

'Holly, don't worry,' soothed Josh.

'How can I not worry? That was our last hope.'

'Don't be silly. No hope is the last hope. And, anyway, Sophie hasn't handed over the money yet.'

I shrugged.

'I don't see what good that's going to do.'

'There might be new treatments, new ways . . .'

'We might as well just face facts, Josh. He was mine, and now he's gone. Could you leave me alone for a bit, please?'

'OK then.' He got up and started to walk away.

'Ehm . . . I didn't mean for you to actually go.'

'Oh, no, of course you didn't. Hang on.'

He sat back down beside me and put his arm around me in a comforting way. Sophie was remonstrating with Roger and Candice, who looked to be giving in.

'OK, everyone,' said Roger finally through his megaphone. He seemed to have aged about ten years. Of course, all the staff were still around Carl's bed, but he waited until they turned back to him. 'We will now have a short presentation of a cheque to the high-dependency unit of St Hugh's from Sophie Masterton-Willis LLB.'

'Do you want some background music?' shouted one of the Spangles, to some guffawing.

Smiling graciously, Sophie snatched Candice's microphone and walked dead centre into the middle of the ward. The cameraman trained his camera on her alone.

'Thank you all so much for coming,' she said. 'Under this

government, hospitals have been sadly neglected. That is why the private sector, as well as the charity of good people like myself, is needed to bolster up the whole sorry structure – which, of course, we all hope will eventually lead to an entirely private system that can remove this wretched burden from humble taxpayers.'

Josh nudged me. There, hanging back at the entrance to the ward, was Kate, looking uncharacteristically shifty.

'She came!' said Josh. 'Shame she missed the best bit!'

Kate appeared to be beckoning some people up the stairs, putting a finger to her lips.

'And that is why I, Sophie Masterton-Willis LLB, have decided to donate to St Hugh's the sum of –' Sophie held up the enormous cheque – 'fifty thousand pounds!' She raised her arms triumphantly, waiting for the round of applause.

Quick as a flash Kate entered with, as I counted, one two three four five six Jameses. They lined up behind Sophie, in full view of the camera.

'Now!' shouted Kate.

Six Jameses lowered their expensive Savile Row trousers and Calvin Klein boxer shorts, revealing six skinny white British arses to the camera, and waggling them about vigorously.

Instantly, there was a storm of applause. Sophie smiled graciously and bowed towards the camera. The Jameses waggled their arses even more fervently.

'Excellent,' said Kate. 'You all keep your jobs.'

As the applause continued, Sophie's smile began to waver. When it sank in that the eyes of the crowd weren't exactly on her, the grin disappeared altogether and she slowly looked round.

She went dangerously pale.

'Can we stop now?' one of the Jameses was saying. 'All the blood is rushing to my head.'

'You . . . you . . .' Sophie said to Kate. Then her face twisted. 'But . . . but *why*?'

Kate stood up straight and trembled. The camera swivelled so it was trained on both of them. Kate took a deep breath, paused, and then opened her mouth.

'Well, Sophie, one reason . . .' she said in a wobbly voice, 'is because you're a big evil fascist.'

'Nothing wrong with that,' said Sophie.

'And the other is . . . that you're stealing the man I'm in love with and being horrible to him!' Kate's voice went very high at this and finished off in a bit of a squeak.

There was a gasp from the crowd. I glanced at Josh. His face was a picture of confusion as he tried to work out who she meant.

'What?' said Sophie. But it was too late. Kate was striding across the ward to Josh. He looked at her for a few seconds.

'What . . . what, *me*?' he asked in disbelief.

'Why do you think I live in your shitty, awful flat, you moron?' said Kate, biting her lip.

'I quite like it,' said Josh.

'Do you quite like me?' asked Kate quietly.

'Cor! Yeah!' said Josh.

'Oh for fuck's sake!' said Sophie. 'I was going to marry him, you idiot. Perfect constituency wife he'd have made. Scones for the village fair and everything.'

'Well you can't,' said Kate, kissing him.

'This is *definitely* my week,' said Josh, kissing her back.

Sophie paused and looked around her.

'Well, fuck you all very much,' she said. And she ripped up the enormous cheque, leaving it in pieces on the floor, then stomped out of the ward.

'Oh my God! The money!' shouted Josh. Everyone looked horrified. Then one of the Jameses picked up a piece of the cheque.

'Fifty thou? Was that all?' he chuckled. 'God, that wouldn't even make a dent in our bonuses, would it, boys?'

'Not likely!' They started pulling out their cheque books.

'Well, I'm giving ten.'

'You limpdick! I'm giving fifteen!'

'You utter homosexual! I'm giving twenty!'

'Just a thought,' said Dr Hitler, 'but does anyone mind if I give the patients their anti-dying medication now?'

*　　*　　*

An hour later, things were getting back to relative normality, although no one had taken the Christmas tree down.

The camera crew had left with Candice, utterly jubilant, clutching Roger's arm and whispering, 'BAFTA, darling, no doubt about it at all.'

I apologized to Chali that she didn't get to play more of her songs, but she brushed it off, saying that Dr Hitler had asked them to play the doctors' summer do, and that they were definitely on their way *this* time.

Kate and Josh had disappeared somewhere, so I didn't want to turn up at home too quickly.

There was lots of fuss at Carl's end of the hall, which meant that God and Addison and I were left to our own devices, but I didn't think I had many more devices to give. I simply sat there, staring out of the window, humming a made-up song to myself, trying to ignore my rising panic.

At about four o'clock, Finn popped his head round the curtain.

'Did I miss it all?' he said.

I nodded.

'Kate made me promise to come, but I really, honestly wanted to stay out of the way of the mooning.'

'Why? Have you got a mutant arse?'

'No! I think I've got quite a nice arse.'

'Turn around,' I ordered. He did so. He did, in fact, have a lovely arse.

'I just don't like shoving it in people's faces, if you know what I mean.'

'You mean, you don't like getting your arse out on national television?'

'Something like that.'

'You are weird.'

He looked at Addison.

'So, no change then.'

I shook my head. 'Oh, Finn. Why the hell couldn't you be a

264

medical doctor? Why the hell couldn't you have trained to sort this out?'

'I don't know,' he said. 'I'd change it if I could, I promise you.'

I sniffed.

'Would you . . . I mean, would you like to go for a drink or something?'

'Of course not,' I sniffed.

'No, of course not. OK. Maybe I should go.'

'Maybe you should.'

'I'm sorry, Holl.'

'Everyone's sorry,' I said. 'Nobody helps.'

Home was empty. I made myself five jam sandwiches and sat by myself on the fire escape eating them slowly. I felt completely wrung out, and toyed with the idea of sleeping in – after all, I'd probably lost my job. But when it came to it, I couldn't.

The next morning Chali was waiting by the door of That Special Someone beaming broadly as I wheeled up.

'What are you doing here at this time?' I asked incredulously – it was only twenty-five minutes after the shop was due to open.

'Ding dong!' she shouted. 'The witch is dead!'

'Which witch?' I asked.

'The wicked witch! Ding! Dong! The wicked witch is dead!'

Chali took my bike off me and proudly led it into the shop.

'Wake up, you sleepyhead! Rub your eyes, get out of bed!'

'OK, *OK*,' I said. 'I get it!'

'Ding! Dong! . . .'

'I *get* it. What happened?'

'Well,' said Chali, measuring out two disgustingly large spoonsful of coffee from Mrs Bigelow's private stash and ripping open a forbidden packet of bourbons with her teeth, 'this little boy came in the shop yesterday, right, with Biggers in charge? Turned out one of his friends had been run over by a car. And he didn't have enough money to pay the delivery charge.'

'No way,' I said.

'Utterly way. So, anyhow, Biggie told him he couldn't have the flowers, and it turns out his father owns a whole chain of conferencing suites.'

I shook my head in disbelief.

'And?'

'And, the dad phones my uncle and . . . she's gone! Gone gone gone! See, I told you that strike was a good idea.'

'Yes, good meaning "lucky" rather than "moral" or anything,' I grumbled, hauling out the displays.

'But don't you see? My uncle's given me the shop! It's ours! You can run it when I'm off doing world tours!'

'Which will be never,' I said, straightening up. 'Still, that's really good, isn't it?'

Chali nodded enthusiastically.

'I mean, we could really make something of this place,' I said, warming to it. After all, if my love life was over for all time, I was going to have to throw myself into my career. 'We could start doing trendier events . . . try and get into, you know, *Hello*! magazine and stuff like that. Send free samplers off. Start a mailing list . . .'

'Ah,' said Chali, 'actually I was rather hoping that it would mean even more slacking off for us.'

'No, no. We could really go places with this place.'

'Do you think the band could play here? So it could be like a flower shop-cum-gig? Kind of a place for the kids to hang out.'

'That', I said, 'is just about the worst business idea I've ever heard.'

Her face fell.

'OK, what about we grow opium poppies here and pretend we're selling flowers?'

'Actually, now I think about it, maybe you were on to a winner with that gig/flowers thing.'

'Yeh?'

'Yeh. It'll be brilliant.'

'I know,' she said. 'And now, as a celebratory gesture, I'm going to shut the shop for a day.'

'You're going to shut the shop on our first day of business?'

'I'm a very positive employer.'

'You're a very optimistic employer.'

'Well, I'm an employer with a rehearsal to go to. It's my new band, made up of tramps playing cardboard percussion instruments. Apparently MTV think it's the new big thing.'

'And a homeless tramp told you this, did he?'

'Uh huh.'

'OK. Where are you rehearsing?'

'King's Cross . . .'

She got sight of the look on my face.

'Huh. Well you won't be grinning when we're playing Wembley.'

'Not unless I'm doing the flowers.'

'Tramps don't like flowers. Unless there's nothing else to eat.'

It was only eleven o'clock in the morning. What exactly did I do with myself before all this, I wondered? Maybe I knew a lot about *Hollyoaks*. I slalomed wearily into the hospital, carrying a copy of *SFX*, the magazine for lonely boys.

The smell of disinfectant seemed to be weighing me down. After the uproar of yesterday, even the corridors seemed quiet. Sighing loudly, I flounced through the doors. Addison was sitting up on the end of the bed.

I turned round and walked straight back out to find the right ward.

I stopped, smacked my head then turned around and walked in again.

My heart and my throat started fighting each other.

My throat won.

'ADDISON!' I screamed at the top of my voice and threw myself pell-mell towards him.

He looked up with a confused expression on his face.

'Hey, Speedy Gonzales,' said Stephen, deftly catching the back of my dungarees. 'If you knock him over again I will have to kill you.'

'Bha baha baha haha . . .' I said, arms flailing. Addison continued to regard me steadily. I couldn't read the expression on his face. Stephen put a restraining hand on my arm.

'Go gently, OK?'

'Buh huh huh huh,' I spluttered.

'Cnif Yarh Bah F!!!' I shouted as, slowly, from behind the curtain, a large – very large – figure emerged, and put a mirror-image protective hand on Addison's arm.

'Clahf . . . Clahff.'

'Do you need a paper bag to breathe into?' asked Stephen.

I struggled to regain control of myself.

'That's . . . that's *Claudia*!' I announced, panting desperately.

'Claudia Finkelman; yes. Apparently so,' said Stephen. 'She arrived about three o'clock this morning, sat with him, and . . . well.'

'Oh *God*!' I said. 'That's . . . that is so *unfair*!'

'Do you want to hear how he is or not?'

'Oh God,' I said again. 'Yes. Of course. I hate myself.'

'Put a brave face on it,' said Stephen. 'The physio and the neurologist have both checked him over, and it's not too bad. He'll have a bit of short-term memory loss, and his muscles will need to get used to not being asleep, but, on the whole, it's looking pretty good.'

As we were talking, I was taking little baby steps closer to the bed. Now I was close enough to speak.

'So, be brave,' Stephen whispered in my ear.

'Hey,' I said bravely.

'Hello,' said Claudia. And not in a friendly way either. In real life she was, if anything, freakier than on the computer. She was that big way only Americans get: so heavy it's as if your legs are pointing in the wrong direction from the knees downwards. Her hair was pinned back with two kirby grips, and her spectacles were huge, Deirdre Barlow-style. She was wearing an outsized *Red Dwarf* T-shirt.

'Hey,' said Addison, turning his big brown eyes on me.

I took another step towards him. Claudia hovered protectively.

'How are you feeling?' I asked, trying to control my quavery voice.

'Sticky,' he said.

I nodded. 'Here – I brought you this.' And handed him *SFX*, not knowing quite what else to do.

'Oh, great – I love this. Look, Claudia, there's an article on number science.'

'Is it an imaginary one?' she replied, and they both sniggered for some reason. I held on to the back of a chair for support.

'So . . .' I said. 'I mean, what happened?'

'I couldn't . . . you know,' said Claudia, 'just stand by while no one did anything for Add.'

I nodded my head gravely.

'You know, this is my first time out of the house in six years. And I made it to a different country.'

'You were very brave,' I said, through gritted teeth.

'I know.'

'Then what happened?'

'Well, I flew over, and arrived last night, and they let me in.'

I wouldn't keep out a monster that arrived at three o'clock in the morning, would you? I tried to quell such uncharitable thoughts, but it was impossible. My whole body felt hollowed out by misery. I wanted to take Addison's place on the bed and lose consciousness for a few months or so. It would definitely be easier than dealing with this. Hook me up, and wake me in time for one of those lovely global-warming summers we're always being promised.

'And I sang you your favourite song, didn't I, sweetheart?'

Addison looked faintly bashful.

'Which is?' I asked politely.

'Oh, a wunnerful British band called Take That. They've got a little song called "Back for Good"? I don't know if you've heard of it.'

'No, I've never heard of it,' I said quietly.

'Well, it's our song, isn't it, sweet pea?'

Addison shrugged and nodded.

'When you were . . . asleep,' I said, taking a deep breath, 'did you . . . did you know anything that was going on around you?'

He shook his head. 'Sorry, no. They told me you came to see me a lot.'

'Oh well, I popped in now and again. It's just as well you didn't hear me, really. Usually I was telling you how big your nose was.'

'She was vicious,' said Stephen, backing me up.

'When's Magda getting back from the phone? Does she have to inform every single one of your Croatian relatives?' asked Claudia. 'We're moving,' she informed me.

'Where?' I said, my *Misery* fears resurfacing.

'I can't walk very well,' said Addison. 'Claudia's putting me in a private hospital to rehabilitate.'

'I figured the food in here was probably bad enough through a tube without having to stick it in your mouth for four weeks,' said Claudia. 'And they need the bed here.'

'That's good of you,' I said, because it was.

'Well, he's my problem now,' she said, trying to make a joke out of it. 'And it saves on hotel costs if they'll let me stay in the room.'

Had I been a better person, I would have offered her Addison's room. I'm not.

Stephen insisted he was taking me to the pub for a brandy when he came off shift at lunchtime, so I had to stand back and wait while they packed everything up, trying desperately to hold on to my tears until they had all gone. 'I have a flower shop,' I told myself fiercely.

Magda was a different person, laughing and crying simultaneously, covering Addison in kisses every time he blinked. She and Claudia went on ahead with the carefully packed *Star Wars* miniatures, whilst a porter loaded Add into a wheelchair and began to transfer him to what was presumably a luxury ambulance.

'Well, I guess we'll see you soon,' I muttered.

'We?' said Addison, turning round.

'Uhm . . . yeah, me and Han Solo.' I took the figure out of my bag. 'We've been working together on this one.'

Addison hesitated.

'I didn't want to say this in front of Claudia,' he began, slowly reversing his wheelchair until he was next to me, 'but sometimes, when I was . . . asleep . . . things swam in and out . . . It was like diving very deep down in the ocean, down further than the fish and the submarines.'

'Like in *The Abyss?*' I suggested.

'The director's cut?'

'But of course.'

He half smiled, then took a deep breath and went on:

'And occasionally, I surfaced. And when I surfaced, you were always there.' He paused and looked away. 'And I did call out to you.'

I leaned over him and stroked his hair.

'Not loudly enough,' I said, the tears welling up.

'You were too far away,' he said, his own eyes watering. He kept his face turned away and rubbed his forehead fiercely. 'You were swimming in a different sea.'

I hugged him and let my tears run through his hair.

'Oh, Add,' I said. 'I'm so sorry.'

'No, I am,' he said.

'No, I am.'

He shook his head, and for a time we couldn't speak.

'I think Moby Dick's waiting for you,' I said finally, swallowing hard and glancing towards the door.

He followed my gaze, then took my hand.

'It's . . . it's hard to explain,' he said.

'Same sea?'

He shrugged. 'Same universe, maybe.'

I handed him Han Solo. 'Well, better take him with you. He's very good for people in sticky spots.'

'I'll remember that,' he said.

'Ehm, sorry but, like, the meter's running,' said the porter.

'Sure,' I choked, and let Add go. Behind me, the nurses were already expertly stripping the bed, wheeling away the tubes and the wires. I waited till they'd finished, then sat on the bed to wait for Stephen, feeling the springs under my hands. I still wanted to curl up on it. It felt like all I had left.

'We're going to be needing that bed,' warned Dr Hitler, flitting past me.

'God?' I whispered.

There was no answer.

'God? Really, I could do with a bit of spiritual guidance right now.'

There was a snorty sound from the next bed.

'God?'

God was lying flat out on the bed with an oxygen mask on. He was very grey and shrunken.

'God?'

He feebly motioned for me to take his oxygen mask off. I checked around for Dr Hitler, then, when she was nowhere to be seen, did so.

'How are you?'

'God is dead,' he said, every syllable coming with a very nasty rattle.

'Don't be ridiculous! Come on, do a miracle.'

'I did one,' he said laboriously. 'Sorry it didn't make you happy.'

'Oh that,' I said. 'Never mind, eh? Just make yourself better.'

'Not a lot of point in that,' he said. 'The world's a pile of shit.'

'Well, that's true,' I reflected. 'But still . . .'

'Neh,' he said. 'I tell you what I'd love, though . . .'

Fuck it, I thought, and opened his locker. Sure enough, there was a half-bottle of old-looking Scotch inside.

'I'm not putting it down your feeding tube, though,' I warned him. 'I may be a disaster area, but I'm not a murderer.'

'No, that'll be fine. Just lift me up a little . . . that's it. Would you like some?'

'I wouldn't mind.'

So I took a swig, then very carefully held up his head and le

God sip a few drops, which he did with a bit of coughing, but eventually he managed to get some down.

'Oh, better,' he said. 'Well, I think it's just about time I was popping off.'

'Don't you have any family you want me to contact?' I asked, stupefied.

'Every living thing is my family,' he said. 'Besides, they all fucked off to Australia.'

He snuffled a bit more and settled down in the pillows. I sat with him and let him have sips of whisky as often as he could manage them.

'You should go now, lass,' he said. 'I think you've a life to be getting on with.'

'I'm not sure I feel like it at the moment.'

'No. But do you want a last bit of advice from the mouth of the creator himself?'

'Yes please.'

'Hmm.' He appeared to fall asleep for a second, then woke up with a grunt.

'Hmm . . . advice. Right. Ehm, wear sunscreen?'

'I think that's been done.'

'No, really? Hmm.' He launched into one of his deathly coughing fits. 'How about – love they neighbour?'

'I adored your neighbour,' I said sadly. 'Didn't help me much.'

'Yes, right, right, I see.'

He paused again.

'Goodbye,' he said quietly. And suddenly, the terrible wheezing stopped. An instant later, one of his machines let out an alarm.

'DOCTOR!' I yelled, leaping up.

'Are you *squatting* here?' asked Dr Hitler, throwing herself up the ward behind the crash cart.

'No . . .'

'Well, please, could you leave? I'm not sure you're a good influence. But if you see that fat girl again, could you send her back in?'

*   *   *

273

I ran out of the ward, blinded. Stephen wasn't around, but I had to get out. I stumbled through the corridors, realizing that people were looking after me with concern. I pushed past them all.

'Hey!' shouted a familiar voice. I ran on.

'Hey!'

'Leave me alone,' I shouted and ran on. It quickly became obvious that someone faster than me was chasing me. I made it as far as the bicycle but couldn't undo the lock in time.

'Physically chasing women,' said Finn, out of breath, leaning his hand on the wall in front of me, 'there's a new macho experience for me. Would you like me to go and wrestle a bear now?'

I straightened up slowly and shook my head.

'What's the matter? Magda phoned Kate at work . . . Oh.'

I welled up.

'It was that other girl, wasn't it?'

'It's fine,' I said chokingly. 'It's better than fine, actually. It's great. I mean, he's alive. He's OK. At least . . . well, at least I won't be going to prison for manslaughter.'

He nodded. 'Always something, I suppose.'

I bent down again to try and unlock my bike.

'Where are you going now?'

'I don't know,' I confessed.

'Huh,' he said. Then, after a pause: 'Would you like to come with me?'

'Where are you going?' I asked timidly.

'Well, it's a beautiful day, so how about staying inside and reading improving captions?'

'That sounds all right,' I said.

'The Science Museum?'

I nodded.

He held out his hand and I took it.

*　　*　　*

The Science Museum was practically deserted, and eerily,

stunningly beautiful. I wandered through the massive atrium, hitting knobs at random and fiddling with things. Finn regarded me calmly.

'Did Madeleine get you in cheap for this too?' I asked, in what I thought was a deeply casual manner.

He laughed. 'I don't really see her . . .'

I looked at him. 'Were you ever seeing her?'

He shrugged. 'Not . . . maybe not as much as I mentioned her in your company.'

I stared at him in consternation.

'Sorry . . . sorry, am I getting this straight? Were you using a cell mitosis biologist to try and make me *jealous*??'

'Did it work?' he asked.

'Well, you know . . . yeah.'

He twisted slightly nervously.

'Holl, I don't . . . I mean . . . if you're still in love with Addison, I wouldn't want to ask you out or anything . . .'

I pushed a big red button that made lots of lights twinkle on and off behind us.

'I think . . .' I said shyly – examining my reasons for doing things was never one of my favourite jobs – 'I think, maybe I was just in love with an idea of him.'

'I think so too,' said Finn, doing something very clever to the machine, so the lights made pretty sparkling patterns.

'Sometimes,' I went on, 'maybe the things you really want are . . .'

'A bit boring and nerdy?' He brushed his gorgeous dark hair out of his gorgeous dark eyes.

'Closer than you think.' I seemed to remember saying that before. 'Oh wow!' I announced, struck suddenly. 'I don't need to pretend to know lots about *Star Trek* any more!'

'And you already know lots about spaghetti.'

'Well, I certainly eat a lot of it.'

'That's what I meant.'

'Wow. Do you think I could have a true scientific heart?'

'I think,' mumbled Finn, looking down, 'you could have this true scientific heart.'

We wandered hand in hand, feeling as small as children, across the Perspex bridge over the massive vaulted Victorian hall, looking on all the great machines and massive works that filled the space.

'That reminds me,' I said, gazing out over it all, 'I meant to tell you before: God died this morning.'

'Oh, I don't think he did really,' said Finn, leaning out with me. 'He's probably just off playing dice somewhere.'

Epilogue

The end of July was beautiful. To celebrate it, and us, we staged an Addison-napping from his plush private hospital and took him to Hyde Park for a picnic. He grumbled all the way, but we insisted: he hadn't had his long-promised birthday party.

Add was improving, slowly. He had a tendency to forget things, and couldn't walk very far, but we were being cautiously optimistic. And his personality didn't seem to have changed, if his antipathy to being out in the open air was any guide. We needed five rugs so that none of his exposed flesh touched the grass.

'I'm going to be sick,' I said, looking up at Finn from my vantage point of his lap.

'Well, you shouldn't have eaten four Penguins, should you?' he said mildly, and continued examining a disgusting caterpillar he'd just picked up.

Kate poured some more champagne for us. She and Josh had

a proper hamper filled with goodies, we had a plastic bag full of tangerines, and Claudia was having a McDonalds.

'I want to propose a toast to us . . .' Kate began. Suddenly, I spotted two people walking towards us.

'Fuck! Fuck! Fuck fuck!' I yelled, sitting upright.

'Well, Holly's pretty much summed up what I was going to say,' said Kate, raising her glass.

'No, look! It's Carol and Farah!'

'We all have to hide!' I yelled. 'Up!'

'Great!' said Josh.

'Let's hide behind Claudia,' I said quietly to Finn, who batted me on the nose.

'Under the blankets!' said Josh.

'Umm I don't think . . .' said Addison.

Carol and Farah were definitely heading this way.

'Quick! Roll Addison!' I ordered, and with much sniggering, we did so, then dived under. Of course, trying to lie very quietly and flatly anywhere is a recipe for disaster, so we giggled helplessly whilst trying to tell each other to be quiet.

'I mean,' Carol was saying, as they drew near, 'this park is a disgrace. Look, somebody's left a wheelchair over there.'

'And a picnic!' said Farah, hopping along. 'Ooh, look, bananas!'

'It's disgusting.'

'You're disgusting!' I said, before Finn clapped a hand over my mouth.

'Did you hear something?' said Carol. 'Oh, let's go. Farah, do you think you could fit up our chimney with a long-handled broom?'

As they walked off, I crept out, grabbing Finn by the hand.

'Don't come out yet,' I hissed to the others. 'They're not quite gone.'

Finn put his arms around me, and we moved a little away.

'It is nice,' I said, putting my arms around him back, 'to get you alone.'

He grinned at me.

'In the open air of the busiest park of the busiest city in a rapidly overpopulating world . . .'

'. . . where, for me,' I said, stopping him with a kiss. 'There is no one else but you.'

Then I kissed him again.

'Holly! Are they gone yet?' yelled Josh.

'Yes – I've got grass up my nose and Claudia smells!' shouted Kate. 'Sorry, Claudia.'

There were loud kissing noises.

'Huh? I wasn't listening,' said Claudia.

We looked around to the four forms wriggling under the blanket. Suddenly Claudia yelped.

'Gosh, sorry,' said Josh. 'Thought you were Skates.'

'You did not!' said Kate crossly.

'Ow!' said Josh.

COSMOPOLITAN

STILL THE WORLD'S BEST SELLING MAGAZINE

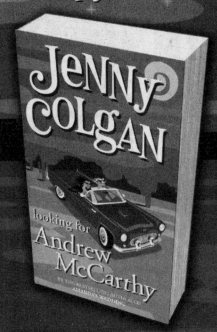